LAMENTATION:

An Immigrant's Dilemma

LAMENTATION:

An Immigrant's Dilemma

Cyril U. Orji

CONTENTS

DEDICATION

To my wife Adanma and our children:
Uzoma, Obinna, Uzoamaka and Uchenna

PART I

1

IKEM'S ASSIGNMENT

It was a hot summer day. The sun had started its westward descent. The air was still and as dull as ditchwater. Chicago, this afternoon, was the sticky city rather than the windy city. Nkechi was glad to be back from work. After an hour in the kitchen preparing dinner, she was tired and felt as weak as water. The family dinner was macaroni and cheese. Of course, Nkechi always had a pot of *egusi* or *ogbono* soup in the freezer as backup in case she didn't feel like preparing an American dish. She belonged to that class of Nigerians who must "swallow" something everyday. Steak, burger, spaghetti or cold sandwich didn't cut it. They had to swallow their *fufu*.

After dinner, Nkechi made one last pass through the kitchen to be sure that everything was in order. But nothing was. The dishes were dirty. The floor was flooded. The sink stank.

"What kind of world is it that a parent prepares dinner, serves food, and does the dishes, while children sit by and do nothing?"

That was not the first time Nkechi had posed this question to an empty room.

"*I-k-em!*" she screamed. Her voice bounced off the wall and returned to her. There was no answer. She thought she heard some noise, but instantly a deadly silence seized the house. It became as silent as a grave. She tiptoed toward the refrigerator in the kitchen, pulling her wrapper up with both hands to avoid the floor that was flooded. The milk, water and egg yolk that had spilled on the floor appeared to have been properly mixed by the many feet that walked over them. She peeped into the refrigerator that was left wide open. Three open cans of soda and a plate of melted ice cream greeted her.

"*I-k-em!*" she screamed again, this time raising her voice a few decibels. She stared at her dirty kitchen, her face livid. She thought she knew where they were. Ikem and Kelechi were children of TV and addicts of video games. But she didn't want to believe herself. It could not be. For the dinner table was still set except that the food was gone. How could the children leave the dinner table and go to the basement to play video games? The plates, the pots, the cutlery—everything was still on the dinner table.

She walked toward the door that led to the basement. Looking away from it as if to avoid some scary sight, she screamed even louder, "*Ikemefuna.*"

"*What?*" answered a voice from the basement. She heard footsteps running up the basement staircase. She knew they must all be there. Playing Sega. Most likely. She looked around and saw that Ikem stood by her.

"Didn't you hear me call you?" she bellowed angrily.

"I did."

"And what did you do?"

"I answered you, Mom."

"You answered who?"

"Mom, I swear, I answered you."

"Shut up. How many times will I tell you to stop answering me *what* whenever I call you? What is *what*? Is that the only way to respond to your mother—*what*?"

Ikem stood there as quiet as a mouse. Her mother broke the silence.

"Where's your father?"

"He's upstairs."

"Call him for me and come back here."

They all stood quietly in the living room. The air was tense but quiet. Ikem's father, Chinedu, knew what was amiss. It was a constant problem in the house. The children would not do the dishes or clean up after dinner.

"Who will wash all these plates?" Nkechi asked, her hands anchored on her waist. "Since I came back from work, I haven't rested even for a second. I prepared dinner and served everybody. You are all well fed, aren't you? Is it too much to expect you, especially Ikem and Kelechi, to do the dishes and clean up after meals? Do you expect me to cook, serve you and do the dishes too? And all you do is play video games?" Shaking her head in disbelief, she muttered, "My God. What am I doing here in America?"

There was an unholy silence in the air. This was not the first time Nkechi had openly lamented and regretted bringing up her children in America.

"Who spilled milk on the floor?" she yelled.

"Kelechi and Nkiru were fighting over the gallon of milk, and it spilled," Ikem explained.

"Ikem was playing with the eggs and they broke," Nkiru added.

"I asked Kelechi to mop the floor and he refused," Ikem said.

"He wants me to clean the egg mess he made," Kelechi countered.

The children stood there looking at their parents, who looked back at them. None of the children made an effort to clean the floor. Nkechi remembered that as a child, she would have immediately started cleaning the floor and not stand there looking at her parents. She didn't know what to do or say. She could only shake her head in disbelief.

Exasperated, she slumped into a nearby chair. She was very angry and looked as pale as the eggshells themselves. This was not the way she had looked forward to bringing up her children. Something was wrong. As a child, once she made eye contact with her mother, she knew exactly what her mother expected of her. In her native Igboland, a general belief was that family members could "talk with their eyes." But that was not the case in America. Not too long ago, Nkechi and her son Kelechi visited Christie, one of Nkechi's friends. Christie had no soda in the house and wanted to run to the grocery and buy some for her guests. Nkechi thought it was unnecessary and said she was not thirsty. She "talked to Kelechi with her eyes" with the hope that Kelechi would also indicate he wasn't thirsty and that a glass of water was fine. Instead Kelechi asked her, "Mom, why are you looking at me like that? I'm thirsty."

Nkechi sat still, no doubt very sorrowful. Her chin rested on her palm and her elbow anchored on her thigh. Her gaze into the distance was as steady as a rock, though she looked at nothing in particular.

"My God, why did I come to America?" she murmured as she shook her head in disbelief at what she felt was happening to her and her children. With a feeling of anguish and pain, she got up from her seat, her two hands forming a dovetail as they rested on her head. She staggered to the restroom with cloudy eyes that had turned red in a short time. She was crying.

Chinedu, her husband, also didn't understand why the children didn't want to do house chores.

"Ikem," he bellowed with rage. "It would take less than five minutes to mop that kitchen. Moreover, I have done dishes in this house almost everyday with the intent to teach you and Kelechi by example. Why on earth is it that any day the dishes are left for both of you, you either do them angrily, and hence badly, or you don't do them at all?"

"It's Kelechi's turn to wash the plates today," Ikem argued.

"No, I washed the plates two days ago. It's your turn today," Kelechi countered.

"I washed them yesterday," Ikem added.

"No, you didn't. Dad washed the plates yesterday."

Chinedu shook his head. His face was sad, grim and angry.

"What rubbish are both of you talking about?" his voice thundered, causing the children to jerk. Clenching his fist and gritting his teeth in anger that forced a stutter, he warned, "If I come back and see those plates and the floor in this shape, I will show both of you what the spirits do with the ear of a goat."

Chinedu had never forgotten that line that he often heard his father say. In those days, coming from his father, it would send chills down his spine. He had no difficulty using the same line with his children and was ready to back it up with action. He walked away angrily from the room and the children rushed to clean up the kitchen.

After pulling herself together from the emotion that overtook her earlier in the day, Nkechi fell asleep on the sofa where she lay brooding over all that had happened. It was almost midnight when she woke up. She remembered how angry she had been and yet restrained herself from spanking the children. She realized this was America and a parent could not spank a child as easily as in Nigeria. A few weeks ago, John, Christie's son reported to his teacher that his mother "threatened to break my head if I didn't eat *fufu*."

John was a very smart child. He was not only as sharp as a razor; he was as talkative as a parrot. He repeated everything he heard the way it was said. His teacher contacted the police, and Christie and her husband were still cooperating in the ensuing investigation. Christie was very angry. Her heart felt as heavy as lead at the thought of she and her husband being involved in a potential child abuse case.

A few days ago, Nkechi had visited Christie who narrated to Nkechi the experience she and her husband had. "How could they think I was really going to break my son's head?" she had asked Nkechi one day. "In Nigeria, a parent would yell and curse, but that didn't mean anything. You were just letting the child know you didn't want him to do certain things."

"My sister, this is America," Nkechi reminded her friend. "They take these things literally. In Nigeria, if someone annoys you, both of you can curse yourselves and yell at the top of your voices. You act out your anger and resolve your differences there. In this country, they look at you as a crazy person when you act out your anger. They internalize theirs and walk away quietly as if nothing happened, but you and I know better."

"They shouldn't take everything a parent says to a child literally."

"Yes, but they do," Nkechi responded. "My husband has taught me to be careful about what I say when these children are present. He reminded me that a stranger who arrives at a city where people are donating ears must cut his own ears and donate too. We are strangers in this place, so we have to watch how they do things here and just follow. We must act like the proverbial fowl that, arriving at a city stands on one leg until it determines that the inhabitants of the city stand on both legs. We have to watch what we say and how we say them for the children will repeat in school whatever they hear at home."

"Tell me about it," Christie said, remembering her own troubles.

"The parrot in my house is even a special case."

"My sister, they're all the same," Nkechi said hoping it would comfort her friend. "That's what they see other children do. It's terrible, but that's the way things are done here. It means you have to bite and chew your words before talking to your child."

*   *   *   *   *

Chinedu and his wife Nkechi completed their schooling a few years ago and should have returned to their country. However, like many other Nigerian immigrants, they decided to settle down in the United States and raise a family. They had four children. Their oldest son was Ikemefuna; their second son was Kelechi; their only daughter, Nkiru and their youngest son, Obioha. It was Chinedu's idea that the family settled in America. Nkechi resisted it because her preference was to return to Nigeria, their native country. But the political situation and economic problems in Nigeria were worsening there by the hour. The army that had ruled the country since Independence was in no hurry to exit the political scene, leaving the country politically unstable. Economically, Nigeria's currency, the *Naira,* had lost nearly all its buying power. From another perspective, their American-born children were getting older, and hence needed exposure to a developed economy like America. Migration to developed countries from developing countries took place mostly at college age, which their children were fast approaching.

Nigeria was also a special case. It was a nation under siege; besieged not by an external force, but by a powerful minority of its own citizens. Nigeria was a nation from which its own citizens fled. Nigerians scattered all over the world will accept any gift from anybody, except a free ticket back to their motherland. It was with this mindset that many Nigerians in diaspora put aside national pride and emotional attachment to their native country, and decided not to return to Nigeria in its present state.

"How much the times have changed," Nkechi told Chinedu. "So, we have settled down to living in America, accepting the system of social security and hoping to draw from it one of these days."

"True," Chinedu agreed. "But, in addition to social security, don't forget there're prepaid burial plans and nursing homes. We may have to start thinking about these before long."

"Tell me about it," Nkechi said, shrugging her shoulders and clapping her hands in disbelief. "So one of these days we may end up in the nursing home. This is unlike life in Nigeria, where old parents live with their children who took care of them. I doubt that these American children, who can't even wash plates after meals, will put up with us in old age."

"It's scary, and we must start to mentally prepare for it," Chinedu admitted, and in a tone that showed resignation to fate, he asked, "Are we sure, Nkechi, that we're doing the right thing settling down here? Sometimes I feel that we're better off in Nigeria, no matter how terrible things may be over there."

Nkechi looked at Chinedu but had no answer. It was a question Nigerians in diaspora dealt with everyday. It was difficult to engage a Nigerian in a discussion that did not end with the Nigerian wondering what he or she was doing in America.

Chinedu and Nkechi reflected on many of the problems facing Nigerian parents in diaspora. Most of these were rooted in the differences between American and Nigerian cultures. They gave Nigerian names to their children to help keep their heritage and hope alive. Try as much as they could to inculcate the Nigerian culture and lifestyle in the children, it was clear that their efforts were not as successful as they had hoped.

"The man was made before he came to America."

This was one of Chinedu's popular sayings, one, which underscored his attachment to his native country.

"So, you're carrying the label, 'Made in Nigeria'," Nkechi joked.

"What about that?" Chinedu asked.

"Well, our car has the label, 'Made in America'," Nkechi responded.

"So, what are you getting at?" Chinedu asked.

"What about Ikem and his siblings?" Nkechi asked. "Where were they made?"

"In our bed," Chinedu helped with the joke.

Nkechi had meant this to be a joke, but in the process, she raised an issue that has beset not only Nigerians, but also people of other cultures now settled in diaspora. Who were their children? Were they Americans or Nigerians? How should they be raised? Should Nigerian parents insist on the strict child development guidelines that characterized their childhood in Nigeria, or should they relax and follow the more liberal policies in America? These were some of the many questions Nigerian parents in diaspora dealt with on a daily basis. For most of them and their families, it was a serious conflict.

The children were also caught in this difficult environment. It was a constant struggle for them to be Nigerians at home and Americans at school. It was difficult for them to eat *fufu* at home and hamburgers at school. It was difficult for them to wear Nigerian clothes to church on Sunday, and to look different from their friends. It was difficult for them to see their friends struggle to pronounce their Nigerian names. Why Ikemefuna, Kelechi, or Nkiru? Why not Bill, Phil, or Cynthia? It was a constant battle.

Ikem and his brother Kelechi were playing Sega. Their younger brother Obioha was also there, but he had long given up on being given his fair chance at the game. Nkiru, their sister, was also there. She was the only girl in the family, and as was quite common, she was tired of combing the hair of her doll that no one was ready to admire with her. Their parents had almost given up on forcing and sometimes pleading with Ikem and Kelechi to be considerate to their younger siblings. Whenever the four children were together, only Ikem and Kelechi would be enjoying themselves. If Obioha cried to be given a chance, the Sega would be left for him and neither Ikem nor Kelechi would want to play with him. They would also be quick to remind Nkiru that she was a girl and that a video game like *mortal combat* was inappropriate for her. But on this day, Ikem had something on his mind. He had a class project, to write a paper describing the childhood of his parents—a topic he knew very little about, but wanted to know everything about.

"I think Dad and Mom should tell us more about their childhood," Ikem said to his brother Kelechi. "I need the stuff for my class project."

"That's cool," Kelechi agreed. "They always talk about their childhood, especially when we do stuff that makes them mad. I think they should be able to help you."

"What do we ask them?" Nkiru wanted to know.

"First, I want to ask them if their parents spanked them," Ikem suggested.

"I can tell you the answer to that one. It's easy," Kelechi responded as he manipulated the buttons on the Sega control panel. He was playing offense against Sega defense in a Sega Cowboys/49ers football game. "Anyway, we can ask about their school, what they did before and after school and general stuff like that. We'll also ask Mom as a girl if she had a room to herself. I don't know why Nkiru has a room all to herself."

"Mom said that it's because Nkiru is a girl," Nkiru's younger brother, Obioha added.

"I think we're getting there," Ikem added. "I know that once we ask one or two questions, Dad will explain even the ones we forgot. It'll be like going to confession. They taught us to ask forgiveness for even the sins we forgot to confess."

"*Wow!*" Kelechi exclaimed. "So, you just tell the priest, 'I know I committed a bunch of sins, but I can't remember any of them, so I ask forgiveness for all of them'? Cool. I can go to confession everyday. It's neat."

"There you go. That's why Mom calls you wise guy," Ikem joked.

It was a snowy and cold Sunday evening. The family had just come back from grocery and their favorite snack, chestnuts were roasting in the oven. They were all seated in the family room waiting for the chestnuts.

"I'm surprised Ikem and Kelechi haven't already gone to the basement to play Sega," Nkechi observed.

"Mom, if we play Sega, we're in trouble, if we don't, we're in trouble. What should we do?" Kelechi asked.

"Wise guy," Nkechi responded. "I've never seen all of you including Nkiru, sitting quietly in the family room like this. Even Obioha, look at him sitting as quietly as a mouse. What are you guys up to?"

"Kelechi and I want to take over the running of this house."

"Fine. Be my guest. When do the bills start going to Ikemefuna and Kelechi?" Nkechi asked.

"Just kidding, Mom," Ikem giggled, making a face at Kelechi.

"You can make any stupid face you like," Nkechi told Ikem pretending to be angry. "I saw the face you made at Kelechi. You haven't said why you're all here."

"OK, Mom. Here's the deal. I need help with a class project."

"Help?" she repeated in an inquiring tone. "What kind of help? Does it involve buying another video game?"

"Mom!" Kelechi chided, slapping his right palm on his forehead. "You're always talking about video games. Video games are cool, but Ikem isn't talking about them now."

"OK, enough of this your 'cool' and 'hot' stuff," their father interjected. "What's the project about?"

"Our teacher asked us to write a term paper on the childhood of our parents. She's interested in parents who grew up in a culture different from American culture. She wants to know how their childhood was different from the childhood of a typical American."

Chinedu and Nkechi exchanged glances.

"So what do you want from me?" Chinedu, asked.

"Our teacher said we should interview our parents. For example, we should find out the type of family they grew up in, the different schools they attended, how they related to their parents, the kinds of chores they did at home, the type of food they ate and stuff like that."

"Mom, did you have a room to yourself like me?" Nkiru asked.

"Shut up, cry baby. We know you have a room. Can you just get lost?" Kelechi yelled at Nkiru.

"Leave her alone," Chinedu admonished. "She's asking what's important to her. It doesn't prevent you from asking what's important to you. By the way, is that the doorbell that I hear?"

Of course, it was the doorbell. Okezie and his wife Ijeoma were at the door. Okezie was Chinedu's best friend, Their friendship had started during their high school days in Nigeria. Now in America, the friendship had continued and had even extended to their wives and children. Nkechi opened the door and welcomed them. Surprised that the whole family was gathered in the family room, Ijeoma asked, "Why are you all here? What's up?"

"My sister, it's Ikem's assignment," Nkechi responded. "I don't know the type of term paper he's writing."

"Mom, I thought he explained it to you and Dad. What else don't you know or understand?" Kelechi politely challenged his mother.

"*Mechie onu,*" Nkechi commanded.

"*Dianyi,* what project is that?" Okezie asked Chinedu.

"There's this woman who teaches in Ikem's school," Chinedu explained. "She's very interested in foreign cultures. I think she and her husband have traveled extensively. She asked Ikem's class to research the childhood of their parents."

"*Wow!* That's a cool project," Okezie joked, scratching his head as he said so.

"You see, Mom, even Uncle Okezie is pretty cool and smooth," Kelechi chided his mother. "Mom, everybody is catching on. You gotta open up, Mom. The next millennium is here!"

Nigerian-American children often referred to any Nigerian adult that was not their father or mother as either Uncle or Aunt.

"*Eh*, 'cool', 'cool' and 'hot' your mouth out of here," Nkechi yelled, flinging her hand in an attempt to spank Kelechi. But Kelechi was an artful dodger, always as agile as a monkey.

"Jokes aside, I think it's an interesting project," Okezie argued. "I think if we just start recalling the good old days, probably just before and immediately after the civil war, Ikem will have more than enough to base his project on."

"True," Ijeoma added. "Another way to approach it would be to look at whatever these children do or don't do today. We can tell them how we did or didn't do similar things when we were growing up like them."

"Don't forget to tell them about the civil war itself," Nkechi interjected. "I think we're all stuck here in America as a result of that stupid war. So, if anybody is looking at what our lives have become in diaspora, I believe the genesis is the civil war."

2
HOMELESS REFUGEES

Nigeria, the most populous nation in Africa, is located on the continent's west coast just off the equator. It has three major ethnic groups: the Hausa, Igbo and Yoruba. The predominantly Muslim Hausa occupy the northern part of the country. The Christian/Muslim Yoruba occupy the west, while the predominantly Christian Igbo, occupy the east. These three regions have become commonly known as the North, the West and the East respectively. Politics in Nigeria has strong ethnic undertones. Therefore, although Nigeria has tried many different political parties and systems in its quest to achieve political stability, the parties have all consisted of variations of the same three ethnic-based parties that the British colonial masters set up before their departure in 1960. Each of the three parties was dominated by one of the three major ethnic groups.

But Nigeria has been under military dictatorship for most of its post-independence life, and has suffered much political turmoil and violence. One of the military coups was preceded by a massacre of the Igbo living in the North.

Chinedu's father, Mazi Pius, or Papa Chinedu as the Igbo would refer to him, lived in Kano, one of the major cities in the North. He worked for the National Electric Power Authority (NEPA). Although it was considered prestigious to work for NEPA, the acronym NEPA was ridiculed by dissatisfied customers as *N*ever *E*xpect *P*ower *A*lways—an indication of the Authority's dismal performance record. Papa Chinedu spent so many years in Kano that his friends generally called him *Mallam*—a salutation reserved for Hausa men. This was in recognition of his fluency in Hausa language and his acculturation to the Hausa way of life.

But then came that fateful day in 1966. Papa Chinedu was spending the evening with his family after the day's work when he heard a big bang on his door.

"*Mallam! Mallam!*"

It was Alhaji Hassan. Although Alhaji Hassan was Hausa, a different ethnic group from Papa Chinedu's Igbo ethnic group, both men were very good friends. Alhaji, as Papa Chinedu often called his friend, brought the news that the massacre of Igbo all over Northern Nigeria was in progress. Igbo properties were being looted, destroyed, and set on fire. However, the friendship between Mallam and Alhaji transcended these ethnic riots. Alhaji would not let harm come to Mallam and his family.

Every second now counted and could be the difference between life and death. In lightning speed, Papa Chinedu and his family disappeared from the house. There was no time to pack or go to the bank for money. They were lucky to just get out of the house alive and they sought refuge in Alhaji's house. Some hid under the bed, others in the attic like thieves, hardly allowed to breathe loudly.

Moments later the looters and executioners arrived.

"Where's Mallam? Where's Mallam?" they shouted, for they knew where every Igbo person lived. They ransacked Mallam's house and burnt it. And so in a very short time, Mallam turned from being one of the most respected men in Sabon Gari Kano to a homeless refugee on the run from a city in which he had spent nearly all his life.

It was late at night and time was of the essence. The situation was degenerating by the minute especially in the metropolitan areas. Mallam and his family had to leave Kano immediately.

The stage was set and the actors were ready. Here was Papa Chinedu's chance to justify the nickname Mallam by which he was commonly known. He was as hairy as a gorilla, but he shaved his hair completely to help the disguise. Given his fluency in Hausa language and his ability to mimic the accent of a typical Hausa person, he passed easily as Mallam Jibril. Alhaji Hassan and his wife together with Mallam Jibril and his wife were "escorting some children to safety because their parents were murdered earlier in the day." The children were Chinedu, then almost a teenager, and his younger siblings, Ugochi and Patrick.

Mallam was still in shock. He couldn't believe he was on the run from Kano. He didn't know where he was running to, for Kano was home to him. The journey started at pitch dark when the city of Kano appeared to have calmed down. It was too dangerous to take a car out of the city since Hausa soldiers still manned most of the roadblocks. Alhaji Hassan and Mallam Jibril knew Kano as well as anybody. They knew the shortest route out of the city and before sunrise, they were safely outside the city's borders.

Alhaji Hassan was one of those Hausa who did not trust the banks. He kept all his money at home, and in the present circumstances it served him well. He took as much as he thought necessary in this campaign to save the lives of his friends. The party carefully chose the routes, avoided hastily set up military checkpoints, and detoured off the road when necessary.

But they ran into a few problems.

"*Everybody commot for car,*" an angry looking Hausa soldier with scores of ethnic marks on his face barked, ordering everybody out of the car in pidgin English, the dialect of the English language that was very popular in Nigeria.

"*Who be yamiri?*" another shouted as they frantically scrutinized every face in an attempt to identify who among the car occupants were Igbo. The Hausa stereotypically referred to the Igbo as *yamiri*, a contraction of a common Igbo request, *yem mmiri,* which translates to, "give me water."

Everybody in the car spoke fluent Hausa. However, faking sleep was the anodyne their parents had prescribed for Chinedu and his siblings to keep their fears under check at military checkpoints. The adults engaged the soldiers in what appeared to be a friendly conversation. There was laughter and a considerable placing of the right palm on the chest, a gesture to Allah, typical of Nigeria's Muslim North. The soldiers looked suspiciously at the apparently sleeping children, but said nothing. Bribery in Nigeria is as old, if not older than the country itself. Something exchanged hands between Alhaji Hassan and one of the soldiers, and the group was waved on. One or two more such incidents were encountered, but the group got by easily.

It was a journey that lasted nearly six days and six nights. On the sixth night, the party members separated. They were now in one of the border towns between the North and the East. It was an emotional parting and Alhaji Hassan showed great emotion. By mid-day, Mallam Jibril had re-transformed to Papa Chinedu again. His family was safe in one of the eastern villages north of the premier university town of Nsukka. With a heart full of both sadness and joy, Alhaji Hassan and his wife started the journey back to Kano—of course, this time by conventional means. They were saddened by the unprepared departure of a well-respected member of the Sabon-Gari community. But Papa Chinedu's situation was much worse than Alhaji understood. For Papa Chinedu was returning to a place where he didn't own anything. Although he sometimes returned to Enugu at Christmas, he did not have a house either in Enugu or his village. If this were America, he would be a native of Kano, for that was where all his life was. The sadness of that unprepared departure notwithstanding, they were happy that Papa Chinedu and his family were alive, for once there is life, there is hope.

*   *   *   *   *

Papa Chinedu and his family had barely settled down to a new life in Enugu when the Nigerian civil war started. The war continued for several months. Like many other returnees from the North, he and his family were having difficulty adjusting to the daily changes necessitated by the war. For example, it was not possible to secure good accommodation in Enugu. Being the seat of government, Enugu attracted most of the returnees from the North. Housing was therefore scarce. In addition, Papa Chinedu did not have enough money on him. He was living on the meager amount his friend Alhaji gave to him. Moreover, although NEPA was a federal authority, the NEPA office in Enugu could not absorb all the returnees from the North. Thus in a sense, Papa Chinedu was out of work.

It would have been a day like any other day in Enugu, but the air was pregnant and uneasy.

"*Ka-gbim, ka-gbim, ka-gbim.*"

Most people were engaged in the only available pastime, listening to Radio Biafra, which narrated endless victories in various war sectors. But those sounds were quietly troubling.

"*Ka-gbim, ka-gbim, ka-gbim.*"

No one said anything, but there was concern on every face. But why the concern? After all, only recently, the midwest region was liberated becoming the Republic of Benin. So, the war was clearly going "our way."

"*Ka-gbim, ka-gbim, ka-gbim.*"

Christian, a tall slim boy, was Chinedu's friend and lived not far away with his parents. He was also in high school, but with schools closed due to the war, he had returned home to his parents. Chinedu and Christian were listening to the radio when those sounds were heard.

"That must be our people testing their mortar and artillery," Christian broke the unholy silence seemingly reassuring Chinedu whose face had assumed a troubled look.

"Yes, I heard that our people developed a new artillery used in the Mid-west campaign," Chinedu added. "However, I don't know why they're testing it in the afternoon very close to Enugu."

"That's okay. I don't see anything wrong with it," Christian argued. "It's fine, provided it's used to destroy the Nigerian vandals."

Just as Christian was completing his comment, the wail of a siren was heard. It wasn't clear whether it came from the distance or from Radio Biafra.

"*Phew, phew, ka, ka, ka, ka. Phew, phew, ka, ka, ka, ... gbim, gbim, gbim.*"

Two Russian MIG fighters and a bomber were over the skies of Enugu. The booming of artillery guns and blasts of explosions deafened the ears of Enugu residents. The radio station went dead. Confusion was in the air. The enemy had launched a combined air and artillery attack on the city of Enugu. It was pandemonium in the streets. Enugu had no air raid bunkers. The city had little, if any, air defense system. The residents had no experience in reacting to such an emergency and for what looked like an eternity, the Nigerian planes came and went, picking their targets at will.

It had been a bright sunny day, but the sun now on its western journey was blanketed by a cloud of smoke, forcing premature darkness on the city. Even when real night finally arrived, the galaxy of stars that graced the skies of Enugu this time of the year was noticeably absent. They were in mourning. The war had reached Enugu.

The artillery fire intensified. It was now clear that it was not "our people." Our people were not "destroying the vandals" as Christian had hoped. It was the other way around. Just as Papa Chinedu and his family left Kano unprepared, they were leaving Enugu unprepared.

The milky way, more commonly known as "milliken hill," was the primary corridor into and out of Enugu. The enemy had taken over milliken hill and from there was bombarding Enugu with mortar and artillery fire. Enugu residents, with their life belongings packed into one or two suitcases, formed a marching brigade retreating to Awgu, a small city about thirty miles east of Enugu. This was the secondary corridor into and out of Enugu. Papa Chinedu and his family were part of this convoy.

Just as quickly as lightning strikes, the once happy and prosperous city of Enugu changed forever. Only a few hours ago, people had been performing their daily activities as much as the general war climate allowed. No one ever thought that, after the flight from the North, people would once again pack their life belongings in a head bundle and endure another flight for life. But that was happening. There was no chance to take a last look at one's home. Many who insisted on doing that didn't get out of Enugu alive. For many like Papa Chinedu, this was their second unprepared flight for life within a period of six months.

After a day's journey, during which many abandoned some of the heavy boxes they carried, Papa Chinedu and his family found themselves in a refugee camp in Awgu. By this time the situation was becoming clearer. Enugu had fallen to the enemy. Radio Biafra now confirmed that some saboteurs had conspired with the enemy in the fall of the Republic of Benin and the city of Enugu. The war had turned irreversibly for the worse. Radio Biafra, however, urged the people to withdraw tactically from Enugu to allow the gallant Biafran forces enough space to flush out the enemy in a couple of days. But the couple of days had turned into couple of weeks, and there was no sign of returning to Enugu. Instead more ground was being lost. The Igbo say that a sleep that lasts four days has become death.

For Papa Chinedu, it had been the fastest six months of his life. He and his family had gone from being very comfortable in Kano to being homeless in a refugee camp in Awgu. Julius was also a returnee from Kano, so he knew Papa Chinedu very well. But unlike Papa Chinedu, Julius did not leave behind any wealth in Kano. He had been poor all his life, in fact as poor as a church mouse. Among the scores of people packed in the open refugee camp, he recognized Papa Chinedu. Tapping his brother Udenta on the shoulder, Julius whispered to him, "I knew that man in Sabon Gari Kano. He didn't live in a house like this."

Udenta nodded his understanding, adding, "When a rich man loses his wealth, he understands what was denied a poor man."

After it became clear that the return to Enugu was not imminent, many of the refugees decided to leave the camp and return to their respective villages. At this stage of the war, the remote villages were relatively safe. The war theater was mainly in the big cites, such as Enugu, Nsukka and Onitsha.

But Papa Chinedu and his family remained in the refugee camp. Although their village, Amuvi, in Arochuku, was relatively safe, Papa Chinedu could not return to the village. He and his wife Teresa knew why. For despite his success and, to some extent, his wealth, Papa Chinedu failed in one key attribute that characterized the Igbo ethnic group in Nigeria: he did not build a house in his village. To the Igbo, this was unacceptable. The Igbo believe that beauty must start from within and radiate outwards. Papa Chinedu was aware of this. But at this point, the harm was already done, and he could not do anything about it. As he lay down on the floor at the Awgu high school refugee camp, tears rolled down his cheeks. He was lamenting his life. His tens of houses in the North were useless now. As the Igbo would say, Papa Chinedu had washed his hands to crack kernels for chickens. While brooding over his misfortune, he was unaware that his son Chinedu was watching him closely.

"Papa, o-gini?" Chinedu was visibly shaken to see tears rolling down his father's cheeks. He had never seen his father in such a state.

Chinedu's mother had just returned from the Red Cross Center, where rations were distributed to refugees once a day. She knew what was going on in her husband's mind. Before she could offer an explanation to her son, the air raid siren went off. This was by now a familiar sound. With lightning speed, everybody dashed into the familiar bushes to take cover. But this was an air raid that would forever live with Chinedu. The bombers flew very low, dropping tens of bombs randomly over the city of Awgu. It was rumored that one of the Biafran divisions defending Enugu had retreated and was now stationed in Awgu.

"Ka, ka, ka, gbim, gbim, gbim."

That was the familiar sound of the fighter-bomber. From where he took cover under a tree, Chinedu observed a huge smoke screen from a crate that formed about 50 yards away. There was blood all over the place. Limbs, legs, arms, and other human body parts littered the field like garbage. A bomb had made a direct hit on a poorly constructed bunker, where scores of people had taken cover. This war was getting worse by the day. Chinedu had never seen human body parts littered in a manner in which not even human waste would be littered. He too could have been a casualty. In fact, his father, who was taking cover about ten trees away, had been refused entry into the bunker because the bunker had been already filled to capacity by the time he had arrived.

After an hour of sustained attack, the air raid ended. However, many, including Christian, did not survive the attack. He was one of the first to get to the bunker. Christian and Chinedu had been close friends at Enugu. Their families left Enugu together. It was only by chance that the two did not go to the bunker together. Chinedu was frantically searching for his friend, but he was no where to be found. Christian had become a war casualty.

Everybody in the bunker was killed instantly. Although properly camouflaged, the bunker appeared to have been directly targeted. Were the enemy bombers targeting civilians or did they think that the camp housed soldiers? Families were wiped out instantly. People were in a state of shock and disbelief. Many of the dead could not be identified. There was wailing and crying. Desperation and hopelessness were in the air.

But many had also lost the will or ability to cry. The tragedy and loss were beyond their comprehension. Mazi Iloka sat numb, his elbows anchored on his thigh, supporting both palms carrying his chin. His appearance indicated his hopelessness and he looked as feeble as a child. Everybody in the camp knew him, for his son Chukwuma, was recently reported killed in the Nsukka sector. Chukwuma was an Engineering senior at the University of Nigeria Nsukka before the outbreak of the war. Mazi Iloka's wife, Maria, and her other four children were all killed in the bunker. Mazi Iloka was left alone. A family of seven only two weeks ago was now reduced to a family of one. The world had collapsed under Mazi Iloka's feet. His life was finished and was no longer worth living. He sat numb and dumb, unable to accept condolences. The following morning, Mazi Iloka was found hanging from a tree. He had committed suicide.

For Papa Chinedu and the other survivors, there was no remaining in that refugee camp. Awgu was now a war front and the refugees must move. To where? Papa Chinedu had no idea. But they must leave Awgu. Their life belongings once again on their heads, they continued their journey to nowhere towards Okigwe and Owerri.

At dawn, the fighter-bombers revisited Awgu. The wandering refugees scuttled for shelter in the shrubs along their route. Luckily for them, the planes were headed into Awgu. News reaching them later indicated that this particular attack was worse than that of the previous day. This time the planes attacked *Orie* Awgu. This was now the only market within a thirty-mile radius since the fall of Enugu, which had forced the closure of Ogbete market. With no anti-aircraft fire, the bombers flew as low as roof tops, dropping tens of bombs in the market while the fighters roamed about gunning down any moving object in sight. Awgu literally became one massive graveyard after this second day of continuous bombardment.

With the passage of time, most of the major cities in Biafra were captured by the Nigerian forces. This meant that, like other refugees, Papa Chinedu and his family were constantly on the move from one refugee camp to another in a shrinking Biafra. They were now living in a refugee camp at Girl's Secondary School Ovim. Life had become unbearable. Malnutrition, which manifested itself in the form of a disease called kwasiokor, was killing nearly as many numbers as those killed at the war theaters. Human beings and human skeletons mingled, and it was becoming difficult to differentiate one from the other.

The options left to Papa Chinedu were few. He knew that his family could not survive another month in the refugee camp. Kwasiokor was much nearer than farther away. And so, after their prayers one Sunday morning, he summoned his family to a meeting. He narrated to them the story of the biblical prodigal son, telling them that, in a sense, he saw himself as a prodigal son of Amuvi. He recalled the tens of houses he owned in Kano, Zaria and Kaduna, but not even a piece of land in his village. He felt like one who had wasted his wealth and his life. He was prepared to return in humility and "ask his people's forgiveness."

"We're returning to Amuvi," he told his family. "It's better to die there than in this refugee camp. I look wasted and humbled, but as long as there's still a breath of life in me, I won't lose hope."

His wife was heartened by his courage. She momentarily felt as good as gold forgetting their plight. She went into the bathroom, cleaned her face and, with all the energy in her body, smiled at her children. It took a great deal of energy to find a reason to smile or laugh in their present circumstances. She became philosophical.

"We can't lose hope," she told them. "Our earthly possessions may have gone from riches in Kano to rags in a refugee camp, but let us look at the bright side. Think of God's miracle that brought us out of Kano. We were about the only family that suffered no losses during that air raid at the refugee camp in Awgu. Over two years into this war, we're still all alive and together. How many families in Igboland can say that? Not many, I believe. God is great. Let's count our blessings and name them one by one. We will be surprised at what God has done for us. We didn't commit any offense against the gods of our forefathers, so from that point of view there's nothing to be ashamed of. It's time to return to Amuvi."

Papa Chinedu was encouraged by the renewed strength in his wife. She had always been his support in difficult times. The war was taking a great toll on him, so his wife knew it was time for her to assume much of the responsibility for their family. And though his body was feeling otherwise, Papa Chinedu felt spiritually strong and determined never to give up this renewed courage and strength.

"Chinedu, get our things together," he said. "We're going home."

Of course, there was not really much to get together. All the family belongings fitted into two or three bags. In a short time Papa Chinedu and his family left the refugee camp in Ovim on the way to their village Amuvi. Transportation by car was virtually non-existent. The army had commandeered every road-worthy car or motorcycle. The only means of civilian transportation in Biafra was by foot and, in some cases, by bicycle.

But luck was on their side. They found space in an old lorry that took them from Umuahia to Ohafia. Ohafia was about forty miles away from their final destination. Given the existing conditions, this was "a short walking distance." By this time, the enemy had taken over virtually all the major cities and roads in Biafra. Cars and lorries traveled via former bicycle routes and, in some cases, through farmlands. The farther away one traveled from conventional roads, the better chance one had of not running into the enemy, for that would be a death sentence for any able-bodied man in the group.

There was no limit to the capacity of a bus or a lorry. Anybody who could find a place to stand or hang on to, did just that. Papa Chinedu was becoming weaker by the day. He was lucky to find space to sit on the floor. Others stood and the rest hung onto the platform. It was a dangerously overloaded lorry, but everybody was glad to give his or her feet some rest from the tens of miles they had walked.

To say that the roads were bad was an oversimplification of their state. These were no roads. With the rainy season just ending, drivers maneuvered their vehicles through the swamps that passed for roads by retracing the path of the previous vehicle. The less swampy areas were as slippery as eels. Continuously rocking from side to side, their lorry snailed along, doing probably no more than 20 m.p.h. And then it happened. The tilt was gradual. Chinedu, who was one of those hanging on the lorry platform saw it coming. They had an accident and their lorry had lost balance. The passengers were thrown out of the vehicle as water is thrown out of a cup, emptied into a cassava farm.

And because the lorry was traveling slowly, it was possible for those hanging onto its platform to jump to safety. They became the emergency team, rescuing those trapped in the wreck. As passengers were pulled out, Chinedu kept looking for his parents. There was his mother, fine, but where was his father? They were getting very anxious and had actually started to cry, believing Papa Chinedu was dead, when they saw, at the bottom of the pile, a man in a slumped position unable to move.

"Papa, Papa," Chinedu shouted to his father. "Papa, Papa, please answer me."

Papa Chinedu was weak. He could not answer, but with all the strength in him, he managed to raise an eyelid. He was alive and the last person pulled from the wreck. Nobody died in the accident, but Papa Chinedu was the most shaken. He was given some food to eat. At that time in Biafra, food was the "first medicine" administered to a sick person, and for Papa Chinedu, it was a welcome medication. The tilted lorry was pushed back up onto the road and the journey resumed.

After a few more days on the road, Papa Chinedu and his family arrived at Amuvi, Arochuku. Sadly, once in the village, Papa Chinedu didn't know where to go. But word had reached home that he had finally decided to return. The village was ready for him. The villagers found a place for him and his family. For the first time in a very long period, Papa Chinedu and his family had a good meal. The villagers came to welcome them, for this family was considered lost, but now found. The story of the prodigal son, which he had narrated to his family just a few days before, had come true.

They settled down very quickly. An adage says that east or west, home is the best. It was actually the best for them. They learned the survival techniques at home. During the day, able-bodied young men and women went into the bushes to hide, thereby avoiding accidental contact with enemy soldiers. At this time, most of Biafra had been overrun and enemy soldiers wandered freely everywhere looking for women, who either followed them freely or were abducted. However, Papa Chinedu and his family had survived the war. They stayed in the village until the war finally came to an end.

Papa Chinedu was humbled by this experience and he quietly committed himself to quickly build a house in the village and to become more active in what goes on in the village. When he returned to Sabon Gari, Kano, his friend Alhaji Hassan and his family were excited to see Mallam alive. Alhaji had saved all of Mallam's houses in Kano, Zaria and Kaduna. In fact, Papa Chinedu received the rent Alhaji had collected over the three war years. So, just as quickly as he had lost everything he had, Papa Chinedu was quickly getting everything back. It was almost as if nothing had happened. He returned to the NEPA office he had left nearly three years ago. Although the house he lived in was burned by the rioters and looters, he quickly reclaimed all the others.

But the experiences were still fresh, and as a precautionary measure, Papa Chinedu decided to leave his family in Enugu rather than take them to Kano at this time. No matter how glad he felt about getting his property back, he knew it was pure luck. And in truth, it was. Not every Igbo came back alive to reclaim his property. As a result of this war experience, Papa Chinedu decided that his family would now stay in Coal Camp Enugu. He would stay in Kano and make frequent visits to Enugu especially during his annual leave in December, at which time the entire family returned to the village for Christmas.

3
COAL CAMP

C oal Camp was one of the older communities in Enugu. Although people of different professions live there, Coal Camp got its name partly from the fact that coal miners had lived there originally. It was a community in which everybody knew his or her neighbor and everybody was his or her neighbor's helper. Coal Campers believed that it took a community or a village to raise a child, hence they supported each other in the difficult task of bringing up their children.

Nwakego was a distant niece to Mama Chinedu and now lived with her. In addition to helping with housework, she attended a school of stenography, commonly referred to in those days as "commercial school" to distinguish it from the more formal "secondary or high school." Her parents also believed that by living with Mama Chinedu in Enugu, Nwakego would be well trained and also be exposed to potential suitors. Patrick and Ugochi were Chinedu's younger siblings and also lived with their mother. Chinedu was then a high school student and spent the holidays with her mother and siblings in Coal Camp. Papa Chinedu had returned to Kano.

Coal Camp inhabitants ranged from the poor to the lower and upper-middle class, and even some rich families who owned their homes. When a person owned a home in Nigeria, the person paid for it in cash. It was not common at that time to take a loan from a mortgage broker or a bank as done in Western societies. The upper-middle class lived in units called *flats* while the lower-middle class lived in units called *one room* and *two rooms*. The very poor either lived with relatives or moved out of the city.

Coal Camp residents lived in buildings called yards. A yard contained either flats or one room and two room units. A yard had a main building or main yard and a backyard, with the backyard considered an annex to the main building. A yard contained about twelve living units, and each unit was rented by a family. It was common to have four or more children in a family.

One of the tenants that lived in the same yard with Mama Chinedu was Papa Uchechukwu. He had four children and his oldest son, Uchechukwu, who was Chinedu's peer was known for his bowleg. In fact, his friends often made a joke of him and claimed that he waddled like a duck. Olunwa, Uchechukwu's sister, though younger than Nwakego was very fond of Nwakego whom she saw as her older sister. Uchechukwu's other siblings were Chioma and Ifeanyi. These younger ones were respectively, Ugochi and Patrick's peers.

One afternoon, Olunwa and Nwakego gossiped about their mutual friend Stella whose family had moved from their one room unit into a flat.

"Did you hear that Papa Stella and his family have moved into a flat?" Olunwa asked Nwakego.

"No," Nwakego responded.

"My mother told me that Stella's uncle rented a flat for them," Olunwa explained. "Stella is now making *iyanga* to me."

A flat was identical to an apartment in the United States with self-contained utilities and facilities.

"Good for her, but why the *iyanga*?" Nwakego asked. "They won't be the first or last to live in a flat."

Nwakego was known to be unhappy because Mama Chinedu preferred to live in one room instead of moving into a flat. On reclaiming his property in Kano, Papa Chinedu wanted to move his family into a more comfortable unit in Enugu. However, his wife was adamantly opposed to it. She still had memories of the refugee camps during the war and would rather direct her family's resources to investing in their village.

"There are more important things to do with money," she once told her husband when they discussed whether the family should move into a flat. "I don't want to move into a flat or a house in the town only to move into a refugee camp should another war break out."

Recently she bought a "six spring" bed, which was squeezed into one end of her living unit. Her son, Chinedu was back on Christmas holidays and she didn't want him to sleep on the floor with the other children. The common practice was that parents slept on a bed, and children slept on mats spread on the floor. However, with his new status as a high school student, Chinedu deserved more respect.

A one-room unit was partitioned with a curtain or blind creating an inner area, the bed area, that housed the parents' bed. At night, the children slept on mats spread on the floor in the outer area. In the morning, the mats were rolled up and stored under the parents' bed. The common household furniture included sofa-like seats called "cushion chairs" and foldable chairs called "back chairs." A "woman bench" was used mostly by women in the kitchen. It was made from a flat piece of wood, about a square foot in size, resting on four wooden legs about twelve to fifteen inches high.

Unlike self-contained flats, tenants in one and two room units shared facilities and utilities. Typically, there were two bathrooms and two toilets in a yard. These were attachments erected in the backyard area. It was common for the cleaning of the facilities to rotate on a weekly basis among the family units that used them.

A bathroom had no shower or bathtub. In place of the shower, a bucket of water was used, and the person taking the shower squatted to scoop water from the bucket with both palms. Bucket toilets were used. A bucket toilet resembled an adult potty trainer kit for general use. However, unlike a potty trainer emptied after every use, bucket toilets were emptied at night by night soil men. They were so called probably because of the way they disposed the human excrement in big holes dug in the ground where it eventually became soil fertilizer.

The kitchen was a small, open building without partitions with about a square foot's area assigned to each living unit. This area was just big enough to hold the tripod under which the cooking fire burned. The most common type of cooking tripod was erected by bringing together three blocks of sun-dried earth and making a fire in their midst. The less common type of tripod was made by welding three metallic rods onto a metallic ring on which the cooking pot was placed. Cooking fire was made using firewood. Blenders and grinders were uncommon; instead, wooden mortar and pestle were used to pound and grind food items.

The space between two buildings, or yards, was referred to as a backyard, and this was distinguished by context from the living annex also referred to as a backyard. The backyard served a number of useful purposes. Every family kept its firewood in the backyard. Families that fermented *cassava*, a very popular staple food item, also kept the clay pots used for the fermentation in the backyard.

A corridor at the center of the main yard provided access to the living units in the main building. This corridor was also a thoroughfare to the backyard. A door connected the kitchen area to the backyard area. This door served dual purposes. First, it provided access to the backyard from the kitchen area so that tenants easily accessed their firewood from the kitchen area. Second, since the kitchen area shared a common open space with the backyard living units, the door also served as an alternative method of access to the backyard living units. In many yards, the unwritten rule was that children used the backyard door while parents used the main yard entrance.

A common cause of conflict between the main yard and backyard tenants was the foot traffic and noise that resulted as the backyard tenants entered and left the yard. Often, children spilled water on the corridor in the main yard and the water seeped into the living units of main yard tenants.

One day, Uchechukwu's bucket of water fell and the water seeped into Mama Chinedu's room. She complained to Mama Uchechukwu about this.

"Mama Uche, please remind Uchechukwu to always take the backyard whenever he is carrying water. I have been mopping the corridor nearly all evening."

"Did he spill water again in the corridor?" Mama Uchechukwu asked.

"I think he was playing and forgot the bucket of water on his head," Mama Chinedu explained. "We thank God that he was okay, because when I heard the bucket fall, I thought it fell on his leg."

"It would have been better for him," Mama Uchechukwu replied. "Uchechukwu will play while carrying water, while eating, while going to school."

"My sister, don't worry. All these children are the same," Mama Chinedu added.

Electricity was another shared resource in a yard. A yard had one electric meter and, at the end of the billing cycle, the tenants got together to determine the amount due to each person. Electrical appliances, like the iron, the refrigerator, and the microwave oven, were uncommon. Most people had just a light bulb in their homes. Thus, to determine the amount due by each person was straightforward.

But this was not always as easy as it seemed. Some tenants tried to cheat others either by secretly using a prohibited appliance like an electric iron or by not turning off the light bulb at the generally agreed time of 7 am. Electric irons were prohibited because it was felt they consumed too much energy, thus resulting in high electric bills.

Papa Uchechukwu was a domineering figure in the yard. He did not go to school when he was a child, but lately attended adult school, commonly referred to as "night school." His newly acquired status as "an educated man" was instrumental to the great influence he had over other tenants. He was known to leave the light bulb in his house on all day, and this became a common source of conflict with other tenants.

"Papa Uchechukwu," Mama Chinedu called. "Please turn off the light in your house. It's almost 12 o'clock and your light is still on. This is the reason our electric bill keeps rising every month."

But Papa Uchechukwu had a ready answer. "Actually, what matters to the cost of electricity is turning it on and off," he told Mama Chinedu. "Leaving the light on throughout the day doesn't matter. The meter reads only when the switch is turned on and off."

That did not make sense to her; however, she did not have sufficient knowledge to argue. But Chinedu, who was standing by, was even more uncomfortable with that explanation. He thought he remembered learning something called kilowatt-hour being the unit of energy that NEPA charged.

"Papa Uchechukwu, are you saying that it doesn't matter whether a 40 watt electric bulb burns for six hours or twenty four hours?" Chinedu asked.

Papa Uchechukwu knew he was in for some educated trouble.

"My son, it's the women who keep turning the light on and off every minute, who cause the problem," Papa Uche explained, walking away to avoid further discussion.

The matter was later resolved during a yard meeting. It was also revealed that Papa Uchechukwu was secretly using an electric iron. It was reaffirmed that every light must be turned off by 7 am and turned on no earlier than 7 pm. The ban on the use of electric iron was reconfirmed.

Electric power was not the only shared utility. Tap water was dispensed in public utilities called pumps. Tap water was scarce, especially during the dry season. Probably, not unrelated to its hilly location, the public pumps in Coal Camp had sufficient pressure to dispense water only very early in the morning or very late at night. Long lines formed at the pumps as early as 4:00 am or as late as midnight. Coal Camp residents were notorious for not maintaining order at the pumps. Hooligans caused chaos by disrupting the queue's order. A fight usually resulted, although, quite often, there was no one brave enough to challenge them. Eventually they left, at which time order was restored.

Nwakego was a very strong girl. Although Mama Chinedu had warned her against it, Nwakego never shied away from challenging boys. She was the type of girl who snubbed boys and once boasted to a boy that he could not see any green in her eyes. Chinedu was at the other extreme. He easily showed an antagonist a white feather leading many to believe he was a coward. He was not considered enough of a deterrent against anyone who dared to beat up his younger siblings, Ugochi and Patrick. His mother once said he was *utala ede,* a type of *fufu* characterized by its softness. But Nwakego was different. She would fight anybody who dared touch Ugochi or Patrick.

Mike and his parents lived in the same yard with Mama Chinedu. Mike was Chinedu's peer, though, not necessarily one of his best friends. He was considered a bully in the yard. Noticeably bigger than his peers, his springy strides were enough to terrorize any opponent. Once angry, his eyeballs seemed to protrude which he used to frighten younger kids. He was known to be quite stubborn and as obstinate as a mule. Once he determined what he wanted, he stuck to it like glue. Mike beat up every child, and unlike other big boys who helped their yard members to fetch water at the pump, he cared only about himself. When he arrived at the pump one fateful day, it turned out that the person he out-muscled was Patrick. Patrick went home crying.

"Why are you crying?" Nwakego asked, already guessing what had happened, given that Patrick was carrying an empty bucket.

"Mike pushed me away while I was fetching water, and when I said I was going to call Chinedu, he beat me up," Patrick explained.

That was all Nwakego needed to hear. Mama Chinedu, who could have restrained her, was not at home. Nwakego dashed into the house to prepare for a fight. She came out wearing, not one pair of underwear, but several layers. Her mature breasts were protected with four bras. She tied her long, plaited hair back with a couple of head ties. She was ready for a showdown with Mike.

Once at the backyard, she assumed a posture she knew infuriated Mike and other boys whose advances she often snubbed. She anchored her hands on her waist, and given how tense she was, she kept rocking her hips and her right leg, which was resting on a pile of firewood. Although her heart throbbed like lightning thunder, the pride and arrogance in her posture would have made a peacock appear humble.

Word immediately spread that Nwakego was waiting to fight Mike. Most people would consider it madness for her to challenge a boy, especially one much bigger than she was, and probably much stronger. But not Nwakego. Because she always snubbed Mike, who liked to flirt with her, Mike was looking for a chance to beat her up. A girl either allowed a boy to make a pass at her, or the boy beat her up in the yard. It was not too long before Mike returned carrying his bucket of water.

"What did my brother Patrick do to you?" Nwakego asked Mike, pushing him so hard that Mike's bucket fell off his head, flipping as it bounced off a pile of firewood. The splash of the water was so forceful that the two combatants were drenched and the noise attracted the attention of those in the kitchen area. Mike was in a rage. Nwakego had caused his bucket of water to spill. Nwakego pushed him first. What further justification was needed to beat her up?

Those in the kitchen area rushed to the backyard, but they were too late. Nwakego and Mike were locked arm-in-arm in a fistfight. No one had seen Nwakego in a fight before. She was a young woman with fully developed breasts. What if Mike tore her underwear or her bra? That was one primary reason a young woman should never fight. Her opponent would always go after her underwear, her bra, or her hair.

But not Nwakego. She was quite prepared. Mike grabbed her underwear, but could not tear them. He next went for her hair and breasts, and Nwakego countered with a bite, leaving deep marks on his arm. The Igbo say that once a fight starts, even a bite is fair game. Mike was hurt and screamed like a seagull while he pushed Nwakego off.

"You bit my hand, you mad dog," he roared, charging forward angrily for the kill. But that was exactly the way Nwakego had scripted the fight. Those who knew her well understood she was as brave as a lion and could be as agile as a monkey. She took a quick side step, ducking as she made her move. She stooped down as low as Mike's knees, waiting for him. He dashed straight into her waiting hands and was caught off balance. Mustering the strength of a horse, Nwakego lifted him up to the heavens and flung him hard onto a pile of firewood. Not allowing him chance to gather his breath, Nwakego pounced on him like a hungry wolf and started to beat the hell out of the bully. The entire neighborhood went into a frenzy.

"*Gbatanu-o, Nwakego egbu-e Mike*," one of the first women at the scene shouted, urging the neighbors to come and see how Nwakego was "killing" Mike. With Nwakego having the upper hand, no one was in a hurry to separate them. It was not until Mike started crying out to the bystanders to separate them that a few good Samaritans took action. That fight remained the talk at Coal Camp for a long while.

Papa Uchechukwu was one of those who rushed to the backyard. He always admired Nwakego. "She should have been somebody's son," he always said of her. "*Agu nwayi*," he praised her now, calling her a lioness.

Nwakego was either too shy or too tired to accept any compliments.

"She's the dried meat that fills the mouth," he further called her. Shaking his head and smiling as he walked away, he added, "If only she was a boy, you could take her alone to face a village. I think God gave her the wrong genitals."

Mama Chinedu did not know how to react to the story when she heard it upon her return. She merely wondered what could have happened if Mike had succeeded in stripping off Nwakego's underwear and bra. That fight was two holidays ago. One thing it guaranteed was that Patrick and Ugochi were always allowed their turns at the public pumps. Most children also believed that Nwakego had "single bone"—a phrase commonly used to characterize very strong people.

But the water scarcity with its associated fights in the pumps was seasonal. The rainy season was hardly anybody's favorite because of the inconvenience it presented to people as they performed their daily activities. A rainfall meant that the firewood in the backyard became wet and, hence, did not readily burn, which made cooking very difficult. Generally, the mortars and pestles used in pounding food were kept outside. However, during rainy periods, they were squeezed inside the kitchen because tenants could no longer use the open backyard space. This caused further inconvenience in the already crowded kitchen.

But not everybody cared about this discomfort. The children loved the rainfall. Equatorial rainfall was often so strong that it fell like torrents from heaven. The children called it "water from heaven" and always looked forward to such heavy rainfall. The rains also meant that the children did not have to fetch water from the pumps. Rainwater was collected and, because it was water from heaven, it was considered purer than water from pump.

To facilitate the collection of rainwater, curved sheets of zinc were placed at the corners of a roof to form a gutter. The rainwater was directed in a concentrated form to the lower end of the tilted gutter, forming a natural pump. Therefore, in a sense, every yard had its own pump during the rainy season. Children loved fetching rainwater, which seemed like play in the midst of work.

This day was no different from any other. It was raining hard in Coal Camp, droning with insistent ardor upon the zinc roofs. The children were holding hands, dancing in a circle and singing their favorite rain song:

Akpankolo, kpankolo
akpankolo, kpankolo
udume, ogene
udume, ogene

onye omalu
du ya ya ya du ya

At the end of the song, whoever was the last to sit on the floor, went in the middle of the circle for the next round.

The children usually sang the songs after all pots and pans had been filled with water. This was the second day of continuous rainfall, hence every container was quickly filled. The only thing Ugochi could think about filling up were the plates, especially the bowl-like ones used for *fufu* soup. When she ran inside to fetch them, her mother noticed that she was shivering and that goose bumps covered her body.

"Chinedu," she called. "Tell everybody to get out of that rain. They have played enough and if care isn't taken, the cold will enter their body."

That was not the first time she had warned them not to play in the rain. This time she enforced it by standing at the door until every child left the rain and entered the kitchen. The shivering children stayed close to the fire, rubbing their hands and doing whatever they could to beat the cold. Mama Chinedu also went to the kitchen to ensure that Ugochi was warm and did not become sick.

Children went into the kitchen for other reasons too. The rainy season was the season when fresh corn and *ube* were harvested. The corn was roasted in the fire and *ube* was placed some distance from the fire so that it did not burn. *Ube* needed to be softened, not burnt.

There was a good way and a bad way to roast corn. Whenever Nwakego wanted her corn done quickly, she removed the corn leaves so that the roasting proceeded speedily. But according to Mama Chinedu, that was the bad way to roast corns.

"I've told you to stop roasting corn that way," she yelled at Nwakego. "When you remove the leaves, the corn simply chars, and it doesn't mean that it's well roasted. I've told you that corn roasted this way causes cough. You must roast corn with the leaves so that the roasting is gradual. Do you hear me?"

"Yes, *ma*," Nwakego responded.

"I don't think you do. I've said that your ears are for dressing and not hearing. I'll cut them out one day and give them to you since you don't use them. The next thing you'll do is to put the *ube* in hot water to soften it. I've also told you not to do that. You must leave the *ube* by the side of the fire to gradually soften. You're always very impatient. At this rate, I'm sorry for the man who will marry you because you'll give him uncooked food."

Nwakego was always upset whenever she was yelled at in public. However, there was nothing she could do about it.

Children also looked forward to the rainy season because of the fairy tales, or *iro*, they told themselves or their parents told them as they sat around the fireplace. The tortoise, a popular character in most *iro*, was a very crafty animal and the Igbo say that there is no *iro* without the tortoise. Nwakego was, however, known to dislike any *iro* that featured the tortoise. She went to great lengths to ensure that the tortoise was not featured in any *iro* she told. But this night she was not in the mood for an *iro*. She was still unhappy that Mama Chinedu yelled at her for the way she roasted corn.

Mama Chinedu knew that one could not keep Nwakego off *iro* for a long time. But she needed time to calm down for the scolding given to her, so Mama Chinedu volunteered the first *iro*.

"Actually, it's a song you all know very well," she told the children. "It isn't *iro* in the sense you all know it. We'll use the song to learn the features of animals. For example, I can start naming animals that fly. For example, a bat flies, a sparrow flies, a kite flies, but a monkey doesn't fly. You remember how the song goes?"

"Yes, *ma*," the children responded.

"OK. Remember that everybody must respond to every line. Therefore, the only time one is allowed to be silent is when I give a wrong response such as saying that a monkey flies. If I sing that a bat flies and you don't respond, then you're wrong. The first person caught with a wrong answer will tell the next *iro* and we'll go around in a clockwise rotation from that person. Do you all understand?"

"Yes, *ma*," they responded again.

Mama Chinedu's song went like this:

Anu one n'ukwu ino (which animals have four legs)
chorus: n'ukwu ino (four legs)
Anu one n'ukwu ino
n'ukwu ino (four legs)
nkita n'ukwu ino (a dog has four legs)
n'ukwu ino (four legs)

ewu n'ukwu ino (a goat has four legs)
n'ukwu ino (four legs)
efi n'ukwu ino (a cow has four legs)
n'ukwu ino (four legs)
atulu n'ukwu ino (a sheep has four legs)
n'ukwu ino (four legs)
okuko n'ukwu ino (a fowl has four legs)
n'ukwu . . .

Nwakego was caught. Although she did not complete the response, the fact that she started to respond meant she was wrong. So, according to the stipulated guidelines, the next *iro* was hers. Luckily she had cheered up by then.

This night she chose to tell the story of a stubborn woman who refused to address her husband as *my husband.*

"She always called him *that husband,* instead of *my husband,*" Nwakego narrated. "This was a sign of disrespect. Many people knew this woman to be a bad woman."

"Did she die because of that?" Chinedu asked.

"Be patient," Nwakego advised. "That's what the story is all about. The one important lesson in the story is that no woman should disobey or disrespect her husband."

"What if she did?" Chinedu asked.

"Allow her to tell us the story," Uchechukwu screamed at Chinedu. "I want to hear the story, and if you keep asking questions she'll never tell it."

"She was a bad woman," Nwakego continued. "One day, her husband went to the evil forest and reported her to the evil spirits. As her husband was leaving for the farm, the evil spirits sent their leader to punish this woman. Remember that the leader of the evil spirits has seven heads and seven tails."

"What did the evil spirit do?" Uchechukwu asked.

"You have to shut up and listen to the story," Chinedu jeered at Uchechukwu.

Everybody laughed because Chinedu just paid Uchechukwu back in his own coins.

"The evil spirit commanded her to address her husband as *my husband,*" Nwakego continued.

"Did she?" Uchechukwu followed up, ignoring Chinedu.

"No, she didn't."

"What happened?"

"The evil spirit used one of its tails to dig a hole in the ground. Immediately, this woman started to sink into the ground. It began with her feet, her legs, then her knees, her buttocks . . ."

"All her body?" Chinedu asked

"Not yet," Nwakego explained.

"What did the woman do?" Chinedu asked.

"She started singing a song. Here's the song she sang. The chorus you will sing is *E-ne-ne*. Do you understand?"

"Yes, we do," the children responded.

Nwakego started the song.

"*Di, ihe nuhu, di ihe nuhu, dika ijewe ugbo?*" *(That husband, that husband, so you are going to the farm?)*

"*E-ne-ne*," the other children responded in chorus.

"*Di, ihe nuhu, di ihe nuhu, dika ijewe ugbo?*"

"*E-ne-ne.*"

"*Ukwu'm atulu onu n'okwere nweputa.*" *(My feet have sunk into the ground and cannot come out.)*

"*E-ne-ne.*"

"*Afo'm atulu onu n'okwere nweputa.*" *(My stomach has sunk into the ground and cannot come out.)*

"*E-ne-ne.*"

"What happened? Did her husband help her?" many of the children asked in unison.

"No," Nwakego responded. "Her body continued to sink into the ground. The evil spirit told her she was going to die unless she addressed her husband properly and promised to respect him from that day."

"What did she do?" Chinedu asked.

"She kept on with her song. Her neck sank. Her chin sank."

"*Chei!*" one of the children exclaimed, her eyeballs seeming to protrude as they focused on Nwakego. She was clearly becoming frightened as she imagined how systematically this woman approached death.

"The evil spirit spared her mouth to give her the last chance to change her song," Nwakego explained. "Her ear sank. Her head sank and finally when her eyes and mouth were about to sink, she became terrified."

"What did she do?"

"She changed her song."

"What did she sing?"

"*Dim nuhu, dim nuhu, dika ijewe ugbo?*" *(My husband, my husband, so you are going to the farm?)*

"*E-ne-ne.*"

"*Dim nuhu, dim nuhu, dika ijewe ugbo?*"

"*E-ne-ne.*"

"*Isi'm atulu onu n'okwere nweputa.*" *(My head has sunk into the ground and cannot come out.)*

"*E-ne-ne.*"

"At this point, her body started to come out of the ground, head first. She kept singing the song until all her body rose from the ground. She thanked the evil spirit and promised never to disrespect or disobey her husband again."

Everybody always liked Nwakego's stories. The usual applause was interrupted by Patrick, who was screaming, holding his stomach and screaming even louder.

"Patrick, Patrick, *o-gini?*" his mother shouted trying to find out what was wrong with her son.

"Olunwa said that *udala* will grow in my stomach," Patrick told her mother. He continued to cry, holding his stomach with both hands. "I don't want *udala* to grow in my stomach, I don't want *udala* to grow in my stomach."

The problem was that Patrick had mistakenly swallowed an *udala* seed. *Udala* was the delicious fruit from the *udala* tree. An *udala* fruit had many seeds and it was considered an art while eating the fruit, to separate a seed from its protective coat in one's mouth rather than with one's hands. The protective coat was the edible part. However, small children not quite versed in this art often find themselves swallowing the seed along with the protective coat. This was what had happened to Patrick.

"Olunwa, come here," Mama Chinedu shouted. "How many times have I warned you to stop frightening small children with your stupid jokes? Who told you that *udala* will grow in his stomach because he swallowed *udala* seed? Or did you just want to make him cry?"

Olunwa was well-known to always come up with jokes to frighten smaller children. She had no answer to Mama Chinedu's question. Mama Chinedu calmed her son down and assured him that the seed would pass out when Patrick went to toilet the following morning.

4
CITY LIFE

The children fought and screamed at the public pumps. The horns of the buses blared and their brakes screeched as they stopped to pick passengers up. The traders hurried to the market and kiosk owners in the city opened them for early morning business. The church bells chimed and parents hurried to morning mass, and from there to work. This was morning in Coal Camp and one had to search hard to find an idle person. Morning in Coal Camp was so full of life that one thought the city had been awake for several hours.

Mama Chinedu, while primarily a homemaker, had a very successful early morning business—frying and selling *akara*.

Preparing *akara* was labor intensive. The black eye beans from which *akara* is made, were soaked in water during the night. In the morning, the skins were removed and the seeds blended into a thick paste. The paste was molded into appropriately sized balls and fried in a deep pan of oil.

There was a blender in Coal Camp at a place called *Igwe okpa.* The name was coined from *igwe*, or machine, and *okpa*, a popular bean species also blended like the black eye beans for *akara.* Chinedu's mother served a one-menu breakfast that consisted of *akara* and *akamu.* *Akama* was the local equivalent of custard, and was usually drunk with *akara* at breakfast.

It was early in the morning. Chinedu and Nwakego just woke up and were ready to go to Igwe okpa to blend the bean seeds for the day's *akara.* Going to Igwe okpa was one of the early morning activities in Coal Camp.

"I'm leaving you," Chinedu shouted loudly at Nwakego who was known to take almost half an hour to stretch herself out of her sleep. It was early in the morning and the rush was on to be among the first at Igwe okpa.

"Where's your *aju?*" Chinedu screamed at Nwakego.

Still nearly half-asleep, and rubbing her eyes with the back of her left hand, Nwakego picked up an old rag and folded it into a circular pad called an *aju.* The pad served two purposes: it provided a cushioning effect to a person's head so that the weight of the item carried was not directly felt on the head, and it also provided a base which helped to keep the item balanced. With the item properly balanced on the head, the carrier did not have to use his or her hands to hold the item in place. However, carrying a pot on the head without holding it in place with at least one hand is an art. Many pots have broken because young girls preferred to place their hands on their waists making *iyanga* instead of holding their pot securely.

With Nwakego still half-asleep, Chinedu snatched the pad from her, forced it on her head, and helped lift a pan of beans to her head. This has become a daily routine, and the forceful placement of the pad on Nwakego's head was yet another way to actually wake her up from her sleep. Since only Nwakego was around, Chinedu had to lift his own pan to his head. This was a tricky business. With his own *aju* positioned on his head, he knelt down on both knees. Next he raised his left knee, lifted the pan on to that knee, and mustering horse-like energy, lifted the pan from the knee to his head. Unfortunately, the pan did not clear the *aju* and hence brushed it off.

Chinedu angrily lowered the pan to the floor.

"How many times will I tell you to hold my *aju* as I lift the pan to my head?" he barked at Nwakego.

That was the trick. With Nwakego's pan on her head, she was supposed to hold it in place with one hand, and use the other hand to hold Chinedu's *aju* in place as he lifted the pan to his head. However, it was actually Chinedu's angry voice that finally woke Nwakego. Prior to that, she was in a state Mama Chinedu referred to as *rahu ura, muru anya*—sleeping with her eyes open. With Nwakego now fully awake, and doing what she was supposed to do, it was easy for Chinedu to lift his own pan of beans to his head. With one hand, he grabbed an empty bucket that would be used to secure a position at the pump.

Nwakego and Chinedu were always among the first to arrive at Igwe Okpa. The blending machine was fully service-operated, a process that could be likened to airline passengers checking in their baggage at the terminal. Each person moved along with his or her pan of beans until a server or operator, as they were more commonly called, was reached. The operator poured the seeds into the funnel-like container of the blending machine and used the volume to estimate the cost of the blending. The machine operator was also the cashier. However, well-known customers like Nwakego did not pay on the spot. Mama Chinedu eventually paid off-line.

While Nwakego and Chinedu were off to Igwe Okpa, Mama Chinedu prepared to open for business herself. She started warming the usually pre-cooked frying oil in a big frying pan called *agbada*. She also barked orders to Patrick and Ugochi.

"Patrick, are you awake or still sleeping?" she shouted loudly. "If you don't sweep off that place in a minute, thunder will break your head for you. Ugochi go and arrange the forms."

Unlike Nwakego, Patrick and Ugochi were light sleepers. They were already wide-awake and quite alert. As swiftly as birds, they set up the breakfast area for their customers. Their next assignment was to go back and sweep the house.

Nwakego and Chinedu returned with two basins of blended bean seeds. The next step was to further blend them in smaller portions in a mortar before frying. Nwakego sat astride the mortar with her wrapper properly placed. This was important because women did not normally sit astride; they sat with their legs placed together. But to properly blend the bean seeds in the mortar, she had to sit astride and hold the mortar in place with both thighs. Holding the pestle with both hands, Nwakego commenced a rotational motion with the pestle to finally blend the paste. It was at this stage that salt, pepper, onions and other ingredients were added. Water was also added to achieve the proper concentration. Mama Chinedu dipped her forefinger into the paste, touched it with the tip of her tongue to decide if the taste was fine. When finally blended and Mama Chinedu was satisfied with the taste, the paste was transferred into a hand-held calabash. From this calabash, appropriately sized balls were made and dropped into the *agbada*. Halfway through the frying, each ball was turned over to ensure proper frying.

A kettle of water was placed by the side of the fire on which the *akara* was fried. Although the kettle was not directly on the fire, the intensity of the fire was such that the water boiled very quickly. This was used to prepare *akamu*.

Timothy Ani was a regular customer. Tim was a successful textile trader at the Ogbete market and December was a busy month for his business. He was a few minutes early this morning and appeared somewhat in a hurry. Everybody in the neighborhood knew Tim for he was considered a short man, only about 5ft fall and often smoked a long pipe. Many believed that but for his long pipe and cowboy hat, Tim could go unnoticed in a crowd.

"I'm going to Onitsha," Tim volunteered without being asked. "Give me twenty *kobo* worth, and don't forget to put *jara*."

Adding *jara* to a sale was very common in Igboland. *Jara* was the small quantity given in addition to what was purchased. For example, if five balls of *akara* sold for ten kobo, the seller would add one or two extra balls as *jara*. Tim wanted to make sure that his *jara* was not forgotten for buyers often patronized sellers who were generous with *jara*.

"Do you want *akamu*?" Nwakego asked.

"No, I won't wait for *akamu*," Tim replied. "I'll buy Silas bread or Ejidike bread at the motor park."

Akara was also eaten with bread. This was the case when a person was in a rush and didn't have the time to wait for *akamu*. In such a situation, the person bought *akara-to-go* and ate it sandwiched between two slices of bread.

"I thought you went to Onitsha two or three days ago?" Mama Chinedu asked.

"Yes, I did," Tim replied. "But you know that this is our season," he added allowing a small smile to show satisfaction at the brisk business traders were doing. Ogbete was the main market in Enugu. However, Otu in Onitsha, and Ariara in Aba, were much bigger markets than Ogbete. As a result, traders in Enugu periodically traveled to Otu or Ariara to purchase goods to resell at Ogbete.

"I may see you in the market," Mama Chinedu told him. "I'm also going to Onitsha. I've run out of beans, and I need to buy Christmas clothes for these children."

"I will definitely see you in the market," Tim replied.

Ugochi immediately wrapped the *akara* for Tim and added *jara*.

"Buy me something at Onitsha," she said as she handed the wrapped *akara* to Tim. She almost forgot to receive the twenty *kobo* from the customer. Tim smiled, handed her the money and hurried away. Once Tim was out of earshot, Nwakego complained about the *jara* Ugochi had put for Tim.

"Mama," Nwakego called, "did you see the *jara* Ugochi put for Timothy?"

"Yes, Ego," Chinedu's mother replied. She often abbreviated names. Nwakego was Ego and Ugochi was Ugo. "I have asked Ugo to do nothing but wash the plates and spoons, but she won't."

"Somehow she recognizes people going to Onitsha," Chinedu added. "She bribes them with *akara* and asks them to buy her something."

"Leave me alone," Ugo cried, as she flung her hands towards Chinedu.

"No one is holding you," their mother said. "But don't seek people's favor with my *akara*."

*   *   *   *   *

Mama Chinedu was almost ready to set out for Onitsha. Nwakego was busy frying *akara*, preparing *akamu,* and in an absent-minded manner, responding "yes, *ma*" to the scores of last-minute instructions from Mama Chinedu. This was one thing she hated because she felt that she no longer needed those microinstructions.

Many of the buses that serviced the Enugu-Onitsha route had names with special significance to their owners and operators. Most people knew that *Mazi* Igbokwe had gone through many ups and downs in life. He once acknowledged that he had eaten from "the table" and from "the floor" and has decided to take life "one day at a time." Indeed, Mazi Igbokwe was once a successful secondhand clothes dealer but lost all his wealth in one unfortunate incident with the customs agents. He then moved into the transportation business. His fleet of buses was called *No Condition Is Permanent*. Mazi Okoye skipped high school and started transportation business at a young age. With only one bus, he competed admirably against the more established transport magnates who had at least ten buses in their fleet. Mazi Okoye was generally admired for his competitive spirit. His one-bus fleet then was called *The Young Shall Grow*. Many believed that Mazi Uchendu was too religious to be successful in the transportation business. He never missed early morning mass and received Holy Communion everyday. While his friends sought business advise from colleagues or from the local *dibia*, Mazi Uchendu took all his concerns to God in prayer through the parish pastor and catechist. His fleet was called *In God We Trust*. Moreover, some of the operators had taken the names of their buses. For example, most people did not know the easy going Mazi Amala by name. He was *Whether Whether*.

No Condition Is Permanent was one of the early-bird Enugu-Onitsha buses. It blared its horn along Agbani Road picking up traders on their way to Onitsha. *No Condition Is Permanent* recently became the first bus to arrive Onitsha from Enugu everyday. Its main competitor, *Whether Whether,* had not lived up to expectation.

Onitsha-by-air was the name given to the Peugeot 404 and 504 taxis that plied the Enugu-Onitsha route. They got their name because of the near-flight speed at which they drove on the ill-maintained Enugu-Onitsha road. *Man Die Go,* which figuratively translated to "man dies and he goes," was a nickname given to one of the popular drivers on this route who prided himself for surviving a crash with a locomotive as he tried to beat the closing gates at a rail crossing. In today's world, *Man Die Go* would need plastic surgery to reclaim his face from the scars that indicated his many motor accidents.

Given that Christmas was quickly approaching, traders traveled to Onitsha more frequently. The rush was on to catch the early morning buses. The conductor of the *Udoye* bus was hustling market women into the bus. The *Udoye* bus shuttled early morning traders and travelers to the motor park; it differed from *No Condition Is Permanent* in that it was an intra-city Enugu bus, while the latter was an inter-city Enugu-Onitsha bus.

Mama Chinedu waited for Chinedu to bring out her market basket as she gave last minute instructions to Nwakego. But in the process, she missed her bus. "Chinedu," she shouted, "I've missed *No Condition Is Permanent*. The next time it takes you one hour to bring out my market basket, I'll break your head."

"Mama," Chinedu calmly called. "Take *Udoye* to 'round-about' and from there take *Onitsha-by-air*. It costs only two *naira* more, and you will be at Otu Onitsha in one hour."

"Round-about" was a popular, unofficial terminal for *Onitsha-by-air* taxis.

"*Tufiakwa,*" she cursed, clapping her hands in the process. "Do you know that this thing they call *Onitsha-by-air* is a death trap? You must be dreaming if you think I will ever enter it."

"Why not?" Chinedu asked. "They're cleaner and faster."

"Chinedu, advise yourself. Don't advise me. I'll follow *Whether Whether*. He'll be here in a minute. Just keep your eyes open and help Nwakego to make sure everything goes well. Don't allow Ugo to sell *akara* again. If she can keep the plates clean, that's enough. And don't let her go late to school. She must leave everything for you and Nwakego by seven o'clock so she gets to school on time."

Whether Whether pulled up and Chinedu's mother hurriedly bade her children good-bye. Shortly, everybody was seated on the bus. The conductor removed the wooden wedge and yelled the usual *yaa iru*, a signal to the driver that the conductor and the passengers were ready. A bus conductor always carried such a wooden wedge that he placed behind the back wheel to prevent the bus from rolling backwards. In those days, a bus conductor did not enter the bus until the bus was in motion. He would run after the bus before it fully accelerated. On catching up with the moving bus, the conductor would grasp the door, run a few paces and acrobatically leap into the bus. A few lost either timing or control, resulting in a fall with serious head injuries.

"Driver *ka-obanye*, driver *ka-obanye*," the passengers in the bus screamed, requesting the driver to stop and allow a passenger to enter.

The conductor was still running along with the bus when that familiar *ka-obanye* cry was heard. Some of the passengers had recognized a woman running after the bus, one hand holding her flapping breasts, and the other holding a big basket on her head. The bus slowed to a stop; the conductor threw the wedge and helped the woman push her basket under her seat. It was Mama Caro, a light-skinned middle-aged woman who lived in a neighboring yard to Mama Chinedu's. She was Mama Chinedu's competitor in the *akara* business. Mama Caro was also going to Onitsha, and like Mama Chinedu, she left her daughter Caro and her siblings to take care of business that day.

After pulling herself together, she recognized she was sitting next to Mama Chinedu.

"Mama Chinedu, good morning."

"Good morning," Mama Chinedu responded, "I thought you went in *No Condition Is Permanent.*"

"No, I overslept. Papa Caro should have woken me up by the time he left for morning mass, but he didn't."

"Mama Caro, you aren't alone," interjected Angela. "It's this Christmas weather. You wake up and you go back to sleep."

"Angela, good morning," Mama Caro greeted. "Are you also going to Otu today? How's my daughter Ndidi?"

Angela, another middle-aged woman known for her beauty, lived a few streets away. She ran a quick-service grocery very similar to a 7-11 and was also on her way to Onitsha. After the death of several of her children, Ndidi, or Patience, was the name Angela gave to her only surviving daughter. It was believed that the name Angela had stuck with her before she had a child who survived, hence many called her Angela instead of Mama Ndidi.

Although only a sixty-five mile trip, it took the buses about three hours to reach Onitsha. These buses found their niche by emphasizing their differences from *Onitsha-by-air*. Unlike the taxis, they made many stops at the small towns and villages along the Enugu-Onitsha road and were considered generally safe, hence their appeal to women and older people.

Having successfully negotiated the "milliken hill," the bus was now headed to Udi, a town on the Enugu-Onitsha road, where a few passengers on their way to *Nkwo-agu* Udi disembarked. Although Otu Onitsha was a big daily market, there were markets in smaller towns that were held on the native week timetable. In Igboland, there are four days in a native week, namely, *Nkwo, Eke, Orie* and *Afor*. Therefore, while the British colonial masters brought with them the concept of seven days in a week, the Igbo had the concept of four days in a market week. *Nkwo-agu* Udi was therefore, the market in Udi that was held every *Nkwo* day.

While a few passengers disembarked at *Nkwo-agu* Udi, those going as far as Otu continued their conversation. Mama Chinedu and the other women discussed the children who were on holidays.

"Mama Caro, what happened to Cletus' left eye?" Angela asked. Cletus was the son of a neighbor who lived in the same yard as Mama Caro.

"Angela, my dear, I don't know," Mama Caro responded. "His father complained to Papa Caro that Cletus wore that black patch *for show*. His father said that nothing was wrong with his eye."

"What?" Angela shouted.

"Yes, my dear," Mama Caro said. "That's the new thing with these children. We won't even know when something has happened to their eyes."

Cletus was a vacationing high school student. The vogue in town with the high school children was to mimic everything they saw on television or read in magazines, especially *Newsweek,* which came from America. *Newsweek* was very popular and was available in many of the department stores in Enugu, notably, Kingsway, Chanrai, Leventis, and Eastern Shop. A recent issue of the magazine featured the then Israeli general, Moshe Dayan, who of course, wore a patch due to an eye problem. It turned out that every high school student in Coal Camp started wearing a patch on his eye to look like "the one-eyed general." In fact, a few days ago, a boy had asked Mama Cletus whether Moshe Dayan was at home. The poor woman was understandably confused. She had no idea what the boy was talking about. Luckily, Cletus' sister was around and was aware that her brother had picked the nickname "Moshe Dayan." It turned out that the boy who was looking for Dayan was Westmoreland. Westmoreland left word that Dayan should meet him at the DMZ north of the No Fly Zone where he would be playing soccer with others, including Dakota.

Mama Caro and the rest of the women agreed that the world might be coming to an end.

"How can a boy close off one of his God-given eyes with a patch just to be like Dayan?" they wondered.

There was little these mothers could do about teenagers and peer pressure. It turned out that it became more pronounced once these kids got to the fourth level in high school, at which time they studied American history and geography. Saskatchewan was the boy who lived with his parents next door to Angela. There was another called Ohio. Vegas had fought with Dallas the other day. "Wonders would never end," Mama Caro noted.

"These American things have taken the names of the children," Angela pointed out, "and sometimes you don't know who or what they're talking about."

The discussion continued as the bus pulled away from Awka, inching closer and closer to Otu Onitsha.

The bus finally pulled up at Otu motor park. As was the practice, the conductor jumped out from the bus before it came to a full stop. It was part of the trade. In those days, conductors took great pride in displaying their ability to jump in and out of a moving bus. He ran along the bus until it finally came to a full stop, positioned a small "woman bench," as a stepping platform to assist the women as they alighted from the bus.

Mama Chinedu bought beans and onions for her *akara*. Next she went to the textile stall where she ran into Timothy. Timothy, a textile re-seller at Ogbete, always chided Mama Chinedu for buying from Otu instead of from him at Ogbete.

"So, Mama Chinedu, you don't want the Ogbete traders to celebrate Christmas?"

"Why do you say that?" Mama Chinedu laughed, but she understood exactly what Tim meant. "Timothy, you don't look for something in the bag of a person looking for the same thing," she added.

Tim smiled and responded, "Maybe we shall all start frying our own *akara*."

This was a well-known dialogue between them. They smiled and went on with their business. Mama Chinedu was about to leave when Tim remembered he had "something" for Ugo.

"*Biko,* give this to my daughter Ugo," Timothy said, handing Mama Chinedu a packet of cabin biscuit and a few candy bars.

"Thank you," she responded. "Everyone is always thinking about Ugo. What about the others?"

Timothy merely smiled and continued looking over the materials he was buying. Nobody mentioned the extra balls of *akara* Ugo put for Tim earlier in the morning.

Most Enugu women did not like spending time at Otu. They finished their business and left immediately. Otu *Ocha,* like most big markets, was a tough place to go to.

"*Hole am, hole am, hole am.*" This was a familiar cry in the market especially during Christmas time. *Hole am* was the colloquial equivalent of "Hold him" or "catch him," a familiar cry used to pursue pickpockets or thieves whenever they struck. Christmas period was their busy season because of the large crowds in the market.

Not far away, the victim, a young man apparently new to town, had had his money stolen. He had placed the money in an envelope in his side pocket and now it was gone.

"Is his head complete?" Angela inquired. "How can someone expose money to them that way?"

"There are people who are still new to Otu and will display their life's savings to these pickpockets," Mama Caro explained. "What a terrible Christmas awaits him. By the way, did they catch the pickpocket?"

"Catch who?" Angela retorted. "They strike as fast as lightning and melt away in the crowd as quickly as ice melts in a cup of hot water."

"There are more pickpockets here in Otu than in Ariara market," Mama Caro argued.

"Oh yes," Angela agreed. "For some time now, the Ariara traders have fought these pickpockets as tirelessly as a seagull, vowing that none of them would leave the market alive. Two pick pockets were stoned to death in one week, and the survivors fled as quickly as their legs could carry them converging here in Otu. My uncle, who has a tobacco shed, told me that the Onitsha Traders Association will meet to decide on a similar line of action like the Aba traders."

"That would be welcome news," Mama Caro said. "But until then, everybody should try their best and safeguard their hard-earned money."

Every woman who was familiar with the way of life at Otu often "wore" her money around her waist or in her bra. The only way to steal such money was, practically speaking, to strip such a woman naked. Wallets were uncommon and men had special pockets by the waistband of their trousers also making it impossible to steal their money. It was unheard of that any man put money in his trousers side or back pockets while in Otu.

It was about 3 pm when *Whether Whether* departed Onitsha for Enugu. The drive back was uneventful and, before it got dark, Chinedu's mother was at home with her children.

"How was the market?" Nwakego asked.

"Everything was fine, especially if your *chi* removes the pick pockets from your path," Mama Chinedu responded, narrating the story of the man whose money had been stolen earlier in the day.

"Mama, I've told you I'm sick and tired of these pickpocket stories at Otu and Ogbete markets," Chinedu added almost angrily. "The day the traders decide that no pick pocket will leave Otu or Ogbete alive, all this nonsense will stop."

"My son, it isn't as simple as you make it sound," Mama Chinedu explained.

5
CHRISTMAS IN COAL CAMP

This was the year the war ended, and people were gradually picking up the pieces of their lives. It was Christmas season and Coal Camp residents like other Enugu residents wanted to use this first post-war Christmas to celebrate the return to Enugu. Word spread encouraging everyone to stay and celebrate the return to the city they so much loved, had lost, but regained. Everybody complied for Enugu was one big family. Papa Chinedu and his family also complied; they spent this Christmas at Coal Camp, Enugu.

Though it was about a fortnight before Christmas, the festivities were already on. The air was gay and youth groups sang Christmas carols every night in the streets. Every child received new clothes at Christmas. Children took great pains in hiding their clothes so that no one outside the family would see them before Christmas Day. Every child looked forward to that element of surprise and praise when the new clothes were worn for the first time on Christmas morning. They were supposed to have been brought on Christmas Eve by Father Christmas.

In those days, many parents gave their children haircuts. It was considered expensive to go to a professional barber. But one of the distinguishing characteristics of Christmas was that every child was given a new haircut by a professional barber. Patrick was running around in excitement. He had not eaten anything since that morning.

"Stupid boy, go and eat," his mother yelled at him.

"I'm not hungry," the overexcited Patrick responded. Everybody was going to the barber that day, which was better than food. Even Chinedu once claimed that he did not want his hair to grow again after Christmas. Mama Chinedu's *aguba* was well known in the neighborhood. Her haircut did not last more than two minutes to complete. Her *aguba* made every head as reflective as a mirror.

Grown-up girls normally plaited their hair. But at Christmas, some girls stretched their hair, but most permed it. Stretching was crudely performed with Vaseline and a hot comb. Electric irons and electric hot combs were uncommon. The comb was heated in a locally made pressing iron. The local pressing iron was made of metal. Burning charcoal was put into it to make it hot. When the comb placed inside the iron was heated to the correct temperature, Vaseline was lavishly rubbed on the hair and the hot comb then used to stretch the greased hair.

But what really excited girls was perming their hair. Olunwa could hardly wait and always preferred to perm hers, usually on Christmas Eve so that it still looked great on Christmas Day. Hair was permed by applying a chemical relaxer. The chemical was then washed off, leaving the hair "long" and beautiful. But timing was important. If the chemical was washed out too soon, the hair might not be properly permed.

It was Christmas Eve and Nwakego was perming Olunwa's hair.

"I think it has cooked well," Olunwa told her. "It's time to wash it off."

The time between the application of the chemical relaxer and rinsing the hair was locally referred to as "cooking" time.

"No," Nwakego responded, admiring her work on her friend's hair. "It needs to remain a few more minutes."

"I think it has cooked well," Olunwa repeated a few moments later. "I feel some tingling in my scalps."

"That means it's cooking well," Nwakego confidently reassured her. Nwakego was feeling quite excited about this opportunity to play hairdresser. She had never done it before and was boasting loudly that Olunwa's hair was going to be the prettiest on Christmas Day.

"You'll show me your Christmas clothes tonight to thank me for your hair."

"I'm not showing anything to you," Olunwa responded. "Did you show yours to me?"

Mama Olunwa passed by and noticed a bad smell in the air.

"Nwakego," she called. "Start washing that hair, it has cooked long enough."

"Yes, *ma*," Nwakego responded. They entered the bathroom and Olunwa sat on a small stool, bending her head forward in the bucket for Nwakego to rinse.

Nwakego poured the first cup of water over Olunwa's hair and ran her hand through the hair to rinse it. Something was wrong. She trembled fearfully and visibly. Olunwa's hair had come out in her hand. Completely terrified, she screamed, calling her god, "*Chim egbuo-mo!*"

Olunwa was startled by Nwakego's scream. Her mother ran to the bathroom only to scream even louder when she herself realized what had happened.

"*Chim-o!*" she screamed with her hands dovetailed over her head. "What did you do to Olunwa's hair?"

Olunwa ran her hand over her hair to determine what was amiss. Her hand became filled with her own hair. She sprang to her feet and fell on the floor almost at the same time, screaming unintelligible words. She had lost her mind and seemed to be in a trance. Nwakego had over-cooked the perm and it burnt off all of Olunwa's hair. There was no way to save it. Mama Chinedu's razor gave her an *aguba* shave that left her with a baldhead. She cried throughout the Christmas holiday.

*　　*　　*　　*　　*

Masquerades featured prominently as part of the Christmas celebration, and Coal Camp had the best and biggest masquerades in all of Enugu. December 25th was set aside for merriment, to entertain friends, and to watch the small masquerades entertain. December 26th, or Boxing Day was for the big masquerades, the day that the masquerades displayed their *otumokpo* to determine which was the biggest and strongest. *Otumokpo* was the *juju* or voodoo with which each masquerade cursed competitors.

But it wasn't only the boys or men that had entertainment groups as part of the Christmas celebration. Eriko was by far the most popular dance presented by teenage girls. Chinelo was a very pretty girl who lived in a neighboring yard. Her parents had once chastised her for spending too much time in Mama Chinedu's house. The reason was that Chinelo visited Nwakego quite often. Although younger than Nwakego, Chinelo looked up to Nwakego as "a big sister" and hence spent most of her time with Nwakego. Nwakego, Olunwa and Chinelo became known in the neighborhood as the "three girl friends." In addition, Chinelo was also well known because she was the lead singer and dancer of the Eriko group.

It was December 25th morning, and a few blocks away at Ogbunike Street and Goldsmith Avenue, the Eriko group was performing.

Eriko eluwe k'ona elunee
Ee udemu udelele odenigbo ndi-egwu
Unu ma ndi gbalu Eriko gaa na ...

That was the signature tune of the Eriko dance. Chinelo's voice was fresh and clear in the air. Because she was so pretty, it was gossiped that Chinelo was *ogbanje*, one of those evil children who tortured their mothers by dying and returning to their mothers' wombs. But that did not affect her Eriko dance. Her voice in the distance sounded crystal clear and as sweet as honey. And when it came to the complicated footwork associated with the Eriko dance, she was as sure-footed as a goat.

Chinelo had become synonymous with Eriko. She had become the dance itself and many believed she could not make a mistake doing the Eriko dance. And this was not without reason: Once, Chinelo had lost her step and fallen down. However, rather than attempt to get up in shame, Chinelo kept dancing while on the floor. And since she was also the lead singer, she changed the song to:

Eriko elue ani (Eriko is on the floor)
Ndi egwum solunu Eriko lue ani (My fellow dancers get on the floor

with Eriko*)*

Impulsively, her fellow dancers fell to the floor and danced as their leader did. Gradually, she changed the song asking them to get up from the floor, which they did and the dance continued from where it had almost been marred. Those who did not know the inside story still argue that the fall to the ground was deliberate and was a new twist in the Eriko dance.

The Eriko dancers wore wrappers that covered the area between their waists and their legs, and a second smaller wrapper or head-tie that was tied across their breasts. They also wore, around their waists, beads called *jigida*, which rattled and added sound effects to the dance.

The primary musical instrument used by the Eriko dancers was the *udu*. *Udu* was a special clay pot about four to ten liters in volume. It had two openings that produced its sound. The primary opening was considered the big mouth of the pot and was about two to three inches in diameter. On the side, but very close to the big mouth, was the small mouth. The small mouth was about an inch in diameter. The *Udu* was held in place with both thighs and the player used both palms to beat on the big and small mouths producing the desired sound. The metallic gong, or *ogene,* played a very small role in Eriko dance.

The boys presented two classes of masquerades. These were the entertainment and dance-oriented masquerades and the aggressive masquerades that pursued and beat up spectators.

Ulaga, Atunma and *Ojionu* typified the first type. *Ulaga* was a song-oriented masquerade presented by a group of boys. As with most masquerades in Igboland, the *Ulaga* was spirit that came from the dead, and the human members merely sang choruses for the spirit. However, during the rehearsals, which were held before Christmas, a human played the part of the spirit. To closely mimic the spirit, a special mouthpiece called *udude* was used in the songs. *Udude* distorted the voice of the speaker and gave the appearance of the voice of a spirit. The best *udude* was made from a snake's skin. It was always a dangerous adventure looking for a dead snake or going out to kill one for its skin. Uchechukwu played the spirit for *Ulaga* group he and Chinedu formed with a few other boys in their yard.

An interesting situation usually arose when two *Ulaga* groups got into a "challenge." In such a challenge, two *Ulaga* alternately sang songs until one ran out of songs, leaving the other the winner.

It was about mid-day on Christmas day, and a few blocks away, the Abagana *Ulaga* was performing.

> *Mbosi anyi j'elu egwu n'uwani*
> *De nde le le ke ndele*
> *Mbosi anyi j'elu egwu n'uwani*
> *De nde le le ke ndele*
> *Ulaga imalu egwu gi puta ndele*
> *De nde le le ke ndele*

This was a common invitation song for a challenge from one *Ulaga* to another. It was Christmas Day at Goldsmith Avenue and Chukwuani Street and the Abagana Street *Ulaga* challenged Chinedu's Chukwuani Street *Ulaga*. The Chukwuani Street *Ulaga* responded to the challenge immediately.

> *Nee m anya n'isi, nee m anya n'odu*
> *k'unu malu na ugo belu n'oji efelugo*
> *Ugo belu n'oji efelugo*
> *Ugo belu n'oji nwannem o, efelugo*
> *Ugo belu n'oji efelugo*

With this response, a big challenge was on between the two of the best *Ulaga* groups in Coal Camp, the Abagana and Chukwuani groups.

As the challenge continued and spectators cheered both *Ulaga*, Mama Uchechukwu looked for her son. Apparently, Uchechukwu had not finished his chores before leaving the house. His mother saw Chinedu and the other children singing choruses for the *Ulaga*, but she did not see Uchechukwu.

"Chinedu," she called. "Do you know where Uchechukwu went to?"

"I don't know," Chinedu replied avoiding eye contact with her. Of course, he knew, but Mama Uchechukwu had no reason to believe that Chinedu had lied to her. Apparently, the *Ulaga* itself had turned around when Uchechukwu's name was mentioned. If only Mama Uchechukwu was careful, she would have observed that the Chukwuani *Ulaga* waddled like a duck, or as many might argue, like Uchechukwu.

Atunma was also featured on December 25th. It was dance-oriented and differed from *Ulaga,* which only sang, but did not dance. *Atunma* did very little, if any, singing, but danced a lot. Many people loved *Atunma* because it was quite entertaining. The instruments used by the *Atunma* group included the *ogene,* the *udu* and the *ekwe.* The *Ekwe* is a wooden instrument with a hollow center, which produced a crackling sound that blended beautifully with the *ogene* and the *udu.*

The masquerades featured on December 26th did not encourage its members to be in close proximity with the spectators. In fact, they were very aggressive, chasing and beating up spectators. *Okwonma Obiesie* was one of the best in this class. People looked forward to Christmas just to watch Obiesie and his *Okwonma.* The clanking and jangling of the metallic chains decorating the *Okwonma* caused everybody to flee. People fell down, picked themselves up again and ran. Yet, they enjoyed it. The *Okwonma* would block the road, bringing traffic to a complete stop. *Okwonma* could be pleaded off the road by giving money to it. Spectators came from all parts of Enugu to watch Obiesie and his *Okwonma.* *Okwonma* music was provided by an *ogene.*

Iga was another aggressive masquerade that also specialized in chasing and beating up spectators. It was always in motion, and like a bull, it would charge on the spectators only to be restrained by its followers, using a rope tied around its waist. The *Ogene* was also the sole musical instrument for the *iga* masquerade.

Goddy iga was one of the first *iga* in Enugu. *Iga Emesibe* came after *Goddy iga* and was feared and dreaded. Its distinguishing characteristic was its ability to scale any building. *Iga Emesibe* would not engage in a fight when on the ground. To effectively contain it, an opponent must first prevent it from reaching the top of a building, for once it was at the top of a building, *Iga Emesibe* was impossible to contain.

Another masquerade from Coal Camp was *Ojionu Igwe Okpa.* Members of this group were mostly the young men who operated the blending machines at *Igwe Okpa.* The *Ojionu* masquerade was dance-oriented. Like the *Okwonma,* the *Ojionu* carried a lot of *otumokpo* or *juju.* A feature that characterized the *Ojionu* was that a member of its group carried its *juju* in a box. This was unlike other masquerades that either wore their *juju* on their bodies, or held them in their hands. Whenever the box was placed on the ground, it was a sign the *Ojionu* was going to curse another masquerade.

Ojionu Igwe Okpa was the favorite of many for numerous reasons. Primarily, it was dance and entertainment-oriented. Unlike the aggressive *Okwonma*, it did not chase or charge the spectators. Consequently, even women came within close range to watch it perform. Like other masquerades, the *Ojionu* was also a spirit. Two young men played the part of the *Ojionu* during rehearsals. By coincidence, they had identical names—Sunday. To distinguish one from the other, the shorter Sunday was Sunday *uno enu. Uno* is "house", and *enu* is "up". Thus, Sunday *uno enu* was a reference to the fact that he lived with his parents in the top floor of a two-story yard. The taller Sunday was Sunday "Artisan" because his family recently moved to another part of Enugu called the Artisan quarters. Coal Campers recognized the *Ojionu* dance abilities of these two young men. Sunday *uno enu* galloped like a horse while Sunday Artisan trotted like a donkey.

The beauty of the *Ojionu* lay in how the masquerade danced in synchrony with its flutist. The other instruments that supported the flute included the *igba* or drums, and *ishaka* or the maracas.

It was Boxing Day at Agbani Road and Calabar Street and *Ojionu Igwe Okpa* was entertaining the spectators.

"*Ojionu mu o*," the flutist blew. This was a typical signature tune for the *Ojionu*. The *Ojionu* responded, shaking its head and pushing backwards the wooden carving that decorated its head. For this particular *Ojionu*, this was a sign that it was going to give a special performance. The crowd moved backwards to make room for it.

"*Ojionu mu o*," the flutist blew again. The *Ojionu* trotted one half block ahead of its drummers. As always, its flutist was right there with it. The drummers beat harder, the flutist blew harder, and the *Ojionu* danced, making spectators rise to their feet. This particular *Ojionu* often peaked its performance by dancing while rolling on the floor. It would follow this by dancing in a semi-circle shaking hands with spectators—something the audience appreciated. Waving to the East, to the West, to the North, and lifting its *oji* from the earth, the *Ojionu* pointed to, and started moving towards the South.

"This is how Sunday Artisan dances," a surprised woman spectator murmured to a friend standing next to her. "Where's Sunday? Isn't he with them today?" she asked since she could not identify Sunday Artisan among the *Ojionu* group members.

"*Shi-i-i,* please shut your mouth," her friend warned, placing her forefinger on her lips to emphasize the warning. "How can you say a thing like that? The *Ojionu* is spirit."

Trembling frightfully, the two women left the scene immediately in case the *Ojionu* ever understood the conversation that had transpired between them.

Although its style was not meant to frighten spectators, other masquerades including many *Okwonma,* respected *Ojionu Igwe Okpa.* They knew that whenever the *Ojionu* called for its *juju* box, danger was in the air. It seldom did, but when it did, the consequences were grave.

An out-of-town *Okwonma* was on a collision course with *Ojionu Igwe Okpa.* Any masquerade from Enugu should have respected the *Ojionu,* but not the *Okwonma.* Ordering its *juju* box to the ground, the *Ojionu* lifted its *oji* from the earth, took a *juju* wrapped with palm fronds from the box, danced around in a circle, and, pointing at the *Okwonma,* thrust the *oji* into the earth. The *Okwonma* was pinned to where it was standing and could not move. This was a powerful *juju* that only the *Ojionu* and *Okwonma Obiesie* possessed. They could pin an opposing masquerade and hold it motionless in its spot. Seeing their masquerade motionless, the members of the out-of-town *Okwonma* offered some sacrifice to placate the *Ojionu.* The *Ojionu* later unpinned their *Okwonma.*

Inyiagbaoku was another big masquerade but it came from a town at the outskirts of Enugu called Udi. *Inyiagbaoku* was feared because it was one masquerade that withstood *Okwonma* Obiesie and *Ojionu* Igwe okpa. The members of the *Inyiagbaoku* masquerade produced good music with their sole musical instrument, the *ogene. Inyiagbaoku* was such a powerful masquerade that no woman ever dared to look at it. If the masquerade was in a neighborhood, every woman must run and take shelter until the masquerade passed. *Inyiagbaoku* was also well known for warning people or other masquerades before it cursed them. It did this by singing its war song:

Meji nye egwu ogbana wa (scare him so he'll flee)
Meji nye egwu ogbana wa
Oke nmawu n'abia gbana wa (run, a big masquerade is coming)
Meji nye egwu ogbaba wa

Once the *Inyiagbaoku* sang this war song, the streets became completely deserted. Only other powerful masquerades like *Okwonma* Obiesie and *Ojionu* Igwe okpa stuck to their turf.

Another big masquerade from out of town that was respected was *Okwonma* Akpugo. Like Udi, Akpugo was a town at the outskirts of Enugu. The distinguishing characteristic of this group was their beautiful *ogene* music. It was generally believed that of all the *Okwonma* of that era, *Okwonma* Akpugo had the best *ogene* music.

Biggie-belle, or "big belly" was an unconventional masquerade. It neither sang nor danced and did not have group members, although it was common for it to attract a large following among boys. It was a masquerade in the form of a caricature of a naked man with a big stomach. Its distinguishing feature was its unusually large penis, which it always held in its hand while chasing or sneaking behind young women.

Obiagu Road was the melting pot for all masquerades that considered themselves powerful. A common saying in Enugu was that on Boxing Day, all roads led to Obiagu Road. Generally, the masquerades from Coal Camp could go anywhere at anytime. The other masquerades that ventured into this "war zone" were *Okwonma* from Akpugo and *Iyiagbaoku* from Udi.

And so Enugu residents will forever remember this first post-war Christmas that they used to celebrate the return to Enugu. But after this Christmas, Enugu residents like other Igbo, embarked in what became known as "mass return." This meant that every family returned to the village at Christmas. In a sense, "mass return" celebrated the fact that while families couldn't survive the war in Enugu, they did so in their villages. Thus, in subsequent years, Enugu at Christmas, looked as deserted as a College campus during summer vacation; every family returned to the village. Papa Chinedu was one champion of this concept. He never failed to return to Amuvi, Arochuku, at Christmas.

6

CHRISTMAS IN AMUVI AROCHUKU

It is said that when the ant stings the buttocks, the buttocks learn. Papa Chinedu had once been stung, and he learned his lesson. No one needed to remind him that east or west, home was the best. The following year, when he returned to Enugu from Kano in mid-December, it was to take his family to his village, Amuvi Arochuku, for the Christmas holiday. This was the first time the whole family traveled home together after that trip from the refugee camp in Ovim. Everybody looked forward to this trip. Even Chinedu's younger siblings, Ugochi and Patrick, looked forward to returning to the village that saved their lives during the war.

The Christmas shopping had been done, and everybody had received a professional haircut. So, it was goodbye to Enugu as they boarded a charter bus that took them to Amuvi for Christmas.

"What a difference a year makes," Mama Chinedu said, but to no one in particular.

Her husband smiled but said nothing. It did not take the children long to catch on to what was going on in their parents' minds.

"I remember the last time we were all together in a bus going home," Chinedu said.

"That's what I was referring to," his mother added.

"I know," Chinedu concurred. "I still remember that if it wasn't for God's mercy, Papa wouldn't have survived that accident."

"My son, I still don't know how to thank God or where to start counting my blessings," Papa Chinedu said.

"It's simple," Mama Chinedu told him. "Keep your hands clean and straight. That's the secret to God's mercy."

"I believe you," Papa Chinedu concurred.

"One more thing," his wife added, "Whenever you can do good, just do it."

Although the road to Amuvi was in a bad shape, it was nothing to compare with the farmlands that were used as roads during the war. Moreover, buses and cars were now available, unlike during the war when the army had commandeered every road-worthy vehicle. More importantly, Papa Chinedu now had a house in the village, and knew how to get to his house!

It was Christmas Eve in the village and the air was festive. The entire village assembled at the Saint Thomas Primary School playground for this year's launching event. Following the war defeat, the Igbo felt that the government was not very responsive to their needs. The response of the Igbo was to raise funds to implement some of the projects they felt the government should have implemented. For example, they raised funds through individual and group levies to rebuild schools, markets and roads. Every Christmas, a project was focused on, and funds raised specifically for that project. The town meeting held to raise the funds was called "a launching" for the project. Thus Christmas in the village became a time for launching self-help projects; it was no longer a time for masquerades.

On his way to Saint Thomas Primary School, where the launching would be held, Chinedu made a brief stop to say hello to a family friend, Mama Nkechi.

"Paul," Mama Nkechi called. "Come and greet your brother Chinedu. Where's Nkechi? Call her to come and greet Chinedu."

Paul was her eldest son. Nkechi, her daughter, was a shy girl. She greeted Chinedu and disappeared almost immediately.

"She'll be entering Queen's High School Enugu next year," Mama Nkechi told Chinedu.

"She passed the entrance to Queens?" Chinedu asked. "That's wonderful. You must be very proud of her."

Nkechi's mother smiled and continued peeling an orange for Chinedu.

Chinedu took the orange with him because he was, by his own count, already late to the launching ceremony.

"Give me a second and I'll go with you," Paul told Chinedu.

"It has to be a second because we're already late," Chinedu responded.

When Chinedu and Paul arrived at the launching venue, it was as noisy as a market. The assembly hall of St. Thomas Primary School was filled to capacity, but Chinedu recognized Okeke and his brother Vincent. They were his distant cousins. At another end of the hall, Chinedu saw his father carrying on a conversation with two distant relations, Mazi Ogbonnia and Mazi Okugo.

A launching was performed with the festive spirit that typified Christmas. During this particular launching, the Amuvi women presented one of their new *ojo-ojo* dance songs as a prelude to the launching. Dressed in their traditional *omu aru* and white lace blouses, the dancers captivated the spectators as they sang and danced:

Umu Amuvi n'abia eh
Amuvi uda n'abia eh
ogo n'ewero obi inwe eh
onye nwere obi inwe naba ah ah eh

Everyone in Amuvi recognized the voice of the women's lead singer, Mgbafor, the wife of Mazi Amechi. In his youth, Mazi Amechi was one of the most handsome men in Amuvi. Over 6' 4'' tall, Mazi Amechi commanded respect. He was a successful hunter who never returned from a hunting expedition empty-handed. The villagers believed he was as strong as the Biblical Samson. Mgbafor was also the most beautiful woman in the village at that time. In fact, she was more commonly known as Uzunma, "the sound of beauty," a name given to her by her husband, Amechi. She had told her parents that if Amechi could not marry her, she would never marry in her life. Even in her early forties and with five children, many believed Uzunma had not lost any hint of her beauty. Many still called her *agbogho,* or "young teenage girl," because like a teenage girl, her breasts still stood upright.

Uzunma's voice was the signal that the *ojo-ojo* dancers were approaching the village square, *agbata uzo ano,* "the junction of four roads." The group was one of the most prestigious in Igboland and their performance never disappointed anyone.

"Paul, I didn't know that your mother danced this well," Chinedu said to Paul as they watched and cheered the *ojo-ojo* dancers. Paul smiled and accepted the compliments on behalf of his mother. Chinedu's mother did not belong to the group since in essence this was her first return to Amuvi for Christmas. She, however, later joined the group.

When the *ojo-ojo* dance ended, it was time to start the official ceremony. Mazi Ogbonnia had become the unofficial master of ceremonies for every event at Amuvi. His eloquence and oratory were second to none. He was the one person to rouse people into action. He took his time walking about the podium and informally greeted many people. He was always as calm as a cat and as crafty as a fox, but everybody looked up to him. "What did he have up his sleeve?" many asked themselves. By the time people thought they were familiar with his jokes and popular sayings, Mazi Ogbonnia always came up with something new.

"If this launching is successful," Okeke pondered thoughtfully, "Ogbonnia must have had something to do with it."

Mazi Ogbonnia cleared his throat. With a fierce look in his eyes, he thundered:

"*Amuvi kwenu!*"

"*Yaa!*" the people responded.

It was a resounding response. The echo and vibrations took some time to settle down. When they did, a grave-like silence seized the hall. Mazi Ogbonnia continued his greeting. Facing a different direction each time, and pushing the air with his right arm, he thundered:

"*Kwenu!*"

"*Yaa!*"

"*Kwenu!*"

"*Yaa!*"

And turning towards the women, he concluded his greetings, "*Oli ihe, oli ihe.*"

And the women responded with the traditional, "*Mazi!*" Actually a small minority of women responded, "*Nwa Mazi!*"

Standing a few feet away from Chinedu was Gloria, one of his distant aunts. Gloria was a leader among those opposed to what she considered the abuse or actually the bastardization of the salutation *Mazi*. Her view was that *Mazi* should be a title earned by deserving men and not a salutation used for every male.

"When did Ogbonnia become *Mazi*? He is *Nwa Mazi*, not *Mazi*," she said almost angrily, emphasizing that *Nwa Mazi*, "the son of Mazi," must be distinguished from *Mazi*.

"*Enyi-die*, you've started this argument again," Mama Nkechi said.

Enyi-die, which translates to "the husband's friend," was how everybody addressed Gloria. She has been married to Mazi Alexander for over 50 years. Prior to her marriage, everybody knew her as *Glory*. She was, indeed, glorious and carried herself with grace that would make a swam appear undignified. Her husband, Mazi Alexander had better ideas. He loved her so much that he gave her the name, *Enyi-die*. He reasoned that one may or may not love one's spouse, but one always loved a friend; hence the name, *Enyi-die*, "the husband's friend."

"That's why I've argued that we should have two separate launching ceremonies," Okeke told his brother, Vincent, who was standing nearby. "We should have ours, and let the women have theirs. Mazi Ogbonnia hasn't said anything, and these women are spending energy on whether he is *Mazi* or *Nwa Mazi*. What difference does it make? What we need here today is money, no more, no less."

Vincent allowed one of his devious smiles. His friends knew he was as cunning as a fox, and had the ability to support opposing sides of an issue at the same time. He was aware that Mama Nkechi overheard Okeke's comments, and he did not want to offend either Mama Nkechi or his brother, Okeke, so he opted for a smile that would not step on any toes.

"I think we know why we're all here," Mazi Ogbonnia said.

Everybody nodded his or her head.

The Igbo say that an issue on which a consensus existed is settled by nods.

"Onye ajulu, oga aju onwe ya?" Mazi Ogbonnia roared questioningly to the people.

" *Mba!*" the people thundered back.

"Onye ajulu, oga aju onwe ya?" he asked again.

" *Mba!*"

Mazi Ogbonnia knew how to rally the people. He remembered that during the civil war, partly fought because the Igbo felt rejected by other Nigerians, a successful rallying cry among the Igbo had been *"Onye ajulu, oga aju onwe ya?"* or "Will one rejected also reject one's self?" The response was, of course, a resounding *Mba* or "No." That cry always appeared to pump up self-pride and confidence among the Igbo. Mazi Ogbonnia was going to leave no stone unturned to insure a successful launching event.

"Che, che, che, Amuvi kwenu!" he roared, cutting through the air with his clenched right fist. This greeting was one sure way to get attention from a crowd.

" *Yaa!*" the crowd thundered back.

"Kwezuenu!" he concluded, slicing the air in a horizontal, right-to-left direction with his left hand.

" *Yaa!*"

There was silence in the air. Mazi Ogbonnia had chosen the short form of the greeting this time. In the long or formal form, the people are greeted four times. In the short form, the greeting is given once or twice. Each form has its place and effect. Mazi Ogbonnia was a master in their usage. Chinedu did not know how the number four was chosen for the formal greeting.

"Mazi Ogbonnia greeted us four times before, this time he greeted us twice," he observed, looking at Paul. "How did they arrive at those numbers, four in particular?"

"I think the first time, the greeting is directed to the East, then the West, north and south in that order," Paul explained.

"So the women are the south?" Chinedu jested.

"It has nothing to do with that. It's simply the tradition," Paul explained.

"And why does he address them as *oli ihe*? Is it also the tradition?"

Oli ihe literally translates to "one who eats or is eating." It could carry the implication of one who does not earn income but simply eats.

It could also be a stereotype.

"Chinedu, it's the tradition, and I haven't heard any woman complain about that."

Tradition was probably Paul's answer to every question. But he was right. The women appeared to enjoy that salutation.

Following that round of greetings, the rowdy hall once again became as silent as a grave. Everyone could hear his own breathing. Mazi Ogbonnia's greetings were producing the intended effect. Every face had also taken on a business-like seriousness. Hairs stood on end. Mazi Ogbonnia paced up and down the podium, taking his time to make eye contact with as many people as possible. He definitely recognized Papa Chinedu in the crowd. His son Chinedu was standing not too far from his father.

"Our people say that a matter previously discussed is settled by nods. Isn't it?" Mazi Ogbonnia asked his audience.

"*Mazi*, it's true," they assured him.

Mazi Ogbonnia continued. "We know how long it has been since the war ended. Unfortunately, whenever there is rainfall, our children can't go to school, because they have no roof over their heads."

Mazi Ogbonnia was an effective speaker and worked his audience methodically.

"Are we going to fold our arms and keep our children at home?"

"*Mba, Chukwu ekwena,*" the people thundered back, suggesting that the people of Amuvi must do something to rebuild their schools.

"Look at the neighboring village of Obinkita. They have rebuilt their primary school. This Christmas, they're laying the foundation stone for a new secondary school. At Easter, they'll have another launching to bring electricity to every house in their village before next Christmas."

Mazi Ogbonnia paused, nodded a few times like one in a deep meditation, and almost immediately, like one stung by a scorpion, he took a few brisk steps to the left, to the right, to the left, to the right, moved his shoulders up and down in a frenzy, resembling one fighting off the evil spirit, and roared again.

"*Che, che, che, Amuvi kwenu!*"

"*Yaa!*" the people thundered back. Having gotten the attention he needed, Mazi Ogbonnia posed the killer question.

"The people of Amuvi, when did Obinkita start choosing before Amuvi?"

The crowd rose to its feet. "Never, never. Not in this lifetime," they shouted. The men shook their heads and beat their chests. The women looked up to the heavens, clasped their hands across their breasts and murmured prayers to the spirit of Amuvi. The atmosphere was intense. Papa Chinedu sprang to his feet, and seizing the microphone from Mazi Ogbonnia, he gave the people a thunderous greeting.

"*Umu Amuvi kwenu!*" he thundered.

"*Yaa!*" the crowd responded.

"*Kwenu!*"

"*Yaa!*"

"*Kwenu!*"

"*Yaa!*"

"*Odozi aku, odozi aku,*" he concluded looking towards the women.

"*Mazi!*" was the unanimous response.

Chinedu looked at Paul and Paul looked at Chinedu. No words were said but the exchange was clear. Chinedu's father had addressed the women almost as Mazi Ogbonnia did a few moments ago. There was no difference between *Odozi aku* and *Oli ihe*. But in Chinedu's mind, it was a stereotype. Though he remembered Paul's argument that no woman had complained about that characterization, it still did not sound right.

"*Umu Amuvi*, it's time for action," his father told the crowd. "The time for speech will come later, but the message now is urgent. I'm starting this launching with a donation of ten thousand *naira.*"

"*Che, che, che, Amuvi kwenu!*" Papa Chinedu roared.

"*Yaa!*" the people thundered back.

The crowd was jubilant. Everybody rose to his feet, clapping, and cheering. Women hugged Mama Chinedu, and Chinedu shook a few hands also. The occasion was off to a great start. Donations poured in, and it looked like the makings of a very successful fundraising event.

Mazi Okugo was on the stage. He was a very powerful and well-respected man in his youth, and always as quick as lightning in everything he did. But after a very long sickness that had nearly killed him, Mazi Okugo was no longer Mazi Okugo of old. He acted slowly with a thinking process that made a snail's motion resemble rocket speed. He had the microphone now and greeted the people.

"*Amuvi kwenu!*" he said.

"*Yaa!*" a handful of people responded. They were those who remembered twenty or thirty years ago, in the days when everybody listened when Mazi Okugo spoke. But many had forgotten or believed that his time had come and gone. At this time, he was nothing but a heavy palm wine drinker who tended to ramble after a few glasses. His brother Nwankwo was always ashamed whenever Okugo spoke in public.

"Who allowed Okugo up there on the stage?" Vincent whispered to Okeke.

"I don't know," Okeke responded. Shaking and scratching his head, he added, "I'm sorry for Nwankwo. Remember that it's the brother of the blind man who feels ashamed, whenever the blind man wants to grab *fufu* but misses the plate and grabs the floor instead."

"*Umu Amuvi*, whether you're listening or not," Okugo stuttered, staggering awkwardly in attempt to steady himself. "This launching is very important. I've always said it. Even during the days of the big oracle, the people of Calabar will come from Oron through the cross-river. You women, listen to me. Do you understand what I'm saying?"

That was typical Mazi Okugo. Completely incoherent.

"Let's put our hands together for our brother, Mazi Okugo," Mazi Ogbonnia said, wresting the microphone from him, while a few young men politely led him off the stage.

By the end of the day, the launching had proved to be one of the most successful ones in Amuvi. Nearly three hundred thousand *naira* was pledged and more than half that amount was collected on the spot.

Chinedu was glad the launching had gone well.

"Papa, I'm happy the launching went fine."

"Yes, my son," Papa Chinedu agreed. "Amuvi is still number one among the nineteen villages in Arochuku. It'll be a shame if Obinkita gets electricity and pipe-borne water before us."

Papa Chinedu did not notice his wife until she chuckled gleefully, fighting back a cough that did not exist. But when her chuckle could not induce the comment she desired, she went on to trigger it with a comment.

"So, it's a competition with Obinkita?" she casually asked, pretending to concentrate on the family dinner she was setting up.

Mama Chinedu was originally from Obinkita but married in Amuvi.

"Mama, are you going back to Obinkita?" Chinedu asked, allowing his own chuckle.

That was not the response Mama Chinedu was expecting. But she had become used to Chinedu knowingly or unknowingly serving as a buffer for his father.

"Chinedu, you're still a small boy, and by the way, I'm not talking to you," she said, sneering at her son.

"Sorry, Mama," Chinedu apologized. "I thought we were all discussing."

That politeness hurt his mother. She did not know whether to apologize for her apparent rudeness to her son or allow him to just keep himself out of the conversation. She decided on the former.

"I didn't mean to be rude, Chinedu," she apologized. "However, it isn't that I'm going back to Obinkita. I know I'm married to an Amuvi man, so I'm now an Amuvi woman. But why is it that the only way to get Amuvi men to own up to their responsibility is to tell them Obinkita did this or that, then they'll beat their breasts and jump about excitedly like a cock chasing a hen?"

There was a little pause. No one appeared to be in a hurry to respond to her comments. Clearly, neither her husband nor her son, who was almost yelled at not too long ago. She continued.

"Amuvi men are the proverbial tortoise who manifests his strength only before the mushroom." She hoped that would trigger a response from her husband. But not Papa Chinedu. He was an expert on the silent treatment. And so he took his time positioning and repositioning the plates of *fufu* and *egusi* soup placed on the dining table.

Again Chinedu threw himself into the middle of his mother's trap.

"Mama, you're not talking as if you really believe you're now Amuvi," Chinedu said, allowing a cunning smile and eyeing his mother from the corner of his left eye. "But, Mama, I'm looking at this whole launching differently."

"*Lijue nsi onu,*" his mother cursed, then walked away angrily, feeling defeated.

His father was quietly appreciative. He has been saved the agony of responding to his wife, because he knew that one argument he could never win against her, was one that involved Obinkita, her village.

"What do you mean by looking at the launching differently?" he asked Chinedu after swallowing the first lump of *fufu*. Hearing her husband's voice and his tacit support for Chinedu, Mama Chinedu looked angrily at them and mumbled something inaudible before going into the kitchen.

With his wife out of sight, Papa Chinedu winked at his son. Father and son exchanged an understanding smile. Chinedu continued with the conversation.

"Papa, how far are we going to go with this launching? Last year, there was launching in all the villages from Ovim to Arochuku. The road from Akara Isu to Ohafia was almost eaten up by erosion. There was launching to fight the erosion. This year the launching was for rebuilding the primary school and Aggrey Memorial Grammar School. There are also launching plans for pipe borne water and electricity. How much money can we raise in these launching ceremonies to take over the functions the government performs in other parts of the country?"

Papa Chinedu did not have a response. Everybody settled down to dinner. It was Christmas Eve, so there would be midnight mass and late-night dances. This was the time to make merry, not the time to worry about Nigeria. Were they not, after all, lucky to be alive to tell the story of the war? How quickly they had forgotten the flight from Kano, the air raid at Awgu, and that last journey from Ovim to Arochuku!

This was one of the more exciting Christmas celebrations at Amuvi. Papa Chinedu was particularly happy about the launching event. Inwardly, he was happy that he had become one of the major players in his village. He returned to Kano with the promise to visit home again before Easter to assess the progress of all the plans that had been put into motion during Christmas. His family went back to Enugu, where Chinedu was a graduating senior in high school and so had to focus on his schooling to do well in his high school examinations.

7
TO THE WHITE MAN'S COUNTRY

A few years had passed and Chinedu had graduated from high school. He worked for one of the government agencies and looked forward to his annual vacation which he spent in the village. The quiet life in the village contrasted sharply with the busy life that characterized the bigger cities. Nkechi, now a high school student at Queens College Enugu, was also on holidays. Probably unknown to himself, Chinedu had become increasingly attracted to Nkechi spending more time at Nkechi's place than in his own place. This attraction was no secret to anyone. Even Paul, Nkechi's brother was aware of this and never allowed Chinedu's visit to alter his plans since he knew Chinedu was actually not coming to visit him. So on this day, Paul had gone to the village market and took his time to come back. Chinedu didn't actually miss him.

"What took you this long in the market?" Nkechi asked her brother. "Chinedu has been waiting for you for a while now."

"I'm sorry," Paul apologized. "I had to do a few other unplanned things in the market."

"That's okay," Chinedu said. "Those things happen. Nkechi hasn't bored me either."

Everybody smiled, but no one said anything. Moments later, Paul broke the silence.

"So, how are your plans shaping out for the university entrance examinations?"

"Study, study and study," Chinedu responded. "I just have to work hard for the examination to The University of Nigeria, Nsukka. It's becoming more and more competitive, especially for the area I want to study."

"What is it?"

"Electrical engineering."

"Good luck," Paul wished Chinedu.

"Thanks, I need all the luck I can get," Chinedu responded, laughing.

"By the way, how's your friend Okezie? Are you guys still in touch since he went abroad?" Paul asked.

"Of course, he writes regularly and I write to him also," Chinedu said. "Now that you reminded me, he wrote to me suggesting that I apply to schools in the United States. But what for? I know I'll get a few admissions, but I don't think I want to put unnecessary pressure on my father to pay my fees in the United States. I've decided to settle for The University of Nigeria, Nsukka or The University of Ife. If things work out, one can still go abroad for graduate work."

But things were to change rather quickly for Chinedu. In a few months, he became a recipient of one of the many government scholarships in Nigeria, which meant he could then study abroad, and his friend Okezie was instrumental in facilitating his admission into an American university. Needless to say that Chinedu was very excited about this, but the people of his village were even more thrilled about this great achievement.

*   *   *   *   *

Chinedu was to depart for the United States in a few weeks. As was customary, his family organized a sendoff party to wish him well on his trip. Sendoff parties were characterized by the sharp contrast in joy and sadness often witnessed in the parties. They were often merry occasions, but there were also tears at the thought of the departure of a loved one. Chinedu's was no different. His mother kept fighting back her tears. She had promised her son she would not cry, neither during the party nor at the airport. However, it was clear that this was going to be one difficult promise to keep.

It was a fortnight to Chinedu's sendoff party, and the *ojo-ojo* dance group members had an emergency meeting to resolve the issue of whether to perform at Chinedu's sendoff. Mama Chinedu had become a member of the group but she was not invited to the meeting since her son's sendoff was the subject to be discussed. Mama Nkechi, of course, had been a member and so was another woman Mgboko, or Mama Ekwutos, who was a mutual friend to her and Mama Chinedu. Ekwutos, her daughter, was Nkechi's peer.

The meeting turned out to be more divisive than many had originally thought. Feelings were strong on either side and emotions were high. The two leading combatants were Mama Nkechi who argued in favor of the dance and Mama Ekwutos who led the group that opposed the idea.

"This is unheard of," argued Mama Ekwutos. "Our policy is that whenever we get an invitation, we allow our members to decide on what to do. I've never heard that because one of our sons is going overseas, we'll perform at his sendoff party without being formally invited."

"Mgbokwo, my sister, you've spoken the truth," Mama Nkechi added calmly. "However, there's always a first time. Papa Chinedu and his wife Teresa are very special people and deserve this special recognition for their son. Moreover, do you know what Papa Chinedu has done for Amuvi since the end of the war?"

It was a heated argument and in the end, Mama Nkechi won. This gave credence to the rumor that both women were strategically preparing their daughters for marriage with Chinedu. Ekwutos was just as pretty as Nkechi, and Mama Ekwutos, like Mama Nkechi, could not wish for another husband for her daughter but Chinedu. Therefore, in a sense, it was not that Mama Ekwutos was against the special respect for Chinedu. However, she considered it tactically wrong to allow Mama Nkechi to take the spotlight and praise. She simply regretted not originating the idea herself. Given that she could not get the glory and praise, her best option, she thought, was to ensure that her primary competitor also did not get it.

Therefore, unknown to Chinedu's mother, there was going to be a performance by the *ojo-ojo* dance group in honor of Chinedu's accomplishment. The Igbo say that the gossip in town runs away from the subjects of the gossip. So while the gossip in Amuvi was about how Mama Nkechi had out-maneuvered Mama Ekwutos in the *ojo-ojo* dance debate, Mama Chinedu and her family, who were the subjects of the gossip, did not hear about it. Many villagers believed that Mama Nkechi did not hide her admiration for Chinedu, and some even suggested that she wanted Chinedu to marry her daughter, Nkechi. It was rumored that there were also other women who wanted Chinedu to marry their daughters. As one of the women once joked: "Who doesn't like a good thing?" The good thing referred to the fact that Chinedu was going to America and the fact that he had received such a prestigious scholarship.

It was the day of Chinedu's sendoff party and it looked like another Christmas. *Jollof* rice was a favorite among children, but the men always thought of rice as food for the birds. Yam was the king of crops, and for a prestigious occasion such as this, pounded yam was prepared in place of the more common *cassava* or *fufu*.

The party was held in Papa Chinedu's compound. No special invitations were extended. It was a party open to all. People came even from neighboring villages. Chinedu's mother made sure that her kinsmen from her village Obinkita came in large numbers. Everybody had a good time. Mazi Okugo always felt merry whenever palm wine and beer were available.

"Papa Chinedu," Mazi Okugo called. "Chinedu is going to the white man's country, so I'm not drinking palm wine here today. I'm going to drink only beer and Schnapps. Tomorrow I'll return to my palm wine at *agbata uzo ano*."

"Mazi Okugo, don't worry," Papa Chinedu responded. "We're ready. Just let me know whatever you want. Come to me personally and I'll make sure that there's enough Star Beer, Guinness Stout and Schnapps for you. Today is today. Do you hear me?" Papa Chinedu concluded, patting Mazi Okugo on the back.

It was an exciting evening and Mama Chinedu was beginning to feel concerned about the absence of many of her friends. Of course, most of her friends were members of the *ojo-ojo* dance troupe. Even her close friend Mama Nkechi was missing. "Where was she?" Mama Chinedu wondered. Just as these thoughts crossed her mind, she noticed that all eyes turned in the direction of Mazi Alexander's house. People were on their feet, and the *ojo-ojo* dance was coming to Papa Chinedu's compound. Mama Chinedu was overcome with emotion. It was a moment she would never forget.

Omu Aro was a special wrapper that featured the Arochuku *Omu* emblem. *Omu Aro* had become almost synonymous with the *ojo-ojo* dance, and it was worn together with a white lace blouse. One of the distinguishing characteristics of the *ojo-ojo* dance was that unlike many other dances, the complex movements associated with it required the involvement of the dancer's entire body. It's complex footwork synchronized with the shaking of the hips, whose rhythm was dictated by an intricate movement of the hands flagging two white handkerchiefs. The tempo of the dance was dictated by a huge metallic gong, the *ogene*. As the tempo rose, the spectators rose to their feet *"Ukwu luo unu ani,"* they cheered, urging the dancers to lower their hips towards the ground. This was the beauty of the *ojo-ojo* dance: to synchronize the footwork, the handwork, the shaking of the hips and the breasts, while lowering the hips to, but not touching the ground.

After the *ojo-ojo* performance, everybody settled down to making speeches, eating and drinking. Papa Chinedu thanked everybody for coming. "Special thanks must go to the *ojo-ojo* dance group," he declared. "You've made my family proud today, and we're forever indebted to you." Turning to his son, he admonished him. "My son, whenever people tell you to continue in your ways, it means you are doing well. Whenever they ask you to change your ways, it means you're doing badly. Everybody here today has asked you to continue in your ways."

"Ise-e-e!" most people in the audience responded. "He's a good son. He's the son of his father."

After a brief pause, Papa Chinedu continued.

"My son, you'll go, and you'll return."

"Ise-e-e!" the crowd cheered.

"We hear that in America, there's no difference between night and day. But our ancestors will lead you and guide you until you return to us."

The crowd cheered and agreed, "*Ise-e-e!*"

"I'll be around for your children, and your children's children. I won't die until you return. I won't," Papa Chinedu emphasized, shaking his head as if he were rejecting and fighting off an invitation from the evil spirit.

The crowd cheered even louder, *"Ise-e-e-e!"*

"But remember what your mother and I told you yesterday," Papa Chinedu added, looking around for his wife. But she was not in her seat.

"Where's Teresa?" he asked.

"She went to the bathroom," one of Mama Chinedu's friends responded from a distance. She was in the bathroom, but not to relieve herself. She had been fighting back tears, but sometimes the tears overcame her and she would sneak outside or into the bathroom to pull herself together.

Papa Chinedu understood what was going on and continued.

"You heard the advice in the *ojo-ojo* song. Were they any different from what your mother and I told you yesterday?"

Chinedu politely nodded, agreeing with his father that the admonitions which the women sang were no different from what his parents told him only the previous day.

"Your mother and I promised that we'll be here for you. But please my son, you're going to the white man's land; beware of their women. Please don't bring them home to us. If you ever marry one of them, I'll die. And when I die, don't come home to bury me for you'll have killed me. Our people do not bury the corpse of a person they killed. Isn't it true?"

"Mazi, you're saying it as it is," the crowd cheered.

Papa Chinedu continued. "Whether your mother will survive it or not, I'll let her speak for herself."

Mama Chinedu who had returned to her seat shook her head, and running her hands through her head and face, clapped them away. Apparently she clapped away the evil thoughts of her son ever bringing home a white woman to the family. Chinedu smiled, and promised his parents that he would not marry any person whom they did not support.

This question of marrying a white woman had resonated strongly in the special *ojo-ojo* tune prepared exclusively for this occasion. The women had prayed that the ancestors would guide and protect Chinedu from all white women, and that when the time came for him to marry, he would return to Amuvi to choose one of his own. It was rumored that Mama Nkechi had a lot of input to the tune.

Many other well wishers spoke and the theme became boring to Chinedu. Everyone guessed what the next speaker was going to say, albeit with different proverbs: "Don't marry a white woman, write home always, mind your books," and so on. Why did everybody want to speak even when they had nothing new to offer? Even Mazi Okugo had a few words too. Chinedu had no choice but to smile through it all. He remembered the proverbial tortoise that stayed seven market weeks in a ditch filled with human excrement. On the last day, the tortoise became impatient asking to be let out quickly. The other animals wondered where the tortoise had been the past seven native weeks. Chinedu would not make the mistake of this proverbial tortoise. He remained the patient Job, pretending to be happy with all the admonition given to him. The end was in sight, he thought to himself.

Nkechi and her family members kept a very low profile. Her mother joined them at the end of the *ojo-ojo* dance. She was one of the more aggressive persons in the village. She not only knew how to go after what she wanted, she also knew when to back off. She had pulled off the *ojo-ojo* dance and thought it was time to recede from the public eye. Moreover, there was yet no formal proposition from Chinedu's family, thus it was prudent for them to keep a respectable distance to protect their daughter's integrity.

Nkechi wore her newest skirt and blouse made from silk material. This was the popular dress of choice for most young women at that time. Her ebony-dark hair was permed and she wore a gold necklace her parents bought for her sixteenth birthday. While many young women of that era took pride in the use of a bleaching body lotion called Ambi to make them look "white," Nkechi remained a worthy apostle of James Brown's "I'm black and proud." Some of her friends called her Ms. Black Beauty. She looked gorgeous in her beautiful, yet simple outfit and kept her distance from the public eye. She was not the girl to betray her parents' trust. There was no doubt that she loved Chinedu, but it was not for a woman to propose to a man in Igboland. These were the thoughts that went through her mind as she sat quietly at one end of the house with her mother. Why can't a woman propose to a man? Was she doing the right thing by staying very low-key? Did she need to be more aggressive with Chinedu? What was the chance that out of sight would become out of mind? Was it possible that Chinedu could meet a white woman and forget her? These questions raced through Nkechi's mind.

Nigerians at home saw every foreigner as white. The distinction between a white and a black foreigner was non-existent. If a Nigerian picked a foreign spouse, then the story became that he married a white woman or worse still, that she ran after a man. The latter was more serious and needed a visit to the local *dibia* to explain what went wrong. There were also unmarried Nigerian women abroad. Did they also pose a threat to Nkechi? There were stories about single women who went abroad to study and never married. Such women, it was said, did everything possible to trap Nigerian men into marriage. These were serious issues that needed resolution in Nkechi's mind. She needed some answers. Her mother was the only one who could help her, but Nkechi did not know how to approach her mother. Finally, she mustered enough strength and murmured to her mother, "Mama, have you talked to Mama Chinedu recently?"

"About what?" her mother responded, or more accurately, snapped back. Her response was swift and hawkish. She had accurately read the thoughts in Nkechi's mind. Nkechi wanted to know if the two women had discussed the marriage of their children.

"No, nothing," Nkechi said, looking away from her mother.

But her mother was angry and furious. "Nkechi, I won't be the monkey carrying its young on the back, not knowing that its young was reaching out and plucking fruits from the tree."

Nkechi did not say anything. The swiftness of her mother's response intimidated her and made her feel almost as hesitant as a rabbit.

"I've told you that you must not spoil our family name," her mother firmly added. "When I got married to your father, his family came formally to my parents. That's the way it's done. Yours cannot be any different, America or no America. Don't you know how people would look at our family if they heard that you ran after a man? Please, Nkechi my daughter, our family name is sacred. You can't soil it."

Papa Chinedu's house was almost filled to capacity, so mother and daughter did not have the luxury of privacy, and the admonition was very brief. Moreover, Papa Chinedu was still on his feet, wishing his son well.

"You've been a good son and have always listened to your parents," he continued. "From the stories we've heard of these white people, they're spirit and almost know what the gods are thinking. But our ancestors will lead you and guide you. You'll bring back their wisdom to help our country. You know how things have gotten worse since the white man left. When they were ruling us, they gave us the Public Works Department that fixed our roads and gave us tap water. Then we cried for independence, and they gave it to us. But what did we do with it? We changed PWD to the Ministry of Works where nothing works. My son, the hope of this country is on people like you."

Papa Chinedu was often at his best whenever he recalled how glorious the colonial days were compared to post independence days. He was one of those that would invite the white man back any day to continue ruling Africa.

"Papa Chinedu," Mazi Ogbonnia called, "Do you think that the white man made us so dependent on himself that, when he left, there was no choice than for us to fall apart."

"Mazi Ogbonnia, don't buy those excuses," Papa Chinedu countered. "We're our own problems."

Mazi Ogbonnia did not appear convinced that Papa Chinedu had the right answers. He waited a few seconds, finished drinking his glass of beer and continued with the conversation. "But, Papa Chinedu, if you like the white man so much, why won't you allow Chinedu to bring back one of his daughters to us?" Mazi Ogbonnia was well known for always bringing up controversial topics. He was one of the very few who would dare to ask Papa Chinedu such a pointed question. But Papa Chinedu had an answer ready.

"Mazi Ogbonnia, there's a difference between the white man in our midst and the white woman as our wife," he countered quickly. "You know very well what happened to our sons who turned down their parents' advice and married white women. They're all now like the biblical Aaron; they're home empty-handed. Their stories are all the same. The white woman refused to live in our villages and returned to her country with her children, leaving our son with no wife and no children. Is that a good thing for a man?"

"Papa Chinedu, I was only joking. I don't think that a good son like Chinedu will ever think of bringing a white woman into our midst. What would he do when his age mates meet at the village square with their wives? Would he bring a white woman wearing long trousers when other women are dressed in their *Omu Aro*? Can a white woman dance *ojo-ojo*? Why in the world would anybody whose head is complete ever do a thing like that? Yes, Papa Chinedu, I agree with you. We like the white man to help us fix our roads and schools, but let him live with his own wife and children, and we'll live with ours."

That was the type of view that Papa Chinedu admired. He allowed Mazi Ogbonnia to have the last word. It was clear that Chinedu had listened very carefully to both of them.

A few other well wishers also spoke and the occasion became informal. Everybody wanted to shake Chinedu's hand and remind him that he must write to them once he arrived in the white man's country.

The first chance he got, Chinedu went over to chat with Nkechi and her parents, which delighted Nkechi's mother. There were, of course, very many young girls of Nkechi's age around. Ekwy and her parents were also there. However, the fact that Chinedu went to seek out Nkechi and her parents sent a strong message to any potential competitors. It was clear that Mama Nkechi held the upper hand in this apparent war with Mama Ekwy.

PART II

8
THE CENTER OF THE WORLD

It was the eve of Chinedu's departure to Chicago. Scores of people traveled from the village to see him off at the small airport at the outskirts of Enugu. It was wonderful to be going abroad, but the lead-like weight of the reality that he would miss his friends bore down heavily on his mind. He presented a happy face, for it would be strange indeed for anyone to give up going abroad because he might miss his local friends and relatives. But it was also known that the graph of the joy of going abroad dropped asymptotically as the departure date was reduced from months to weeks and then to days. The screaming joys of six months ago had turned to somber reflections of the reality ahead and possible loneliness in a new land.

Mama Nkechi and her daughter visited Chinedu's family. They helped Chinedu's mother as she made final preparations for her son's departure the following day. Both women took a last look at Chinedu's

luggage. His mother had prepared *anu-okpo* or dried meat. Even without
refrigeration, *anu-okpo* could last a long time. And since it was well
cooked, it could be eaten as is.

"Chinedu, the meat is in your hand bag," his mother told him.
"You can easily reach it in case you become hungry in the air. You said
you will be nearly two days in the air?"

"Mama, they give a lot of food on the plane," Chinedu assured his
mother.

"True," Mama Nkechi interjected. "But you're never sure the kind
of food they eat in that place. So the meat should help in case you don't
like their food. It's a special *anu-nchi* or cutting grass meat. Your
mother said you like it a lot."

Chinedu smiled for it was a well-known fact that *anu-nchi* was his
favorite meat. No one was sure what Chinedu was going to face once he
arrived in Chicago. What kind of food did they eat there? Mothers were
often concerned about such details.

"Mama, my friend Okezie has been there for more than a year,"
Chinedu reminded his mother. "So, whatever he eats to survive, I'll also
eat."

But that didn't stop his mother from stuffing his luggage with local
food items like yam, dried *cassava*, stockfish, *kola* nut, *egusi*, *ogbono*,
bitter leaf and other food items. Some of the items like yam would
eventually be seized and destroyed at the customs post in Chicago.

The anticipated morning came and Chinedu was about to board the
plane and fly off to America. There were tears in almost every eye. And
while crying, people consoled others not to cry. Chinedu consoled his
mother who must have forgotten her promise not to cry at her son's
departure. When boarding was announced, he hugged her, but when that
appeared to let loose more storm from her eyes, Chinedu threatened to
cry also if his mother did not stop crying. That threat apparently worked.
In fact, it had worked for many others before Chinedu. It was common
knowledge that no matter how much a mother missed her son traveling
abroad, she did not want to see her son shed tears "like a woman" at the
airport. Chinedu also hugged Nkechi, shook his father's hand, and
mustering all the strength in him, bid everybody farewell and trotted
onto the tarmac for the short walk to the plane, which stood about fifty
yards away. When his plane was finally airborne, *en route* to Lagos,
those who came to see him off walked to their cars and buses with heavy

faces as if they were in a funeral procession.

Chinedu's travel to Chicago took him through London's Heathrow airport. He did not know what to expect as the descent into Heathrow was announced. His window seat allowed him to fully appreciate the beauty of landing in one of the world's premier airports. It was a fall evening in London. Darkness had arrived, and the beauty of the city was emphasized by the rows of lights that graced its streets. He recalled the story of London as given in his high school civics text. According to the British author of the text, London was the center of the world, and hence everything revolved around the city.

"That isn't necessarily true," Chinedu recalled that counter-view from his Nigerian born civics teacher. "London is no more at the center of the world than Enugu, Port Harcourt or any city for that matter. When you write your own book, you can make your town or village the center of the world."

Chinedu did not have time to see London. He had just one night's stay in one of the airport hotels. Later in the evening, he found himself seated in the hotel restaurant for dinner. "*Jesus!*" he muttered to himself. It was becoming real. He was in the white man's country. Everything was intimidating. A beautiful young lady came over to his table, poured him a cup of tea, dropped off what eventually turned out to be the menu, said a few things that Chinedu did not understand, and left. But he had a savior. The hotel was quite at home with transit passengers. The hostess came back with a bottle of Coca-Cola, some hard rolls and butter.

"How did she know that I like Coca Cola?" Chinedu thought to himself. He gulped down the first glass, refilled it and started on the bread. The hostess flipped through the menu and after a brief conversation in English and sign language, she smiled at the lonely passenger and left. A short while later, she came back with Chinedu's meal. He could recognize rice and beef, which was fine.

"But how much was the food?" he wondered to himself. He had no idea. But he knew he had more than enough money on him. When the waitress returned, she was able to determine that Chinedu had flown in via Nigeria Airways and thus would have a free meal coupon. Chinedu, of course, spoke excellent English, but the new environment was just so intimidating. From the way he communicated with the waitress, one might think he was hearing the English language for the first time.

However, the waitress appeared to have considerable experience dealing with foreign patrons like Chinedu. She remained polite and calm, repeating herself as often as she thought necessary until the coupon issue was straightened out.

The last major leg of his trip was the flight from London to Chicago. His friend Okezie was at O'Hare airport in Chicago to welcome him. The experience at Heathrow and at the airport hotel in London had calmed him down and Chinedu was now ready to appreciate the white man's country. He had never seen a computer in his life and here everything was computerized. Even the moving walkway must be computerized, he thought to himself.

Systematically, the passengers went through immigration and customs. It was at the customs that his yam and *kola* nut were confiscated. Clearly overwhelmed and intimidated, Chinedu offered no resistance. He finally passed through customs to meet his friend Okezie who was waiting just behind the gate.

Chinedu was relieved to finally meet someone to whom he could talk freely, but he did not know where to start. Was it the tall buildings, the many cars on the expressway, the order in which things moved at the airport? He was just stunned to silence and said little.

"This is a different world," Okezie offered. "You'll get used to it. Everybody went through the initial shock. What about your parents and how did they take your departure?"

Chinedu told as much of the story as he could. It was evening in Chicago and he was already feeling sleepy.

"It's called jet lag," Okezie explained. "It's about midnight in Nigeria now, and your body is still working on Nigerian time."

Chinedu slept like a baby and woke the following morning well rested.

During the next several days, friends trooped in to welcome him. It was really nice, for their small gatherings had everything about home in them. The language was familiar, as were the jokes.

After staying a few weeks with Okezie, it was time for Chinedu to move into his own apartment. Once an apartment became available in the complex that Okezie lived in, they bought the bed, bedcovers, cooking utensils and other appliances that he needed. But Chinedu was surprised that there were already in the apartment, a refrigerator and a range. He thought that Okezie had purchased his.

"Do they buy a refrigerator and gas cooker for every apartment?" he asked as they set things up in the new apartment.

"Yes, every apartment must have at least a refrigerator, a range, and in some cases a microwave oven. But you pay for these things one way or another when you pay your rent."

Chinedu merely shook his head. "This truly is a different world," he murmured.

Okezie had called earlier the telephone company on Chinedu's behalf and the phone was working in two days. But Chinedu had some ideas about what it took to get a phone line in Nigeria. Among other things, technicians would be sent to run a line from the closest manhole to the building where the phone would be installed.

In that era in Nigeria when nobody worked but everybody sat around and waited for his share of the oil money, running a telephone line was a visible activity. On the first day, the technicians went in a big truck and unloaded their equipment. Then they went to lunch and returned from lunch the following day. The second day they opened the manhole, left it uncovered and went to lunch from which they returned on the third day. Probably by the third day, somebody might dig up some earth and cut a few electric wires since nobody had any idea what wires were laid where. Eventually, the wire was run and telephone customer waited for a number to "become available." These thoughts raced through Chinedu's mind.

"How can they install a phone in two days?" he asked. "When will they run the line? Is there a manhole close by? How are they sure a number will be available that quick?"

He asked a few more questions, but stopped when he found that Okezie was laughing at him.

"This isn't Nigeria. If you need two phone lines in this apartment today, and you're ready to pay for them, bingo, they're yours!"

"But how?" Chinedu asked. "When do they install the lines?"

"Listen, this is America. Everything is planned and coordinated. It isn't like Nigeria where the telephone man cuts every cable laid by the water department, who on their part, cut all the electric cables. Nothing is planned in Nigeria. There are no maps to guide the utility company workers. That isn't the case here. When a new building is planned, the telephone, electric, gas, and in fact, all the utility companies are involved from the first day. They all work together so everything fits like a glove. Just relax and enjoy the convenience of your apartment."

Chinedu wiped his face, and went over to the refrigerator and poured himself another glass of champagne.

"Do you know that people in Africa are living in darkness? This country is advanced."

"You haven't seen anything yet," Okezie responded.

Although he was quite impressed with his apartment, living in it was actually one of Chinedu's initial disappointments in America. The concept of a commuter university was at that time uncommon in Nigeria. Part of the fun in university life was the social life in campus hostels. He had looked forward to such an experience, but apparently, that was not to be.

*   *   *   *   *

The more Chinedu saw the wonders of America, the more he thought about his childhood days in Coal Camp. The changes he was experiencing in America presented challenges to him. He was doing his best to catch up, and luckily Okezie was there to lend a helping hand. Okezie took him around town and to different places on campus to get him speedily acquainted with American life. One of the problems Nigerian students faced upon arrival in the United States was adapting to the automation of the American lifestyle. Using a moneychanger was new. Even the cafeteria menu presented its own problems, for they did not understand the names of American dishes. However, Okezie had gone through the process and knew how best to help his friend.

It was a Friday afternoon at school and both friends visited various buildings and offices to further get Chinedu acquainted to his new environment. They had been to the University Center which housed the Office of Foreign Students' Affairs. They had also been to the Engineering Building where the offices of the engineering professors were located. Next they went to a vending machine area for a short break. They needed to use the vending machines, but first, they had to use the moneychanger.

"Just watch me closely," he told Chinedu in their native language as Okezie got ready to use the moneychanger.

"Won't people become offended if they hear us speaking in a

language they don't understand?" Chinedu asked.

"They can go to hell," Okezie responded casually. "This is America. You speak whatever you like, even Spanish."

Continuing in their native language, Okezie added. "Just relax, put your hands in your pocket and be as cool as a cucumber. See the machine on the extreme right, it's a moneychanger. If you insert a dollar bill, it returns coins to you. Just watch me closely as I do it."

Okezie and Chinedu walked up casually to the moneychanger. Unless you understood their language, you would never suspect the on-going tutoring. Okezie used the moneychanger and then it was Chinedu's turn. He had studied Okezie's every move, yet he mistakenly inserted the dollar bill with the wrong face up, and the machine spit it back to him. He immediately broke into a cold sweat. His heartbeat quickened. Two women were standing behind them and were waiting to use the machine. The last thing Chinedu wanted was for anyone to understand that he was a JJC, a "Johnny Just Come," a phrase used in Nigeria to describe someone new.

Speaking in a calm voice, Okezie added, "*Dianyi,* relax. Just turn the bill over, and insert it again."

Unfortunately, Chinedu did more than he was told. He not only turned the bill over, he inserted it with the wrong edge. The result was the same. The machine rejected his dollar bill. Sweat was dripping down his forehead. His heartbeat raced. Realizing that, with the young women standing behind them, his friend might pass out any moment, Okezie took a dollar bill from his wallet, inserted it correctly into the machine. As he did so, he offered what could be considered a defense for his friend: "These machines can sometimes act funny, rejecting bills for no reason."

One of the white women standing behind them smiled as both friends walked away from the machine.

"Do you think she understood what happened?" Chinedu asked Okezie, stepping up his strides so they could get out of view quickly.

"Who cares?" Okezie responded. "She smiled as if she likes you. Some of these white women like black people."

"You saw her smiling at me or smiling at you?" Chinedu countered.

"She was smiling at you," Okezie insisted.

"Did you say they like black people?" Chinedu was not sure he had heard that one correctly. "Why do they like black people?"

"Too much potential energy," Okezie responded.

"What do you mean?" Chinedu asked.

"Come on. You mean you don't know the difference between potential energy and kinetic energy, or how one converts to the other?" Okezie asked cynically.

It was at this point that Chinedu understood it was a joke. "Wonders will never end," he said. "I hope my parents don't hear you in their dream. Do you know what?"

"What?" Okezie asked.

"I understood everything those white girls said, but I always have difficulty when I talk with a black American."

"You can easily identify everyone from his or her accent," Okezie explained. "The black Americans speak in a certain way."

"That's the point I was making," Chinedu cut in. "I think it's so hard to understand them."

"That's exactly what they say of us also," Okezie explained. "The accents are different. After a short time, you'll get used to the way they speak and they'll also get used to our accent. I asked my friend to come with a couple of her friends when we do our group study. I want you to meet some of them."

"Do you study with them? What do you study?"

"You have to start somewhere," Okezie said, smiling as he did so. "There're a few Naija women on campus, but I really don't want to get involved with them. The black Americans are easier to get along with."

Nigerians in the United States colloquially referred to Nigeria as Naija.

"The Naija women are so much after settling down that you wonder why they didn't marry before coming to America," Okezie added.

It was lunchtime and they opted to eat in the school cafeteria. But there was a problem. Even Okezie himself was not quite familiar with the cafeteria menu. There was this thing about an entrée, one starch, and one vegetable. He had no idea what it meant. In Nigeria, starch was used in laundry and dry cleaning. He did not understand what starch had to do with his lunch.

"There are two strategies to use here," Okezie explained. "The first is to stand behind somebody you suspect understands the menu jargon.

Wait for him or her to be served, and when it is your turn to be served, tell the waiter that you want exactly the same dish as the previous person. This way, you don't have to deal with any entrée or starch."

"Suppose it's something I don't want?" Chinedu asked.

"Too bad. Can't help it," Okezie replied. "The second strategy is to be sure you always have a lot of money in your wallet. You just point to the food you like, and pay whatever the cash register rings up. Hey, this is America."

Chinedu shook his head. "This is tough," he said, adding, "I shouldn't have rushed the dried meat my mother had prepared for me."

Okezie smiled. He understood the feeling. "Actually, there's a third alternative," he told his friend, "a McDonald's hamburger. But you already described it as nothing but beef wrapped in bread; you'd rather not eat your beef that way." Okezie smiled at his friend, whom he knew did not like American fast food. "There's still too much Nigeria in you," he added.

Chinedu was as patient as Job as he stood in the line. He was not sure what he was going to do when he reached the server. Most probably the second option that Okezie had offered would be okay for now. His wallet was loaded and there would be no problem paying for any items he picked.

"We have to switch to another line," Okezie said, moving to another line. "The girl serving that line is an Igbo girl. She's a student and works part time here in the cafeteria. Whenever I see her, I switch to her line. At least I can speak to her in Igbo and she can explain to me what's in the menu."

When it was Chinedu's turn to be served, he spoke to the server in Igbo. "Please give me rice."

Leticia smiled. She knew that this was yet another JJC. Leticia had been in the US for a while. She was single, and had helped many Nigerians settle down in Chicago. She served Chinedu a large portion of chicken, some vegetables and a scoop of rice.

Speaking in Igbo, Chinedu said to her. "I asked for rice, not chicken. What am I going to do with that spoon of rice?"

Nigerians were more familiar with spoon measures than with scoop measures.

Leticia smiled again. She understood. In Nigeria, rice was the main course, and chicken and beef were side orders. In America, the case was the opposite. Leticia put two extra scoops of white rice and explained to Chinedu that he might have to pay for that as side order.

Chinedu was grateful and promised to give Leticia a call. Leticia smiled back and added, "That's how you all behave when you're new. Before long, you'll learn from your friends and will join them. Anyway, welcome to America and if you think I can help you in anyway, please don't fail to ask."

Chinedu and Okezie settled down to eat their meals. It was almost like homemade food. Thanks to Leticia, who knew what was good for them. As they ate, Okezie broke the silence that existed.

"You've got to be careful with that woman," Okezie told Chinedu. "Don't mind that we were all smiling over there. It was nothing more than opening our teeth."

"What do you mean? She was very nice to us."

"She's like a big net. Make sure you don't become a fish. She's one of those Naija women who've been here for a while. Her clock is ticking and a sense of frustration is about to settle in. She'll hook any man who crosses her way. You're only a few months old in America and hence, a prime target. They all know me; I can take care of myself."

This was becoming very troubling to Chinedu. Here was a Nigerian woman who was simply being nice to them, and he had to be careful to avoid her. It was also true that he felt committed to Nkechi, no matter how long his studies in America took. So what was he to do? Should he explain to his friend that they were being unfair to the Nigerian women, or should he join the rest of his friends and keep his distance?

9
LEARNING THE RULES

Okezie and Chinedu were seated in a study room in the school library when two African-American women walked in. One was tall, with straight hair. She wore a pair of Nike sports shoes, a pair of blue jeans and a casual white blouse, or actually, shirt. The top buttons of the shirt were noticeably not in place giving Jennifer a sexy look. Her companion looked no less sexy, though, more formally dressed. Her hair was low cut and she wore a shell-pink gown with a tiny yellow rose pinned just above her left breast. The color of her purse was agreeable to the light-gold color of her scarf and shoes. Cynthia seemed more restrained than her friend Jennifer who had taken control of the gathering. Jennifer hugged Okezie and kissed him on the cheek.

"This must be your friend," she said extending her hand to greet Chinedu.

Wiping off the marks left by Jennifer's lipstick, Okezie smiled at Chinedu and said, "Meet my friend, Jennifer."

"I'm glad to finally meet you, *Chi-edu*. Did I say it correctly?" Jennifer asked.

"That's fine," Chinedu responded, smiling and shaking her hand.

"No, tell me how to say it. I want to say it correctly," she insisted.

"You said it correctly," Okezie added quickly, not allowing Chinedu time to respond. "But who is your friend? It's more important than learning African phonetics."

"Oh, I'm sorry. This is my friend Cynthia. Cynthia, you've met Oke-zie once before, I believe. His friend, Chi-edu, came from Africa about two months ago. This is his first semester on campus."

Chinedu held out his hand to Cynthia. They shook hands and Chinedu was startled by the smoothness of Cynthia's hands. He felt like holding on to them a little longer, but, he let them go. She not only looked gorgeous, but every air about her felt fresh and glorious.

"You girls are looking good," Okezie remarked to Jennifer and Cynthia.

"Oh, thank you," Cynthia responded with a smile.

"Something doesn't sound right," Jennifer observed somewhat cynically.

"What is it?" Chinedu and Okezie asked in near synchrony.

"Your friend Chi-edu must have done something to you these few weeks since his arrival," Jennifer chuckled. "I have never heard you compliment anybody before."

Okezie smiled but said nothing.

"When you see something good, there's nothing bad in appreciating it," Chinedu said, admiring Cynthia's outfit.

"Cynthia, in Nigeria, we would say you're dressed to kill."

Cynthia smiled and thanked him. "It wasn't really too expensive," she explained. Everything in Bloomindales was 60% off, during their Easter sales event."

This was new to Chinedu and he asked Okezie to clarify the "sale" and the idea of something being 60% off. These phrases were strange to him.

"This is a marketing strategy in America, to pull the crowds into a store," Okezie explained. "It has to do with the culture of the people. It is like *jara* in Nigeria. Sometimes people don't buy unless the seller adds *jara* and here some people don't buy until an item is on sale."

The discussion had detoured somewhat, but that was okay, for it provided Chinedu with the chance to continue learning about his new environment.

With the sale discussion over, Jennifer returned to working on African names.

"Oke-zie, I told you I love Africa and African names. My daughter's name is Zumuta. I think it's Swahili. Does your friend speak Swahili?"

"No, he doesn't," Okezie responded.

"I thought everybody in Africa speaks Swahili?"

"Who told you that?" Okezie asked.

"Anyway, although I no longer date my daughter's father, I still like the Swahili name. I love to go out with African men. I once dated a guy from Ghana and he was really nice to me, but when his wife came from Africa, he stopped going out with me. I know when Oke-zie's African wife comes, he'll do the same."

Okezie smiled, but said nothing. Chinedu did not know whether he was confused or in a trance. In the first place, he knew that like him, Okezie's fiancée was in Nigeria. But how did Jennifer know about her? And secondly, what did Jennifer mean when she said "my daughter's father?" Wouldn't that be Jennifer's husband? He couldn't believe Jennifer had a child. She looked pretty, elegant, and relatively speaking, young. In his village in Nigeria, it would be an abomination to have a child out of wedlock, but it did not seem to be a problem here.

"How old is your daughter?" Chinedu asked.

"Three years old."

"She must be as pretty as you are?"

"She's a little doll."

"Where's she now that you're not at home?"

"Her grandma keeps her when I have to work or go to school. If her grandma can't keep her, then I have to pay somebody to take care of her."

This was a new one too, Chinedu thought. In his village, there would be a lot of other relatives and friends to take care of one's child without being directly paid. But he was now getting used to how things were done differently in America.

"Cynthia, what about you? Do you have a baby also?"

"I have a daughter. She's almost seven now."

"Wow! You have a seven-year old. How old are you?" Chinedu was becoming brave.

"Twenty one," she said and threw it back at Chinedu, "How old are you?"

"I'm in my mid to late twenties," Chinedu answered.

Jennifer read her friend's mind accurately. Cynthia was wondering why Chinedu had offered his age in terms of mid, late, mean or median. Just give me a number, she thought to herself.

"Cynthia, if you have to date a Nigerian man, that's one thing you have to deal with: he won't respond directly about his age. But every one of them is sweet though," Jennifer said, leaning on Okezie.

"Can we talk academics?" Okezie suggested. "I thought this was meant to be a group study session."

"That's fine," Cynthia added, "Chi-edu, what classes are you taking this semester?"

"I've just three classes, Calculus I, Physics I and Black Studies 100. The Black Studies is an elective."

"What's your major?" Jennifer asked.

"Electrical engineering," Chinedu responded.

"So, they allowed you to take calculus in your first semester?" Cynthia asked, obviously surprised. "Even though you're still a freshman?"

Chinedu did not understand why he could not take calculus. However, before he had the chance to ask for explanation, Jennifer almost shouted, "I'm also an engineering major, but they never allowed me to take calculus until after one year. Oke-zie, I've told you that white folks treat Africans differently than they treat us who are African-Americans."

"You and I have discussed this before," Okezie calmly, yet firmly, responded. "Either you don't listen to me or you've made up your mind what to believe."

"Or you don't want to see my point of view," Jennifer added aggressively, with a hint of cynicism. "I've dated a few African men, and I know they don't want their viewpoint to be challenged. Let me explain to you again that I had to spend two semesters taking college algebra and trigonometry before they allowed me to register for calculus. Your friend has just arrived, and they allowed him to register for calculus in his first semester. Oke-zie, don't you see any double standards here?"

"And those stupid algebra and trigonometry credits don't count towards graduation," Cynthia added. "That's why black American folks need six to seven years to get a Bachelor's degree, and you African folks are allowed to finish in three or four years."

"I don't understand the argument," Chinedu said, confused by the points Jennifer and Cynthia were trying to make. "Why are they not allowed to enroll in calculus?"

"It seems a bit complicated, yet it's quite simple," Okezie added rather calmly. "I can explain."

"You have six ears to feed," Jennifer chuckled gleefully. "They're all yours."

"Anyway, I've gone over this with Jennifer zillions of times," Okezie added. "But in the interest of Chinedu and Cynthia, I'll do it one more time."

"Go for it, baby," Jennifer said sarcastically.

Okezie ignored her and addressed Chinedu.

"Before you enrolled in Calculus I and Physics I, you took a placement test, didn't you?"

"I did," Chinedu responded.

"From the test results, it was determined that you were prepared for Calculus I and Physics I. But not everybody was as prepared as you were, so such people have to take remedial classes such as college algebra and the like, which don't count towards graduation. But come to think about it, what's Calculus I, after all? Isn't it differentiation and integration, things we learned in additional mathematics, or 'AddMath,' as it was commonly called in our high schools in Nigeria?"

"That was my next point," Chinedu hastily added. "Calculus I is actually very boring to me. I've not learned anything new in the class except that dy/dx is derivative, and integration is anti-derivative. Do I have to spend a semester learning nothing but terminology?"

"Okezie, you learned calculus in high school?" Cynthia asked, seeming rather perplexed.

"Yes, Cynthia, and that's what your friend Jennifer has refused to understand," Okezie replied. "I've told her that people come to college with different levels of preparation. Some are better prepared than others. The level of preparation is reflected in the placement tests. This is what determines whether a new student starts out taking remedial classes or is allowed to enroll in credit-earning classes like calculus I and physics I. There are Africans taking remedial courses like you did, so don't take it personally."

Two hours had gone by, and after the heated discussion, no one was in the mood to study.

"I guess we can all stop by Chinedu's apartment and have a drink," Okezie suggested. "It'll help calm Jennifer down. Thank God It's Friday. No one is going to school tomorrow."

"That's a good idea," Jennifer said. "It'll also calm you down too. Does your friend know my favorite drinks, Barcady Rum and Andre champagne?"

Okezie smiled. "Jennifer, we can take care of whatever you want to drink."

The women excused themselves to make phone calls, and Okezie quickly brought Chinedu up to date. "Cynthia is yours. When we get to your apartment, Jennifer and I'll leave. Don't worry about anything. Just have fun and enjoy yourself. You are on a fast-paced 'Learning the rules' program," Okezie added, smiling as he did so.

"But wouldn't she say that she was meeting me for the first time?" Chinedu asked.

"It doesn't matter. That line belongs to Naija women only. These are African-Americans. Just have fun. We'll go to that disco place I told you about. It's in Century Mall at Clark by Diversey and Broadway. She'll spend the night with you, and Jennifer will be with me. We'll drop them off tomorrow."

Chinedu was confused. "They'll spend the night with us?" he asked, his mouth half-open.

"Sure," Okezie replied. "Just one more thing, and this is important. This is where many of our boys go wrong. It's quite common for a man to have a female roommate here in America. In some cases these are just roommates and in other cases, the woman could be a live-in girl friend. However, such an arrangement is uncommon in Nigeria, and I doubt you're interested in that."

"I'm not looking for any roommate," Chinedu added immediately.

"That's fine," Okezie continued. "Here are some ground rules. Be honest, yet firm from day one. If she really wants to know, tell her you have a wife in Nigeria, and you don't want to disappoint her. That's my understanding with Jennifer, and it has worked out fine so far. Incidentally, unlike a Naija woman who wants to hear something sweet, even though she knows it's probably a lie, the American appreciates straight, honest talk."

Chinedu thought about her mother, her father, and . . . He fought back the tears as Nkechi's image rose before him. Was he in a trance? He woke up when he heard Jennifer's voice.

" So what are we doing tonight?"

" Do you like to dance?" Cynthia asked Chinedu.

" Sometimes," was his shy reply.

"That's the way it is when you're new from Africa," Jennifer hastily added. "I remember I almost had to drag your friend Oke-zie to night clubs the first time we started dating. But now, he's almost ready for the *Soul Train* dance contest."

"Oh yes, I watched *Soul Train* on Channel 9 last week," Chinedu added.

Before he could say more, Okezie cut in and explained that his friend liked *Soul Train,* making a face at Chinedu in the process. Actually, Chinedu had considered the dancing in *Soul Train* weird and wild and had just been about to say so.

It was a short drive to Chinedu's apartment on the north side of Chicago. On their way home they stopped at a store and bought the wine and liquor, Barcady Rum, and Andre Champagne. Chinedu had Heineken and Guinness Stout at home.

"Nigerians play big and have a lot of money," Jennifer told her friend. "I won't square you with any of these cheap men around. As soon as Okezie told me it was his old friend from their country, that was all I needed to know. Although Okezie denies it, I think their parents own oil wells in Africa."

Chinedu had heard that joke about students who claimed their parents owned oil wells in Nigeria. He was, however, relieved that Okezie had not claimed that too.

They were now relaxed in Chinedu's apartment. Cynthia lit a cigarette. She had drunk about four ounces of Barcady Rum and two glasses of champagne. She was beginning to feel light-headed.

Okezie and Jennifer excused themselves and went to Okezie's apartment which was in the same complex. Chinedu and Cynthia were alone on the love seat. Chinedu's heart was throbbing. What should he say or do? He did not want to make any mistakes.

"You can touch me and hold me. It's perfectly fine," Cynthia suggested to Chinedu who managed a near-timid smile. Cynthia stood up, undressed and asked Chinedu to do the same. "Jennifer told me Nigerian men are always shy the first time around. Later, they'll demand it as if it's their birthright."

Cynthia surprised Chinedu with her involvement and aggressiveness in lovemaking. When Chinedu finally got out of bed, he felt that "power had gone out of him." Cynthia was a full participant at the act. The Naija woman, Chinedu thought, was quite the opposite. Most of them would almost fake death, behaving as if their duty was only to deposit their body on the bed.

Chinedu caught himself scratching his head as he processed that thought. "Was that really true?" he thought to himself. "Suppose his wife was as aggressive as Cynthia? Wouldn't he start wondering where she had learned it all?" This was an interesting puzzle.

But this was not the time to worry about those issues, he finally told himself. He wasn't even married. However, one thing was clear from this experience with Cynthia. Chinedu believed he had identified a key reason why many Nigerian men, in spite of parental warnings, took American spouses. When later he talked about this experience with Okezie, Chinedu joked: "And this was just with a black woman. I haven't even checked out the other color."

"Not to worry," Okezie replied. "One is like the other."

Things were beginning to fall into place. Was this why some Nigerian men kept an American spouse in America and a Nigerian spouse with "permanent residence" in Nigeria?

The phone rang at about 11pm. It was Okezie. He was coming over with Jennifer and it was time to go to the Century Mall disco. Chinedu was becoming Americanized and learning the rules at a rather fast pace. They arrived at the disco a little before midnight. The place was lively and everybody was having a good time. Cynthia and Chinedu liked standing together, side by side.

"You're so sweet, Chi-edu. I'm glad I met you."

"You're also very sweet, Cynthia. It's wonderful getting to know you."

Chinedu took a sip from his glass of Miller Lite beer, his first American beer.

" This tastes just like water," he complained.

The night was well spent and they were back by 4:30 am. Okezie's phone call woke Chinedu and Cynthia up at about 11:00 am Saturday morning. They continued to have a good time together that day and the women were taken back to their South Side residences much later that evening. On their way back, via the Dan Ryan expressway, Okezie looked at his friend, smiled and said, " Welcome to America."

10
TROUBLED MIND

Chinedu had spent about two years in America. A lot of things had changed during this period. In particular, the situation in his native country worsened, which forced adjustments to his plans. Initially, he wanted just one year to settle down before Nkechi joined him. However, as he learned more about the new culture he was living in, he started to rethink his decisions. At one point, all he wanted was to graduate and return to Nigeria. However, that plan was also changing. With the worsening economic situation at home, graduating Nigerians preferred to settle down in diaspora instead of returning to their native country. This was the beginning of the formation of Nigerian communities in the United States.

These events left Chinedu in a quandary. Although his graduation was drawing closer, he was not sure what to do after that. He was not only worried about himself, but also about Nkechi. Unanswered questions kept flashing through his mind. Should he immediately return to Nigeria upon graduation? But that was against all counsel. If he did not return, what about Nkechi? But given what he had learned about American culture, did he still want to expose her to America?

Chinedu and Okezie were having lunch in the school cafeteria one afternoon when another Nigerian student, Elias, joined them. Elias' wife recently came from Nigeria, but unfortunately, the couple were having marital problems. Elias was glad to pour out his heart to sympathetic ears.

Elias had a Bachelor of Science degree in electrical engineering, but remained a student to keep his Visa current. He was on a student Visa and could not get a job as an electrical engineer. In addition to his campus job, he worked as a store attendant at a local 7-11. He had worked these two jobs and had saved enough money to sponsor his wife to come from Nigeria. When she came to America, Elias practically worked round the clock to put her through school. In fact, he sometimes drove cabs during the weekend, in addition to his other two jobs. She studied and became a nurse.

Elias had just completed narrating how he worked hard to finance his wife's coming to America when his emotion overtook him. He sobbed uncontrollably.

"*Dianyi*, take it like a man," Okezie counseled.

"It's really hard," Elias said.

"I know, but you can't allow her behavior to bring you down," Okezie countered.

Chinedu patted Elias on the back but was unable to say anything. He was also fighting back his own emotion. Elias blew his nose, cleaned his face and continued.

"Once she became a registered nurse, she changed," Elias narrated. "It was clear that she was no longer herself. Even her jokes changed. She once joked that she needed or deserved a husband whose economic disposition was at least at the same level of that of the doctors with whom she worked."

"Was that a joke?" Chinedu asked. "Remember that even if it was a joke, people sometimes say what's really on their minds in the form of a joke."

"I agree with you," Elias said. "Later events bore this out."

"It's crazy," Okezie said. "But how did it eventually get out of hand?"

"As I said before, it became hell in the house," Elias continued. "Apparently, she believed her pay check was heftier than mine. According to her, her mother once said that when a woman becomes the primary breadwinner in a house, the man was no longer fit to be around. I couldn't handle a woman I brought to America and whose school fees I paid, call me a worthless idiot."

"What!" Chinedu exclaimed. Okezie was more familiar with those types of situations and merely smiled. "Called you what?" Chinedu asked again in utter disbelief.

"This has been going on for some time. In fact, people had counseled her to calm down, but she wouldn't listen to anyone. Last week it reached a climax. She was running her mouth right, left, and center. I couldn't take it anymore and I beat the hell out of her," Elias said.

Chinedu kept staring at Elias, his gaze as straight as a ramrod.

"I didn't know it," Elias continued, "but she called 911, and in seconds, the cops were around. To make the story short, I got thrown out of the house."

"What about your two sons?" Chinedu managed to ask after a long silence. He could not believe the story he was hearing.

"They're home with her. That's the American way; she keeps the children."

"You have to leave your house for her?" Chinedu asked. "And she sleeps well at night?"

"Don't worry about that, Chinedu," Okezie said, "This isn't Nigeria where people become sentimental over these issues. The guy's thrown out of the house and I'd say all she's interested in now is child support payment. She doesn't care to recall what Elias went through to get her to where she is today."

Was this the type of environment Chinedu wanted for his marriage? Wouldn't it be better for him to just save himself this problem, get as much education as he could, and then go back to Nigeria and start a normal life with his wife? He did not want his upcoming marriage to Nkechi to end up like Elias!

"This is a girl that your parents married for you at home?" Chinedu was still confused. "If one of them can do that, then any of them can. How does one guarantee against that?"

"It's nothing but exposure to American culture," Elias added.

Chinedu felt quite bitter. He was almost certain the solution was to keep Nkechi in Nigeria. She did not need exposure to this culture. He had an answer, but needed to rationalize it, and the recollection that came to his mind appeared to do just that. A devout Catholic during his childhood days, he recalled an admonition he had once received from a Reverend Father during his first confession and communion. He nodded and smiled as he remembered.

Chinedu had recited all his sins, ending with the usual, "for these and other sins I have forgotten, father, I ask forgiveness for them."

"My son, are you sorry for your sins?" the Reverend Father had asked.

"Yes, Father. I am sorry for them and I ask our Blessed Virgin Mary to pray to Jesus for my soul," Chinedu had said.

"God has forgiven you your sins, but you must promise Him never to sin again."

"Yes, Father," Chinedu had responded, and had been about to leave, but remembered that the absolution and penance had not been given.

"Before I give you your penance and absolution, I want to ask you a question," the priest had said. "Do you see that house over there?" he had asked Chinedu, pointing at one of the buildings in the church compound.

Chinedu had looked in the direction the priest was pointing and had seen the house. It had seemed to him that there was nothing unique about it and he had wondered what relevance it had to his confession. The priest continued with the dialogue.

"Suppose you know that if you entered that house, you're likely to commit sin, what would you do?"

Chinedu had been properly tutored about going to confession, but had not been ready for this one. He was, however, pretty smart for his age, and knew that in the Catholic Church, you could rarely go wrong with the Blessed Virgin Mary.

"Father, I'll ask our Blessed Virgin Mary to pray to Jesus for my soul," he had responded.

"That's good, my son, but that wasn't what I was expecting," the Reverend Father had explained. Chinedu recalled how his heart had started pounding faster. Had he failed in the confession? Were his sins no longer forgiven? As these thoughts went through his mind, the priest had continued.

"When God drove Lucifer out of the Garden of Eden, He didn't take away the powers Lucifer had. My son, Satan still has powers. What you should do first and foremost is not to enter the house. You don't enter the house and start praying to our Blessed Mother. My son, do you understand?"

"Yes, father."

That confession of many years ago came to his mind perfectly now, and Chinedu realized that the Reverend Father had been right. Chinedu also believed that his current thoughts about bringing Nkechi to America were also right. If bringing her to America would destroy his marriage, the best solution was not to bring her to America at all. Yes, he had it all figured out. The next day, without explaining the reasons to either his parents or Nkechi, Chinedu requested that they postpone the marriage ceremony until after his graduation.

11
NAIJA WOMEN

Many months had passed and during that period, Okezie's wife, Ijeoma had arrived from Nigeria. But even her arrival was not enough reason for Chinedu to change his mind about the decisions he'd made about Nkechi.

"I'm beginning to rethink everything about Nkechi joining me," Chinedu told his trusted friend as they walked to the parking lot for their drive home one Friday evening.

"I was just saying to myself that we needed to sit down and talk about that," Okezie responded. "So many things have been going on, and we haven't had the time to reflect on them carefully."

Okezie detoured to a water fountain about thirty feet away. He turned on the fountain quickly, allowing the water to splash on his face as he gulped two mouthfuls of water. He rejoined his friend and after a moment in which no one said anything, Okezie broke the silence. "Aren't you going to say anything?" he chuckled at Chinedu.

Actually, he knew what Chinedu would have said, had it not been for the more serious thoughts on his friend's mind. A few weeks ago, Chinedu had accused Okezie of becoming too Americanized in his water drinking habit.

"If you're thirsty, drink a glass of water. Cease this habit of stopping at a fountain every five minutes to splash water on your tongue."

However, with the current thoughts on his mind, "No," was Chinedu's response to Okezie.

Since Chinedu had declined his invitation for a comment, Okezie returned to their discussion.

"You can't take all these issues either too seriously or too literally. I think it's still the right thing to do to get Nkechi to join you here. There are a number of reasons for that."

"I know it's good to have her around, but not in this culture," Chinedu tried to explain, but Okezie was determined to make his point.

"Just hear me out first," Okezie insisted. "As I said before, there are many reasons why she should come to America. The first is that she can't wait indefinitely for you, and you can't wait indefinitely for her. I think that a couple should stay together to save themselves the temptations they're exposed to when they live apart."

"I'm not yet married," Chinedu added jokingly.

"Well, I didn't know you were still looking around," Okezie understood his friend's joke and continued with his argument. "America changes everybody. The Chinedu that left Nigeria over two years ago isn't the same as the Chinedu I'm now talking to."

"I've no idea what you're talking about. As far as I'm concerned, I'm who I am. Nothing has changed."

"You've changed," Okezie insisted. "I've also changed, so don't take it personally. America imposes a change on everybody. It doesn't matter whether you accept it or not. Therefore, the Chinedu that'll return to Nkechi in Nigeria isn't the Chinedu that Nkechi used to know. In fact, you will probably see a different Nkechi than the one you left in Nigeria."

They were in the parking lot, and Okezie was looking for his car. He had a favorite spot, though it had been taken before he arrived in the mid-morning hours that day. Since his wife's arrival, he had become a latecomer to school. He now arrived at school closer to lunchtime, when all the prime parking spots were occupied.

"Where did you park?" Chinedu asked.

"Probably on level two. I was late this morning, and I left the car at the first available spot I found," Okezie explained and continued with the discussion.

"Because of this change we experience living in America, it's very important to have our spouses exposed to the same environment. Many Nigerians don't understand this point, but that's the biggest reason why my wife, Ijeoma, is here."

Chinedu had never really given a thought to this line of argument, though he admitted that it sounded fairly strong and compelling. However, it was just one factor in favor of his wife coming. He still had to weigh everything to see in which direction the scale would tilt.

"I know that the story Elias told us a couple of days ago is still fresh on your mind," Okezie said.

"It isn't just fresh, it's devastating," Chinedu quickly added.

"I know. I'm not a mind reader, but you aren't the best person at concealing feelings," Okezie added, opening the trunk of his car. They had finally stumbled upon it, because Okezie had no memory of where he had parked it earlier in the day. Actually, a campus police officer had been closely monitoring their movement as they walked through the parking lot, apparently aimlessly and in no hurry.

"Why are you opening the trunk?" Chinedu asked.

"I want you to get in there. It's large enough for you, isn't it?" Okezie joked.

They both smiled.

"I plan to make a stop at the Jewel grocery at LaSalle Drive. Ijeoma wants me to pick up a few things there. This is the time to put our briefcases in the trunk, not at the Jewel parking lot for that would be an invitation for thieves to break into the car."

"Good idea," Chinedu agreed. "However, they probably won't find anything more than my calculus and physics text books."

Okezie was determined to make his pitch for Nkechi, so he picked up the conversation where they had left it.

"We know that what Elias is going through is terrible. He worked hard to bring over his wife, and she threw him out of the house. However, I don't think it would be fair to paint all Nigerian wives in the United States with one brush. That's very unfair to them. There are really some wacky ones among them, but aren't there some wacky men among us?"

"I didn't know that you had become a feminist," Chinedu joked.

Okezie smiled, but continued. "You must look carefully at what our women are going through in America to better appreciate the root causes of the problems Nigerian families are facing. Consider yourself lucky to be informed about these issues before Nkechi joins you. That should make you a better husband, not a scared husband."

"Who told you I'm a scared husband?" Chinedu joked, rolling down the car window as Okezie started the car for the drive home.

"I was going to put on the ac," Okezie suggested.

"No, thanks. I want some fresh air."

"Why? It's hot outside."

"But not too hot," Chinedu insisted, putting his right hand out of the window to feel the air temperature outside. "I need the fresh natural air. I told you before that the ac and the heater make me dizzy. They're not natural."

"That's fine, let's hope you can still hear me with the windows open."

"Go ahead, I can hear you quite well," Chinedu assured him. "We're well known for shouting and screaming even when on the telephone."

"Where did you get that stereotype?"

"It isn't a stereotype," Chinedu countered. "Whenever Nigerians are conversing, don't you notice they're always screaming and shouting at the top of their voices?"

"Chinedu, this is Naija bashing," Okezie protested.

"Forget it then," Chinedu said. "Let's continue with what we were saying."

"I was going to ask if you were aware that a majority of the Nigerian women in the United States suffer from high blood pressure. Has anyone considered why that's the case?"

"Okezie, when did you become a marriage counselor?" Chinedu asked. "Your wife, Ijeoma, just came not too long ago and you no longer sound like the Okezie who complained that Naija women always wanted more than was given to them."

"Yes, we can always crack those jokes," Okezie countered, though not allowing it to dilute the seriousness of the point he was making. "Let me walk you through the life of a typical Naija woman in America."

"I don't understand what you're talking about," Chinedu argued. "Ijeoma has only been here a few months and you're already an expert on Naija women."

Okezie ignored him and continued. "To get a proper perspective on some of these issues, take a moment to reflect on the image we build up in the minds of these women while they are still in Nigeria."

"I thought you were talking about high blood pressure," Chinedu said.

"Yes, I'm getting to it," Okezie responded. "But allow me to stay on this image issue for a moment."

"Take two moments," Chinedu joked. He was, however, interested in what Okezie had to say. He had often felt badly for Naija women himself.

"Think about the many photographs we send to them, and the impressions these leave on them. For example, consider the many pictures you've sent to Nkechi with your two-door Ford Mustang. Clearly, for you and I, that may not mean anything, however, for Nkechi, that car is better than any car she has seen all her life."

"You're mixing up issues, Okezie. What has a picture to do with it? If I send pictures to my wife, does that mean she has to throw me out of the house when she comes to America?"

"No, it doesn't mean that," Okezie agreed. "But I was trying to explain to you the impact the pictures have on the women."

"Like what?"

"Like everything," Okezie countered. "Most of the items in those pictures, though commonplace here in America, are luxury items in Nigeria. So when they see a refrigerator, a television set and a microwave oven in our apartments, the impression created in their minds is not really the right one."

Okezie was absent-mindedly traveling north on Halsted Avenue, having missed his entrance onto the Kennedy Expressway. He was not happy with himself about that, for it meant an additional ten to fifteen minutes on the commute time. Unless one was going for lunch or dinner at one of those Greek restaurants on Halsted Avenue, there was no reason to want to drive through Greek town on Halsted and Adams on a Friday afternoon. Okezie had been patient through the "stop and go" traffic that started at Van Buren and only eased up around Grand

Avenue. The only good side of the mistake was that Chinedu would finally see the Cabrini Green Housing Project around Division and Halsted. Actually, they would go east on Division, through the heart of the project to rejoin LaSalle Drive. Chinedu has heard stories about the crimes committed in Cabrini Green, but had never been there.

Waiting patiently behind the number Eight Halsted Avenue bus before making his turn onto Division, Okezie continued with his analysis.

"Consider, for example, what it takes to own a car in America," he suggested to Chinedu. "It's like owning a bicycle in Nigeria. The guy flipping hamburgers on the grill at the local McDonald's restaurant can afford a used car."

Chinedu smiled. "That reminds me the joke, or actually, the true story about why students buy cars in America."

"I haven't heard that one," Okezie told him. "What is it?"

"When a bunch of high school seniors were asked why they needed cars, they all said it was to get to their jobs on time. But why do you need jobs? they were asked, and do you know the response? To pay for their car notes."

"What a funny cycle," Okezie commented with a grin.

"Yes, it is," Chinedu agreed. "Anyway continue with your thesis."

"You call it a thesis?" Okezie asked, then smiled and continued with his narration. "I was talking about the hamburger flipper and the car he bought. He then takes a picture with the car, using the high rise buildings at Cabrini Green as a background. This is all to impress his wife in Nigeria. There's nothing in the photograph to inform the person in Nigeria that the high rise building is a housing project, and that rich Americans don't live in projects."

"That's true," Chinedu agreed, meticulously studying everything he saw around Cabrini Green. Recently, there had been an increase in crimes committed at Cabrini Green, and the project had been very much in the news. Chinedu did not know what he expected to see in Cabrini Green. Realizing what was going on in his friend's mind, Okezie slowed down, allowing Chinedu time to see the project at close range.

"Buildings that go thirty to forty floors high are rare in Nigeria," Okezie pointed out. "So when these women see them in pictures from America, the thinking is that they must be the best. And sometimes they are. You can recall the many pictures we took of the Sears Tower and

John Hancock building in downtown. This is the image we create in the minds of our wives while they're still in Nigeria. So while in Nigeria, they get the wrong impression of what America is all about."

"You know, it's sometimes good to talk about these things," Chinedu admitted. "You never really give a thought to the implications of your actions. You just think your wife at home needs to see these pictures, and you send them without carefully understanding the impressions they create."

"That's where the problems start," Okezie pointed out. "These women fly in to America to enjoy these fancy cars and high rise buildings. They come to America without the least idea of what awaits them. It's often quite traumatic for them when, within the first two weeks after their arrival, they learn they have to work."

Something in that statement stung Chinedu. He turned and took a hard look at his friend.

"Although I follow your argument," he told Okezie, "I still get confused with some points you make. Why wouldn't they want to work? They were all probably working in Nigeria or going to school."

"It isn't that they don't want to work," Okezie hastily added. "In fact, you may recall that many of them have either graduate or undergraduate degrees from Nigeria. As you rightly pointed out, many of them were respected professionals before they left Nigeria. Some were high school teachers, and others worked in various government ministries. So their expectation of work in America would be for a job similar to what they did in Nigeria, not what they might have to do here."

That explanation gave Chinedu the type of relief an asthma patient gets from his inhaler. He nodded a few times. "That's true. There is work, and there is work."

Realizing that his points were starting to convince his friend, Okezie pressed on.

"I hope you're beginning to see the origin of the trauma. When a young professional with very high expectations is asked to go and train as a nurse's aid, or what they call CNA—I don't quite understand all the acronyms—it can be devastating or 'brain damage' as our friend Elias would put it."

Okezie pulled the car to a stop at the Jewel parking lot.

"Has Ijeoma started already?" Chinedu joked.

Okezie responded quickly, "The truth is that except for those lucky few whose husbands managed to land a good job, the rest of the women married to regular, struggling guys like me, go through the same process. I talk for myself, I don't know about you."

"You don't know about me?" Chinedu would not let that joke go uncontested.

"Well, let me continue," Okezie suggested as they walked through the isles, placing items into their shopping cart. "What's the work of the CNA? The CNA are the nursing aides who do what can be considered the lowest jobs in nursing homes and hospitals. It's the CNA who're responsible for bathing, cleaning and feeding all the old and terminally ill people who have become so weak that they pass human excrement all over their bodies. I know, you might argue that there's nothing wrong with that, since it was what Florence Nightingale had in mind when she started the nursing profession."

"If that was what Florence had in mind for the CNAs, what are the real nurses supposed to do?"

"You have to figure that out yourself. Remember the law of geography: the higher you go, the cooler it becomes."

Chinedu shook his head, and picking up a 6-pack of Guinness Stout, sighed, "This is a tough one."

"Quite tough," Okezie agreed. "Consider the adjustment this woman must make in such a very short time. She was coming to America—the heaven on earth—to enjoy life, not to work in a nursing home. That was the message in all those photographs sent home to her. No one ever told her that America was rough. Now once she stepped out of the plane, she learns she has to become a nurse's aid in a nursing home. It's traumatic."

Okezie allowed this to sink in as they checked out and paid for the items they bought. They were back on LaSalle drive on their way home.

I'll take Lake Shore drive from here," Okezie explained.

"Of course," Chinedu agreed. "Were you considering returning to Halsted?"

"I thought you were still a JJC," Okezie joked.

After a short silence, as he maneuvered through the busy intersection to the on-ramp to LakeShore drive, Okezie continued with the conversation.

"This CNA trauma is only the beginning," he pointed out.

"Remember that, if after nine months you don't have any news to the home front, your mother will want to know what was wrong."

"That's true, Nigerians are still Nigerians," Chinedu agreed. "If the woman isn't pregnant immediately, it must be her fault. Nobody remembers that there are two people involved in the child-making process, so both must be checked out before a finger is pointed at anyone."

"Don't even touch that one. Did you hear this story? A man whose name I won't say, lived at Ogui New Layout with his wife. After two years had passed and his wife couldn't become pregnant she was sent packing in ignominy and chastised as one of those who had wasted her youth and was therefore no longer able to conceive. The man married another wife, and given how pretty his previous wife was, she too was quickly remarried. At the last count, she had five boys and two girls."

"What about her former husband and his new wife?"

"As our people would say when a man tries without succeeding— it's still knock on wood. I heard the new wife has run away."

"You're bad," Chinedu said, laughing as he said so.

"Let me continue with my story," Okezie suggested. "So you have a wife, who has been in America only six weeks and who doesn't yet know how to get around, but she's already in the second week of the nurse's aid training and is already missing her period! Think about the trauma. Getting used to a new environment in a hurry, being pregnant and learning to be a nurse's aid, all at the same time."

"It's tough," Chinedu managed to add.

"You haven't seen anything yet," Okezie added. "Together with the nurse's aid training, she's also registered in a university or community college taking classes. In some cases, she has to take up to twelve credit hours because she's a foreign student and must be full-time. And once the CNA training is over, she starts to work 11 pm to 7 am because she has to go to school during the day. So the Naija woman is a student, a worker, and either she is pregnant or she is nursing a child, sometimes both."

"You mean nursing a baby and being pregnant at the same time?" Chinedu asked.

Okezie looked at him funny and cynically asked, "Of everything I just said, is that the only one you don't understand?"

"Not really," Chinedu responded, "but I can only ask for

clarification one question at a time."

Okezie ignored the comment. "What's more," he continued, "some of us so-called husbands pretend not to understand these problems, and expect our wives to serve us like our mothers served our fathers in Nigeria. We forget that, in Nigeria, our mothers had help. But here, the Naija woman is all on her own. In Nigeria, after a woman has a baby, the traditional *ine-omugo* follows."

"Okezie, you should become a marriage counselor. How do you remember all these details?"

"Didn't you grow up in Nigeria?" Okezie asked.

"Of course I did," Chinedu replied. "I remember *ine-omugo*. That thing spoils women, because they eat a lot. I'm surprised they don't add a lot of weight after that."

"That's the wrong way to look at *ine-omugo*," Okezie pointed out.

"What's the right way to look at it? Don't women eat a lot of food while at *omugo*?"

"I know they eat a lot of food," Okezie agreed. "But that isn't the essence of the process. *Omugo* is the period immediately after childbirth when the woman's mother or mother-in-law comes to stay with her. Many people, like you, forget that for a first birth, this is when the young mother is given the basics of motherhood. This is when she's taught how to take care of a new baby. It isn't the time for her to eat a lot of food. But even if she does, what's wrong with a woman recuperating after nine months of hell?"

"That's probably true," Chinedu agreed.

"But here in America, the young mother is all on her own," Okezie observed. "What do you expect her to do with a one-week-old baby? How do you bathe or clean a tender one-week-old baby? How is breastfeeding actually done? She's learning and doing all these things in a hurry, and on her own."

"Hey, this is America. Everything is rough," was all Chinedu could add this time.

"That's true, but that doesn't excuse certain things," Okezie argued. "Do you know that in Nigeria, a woman who has just delivered a baby doesn't enter the kitchen for a long time because there is help around? Not the case here. I remember this case that happened a few years ago, I believe before you came."

"What happened?" Chinedu wanted to know.

"This Nigerian woman had just had a baby," Okezie started to explain. "I heard that the woman had a little cut during child-birth because her baby was big. That's pretty common, and although the birth is classified normal, the woman still needs time to heal."

"What do you mean by a little cut?" Chinedu asked.

"I can't explain that well. I'm not a doctor. However, I think that it has something to do with opening up the vagina to increase the passage for a child at birth. It's pretty common with women whose kids are big at birth."

"That's fine. I get the idea," Chinedu said.

Okezie continued with the story. "The gossip was that her husband came home from work about a week after the birth and was mad that his food wasn't ready. He failed to appreciate the pain his wife was going through. He didn't care that she was unable to stand up and pick up her six-day-old baby who was crying in the crib. The only thing that mattered to him was that his dinner wasn't ready."

"Okezie, I know I'm not married, but I bet you that this story isn't as one-sided as you're making it. I think Nigerian men are probably among the best husbands around," Chinedu argued.

"I couldn't agree with you more, Chinedu. If I've left the impression that all Nigerian men are bad, then I may have failed in what I set out to do. That wasn't my intention at all."

"If that's so, then make the story balanced," Chinedu admonished.

"The aim isn't necessarily to present a balanced or a one-sided story," Okezie pointed out. "My belief, though, is that Nigerian men are making their case a little more effectively than the women. Therefore, I don't think that my presenting another perspective will hurt. But let me add, that there are definitely some women out there whose way of life, to say the least, is troubling. But my suspicion is that such women are in the minority, and their image can't be allowed to overshadow the image of our wonderful women in diaspora."

"I agree," Chinedu added. "However, I hasten to add that those men whose image you just painted are also in the minority. Their image shouldn't be seen as representative of the many respectful, kind and hardworking Nigerian men in diaspora."

"That's also true," Okezie admitted. "However, that doesn't negate the tremendous pressure under which most Nigerian women live. It's very important that we understand this aspect of the problem, otherwise, we'll never be able to resolve it. And remember that these women generally have very little time to make the transition to this type of life. The net impact of the big change is often traumatic, and for most of them, results in high blood pressure. Sometimes, the situation becomes so unbearable that the woman just snaps. It's understandable. We just need to move on and find a solution to the problem."

"It's tough," was all Chinedu could say.

"True," Okezie agreed as he entered the off-ramp on LakeShore drive onto Foster Street. "Remember also that there are men who go home to marry and lie to their wives about what actually they're doing in the United States. Such women come with even higher expectation only to be devastated by the reality that sets in on arrival."

"I've heard some weird stories. How can you lie to your wife about who you really are? For how long can you hide yourself from your wife?" Chinedu wondered.

"That's the intriguing part," Okezie responded. "In some cases, the blame rests with Nigerian parents and their daughters at home, who would prefer a sweet lie to the bitter truth. Many of our men here are only reacting to that expectation by lying about their identity."

"That can be very serious," Chinedu suggested. "For how long can that type of self-deception continue?"

"Consider the story we heard last week about the guy who went home and told the girl he was about to marry that he was a medical doctor," Okezie said as he pulled into the parking lot of their apartment complex. He put the car in park, but was in no hurry to get out. He wanted to finish the conversation. Chinedu also realized that, once they joined Ijeoma, the tone of the conversation would change.

"When this guy's wife finally arrived in the United States, he told her that he worked in the emergency room and was always on early morning duties. Every morning, he would leave the house at about 4:30 am in a three-piece-suit, only to stop by a friend's house and change into the street clothes he wore to distribute newspapers, *The Tribune* and *The SunTimes*, in the suburbs. That job took him until about 7:00 am and at that time, he went to his second job as a store attendant in a 7-11. He returned to his wife about 5:00 pm in his three-piece-suit and told stories of how terrible the emergency room was on that day. On certain days, he would request additional antiseptic soap to properly clean his hands."

"Come on Okezie, how do you believe somebody did that?"

Chinedu asked, laughing so hard that he was almost hysterical.

"Why is it hard to believe? I can tell you who the guy is, but I won't because it makes no sense," Okezie added. "You must understand that people have different mindsets. There are people who live a false and fake life 24 hours a day, 365 days a year. They just don't care."

"So, what's the situation now?" Chinedu asked. "Did his wife eventually find out the truth?"

"Of course," Okezie responded. "One interesting aspect is that the person who told the wife the truth was the friend in whose house he changed clothes in the morning."

"What?" Chinedu shouted.

"Naija people. What did you expect?" Okezie asked.

"How did this thing play out?"

"Quite naturally, it was a trauma for the wife. Their lives changed. Their house became a war zone. Ultimately, I think, she couldn't stand it and she moved out. To where? I don't know. It's one of the more tragic situations I'm aware of."

"It's unfortunate," Chinedu added, shaking his head in pity.

"Yes, it is," Okezie agreed. "The other part of the story is that I heard that the girl wanted to marry a medical doctor or someone with the 'Dr.' prefix. She turned down other suitors until this guy came around. Unfortunately, she fell for the wrong person."

"This is one of those situations my father would describe as a two-edged sword. It cuts both ways."

"I agree," Okezie added. "Who is to blame? The woman who wants to marry a doctor at all costs, or the man who can't be himself? This is one major reason for all these problems you hear about. If people could just be themselves, we would all be better off."

"True," Chinedu responded.

"You see, we're in America, and America is all about information. Now you have additional information to help you decide what to do about Nkechi. In my own case, the choice was easy. If you think we need to talk some more, that's what friends are all about. But if you ask me what I think, my response is simple: Nkechi should be here *yesterday!*"

12

HOME AGAIN

The conversation with Okezie made a tremendous impact on Chinedu. Doing a 180-degree turn, he was now firmly determined that Nkechi must join him in the United States. However, he would forever regret that he did not come to this realization immediately upon his arrival in America. It would have been quite easy at that time, but now, there were complications such as permanent residency and possibly citizenship.

In addition to these issues, it was also important to ensure that the traditional marriage ceremonies at home were completed on time. To facilitate this, Chinedu decided to travel to Nigeria immediately while he was still an official student. He did not want to run into visa problems upon re-entry. Moreover, he was beginning to feel homesick, and his parents' letters were troubling to him. They suggested they were no longer sure what was going on with him. It was clear his parents thought that perhaps Chinedu had married a white woman and was hiding the fact or that he was having other problems they did not know about. These were some of the standard thoughts that went through the minds of Nigerian parents whose children were abroad. Chinedu was aware of these thoughts, and wanted to put his parents' minds at ease with a visit to Nigeria.

It was welcome news to all when Chinedu called to inform his parents and Nkechi's parents of his plans to visit Nigeria.

"Am I going back with you this time?" Nkechi asked.

"We'll see how things work out. I think the visa process takes some time now." Chinedu couldn't fully explain to Nkechi the difficulties ahead. He was going home to reassure everybody that all was well with him. He had not changed his mind about Nkechi. The traditional marriage would take place during his visit. However, whether she would join him at the end of the trip was not clear. Nkechi was going to join that class of wives in Nigeria commonly referred to as being on "lay away" because their husbands were abroad. However, that was still better than the current uncertainty Chinedu's inaction caused everybody.

Chinedu started thinking like other Nigerians, whom circumstances forced into looking for a permanent residency and well-paying jobs in America. Prior to this time, many Nigerians were interested neither in American permanent residency nor in American jobs. They just wanted to graduate and return to Nigeria where excellent job opportunities awaited them. But the times and circumstances were changing. The job opportunities in Nigeria all seemed to have vanished.

By this time, visiting Nigeria had become a very expensive project. The family system was extended and every member of the family expected a gift. However, from Chinedu's viewpoint, the most important person was Nkechi. Okezie's wife, Ijeoma, would help him to shop for Nkechi. Although she did not meet her in Nigeria, Ijeoma already had a good idea about her from Chinedu's description. Moreover, Chinedu could look at a woman and accurately tell if she was a 36C or 36D. He could be that precise.

This was going to be Chinedu's first trip back home and he did not have much travel experience except for his trip to America. Luckily, Okezie was there to help.

"All you need are the two pieces of luggage the airlines allow with your ticket," he explained. "You can't worry about extra luggage. Everything is available in Nigeria, provided you have the money. You don't need to take much with you."

"That's true," Chinedu agreed. "I heard that the custom people want to be bribed if you carry a lot of luggage."

"They'll ask for a bribe one way or another," Okezie noted. "However, the fewer the pieces of luggage you carry, the easier you can get through."

There was a buzz on the door and a few friends were let in. It was the eve of Chinedu's departure and friends have been trooping in with messages for relatives in Nigeria. Emmanuel, Alfred and Alexander were Chinedu's friends. They have been in Chicago for a few years and were all married. They came to wish Chinedu well in his trip.

"Did you guys come together or is this a happenstance," Okezie asked as he welcomed the three men.

"Actually, I think it's a coincidence," Alexander said. "Emmanuel and Alfred came together."

"Why then is it a coincidence?" Emmanuel asked.

"Only yesterday, you and Alfred met me at Okezie's house," Alexander said.

"That's true," Okezie added. "We were all together in my house yesterday."

"Oh, I see," Alfred said. "So, that's the coincidence. What's the happenstance?"

"First time it's happenstance," Alexander explained. "Second time it's coincidence, and the third time two of you run into me again in the near future, I'll declare it enemy action."

"Alex, there's too much 'Dr. No' in you," Emmanuel said. Everybody laughed heartily.

"Chinedu, how's the preparation going on," Alexander asked. "In a day or two, you'll be a Naija man again, eating real homemade food."

"Chinedu is a bachelor boy," Emmanuel added. "I know he must be looking forward to his mother's *egusi* soup."

"I know," Alfred concurred. "It'd be tough to see what people like him would do if they closed all the McDonald's restaurants in town."

"Alfred, *biko* leave Chinedu alone," Ijeoma, Okezie's wife said. "Chinedu, don't mind them, the young shall grow."

"Ijeoma, it looks like Chinedu will bring *egusi, ogbono, uda* and *utazi* for you," Alexander said. "That'll explain this rugged defense you mounted for him."

They all laughed at Alexander's joke.

"Isn't that a buzz I heard?" Ijeoma asked. "Alfred, *biko*, buzz whoever it is in."

A few minutes later, Mrs. Okafor came in. She was just able to drag in a big carton and was gasping for breath like a person at the finishing line at a marathon. Mrs. Okafor exchanged greetings with everybody and took a seat at one corner of the room.

"Thank God for Chinedu's trip," Ijeoma said to Mrs. Okafor. "That's why we see you today."

"No my dear," Mrs. Okafor responded, "you know that America is rough. You may want to visit somebody but you have to be sure the person has the time for you."

"That's true, my sister," Ijeoma agreed.

"Madam, it looks like that carton is heavy. What's in it?" Okezie asked after the women had concluded their brief conversation.

"Oh, my dear, it's a few small things I want Chinedu to give to my parents in Onitsha," she responded.

Okezie exchanged an understanding glance with Chinedu.

"Madam, Chinedu is not going to Onitsha. He's going to Arochuku. With the state of roads in Nigeria, it may take one full day to travel from Arochuku to Onitsha."

"That's assuming there's gas," Emmanuel added.

"True," Okezie agreed. "We export oil, but we also lead the world in fuel scarcity. This is a Nigerian exclusive."

"You got that one right," Emmanuel responded.

Mrs. Okafor ignored the comments and flipped through a photo album that she picked up from Chinedu's center table.

Okezie walked over and opened the carton. He counted 24 tins of carnation milk, two 5lb bags of granulated sugar, two packets of Perdue chicken drumsticks, three packets of Perdue chicken gizzards, and a few other items. Actually, he stopped looking when he saw the packets of chicken parts.

Okezie heaved a heavy sigh and shook his head in disbelief and disgust. He walked over to the refrigerator and served himself a can of Heineken. Cans of Heineken, bottles of Guinness stout and cans of Coke were properly cooled and the guests were already advised about the self-service protocol in effect. Chinedu was busy packing, hence there was no time to elaborately serve anybody.

After a long silence, Okezie addressed Mrs. Okafor. "Madam, do you have an idea how much those 24 tins of milk weigh?".

"Okezie, *biko* go with your trouble," she responded, clearly annoyed by Okezie. "I have never asked Chinedu to do anything for me until today."

"Madam, I don't think you heard my question," Okezie responded, giving the carton a slight push with his right foot. "I was asking about the tins of milk. Do you also know that there's weight restriction on luggage carried in the plane?"

"You think I haven't traveled before?" she snapped. "I came back from Nigeria only six months ago when my husband took the chieftaincy title. We traveled with twenty pieces of luggage. I don't think it's this small carton for my people that'll cause all the troubles for Chinedu."

"Madam, I'm not talking about your husband's chieftaincy title. But let me try another one. Why are you sending frozen chicken gizzards to Nigeria? Don't we have chicken in Nigeria?"

"*Biko*, Okezie, don't touch that one. My mother likes foreign chicken. Even if Chinedu can't take the sugar and milk, I want the chicken to get to my mother."

Whenever Okezie was angry, he would whistle like a bird. It bought him time to cool down. He did that right now, and when he had calmed down, he picked up the conversation.

"Listen, Madam. The solution is easy. And that's what we've been telling other people too. Chinedu isn't touching any package. Bring whatever you want to send to your people to the airport tomorrow at noon and pay the shipping cost directly to the airline. He's traveling by British Airways, so you can easily find us at their terminal. Your people will have to meet him at the customs checkout in Lagos and take care of their luggage. The only thing he is accepting from people are letters and money. No more, no less."

"Okezie, *biko,* don't become a problem for me this night. It's Chinedu that I've come to see, not you."

"Madam, I don't want to ask you to make your visit brief, but Chinedu and I have a lot of things to get together tonight before going to bed. Chinedu doesn't like to keep late nights," Okezie added as his last word on the issue.

After a short stay during which Chinedu refused to join in the discussion, Mrs. Okafor angrily left, dragging her carton with her and cursing everyone as she did so.

As was anticipated, nobody came to the airline to directly check in luggage for his or her people. Thus, Chinedu had only two boxes with which to contend. After these many years in America, his trip to Nigeria was in no way similar to his initial trip from Nigeria. Chinedu could freely move around Heathrow during the lay over in London. He did not have to drink Coca-Cola or anything given to him; he could confidently ask for whatever he wanted. What a difference Chicago had made in him.

The difficulty in traveling to Nigeria hit home once the descent into Murtala Mohammed airport in Lagos was announced. Some passengers quietly prayed to God for a safe landing. But landing in Lagos airport called for additional prayers. Chinedu remembered praying that he would not be pressed to use the restroom at the airport, since there would be no useable restroom. He prayed that God would guide him safely through the customs agents and their thugs. But he realized that oftentimes the best prayers at the Lagos airport were those that wetted the palms of such people.

The sight of the American dollar had the power to cause momentary loss of self-control in the average customs agent in Nigeria's entry ports. Since Chinedu was not carrying many pieces of luggage, he was able to ease through with only a few dollars.

Traveling by road was no less traumatic. Literally speaking, there were no roads. Potholes and erosion had turned them into death traps. There were neither northbound versus southbound lanes, nor eastbound versus westbound lanes on what were supposed to be interstate express roads. It was more like a free-for-all maneuver of bumper cars in an amusement park. Cars and trucks bumped into and out of potholes, dodging ditches like bullets. In some cases, travelers pushed out cars and trucks stuck in muddy ditches. With no control over settlements near expressways, villagers living around these roads made quick earnings collecting tolls from cars and trucks that must detour through their farmlands in areas where erosion had completely eaten the road.

Although Chinedu was mentally prepared for the deteriorating situation in the country, what he saw overwhelmed him. The situation was becoming worse by the hour. Police or military checkpoints were littered all over the place. It was not clear whether those people were beggars, robbers or law enforcement agents. Chinedu's relations traveling with him had warned him to just "shut up" whenever a checkpoint was reached. It was so easy for someone just back from abroad to betray himself by his speech. That would mean that everybody in the car must come out for the car to be "properly searched." Of course, no one was really interested in searching anybody, for there was nothing being sought. The real issue was whether there was anyone with dollars in the car, in which case, the usual fifty-naira bribe per car per checkpoint would no longer be acceptable. With this state of affairs on the roads, it took almost a full day for Chinedu to travel from Enugu to his town, Arochuku, a distance of just under 150 miles.

13
IBA MEDICINE

Chinedu's return to his village was like the unveiling of a new moon with everybody coming out to welcome him after being away for such a long time. Although America had changed him in some ways, Chinedu himself always argued that the man was made before he went to America. From that viewpoint, he was just at home in the village as he had been before he had traveled to America. His parents were still very strong and healthy, and a neighbor was quick to point out that, "Teresa has been looking like a young girl since the past few days," an indication of the joy felt by his mother.

The traditional marriage was delayed a few days because Chinedu became sick. The news of his sickness had spread like wildfire in the harmattan and villagers trooped in to wish him fast recovery. His father's bed became his sick bed as he lay with Nkechi keeping vigil by the bedside. Mama Ekwutos, or Ekwy or as she was more commonly called visited to wish him well.

"It's all over his body," his mother explained to Mama Ekwy. "They say it's *iba*."

"Has anyone gone to get *iba* medicine?" Mama Ekwy asked.

"Yes, his father and Mazi Okugo went to get some *iba* medicine."

"That's good," Mama Ekwy said. "Mazi Okugo knows the right leaves and barks of trees that make the most effective *iba* medicine."

"True," Mama Chinedu added. "I pray that the medicine helps him. I don't understand this *iba* immediately he came back."

"I think this is the season for *iba*," Mama Ekwy said. "Once he showers with the medicine and drinks it for a native week, he should be all right. Let me take a look at your eyes," she said to Chinedu, gently tugging on his eyelid and inspecting his eyes closely. "This is good," she said. "It hasn't entered his eyes, so I think it was caught on time and he should be all right in a few days." It was always a bad sign for the *iba* to affect the eyes, because then it became serious and often fatal.

No sooner had Mama Ekwy left than Mama Nkechi arrived. She was gasping for breath and appeared to have been running. She placed her left palm on Chinedu's forehead to feel his body temperature.

"His body is very hot," she said to her daughter who sat by Chinedu's bedside. "Get a cold wet towel and place it over his forehead. It should help to lower his body temperature."

When Nkechi left to get the towel, his mother asked Mama Chinedu, "Do you know in whose houses he ate since he came back? People are bad. I think there's something suspicious about this *iba*. I can see it clearly, it's hand-made," she concluded, insinuating that Chinedu may have been poisoned.

"My sister, they're trying to take my only eye," Mama Chinedu replied. "He was very healthy when he returned, and all of a sudden he's dying. He should have stayed back in America. Our people are too jealous and wicked." Turning to Chinedu, his mother asked him, "Can you remember all the places you ate since you returned?"

"Mama, don't ask me those questions," Chinedu responded angrily. "Does it matter where I ate? The next thing is that somebody gave me poison."

"My son, it isn't whether anybody gave you poison," Mama Nkechi said as she, too, inspected Chinedu's eyes by tugging on his eyelid just as Mama Ekwy did not too long ago. "But this world is very bad. This is Nigeria, not America. Your mother is right to find out who you visited and who touched the food you ate since you returned."

Actually, unknown to them, Mama Nkechi had been very concerned about Chinedu's sickness and had traveled to Ohafia to see the famous *dibia,* Kalu, who was regarded as the most powerful *dibia* in the area.

Mama Nkechi, by many standards, was an informed woman. She had a high school diploma. She was a certified teacher, and having spent many years in Enugu was considered a modern woman. However, she was also considered superstitious by her critics, probably not without reason. She was well known in her church, being a past secretary of the League of Mary, a prestigious Catholic women's group generally referred to as *Umu Mary,* Mary's children. However, she was one of those parishioners, who on their way home after consulting with the parish pastor in the church, often stopped to see the local *dibia* to verify what the pastor had said. Such people were commonly referred to as *oje uka ome njo*—those who went to church and sinned at the same time.

Shortly after she arrived at Mazi Kalu's house, Mama Nkechi was ushered into Mazi Kalu's shrine where he communicated with the spirits in a ritual called *igba afa.* Mama Nkechi then narrated the purpose of her visit to Mazi Kalu.

"So, he came back from America to marry your daughter?" Mazi Kalu asked Mama Nkechi.

"Yes, sir," she responded.

"And you and your husband want him to marry your daughter?"

"Yes, sir. We do."

Mazi Kalu nodded, rose from the floor where he was sitting on a mat made from *akpukpo agu,* lion's skin. He went over to his medicine bag, also made from lion's skin and brought a few more cowries, dry pepper and an egg. He came back, sat on his mat and started to communicate with the spirits in a ritual referred to as *igba afa.*

Mazi Kalu was not only a very powerful *dibia,* he was also one of the most accomplished men in Ohafia. He was known to have killed and skinned a lion alone, hence people generally referred to him as *ogbuagu*—the lion killer. Such a man was not only respected, he was also feared. Thus, Mazi Kalu's dual role as a powerful *dibia* and *ogbuagu* made him a dominating figure in Ohafia and neighboring towns.

As he sat down again on his mat, he inspected the items he brought, admired them, nodded his approval and smiled. He looked at his guest, Mama Nkechi, murmured a few words of ritual, picked up the cowries allowing them to drop noisily to the floor. He repeated this process a few times, each time nodding his head like someone who had seen the solution to a perplexing puzzle. Finally, he looked seriously at Mama Nkechi, held his gaze on her for a few seconds, then laughed mildly as he shook his shoulders.

"Your *chi* is alive," Mazi Kalu told his guest. Mama Nkechi heaved a sigh of relief, clasping her hands across her breasts.

"But there's still something a little blurry, though it keeps clearing up. I see the figure of a woman, holding her baby and looking at your daughter. What's her name again?"

"Nkechi," Mama Nkechi responded.

Mazi Kalu nodded, drew some lines on the floor with *nzu*, a whitish stone that resembled a piece of chalk. He picked up the cowries again and dropped them on the floor. He repeated this process over and over, aligning and realigning the cowries with the lines he drew on the floor.

"Do you think there's anybody in Amuvi that wouldn't like a good thing for your daughter?" he finally asked his client.

Mama Nkechi nodded. It was beginning to make sense to her. Moreover, it seemed to confirm her suspicion. She knew to whose figure Kalu referred. She briefly narrated to Mazi Kalu how she had beaten Mama Ekwy in their apparent contest over who would become Chinedu's wife. She recalled the *ojo-ojo* sendoff episode, and many other things that had happened between the two rivals.

Mazi Kalu listened attentively, punctuating his attention with a few smiles. He was a great listener and never interrupted a client narrating his or her problem. When Mama Nkechi was done, he smiled and told her again, "Your *chi* is alive. It's your *chi* that brought you here today. You didn't come by your own power. It's your *chi*. Everything will be all right."

That was just what she wanted to hear. An assurance from Kalu was almost an assurance from God.

"I had a case similar to this from the neighboring town of Ututu a few weeks ago, and we solved it. Therefore, don't worry, it's a very simple matter. Your daughter and her husband will be fine. Nothing will happen to them."

"Thank you sir," Mama Nkechi responded, with her hands still clasped across her breasts.

Kalu smiled again. He knew how to get across to his clients. "I've told our people that whatever we do here is not by our own power. We're here as a messenger of the spirits of our ancestors. Once you believe that, no harm will ever come to you."

"Thank you sir," Mama Nkechi repeated.

Mazi Kalu nodded. He slowly rose from his mat and went outside. Alternately closing each nostril with his left thumb, he blew away the remains of the snuff (tobacco) in each nose. He sat down again, wiping his nose with his left hand and rubbing away the tobacco remains on his left palm with his right palm. Lastly, he cleaned both hands on his thighs and clapped away the remains.

Mazi Kalu was always methodical in his ways. He never hurried his actions.

"Everything will be fine. Do you hear me?" he asked Mama Nkechi

"Yes, sir. Thank you sir."

"Once you bring your concerns to our ancestors, you've done your part. The rest is ours."

"Thank you sir."

"Everything will be fine."

"Thank you sir," was all she could say, her hands clasped firmly across her breasts.

"I'll tell you what to offer to our ancestors. I don't charge any fees and that's why I'm still able to do what I do. I haven't allowed money to come between me and our ancestors."

"Thank you sir," Mama Nkechi responded.

"You will bring the following items for our ancestors: a white cock, a white fowl, four chicken eggs, four feathers, one keg of palm wine that didn't touch the ground, two heads of tobacco and one bottle of gin."

"Yes, sir. Thank you sir."

Mazi Kalu rose to leave when Mama Nkechi remembered that there was no market being held in Ohafia that day.

"Do I have to buy these things, or can I pay for some of them with money? Today is *Orie*, so *Eke* Ohafia isn't in session."

Mazi Kalu smiled and explained to her. "I know that today is *Orie*, but if you talk to my senior wife, she may help you. I don't touch the money. Let me go into the bush and bring a few things, and you should be on your way back to Amuvi very soon."

"Thank you sir."

Mazi Kalu's senior wife brought the necessary items to Mama Nkechi. She had a good stock of them. Mama Nkechi gave her their equivalent in money. Interestingly, there was no haggling. Mama Nkechi was very thankful and explained to her fellow woman her problems as they awaited Mazi Kalu's return.

"This world is very bad," Mazi Kalu's wife said to Mama Nkechi. "But you did the right thing by coming to see *Ogbuagu*. I think this is a very simple matter for him. However, make sure you don't ask him to do anything that'll hurt this other woman. *Ogbuagu* won't do that. He can instead ask our ancestors to take away this woman's bad will towards your daughter and her husband."

"That's exactly what I want," Mama Nkechi responded. "I've never hurt a fly in my life. How can I do a bad thing to a person? All I want is for our ancestors to keep these bad people behind when I'm in front, and keep them in front when I'm behind."

Kalu's wife sighted her husband returning and left Mama Nkechi. "Kalu is coming. Don't worry, everything will be all right," she reassured Mama Nkechi as she stood and left the room.

"You have to do this for three native weeks," Kalu explained to Mama Nkechi, handing her the medicine he had prepared. "Take a little quantity each day, and mix it with *ose oji*, about seven of them, add a little *nzu*, *akawu* and one cowry. When you finish mixing them, put one egg on top of it, and throw everything into the stream in your village. You can either do this before sunrise or after sunset, but it's better if you can do it before sunrise."

"I can do it, sir. That's no problem at all," Mama Nkechi quickly responded.

"Before throwing it away, look towards the direction of sunrise, and mention the name of your would-be son in-law three times, mention your daughter's name three times, then facing the direction of sunset, mention this woman's name—what's her name again?"

"Mgbokwo."

"Good. Call Mgbokwo seven times and ask the gods of Amuvi to drown Mgbokwo's evil thoughts in the river. Having said that, throw the medicine into the river. Do this for three native weeks, then come back

and give me the good news," Mazi Kalu concluded with a smile.
Mama Nkechi thanked him and returned to Amuvi.

*   *   *   *   *

Mazi Okugo had just entered the house with Papa Chinedu. They
brought all the ingredients required for the *iba* medicine and started to
cook them. Mama Nkechi learned that Mama Ekwutos had visited
earlier in the day to see how Chinedu was doing. "That was the time the
medicine man saw her," she told herself.

"What did she come to do?" she asked aloud.

"Mama, she came to see Chinedu," Nkechi responded. "Everyone
in Amuvi knows that Chinedu has *iba,* and people have been coming to
see him."

"They should see themselves first," Mama Nkechi said cynically.
She cautioned her friend, "Mama Chinedu, *biko,* keep an eye on
everyone who comes in to see Chinedu. I don't trust all these people
trooping in here."

Though the people of Amuvi didn't respect Mazi Okugo for much,
they still recognized that no one could administer the *iba* medicine as
well as he did.

"Where's the 'woman bench'?" Mazi Okugo asked. "This chair is
too high. Get me three blankets and some wrappers."

Mama Chinedu went into her room and brought back the blankets
and wrappers.

"Chinedu, remove everything you're wearing except your small
underwear," Mazi Okugo instructed. Chinedu complied and sat on the
woman bench in his father's living room. Usually, the *iba* medicine was
administered in the bathroom or backyard, but for somebody as
"important" as Chinedu, just back from America, anyplace, even his
father's bedroom was adequate.

Every Amuvi person knew how bad *iba* medicine could be,
especially when prepared by Okugo. However, one thing was certain: it
worked. The medicine boiled for about half an hour before Mazi Okugo
brought it down from the fire. He placed the pot of medicine in front of
the woman bench and asked Chinedu to sit astride the steaming pot. He
covered Chinedu with the blankets and wrappers.

"Bend your head over the pot," he told Chinedu. "Once I open the pot, open your eyes and mouth. The medicine needs to get into your eyes, your mouth, your lungs, and into your intestines. By this time tomorrow, you should be drinking palm wine with me at *agbata uzo ano.*"

He slipped one hand under the blanket and removed the cover of the medicine pot.

"*Ewo o, chei, ozugo,*" Chinedu cried in a restrained voice. He was clearly in serious discomfort and would have struggled out of the blankets. However, he understood that such an action would be considered cowardly. Moreover, Mazi Okugo forcibly held down any of his patients who tried to struggle out during the administration of the *iba* medicine. Nkechi was visibly shaken and was looking at Mazi Okugo, almost begging him to remove the blankets.

"I think it's good that he's talking," Mazi Okugo pointed out. "That way, we're sure the medicine gets into his body through his mouth."

Iba medicine was administered for about five minutes. By the time the blankets were removed, Chinedu was completely drenched in perspiration and looked as if he had taken a hot bath. Everyone in the room appeared satisfied. The medicine must have worked. His mother helped him into the bathroom where he took a shower.

Following Mazi Okugo's instructions, Chinedu's parents administered the medicine two times a day, once early in the morning and once late at night, for three days. By the third day, Chinedu was almost completely recovered and started to focus on implementing the project that had brought him home, to marry Nkechi. Mama Nkechi, unknown to anybody, returned to Ohafia to thank Mazi Kalu.

14

WEDDING OBSTACLES

The bride price negotiation and the traditional marriage were rescheduled because Chinedu's sickness disrupted the original plans. The ceremonies would now take place on Saturday, *Eke*, the eve of Sunday, *Uka Orie*. This schedule was not completely by chance, for it was planned to allow those involved in the upcoming event to attend the big *Nkwo* market on Friday. Given the order of Igbo market days—*Nkwo, Eke, Orie* and *Afor*—it was quite common to schedule important ceremonies on a Saturday that fell on *Eke*. The dual advantage was the convenience of the Friday *Nkwo* market as well as the opportunity to rest on the Sunday following the festivities. Legend had it that because of the importance of the *Nkwo* market day, the people of Arochukwu did not bury a dead person on *Nkwo* day. Nothing was allowed to interfere with this big market event.

Chinedu's trip had already been plagued by many unforeseen events. His recent sickness was just one of them. Thus, everybody felt relieved because the most important event that had brought him home was finally about to take place. However, just before his mother departed for the market on this particular Friday, *Nkwo,* there was a loud knock at the front door.

"Mazi Pius," a voice called from outside.

Both Papa Chinedu and his wife recognized the voice for not many people in the village addressed Papa Chinedu as Mazi Pius. It was Ochonma's voice. Ochonma was not an early morning person. For him to come to Papa Chinedu's house this early in the morning meant something was seriously amiss. Nobody in Amuvi called Mazi Israel by his real name. He was *Ochonma,* or one who spends time beautifying himself. But most people believed that Ochonma was a reliable person to call upon in an emergency, provided that he was given the time to properly comb his hair.

"Papa Chinedu," his wife called. "Is that Ochonma's voice that I hear?"

"Yes, I think so," Papa Chinedu responded.

"This early in the morning?" his wife asked.

"I'm equally concerned for a toad does not run in the daytime for nothing."

"That's true," his wife agreed. "The last time he came to us this early in the morning was when Okoro's wife died in labor."

Papa Chinedu opened the door for his early morning visitor. Though physically present, Papa Chinedu had mentally traveled the entire village, trying to determine what must have happened. He could not determine what it was, but he was sure something was wrong. He offered *kola* nut to his guest. Ochonma touched the plate of *kola* and thanked his host.

"Let's not break the *kola* nut now," Ochonma said. "I'll take mine along. The morning is still young."

"That's true," Papa Chinedu agreed.

Ochonma cleared his throat and wiped his forehead.

"What has happened?" Mama Chinedu asked unable to control her anxiety and curiosity any longer.

It was clear that something was wrong and Ochonma prepared his hosts for the bad news.

"Our people say that, when a serious situation arises, the way to handle it often presents itself.".

"What is it?" Mama Chinedu asked.

"Nwamgbo has paid her dues," Ochonma solemnly announced.

Papa Chinedu's head dropped. Everybody sat speechless and motionless.

Nwamgbo's death was serious for Papa Chinedu and his family. She has died on *Nkwo* day, and since she could not be buried that day, her burial must be deferred until the following day, which would conflict with Chinedu's marriage.

"I'm really getting worried about Chinedu's trip," his father said shaking his head in disbelief at the bad news.

"Nwamgbo has died at a very bad time but there should be a way to deal with it," Ochonma said, hoping his words would serve to lift the spirits of his hosts who were visibly disturbed.

"I don't see how," Papa Chinedu argued. "Our people say that the branch which hangs onto other branches and refuses to fall directly to the ground looks for an innocent passerby to kill."

"True," Ochonma said with a sigh.

"Chinedu's trip has refused to succeed or fail. Yesterday it was his *iba*, today it's Nwamgbo. Who knows what the obstacle will be tomorrow?"

"Let's not despair," Ochonma implored his host. "There's always a way out of every difficult situation."

There was, in fact, a way to deal with the current situation. The death announcement could be withheld, allowing Chinedu's previously planned event to proceed and the burial to take place later. However, Nwamgbo had been sick for a long time, hence this option was not very attractive. A person who died after a prolonged sickness needed to be buried immediately, otherwise the corpse might "spoil." The situation was a real crisis given that Chinedu's stay was coming to an end and he did not have the luxury of extending it much further.

"A small group is meeting at Mazi Kanu's house and we should go and join in their deliberations," Ochonma said.

A number of people had gathered at Mazi Kanu's house before Papa Chinedu, his wife and Ochonma arrived. Mazi Kanu was one of the most respected men in the village. He was Papa Nkechi's cousin, although Nkechi loosely referred to him as her uncle. Papa Nkechi and his wife, Mama Nkechi were also present, and so was Mazi Okoronkwo, one of Papa Chinedu's distant cousins. The room was quiet as greetings were exchanged in low, hushed tones. They deliberated quietly and in the end a crisis containment team led by Mazi Kanu and Mazi Okoronkwo was formed to address the situation.

"We'll see *Eze* Aro," Mazi Kanu advised. "There should be a way out of this. Many years before the war, a death occurred on the eve of the *ikeji* festival and we were able to handle it."

"True," Mazi Okoronkwo agreed. "You're a true son of Amuvi."

Mama Chinedu had been sitting quietly through this informal, yet very important meeting. Though the deceased was a good friend of her family, she was frustrated about the delay over her son's marriage. She was happy to see Mazi Kanu and Mazi Okoronkwo leading the effort to contain the situation. These were the two men to look for in such a difficult situation.

"Mama Chinedu don't worry," Mazi Okoronkwo told her. "Mazi Kanu and I have stepped into the middle of this problem. We shall be there until the end is reached."

Mazi Kanu smiled. He was not one to shy away from difficult tasks. Everybody in Amuvi knew that all seemingly impossible tasks belonged to Mazi Kanu and Mazi Okoronkwo.

"Don't worry, we're here," he assured Mama Chinedu.

"Of course," Mama Nkechi, who was also sitting quietly at one end of the house, chuckled happily. "Were you men going to leave it for me and Teresa? If an egg is used to crack a kernel, the shame belongs to the stone."

"Mama Nkechi," Mazi Okoronkwo called. "I don't always agree with you, but in this case, you have my vote. If Mazi Kanu and I can't do it, the shame belongs to us."

Everybody laughed and seemed to relax. Although no solution was yet in place, a sense of relief was in the air.

"The process is simple," Mazi Kanu explained. "We'll see *Eze* Aro with the following items: *ito otu aka nabo,* two bottles of hot drink, two cartons of beer, two crates of mineral, one he-goat, one she-goat and two heads of tobacco. *Eze* Aro will perform rituals that will allow us to bury the dead today after sunset."

"Mazi Kanu, you've spoken well," Mazi Okoronkwo said. "It's still good to have people who know the custom around. The day Amuvi is left with only these *onatara Aro n'ukoni,* our neighbors will deny us our share."

The comment was a clear reference to people like Papa Chinedu who were still haunted by the ghost of their inability to return to their village until after the civil war. Such people were often described as *onatara Aro n'ukoni*, or "those that returned to Aro in the afternoon," differentiating them from those that had been in the village even before the civil war, and hence had a better understanding of the custom.

"That will be an abomination. A man denied his share in the gathering of his brethren is no longer a man," Mazi Kanu added.

"True," Mazi Okoronkwo agreed. "We'll proceed as you have suggested. We'll see *Eze* Aro, and after sunset, he can declare our market day, *Nkwo,* over, allowing us to bury the dead. The burial then is on *Eke* day, which complies with the directives of *ndi-ichie-aro*."

The two families involved in the wedding were happy when word spread that preparations would continue as if nothing had happened. A delegation went to see *Eze* Aro as planned and another committee assisted the family of the deceased so that burial would commence once *Eze* Aro performed the necessary rituals.

It was late in the evening when *Eze* Aro arrived at Amuvi. His council of chiefs and a few other titled men were with him, and each had been "seen" during the day with one bottle of a hot drink to ensure full cooperation. *Eze* Aro started by greeting the small crowd that gathered for the ceremony.

"*Aro kwenu!*"

"*Yaa!*" the titled men responded.

"*Amuvi kwenu!*"

"*Yaa!*"

"*Kwenu!*"

"*Yaa!*"

"*Kwezuenu!*"

"*Yaa!*"

This was a very important ceremony to which women were generally not welcome. *Eze* Aro explained what the ceremony was about and everybody nodded in agreement.

"Our people say that a matter already discussed is decided with nods," *Eze* Aro told his audience.

"*Ndewo* Mazi," his audience said in greeting implying their concurrence.

Eze Aro performed a few rituals, and facing the direction of sunset, he asked the titled men, "What day is today?"

"*Nkwo*," they responded.

Eze Aro nodded in agreement. Repositioning his chieftaincy cap properly on his head, he looked at his council of chiefs and elders and asked them, "Does anyone see the sun anymore?"

"Mazi *odighi*," they responded, indicating that no one saw the sun.

Eze Aro picked up his staff, murmured a few more incantations and, facing the elders and titled men, he declared:

"*Ndi Mazi*, in accordance with the power and authority vested in me as *Eze* Aro, and with all of you, the representatives of *ndi-ichie-aro* as witnesses to the fact that the sun has set, I hereby declare that our market day, *Nkwo,* is over. *Aro kwenu!*" he greeted.

"*Yaa!*" the elders responded.

"*Amuvi kwenu!*"

"*Yaa!*"

"Nkwo is over, it's now Eke, I salute you," *Eze* Aro declared, taking his seat.

The titled men greeted themselves and word spread around town that *Eze* Aro has declared *Nkwo* market day over and Nwamgbo could therefore be buried.

The people of Amuvi gathered to bury her. Actually, before *Eze* Aro came to perform the ceremony, gravediggers snuck in to get an early start on their jobs, so that, by the time the people gathered, the grave was ready. Of course no one asked if the grave had been dug on *Nkwo* day. Only key burial rites were performed for this particular funeral. The other rites were deferred until the *izu ato* and *izu asaa* ceremonies, performed three and seven market weeks after the burial. Legend had it that the spirit of the dead continued to visit the house where the dead person lived until these ceremonies were performed. Consequently, they were taken very seriously as they represented the acts that allowed the dead to finally rest with their ancestors.

Although it was getting late, Papa Chinedu and his family took time to visit with Onwuasoanya, the son of the deceased. Onwuasoanya had returned from his station when he received news that his mother's condition had worsened. Onwuasoanya had lost his father many years ago and being the oldest son in the family, he was responsible for his mother.

"Mazi, Ndewo," Onwuasoanya greeted Papa Chinedu.

"*Bekee,* how are you?" Papa Chinedu responded.

Mazi Onwuasonya was often called *bekee,* or "white man," because he had a certain elegance and dignity in his character. Onwuasoanya also greeted Chinedu, talked briefly about his *iba,* and the traditional marriage coming up the following day.

"I didn't expect you to make time to come to my mother's burial tonight," he told Papa Chinedu. "I know you must be busy preparing for Chinedu's marriage tomorrow."

"That's true, *bekee,*" Papa Chinedu responded. "But your mother's death truly saddened us. She was very fond of Chinedu and we're quite sad that she died at this time."

"Death comes when it chooses," Onwuasoanya responded. "My mother suffered a lot. My hope is that she's now resting in peace, if there's peace there."

"She lived a very good life," Mama Chinedu noted. "I've no doubt she's resting with the angels in heaven."

15

FOLLOWING THE RIVER

With Nwamgbo's burial behind them, it was time to proceed with Chinedu's traditional marriage. Loosely speaking, two acts constitute marriage in Igboland. First, both parties must agree on a bride price and the bride must accept the bridegroom's marriage proposal by publicly offering a glass of palm wine to him. Second, there is the *mmaya ukwu*, or "big wine" ceremony. In this ceremony, the bridegroom's family treated the bride's family, or sometimes, the bride's village to a big feast. Since it took a village to raise a child, the *mmaya ukwu* ceremony was a way to acknowledge the village for the work it did to raise the child. Given that Chinedu was traveling back to the United States, both families had agreed that the *mmaya ukwu* ceremony would be performed in his absence.

Many Igbo are Christian, thus, many traditional marriages are followed by the western-type "church" wedding. However, from a strict traditional viewpoint, an Igbo marriage became official after the rites in the traditional marriage ceremony were performed.

Papa Nkechi had invited his relatives to attend the ceremony. His cousin Mazi Kanu was designated as the official leader and spokesperson for their family. On her own part, Mama Nkechi had also invited some of her friends to help her cook and wait on her guests. Dibugwu, and Mama Nwoye were among those that came. The two women were Mama Nkechi's peers and had been her friends since childhood. Like most of the villagers, they had looked forward to this day.

Before the event started, the women talked about some unique marriages that had taken place in the village. In particular, Mama Nwoye recalled the marriage of the daughter of one of their mutual friends, Mgbeke, also known as Mama Adaugo.

"I hope your daughter won't do to you what Mgbeke's daughter did to her," Nwoye's mother said to Mama Nkechi.

Everybody laughed heartily because this was a well-known story in the village. One person, however, did not remember the story.

"I'm surprised everybody remembers this story except me," Dibugwu noted.

"You remember that Mgbeke's husband died young," Mama Nwoye recalled. "Mgbeke single-handedly brought up their children."

"Yes, I remember that very well," Dibugwu responded.

"She struggled to make ends meet. In fact, for most of her life, she never ate breakfast. She always left whatever was available for her children telling them that she didn't like to eat in the morning."

"Mgbeke suffered a lot to raise her children," Dibugwu recalled.

"Eventually, her daughter Adaugo became married," Mama Nwoye said.

"She was very beautiful too," Dibugwu noted. "Maybe that was why her father called her *Ada-ugo*, 'daughter of the bird *egret*,' one of the most beautiful birds to ever grace the sky."

"She married a very wealthy man," Mama Nwoye continued. "Do you know what happened when Mgbeke went to spend the Christmas with Adaugo and her wealthy husband?"

"No," Dibugwu replied.

"Everybody knew that Adaugo's husband loved his mother-in-law very much and wanted to do everything to make Adaugo's mother happy. He killed a cow for the Christmas party, bought eggs for breakfast and filled the refrigerator with every type of drink one could think of. He wanted to make every day of Mgbeke's visit a party."

"God really heard her prayers," Dibugwu said, noting that, "Mgbeke deserved a rich in-law given all she suffered for her children."

"True," Mama Nwoye agreed, "but listen to the story first. The first morning following Mgbeke's arrival, Adaugo made breakfast for herself and her husband but not for her mother."

"What?" Dibugwu exclaimed.

"When her husband asked why she didn't prepare any food for her mother, Adaugo responded that her mother did not eat breakfast. She explained to her husband that all the years she lived with her mother, she never saw her eat breakfast."

"What did Mgbeke do?" Dibugwu asked.

"She sat there calmly as a cat, dying in silence. Throughout her stay with Adaugo and her husband, Mgbeke didn't eat breakfast."

"My sister, that won't happen to me. I'll speak out," Mama Nkechi said.

"I agree with you, my sister," Dibugwu said. "How can I be at the stream and allow soap to enter my eyes?"

Papa Chinedu and his group arrived in the late afternoon hours. Some of the men that came with him included Mazi Okugo, Mazi Ezuma and Mazi Nwosu. These were all his cousins whom Chinedu loosely regarded as his uncles. Another important member of this group was Mazi Ugorji, Mama Chinedu's younger brother who came from their village, Obinkita. In addition to the wives of these men, Mama Chinedu invited some of her friends and relatives from her village, Obinkita. It was a party of about twenty-five persons.

In Igboland, the bride price negotiation was often a lengthy event. Nothing was allowed to conflict with it, and the process stretched everybody's patience to its limit. The negotiation often lasted late into the night and sometimes until the early hours of the following morning.

Kola nut, or *oji* as the Igbo call it, was presented and blessed.

"He who brings *kola* brings life," Papa Chinedu prayed, as the plate of *kola* nut was handed to him.

"*Isee!*" the people responded.

"May God replenish tenfold the source from which this *kola* came," he added.

"*Isee!*"

"It's our life."

"*Isee!*"

"It's for our posterity."

"*Isee!*"

"May our visit to your place be a good one."

"*Isee!*"

"May the pot of wine that will cause trouble between us break before we drink from it."

"*Isee!*"

Papa Chinedu offered more prayers. He took one *kola* nut, looked around, and following the tradition, handed back the plate of *kola* nut to Mazi Nwafor, their host saying as he did so, "Mazi Nwafor, the king's *kola*, is in the king's hands."

"*Ndewo*, Mazi," Mazi Nwafor greeted, accepting the plate of *kola* nut.

Generally, after an elderly person blessed the *kola* nut, the duty of breaking and distributing it was delegated to a younger person.

"*Biko*, where's a young man to break the *kola* nut?" Mazi Nwafor asked, looking around for a person to give the assignment to. He asked Chinedu to break the *kola* nut. "Chinedu, come and break the *kola* for us. Do you people eat *kola* nut in America?"

Everybody laughed at the thought. Mazi Okoronkwo, who was a leading member in Chinedu's group thought it was inappropriate for Chinedu to break the *kola* nut.

"Mazi Nwafor, *biko*, let us leave this American boy alone," Mazi Okoronkwo said. "He might break our *kola* with his left hand."

Everybody laughed again at the thought of a person breaking a *kola* nut with his left hand. In Igboland, doing anything with the left hand implied doing it incorrectly.

"Afamefula, come and break the *kola* nut for us," Mazi Okoronkwo instructed his eldest son, Afamefula, who was in high school but came home for this important event. His father always wanted him to be present at every traditional event, and also wanted him to follow in Chinedu's footsteps to America. Afamefula, which meant, "may my name never be lost," was a common name in Igboland. It was a prayer to God, asking for a son to ensure that the family name would never be lost. At marriage, a woman dropped her maiden name and assumed her husband's name. Afamefula was Mazi Okoronkwo's seventh child, the first six being all females.

Afamefula was about to break the *kola* nut when Chinedu's uncle Mazi Ugorji complained that he "did not see" the *kola*. Mazi Ugorji, the younger brother of Chinedu's mother, came from their village Obinkita for this ceremony. Unfortunately, when the *kola* nut was presented, Papa Chinedu forgot that everyone in the house was not from Amuvi. This could have allowed him to assume that everyone present "had seen" the *kola*. However, if there was a person from another village or town, the *kola* had to be presented to such a person. The person then had to take one *kola* nut home to his people. This was a confirmation to the people that their emissary had participated in the event to which he was sent. This was a tradition the Igbo observed meticulously.

"Papa Chinedu, how can you forget your in-law?" Mazi Kanu asked. "Mazi Ugorji has a right to levy any fine on you and can even take his sister until you go and plead with the people of Obinkita."

Chinedu's mother smiled, happy that her brother was scoring points against the Amuvi people. She still felt loyalty to her original village.

"Mazi Ugorji, I'm on the floor," Papa Chinedu said to his in-law, stooping in the process as a sign of respect.

"Mazi, get up," Mazi Ugorji responded, smiling as he did so. It was a sign of respect for a person of Papa Chinedu's stature to stoop and apologize to a much younger person. Mazi Ugorji accepted the apology, and the process of passing the *kola* nut around was resumed. After the *kola* nut went around "correctly," it was blessed again before Afamefula broke and distributed it.

The ceremonies were ready to begin in earnest. The Igbo believe that a child belonged to all the people in the village. Thus, it took a village or an entire community to raise the child. Consequently, when the child reached adulthood, his or her marriage was a community or an extended family affair. While the parents of the bride and bridegroom made the ultimate decision on bride price, they did not participate openly in the deliberations.

The two sides had chosen their spokespersons. Greetings were exchanged, and Mazi Okoronkwo who spoke for Papa Chinedu's party, addressed the gathering.

"*Amuvi kwenu!*"

"*Yaa!*" everyone responded.

"*Aro kwenu!*"

" *Yaa!*"

" *Kwenu!*"

" *Yaa!*"

" *Oli ihe, oli ihe!*"

" *Mazi!*"

"Mazi Nwafor and family, I salute you," Mazi Okoronkwo said. "Our son, Chinedu, came back from the white man's land because of what he saw in your family. We must all commend him. He's the son of his father." Addressing Chinedu, he continued, "You're a good son. You've followed the river, and you'll find the sea. You've stayed alone rather than join ill company. My son, you've washed your hands and you'll eat with elders. *Amuvi kwenu!*"

"*Yaa!*" the people responded.

Everybody nodded in support of Mazi Okoronkwo's speech. They were happy that Chinedu had returned to choose a wife from among his own people. Many recalled the admonition given to him during his sendoff party by the *ojo-ojo* dance group.

Arochuku had a long progressive, yet non-binding bride price tradition. The bride price for every Aro daughter, regardless of education or family status, was *okwa isii*. During the British colonial era, *ofu okwa* was two guineas or two pounds and two shillings, and *okwa isii* was twelve guineas or twelve pounds and twelve shillings. In modern currency, *okwa isii* was twenty-five *naira*. Given the economic crisis in the country, this was worth much less than one American dollar.

With or without *okwa isii*, the process of negotiating a bride price was lengthy. The process was made exceptionally difficult for the bridegroom to show the love a bride's family had for her. It was also common for families to make unnecessary demands from their prospective in-laws in the name of the other "necessary" customary rites associated with marriage. Negotiating the details of such rites tended to prolong the already lengthy process.

Mazi Kanu who spoke for Papa Nkechi's side initiated the negotiation at about 7 pm.

"*Amuvi kwenu!*" he greeted.

"*Yaa!*" the people responded.

"*Aro kwenu!*"

"*Yaa!*"

"*Kwenu!*"

"Yaa!"

" Oli ihe, oli ihe!"

" Mazi!"

"Mazi Okoronkwo, I've heard everything you said," Mazi Kanu responded after his greetings guaranteed the silence he sought. He cleared his throat and took a sip from his glass of *aka mere*. *Aka mere,* which meant "made by hand," was the name given to the locally brewed gin, because it was literally made by hand, to distinguish it from the white man's gin, which was made or brewed by machine. Mazi Kanu was often referred to as *onye ocha nna ya di oji,* "a white person whose father is black." The meaning of this praise name depended on the context in which it was used. Mazi Kanu was known to always behave "big" and with elegance. In those days, the dominant viewpoint was that the white colonial masters were the "big" people in society and that they behaved with elegance and dignity.

Although palm wine was the common drink of the people, Mazi Kanu did not drink palm wine. He drank gin or "hot drink" as it was called, because the white man drank gin. Given that Gordon gin was very expensive, it was rumored that Mazi Kanu saved an empty bottle with the original Gordon gin label and refilled it with the locally brewed *aka mere*. Thus, only those who knew him well understood he was drinking *aka mere,* not the original Gordon gin like the white man. He took another sip from his glass. He was in no hurry. He licked his lips to emphasize how different his gin was from the palm wine which the rest of the people drank.

"Mazi Okoronkwo," he continued. "There's no amount we will ask from you that will be enough for our daughter. So, we've decided to make this very brief and simple. You'll give us five hundred thousand *naira* as a bride price. That's it, and if it's okay with you, this thing is over, so let's start drinking. *Amuvi kwenu!"* he greeted, taking his seat.

"*Yaa!"* the people responded.

"*O me ka nna ya,*" one member of his group shouted, praising Mazi Kanu as "one who behaved like his father," a very high praise among the Igbo.

"*Onye ocha nna ya di oji,*" another person greeted.

Everybody got up to shake Mazi Kanu's hand and thanked him for speaking well. Mazi Okugo was in Papa Chinedu's party, but he was in no hurry to shake Mazi Kanu's hand.

"Go and greet Mazi Kanu," Mazi Ezuma told Mazi Okugo. "They won't ask you to contribute to the bride price."

"Okugo is the clay pot that feels threatened whenever a stone is thrown," Mazi Nwosu, who was sitting next to Mazi Ezuma, joked.

"Must you bring me into this?" Mazi Okugo said haltingly to Mazi Nwosu. "I know my name is always sweet and that's why I've kept quiet. The bat says he knows how ugly he looks, hence he chooses to fly at night. Did you hear me say anything about money?"

"Mazi Okugo, I was joking. Nobody is talking about money."

"Yes, you're talking about money," Mazi Okugo sneered. Mumbling angrily, he added, "How much did Kanu pay for his wife? Looking at the mouth of a grown up, you'd think he hadn't sucked his mother's breast. He wants five hundred thousand *naira*. Why doesn't he want Chinedu's head?"

Mazi Okoronkwo did not allow Mazi Okugo's comments to distract him. Instead, he thanked Mazi Kanu and requested permission to go outside and confer with his group in order to come up with a counter offer or accept the offer on the table.

One did not have to look far to see what bride price negotiation in Igboland had in common with American football and used car salesmen. Before every play, the offense led by the quarterback went into a huddle to iron out the next play, which was exactly what Mazi Okoronkwo and his group were doing. Once out of the huddle, they would put a counteroffer on the table. This was similar to the behavior of a used car salesman, who shuttled between the buyer and his manager in the process of presenting and accepting counteroffers.

Fifteen minutes had passed before Mazi Okoronkwo and his group reentered the room.

"*Che, che, che, Amuvi kwenu!*" Mazi Okoronkwo called in greeting.

"*Yaa!*"

"We've heard what you said," he told Mazi Kanu. "We'll show you that we're men who've come to you prepared. I'll keep it simple. Our offer is ten thousand *naira*." Looking at the other members of his party, he sought their confirmation by asking, "Have I represented our views correctly?"

"Mazi, that's what we agreed on," other members concurred.

"*Amuvi kwenu!*" Mazi Okoronkwo said again in greeting and took his seat.

"*Yaa!*" the people responded.

Everybody shook Mazi Okoronkwo's hand and thanked him for speaking so well. After that, the serious aspect of the business at hand continued.

Mazi Kanu described the ten thousand-naira counteroffer as an insult, and an indication that Mazi Okoronkwo's group was not serious about the marriage at hand. He said he was leaving since there was no need to waste his time with "people who were not ready to marry a wife for their son." Mazi Okoronkwo countered that he "didn't see who Mazi Kanu was selling for five hundred thousand naira." He also threatened to leave unless Mazi Kanu and his group became more reasonable.

It was about 9 pm and the two sides were still over four hundred thousand *naira* apart. The women were growing impatient, because no one would eat the food they'd prepared until the bride price had been settled. Of course everyone ate a light dinner before the negotiation had started, but the feast had to wait until success had been achieved.

It was about 10 pm., and still very little progress had been made. Chinedu was very sleepy, but Mazi Kanu warned that he wanted Chinedu within view.

"Where's Chinedu?" Mazi Kanu barked.

"He's here," his mother responded.

"Let him come and sit where I can see him," Mazi Kanu commanded. "We're all here for him and he must be a part of what's happening."

The parties reached a stalemate at about 11 pm Mazi Kanu left for home without saying a word. It couldn't get any worse. As was common, a bipartisan committee of peacemakers was formed. They were able to plead with Mazi Kanu to return to the negotiation and succeeded with a bottle of English Gordon gin, which he stowed safely in his bag because it belonged to him exclusively.

After he returned, another round of counteroffers was completed, yet the two sides were still very much apart.

"I have met you before in negotiations such as this," Mazi Kanu reminded Mazi Okoronkwo. "But these people you brought to us today are very stingy. We thought their son came from America? Is his own America different? We know everybody in America has so much money he doesn't know what to do with it. Moreover, our daughter is worth over five hundred thousand *naira,* and you people are pricing her as if you were buying *okuko ojugo.*"

"Not true," Mazi Okoronkwo countered. "We've come to you as men, but the way this is going, we may have to go home, think it over, and send word when we're ready to continue."

There was no movement from either side. Everybody was tense because what would happen next was unclear. There was a good chance that the negotiation could fail. It may be that Mazi Nwafor and family wanted to squeeze out every dollar with which Chinedu had returned. Could it be that his three years in America had shaken the trust they had in him to the extent that they wanted to get as much money from him as possible?

The two sides returned to their respective huddles to figure out how to break the stalemate. They were still in the huddle when Mazi Nwafor's clock chimed midnight. When they reassembled, Mazi Kanu greeted them.

"*Che, che, che, Amuvi kwenu!*"

"*Yaa!*" the people responded.

"*Aro Kwenu!*"

"*Yaa!*"

"*Kwenu!*"

"*Yaa!*"

"*Oli ihe oli ihe!*"

"*Mazi!*"

"Mazi Okoronkwo," Mazi Kanu called. "The night has gone far. In fact, that chime of the bell tells me it's now Sunday, *Uka Orie,* isn't it?"

"Mazi, it's a new day," the people responded.

Mazi Okoronkwo sat still, his left elbow resting on his thigh, and his left palm holding his chin. He gazed at nothing on the floor and listened attentively to Mazi Kanu. He had been in these types of negotiations before and had seen a lot of dashed hopes. But it was clear that in a short time, this bride price negotiation had to end. He was not sure which way it was going to go. He remained calm.

"What we've done here today, actually since yesterday," Mazi Kanu explained, "is to show you people the love we have for our daughter *Nkechinyere.* You know she's one of the best daughters God has given to Amuvi. Our actions will guide your son, Chinedu, so that he realizes that Nkechi has people behind her."

"*O me ka nna ya*," one member of his group said again in praise.

"*Onye ocha nna ya di oji,*" another greeted.

"*Okwulu oha*," or "one who speaks for everybody," yet another person called him.

Mazi Kanu took a sip from his glass of *aka mere*, cleared his throat and greeted the people. "*Che, che, che, Amuvi kwenu!*"

"*Yaa!*" the people thundered back.

"Mazi Okoronkwo," Mazi Kanu called. "You're a full-fledged son of Amuvi. You know the custom, don't you?"

Mazi Okoronkwo offered a non-committal smile. He knew the custom very well, but would not commit to anything until he heard Mazi Kanu completely. Didn't they say that the devil is in the details? In recent times, people had claimed adherence to the *okwa issi*, but behind the scenes, the bridegroom was forced to accept other financial commitments. For example, it had become common to ask one's in-laws to pay school fees for his brothers-in-law.

"Your son will marry our daughter Nkechi," Mazi Kanu declared. "Our bride price is *okwa isii Aro*. 'No more, no less.' *Che, che, che, Aro kwenu!*"

"*Yaa!*" the people cheered.

Mazi Kanu was about to take his seat, but he just didn't. There was joy in the air. The people hugged and greeted him. From the way he summarized the negotiations, Nkechi's parents simply wanted *okwa isii Aro*. They didn't want Chinedu to pay anybody's school fees or commit to any other financial responsibilities. That was the significance of the "no more, no less" phrase Mazi Kanu had used.

For the first time since the *kola* nut incident, Papa Chinedu came out openly and greeted everybody. Chinedu hugged Mazi Kanu, shook his hands, and greeted him with a bottle of Andre champagne from America. Since the champagne was foreign, the people's perception of its value was very high. Mazi Nwafor also came out and accepted the people's greetings. It was true that Mazi Kanu was the lead spokesperson, but it was also clear that Mazi Nwafor had made all the decisions off-stage. The air was festive but there was still one important ceremony to perform.

"*Amuvi kwenu!*" Mazi Kanu greeted again.

"*Yaa!*" the people responded.

"My assignment isn't yet done."

Everybody knew to what he was referring. The bride price was settled, but Nkechi had yet to openly accept Chinedu's hand in marriage before the people, which made the marriage official. Chinedu sat among his friends and people in his age group. They surrounded him, making access to him difficult. This was deliberate, because in this part of the ceremony, Nkechi had to find a way to get to Chinedu and nobody was interested in making it easy for her.

"Where's Nkechi?" Mazi Kanu asked.

A shy little figure was led out from one corner of the house by her peers. Mazi Kanu handed her a glass of palm wine and asked her to take a sip, which she did.

"Now listen very carefully," Mazi Kanu instructed. "There're many people here tonight. Look very carefully and offer this glass of palm wine to the person you've chosen as your husband."

This was the fun part. There was suspense in the air as Nkechi started to look for Chinedu. Of course, Chinedu's age mates were deliberately obscuring him to make it difficult for Nkechi to find him. Some men jokingly asked Nkechi if she sought them, but eventually, she found Chinedu. Following the tradition, she knelt down on both knees and handed the glass of palm wine to him. Chinedu drank the palm wine, embraced his wife, and the marriage was thus complete. It was party time.

According to tradition, the bride price was never completely paid so that the bridegroom would always remain indebted to his in-laws. Chinedu's parents gave the sum of twenty-three *naira* to Mazi Nwafor as a partial payment of the bride price.

"Mazi Nwafor, we still owe you two *naira*," Papa Chinedu explained.

"It's the custom, my in-law," Mazi Nwafor agreed.

As the people ate and drank, they talked about the richness of the marriage custom in Arochuku.

"This is what a marriage ceremony should be like," Mazi Ezuma pointed out. "It's not the nonsense they do at Abako." Abako is a neighboring town to Arochuku.

"What do they do there?" Mazi Ugorji asked.

"You haven't heard about their custom?"

"I don't know which one you're talking about. Every town has many customs."

"In Abako, a marriage isn't complete until the young bride completes a native week trial live-in with the family of the groom," Mazi Ezuma explained.

"Oh, yes. I have heard about that," Mazi Ugorji recalled. "But is it really bad?"

"Yes, it is," Mazi Ezuma added emphatically. "Didn't you hear what happened to the daughter of their chief who became married recently?"

"No."

"She went to live with her parents-in-law, and one day they prepared a crab soup for her," Ezuma narrated. "You know what it sounds like when you chew a crab."

Mazi Nwosu was also listening to the story. "Oh, yes, I know what you mean," he chuckled. "The noise is worse than the noise made by that thing Chinedu brought from America. I don't know what he calls it."

"Mazi Nwosu, you're right," Mazi Ezuma laughed. "When Chinedu chews that thing, you can hear his mouth at *agbata uzo ano*. Everything sounds *karam, karam, karam*. You would think two elephants were fighting on dry harmattan leaves."

"I forgot what Chinedu called it," Mazi Nwosu said, thinking hard to remember. "I know he said it's made from *ji-oyibo*, white man's yam."

"Potato, yes, I remember, potato-chip. That's what he called it," Mazi Ezuma said.

"That's true," Mazi Nwosu laughed. "Maybe the chief's daughter should have asked Chinedu how to chew the crab. I guess if you can chew that potato thing, you can also chew crabs."

"Well, the young bride was very shy," Mazi Ezuma continued. "But she wanted to eat the crab, otherwise, her parents-in-law would accuse her of being rude and not eating the food prepared for her."

"So what did she do?" Mazi Ugorji asked.

"She had a plan," Mazi Ezuma explained. "She buried a small piece of the crab in every lump of *fufu* that she swallowed. Gradually, but steadily, she swallowed all the crab. But her parents-in-law didn't know what was going on until she thanked them, indicating that she had finished her meal."

"What!" Mazi Nwosu exclaimed, laughing as he did so. "Anyway, our people say that the music you can't dance to with your feet, you shake your head in response to. If she can't chew it, she can swallow it. What happened after that? I know your story isn't finished."

"No, it isn't finished," Mazi Ezuma agreed. "The next morning, her parents-in-law took her back to her parents. They claimed that their son wouldn't marry a woman who could finish a plate of crabs without anyone around hearing the noise when the crabs were chewed. Such a woman could kill and bury a person without anybody around knowing what had happened."

"That's really a stupid custom," Mazi Ugorji said and Mazi Nwosu agreed.

The festivities continued and Nkechi's mother was very happy that this day went successfully. Chinedu was happy that all things considered, his trip had been a success. While the people ate and made merry, Chinedu and Nkechi sneaked into Papa Nkechi's room for a quiet talk about their future.

"Why am I not going back with you?" Nkechi asked.

"The American embassy has tightened issuance of F-2 visas," Chinedu said.

"What's F-2 visa?"

"That's the type of visa they'd give to you since I'm on what is called F-1 or student visa. In other words, you're the wife of a student."

"So, they tightened it when it was my turn to get one?" Nkechi asked sobbing as she said so.

"No," Chinedu comforted her. "I'll be graduating very shortly and will easily find a job. With that I'll get a green card and your visa would be automatic at that point."

"How long will that take?" Nkechi asked.

"Not too long," Chinedu said. "But that's the only sure way now. You can just assume they no longer issue F-2 visas. Don't worry Nkechi, once I return to Chicago, I'll start to work on it."

"Are you telling me the truth?" Nkechi asked.

"Of course," Chinedu reassured her. "I'll also start to make plans for our church wedding in Chicago. The traditional marriage is for our parents and the people of Amuvi, but the church wedding is ours and our friends'. It'll be in Chicago. What do you think?"

Nkechi leaned on Chinedu and sobbed more. She was, however,

excited about the thought of her church wedding in Chicago.

It was a difficult and emotional moment, but Chinedu was able to convince Nkechi that he had the right plans to get her to America. What he didn't tell her was that in Chicago she would now be classified a bride on lay-away.

Their parents were not as concerned as the young couple, for in their parents' minds, there was really nothing wrong for Nkechi to wait for her husband for a couple of years. The important ceremony had been performed and everybody knew that Nkechi was Chinedu's wife.

Chinedu's visit was over in a few days. He returned to Chicago and told Okezie how he almost died of *iba* and the *iba* medicine that Mazi Okugo prepared for him.

"Did you take all the medications and vaccines you were supposed to take before traveling?" Okezie asked.

"What medication? I didn't take anything," Chinedu responded.

"Jesus!" Okezie exclaimed. "You mean you didn't even take yellow fever and cholera vaccines?"

"No. Was I supposed to?" Chinedu asked, even more surprised than Okezie.

"You're lucky you didn't get yellow fever or cholera," Okezie explained. "Yellow fever sometimes colors both eyes and can be fatal if it isn't caught on time. Many people made the same mistake you did, and for some of them, it was fatal. For such people, the story at home was that they were poisoned."

"My mother and Nkechi's mother insinuated that."

"I can relate to that," Okezie responded. "The truth, though, is that after so many years in America, your body needs a gradual readjustment to the water and food in Nigeria. Those vaccines, and in particular, the malaria medicine can be very helpful. I'm sure that you got the malaria from the mosquito bite at home. Thank your God you're alive to tell the story."

Chinedu did feel thankful, although he would probably never understand the role Kalu Idika of Ohafia had played in his recovery. Or was it just Mazi Okugo's *iba* medicine?

16

LAY-AWAY BRIDE

After Chinedu returned to America, it was up to Nkechi to either move in with her mother-in-law or stay with her parents. She was given that option primarily because of the very strong friendship between her mother and her mother-in-law. Nkechi loved her mother-in-law as much as she loved her own mother. She chose to split her time between both women.

Mama Nkechi and her newly-married daughter paid a visit to Mama Chinedu. While Nkechi looked over a family photo album, her mother and mother-in-law talked about differences in marriage customs now and when they were Nkechi's age.

"How quickly things are changing!" Nkechi's mother said to her friend and in-law, Mama Chinedu.

"What do you mean?" Mama Chinedu asked.

"I was thinking about Nkechi staying with you. Many years ago, actually before our time, it was required of every young woman to live with an older woman to prepare her for living with her husband," Mama Nkechi responded.

"Yes, that's true. It was called *ije ozuzu*. By the time we were Nkechi's age, the custom was beginning to die, especially in the big cities. I don't remember if you went to *ozuzu* after you met Papa Nkechi, but because Papa Chinedu was living in the north at the time we married, he sent me to his niece at Nkalagu," Mama Chinedu recalled. Nkalagu was a city about 50 miles from Enugu.

"Oh yes, I remember," Mama Nkechi said. "Papa Chinedu was already living in the north before he married you. Like father, like son. He was in Kano and sent you to Nkalagu, and Chinedu is in America and sends Nkechi to Enugu."

They smiled at the unintended coincidence. None of the women realized that in America the joke would be that Nkechi was on "lay-away."

Although Nkechi flipped through the photo albums, she listened attentively to the conversation. "What is *ije ozuzu?*" she asked.

"Oh, I'm sorry, my daughter," her mother-in-law responded. "It's the time a young woman lives with her mother-in-law or another older woman to prepare her for living with her husband."

"Things have changed," Mama Nkechi told her daughter. "These days, a young girl starts to live with her husband even when she doesn't know her left hand from her right hand."

"Mama, I know my left hand from my right hand," Nkechi protested. "I'm no longer a baby."

The mothers laughed over Nkechi's protest and continued their conversation.

"The day I came back from *ozuzu* was one of the happiest days of my life," Mama Chinedu recalled. "It was a big ceremony. Other married women escorted me to my husband's house with songs and dances. It was like being initiated into the marriage club. Some people believe that the day a woman returns from *ozuzu* is the day she is supposed to 'know her husband' for the first time."

"Did you say they prepared a song for someone returning from *ozuzu?*" Nkechi asked.

"Yes," Mama Nkechi and Mama Chinedu responded, almost in unison. "It was a common song and everybody knew how to sing and dance to it."

Mama Nkechi remembered the song very well even though she did not go to *ozuzu* in the sense that Mama Chinedu did. She started singing and dancing to it and Mama Chinedu immediately joined her.

> *Mrs jelu ozuzu be ndi ocha, onaba be di ya*
> *onaba, ona no, onaba, onaba be di ya . . .*
> (The Mrs. who went for training in the white man's
> house is now going back to her husband . . .)

The two women sang and danced, enjoying the recollection of their youth. Such memories always drew fire in Mama Nkechi's blood. Whenever she felt this way, she would go to a mirror and admire herself. She did that right then, spinning around to catch her reflection in the mirror and whistling one of her favorite expressions, "The girl is good." As she spun around, she shook her shoulders and waist in the process, pushing her chest forward, and remembered that once upon a time, those breasts stood upright.

Pretending not to observe her mother, Nkechi asked her mother-in-law, "Did you go to America, the white man's country for *ozuzu*?"

"No, my daughter," Mama Chinedu responded. "I've never gone beyond Enugu, Nkalagu and Kano. It was only a song. Don't take it too literally."

* * * * *

Chinedu had completed his first degree and was now in graduate school. He also worked full-time as an engineer with the IBM. It was a weekend and Okezie visited his friend after he and his family had done their shopping. He wanted to discuss how best to speed up Nkechi's visa application. It turned out that it was the same issue that occupied Chinedu's mind and Chinedu was the first to start off the conversation.

"It's time to start doing something about my residency," he said to Okezie. "I'm afraid that Nkechi could be in Nigeria for the next three years, if not more. I don't think I can take that, Nkechi is also becoming impatient, and rightly so."

"I think the solution at this point is obvious," Okezie said.

"So what do I do?" Chinedu asked.

"The shortcut to residency in America today is to get an American spouse."

"How can I do that? Marry an American while Nkechi is in Nigeria?"

"Not to worry. Everybody does it," Okezie said matter-of-factly.

"I don't understand," Chinedu insisted.

"It's easy. I did it too."

"You did what?"

"That's the main reason I'm indebted to Jennifer," Okezie explained. "She helped with my green card. I explained my situation to her and before I had time to explain in detail, she started to laugh and asked, 'So you want me to marry you, and we'll divorce after you get your green card?' "

"That was gutsy on her part. What did you say to her?" Chinedu had not known these details about his friend's life.

"In two weeks, we were married. At that time, a person received his green card immediately. I think that now you have to wait for it in the mail. But still, it comes within only a few months."

Okezie's explanation was interrupted by a phone call. Chinedu answered it and, after a few smiles and exchanges, hung up.

"That was Cynthia," Chinedu told Okezie. "She wants to stop over with Jennifer to kill some time here."

"So they're both coming over?" Okezie asked surprised at the coincidence.

"That's my understanding," Chinedu responded.

"This is becoming interesting. You haven't gone out with her for a long time, and she's about to resurface when she just might be the one person who can help us."

"What happened after you married Jennifer? Are you still married to her?"

"No," Okezie responded. "We divorced after six months, and I was able to file Ijeoma's papers."

"Does Ijeoma know about this?"

"Yes, she does. In fact, she's friends with Jennifer."

"American women are more open-minded than our Naija women. Do you think a Naija woman would do what Jennifer did for you?"

"I doubt that," Okezie responded.

Okezie's visit was brief and Chinedu walked to the grocery store to buy drinks for the guests he expected. Cynthia and Jennifer arrived just as Chinedu was coming back from the store.

"Where did you go to?" Jennifer asked.

"I just walked to the store to pick up a few things."

"So, we'd have stood out in the street waiting for you?"

"I knew I'd be back before you arrived," Chinedu explained. "It's at least half an hour to forty five minutes from 95th and Dan Ryan to this place."

Chinedu and his guests took the elevator up to his apartment.

As they settled down to drinks, Cynthia asked Chinedu casually, "Why are you behaving like your friend Oke-zie, whose wife has come? You don't want to see me again?"

"What do you mean?" Chinedu pretended not to understand.

"You don't call me again. You don't see me again. Who's the new girl in town?" Cynthia joked, but Chinedu could tell that she really wanted to know why he'd been ignoring her.

"Not at all," Chinedu explained. "Combining a full-time job and graduate school isn't easy."

"That's exactly the Nigerian man," Jennifer cut in. "When he doesn't want to see you, he remembers his job and his grades. Find a new line, Chinedu, that one is old. By the way, how's your friend, Oke-zie? Enjoying his African wife?"

Chinedu carefully chose which of the statements he wanted to respond to.

"He's fine. Just fine. He was here a few moments ago," Chinedu said as he picked up the phone to tell Okezie that Cynthia and Jennifer had arrived.

"How's *I-ji-oma* and the baby? Did I pronounce it well? She's really a sweet girl. I like her a lot. I think she's an excellent wife for Okezie. When is your own wife coming?"

As Jennifer fired off these questions, Okezie and his family arrived. Okezie's son was about six months old. Ijeoma was having difficulty pushing the stroller through the door and required Chinedu and Okezie's help. They all knew each other, except that Jennifer and Cynthia had not seen Okezie's son before.

Ijeoma was casually dressed. She wore a blue jeans skirt with a blue jeans blouse to match. Her hair was braided and she wore a pair of gold earrings, but no necklace. Although she schooled in Nigeria and hence spoke excellent English, Ijeoma had mastered American slang and could easily pass as an African-American.

"He's so cute," Cynthia said of the baby squatting to take a closer look at Okezie's son, Nweke, in the stroller.

"Yes, he is," Jennifer agreed. "I'm so sorry, I-ji-oma. I kept promising I was gonna come and see your baby, but I kept getting caught up with so many things. I'm still gonna come see you. I've got to get the baby something, especially since I missed your baby shower. I'm really so sorry."

"Not to worry," Ijeoma responded. "How have you all been?"

"Just fine, just fine. I can't complain," Jennifer responded.

"Even if you complain, they won't listen," Cynthia laughed.

"That's right, baby. And those who listen can't even help me," Jennifer completed the joke.

"This one is new," Okezie said about the joke. "I haven't heard it before."

After a brief stay, Ijeoma excused herself and the baby. She knew what her husband had planned to request of Cynthia, and she felt it was inappropriate for her to be there when he did.

"When is your wife coming?" Cynthia asked Chinedu, after Ijeoma left. She knew a lot about Nkechi having seen her picture a few times. Actually, Nkechi's pictures were all over Chinedu's apartment.

"Nkechi is just fine," Okezie responded even though the question was not meant for him. "She hopes to be here as soon as the embassy gives her a visa."

"You've got an American embassy in Nigeria?" Jennifer asked.

"Yes. But you don't get a visa through the drive-thru window in Nigeria. It's a tough process. You know Chinedu is still on a student visa."

"Chi-edu, you don't have a green card?" Cynthia asked.

Chinedu shook his head.

"I thought every Nigerian man already had a green card. You've got one Oke-zie, don't you?"

"Well, I do. Actually, that's one . . ." Okezie was about to explain further before Jennifer interrupted.

"Actually what? You want Cynthia to get Chi-edu a green card the way I got one for you?"

Okezie knew Jennifer to be bold and outspoken, but this outburst took him by surprise. Jennifer continued before getting an answer. "Listen, you Nigerian smart guys. You want your African wives, and you want an American green card. That's fine, but now it's business. Cynthia will help Chi-edu, but he must pay her a thousand bucks."

Even Cynthia was taken by surprise. Only Jennifer seemed completely at ease with herself and the fact that she was clearly in control of the situation.

"If we wanted to play games with you," she continued, "we would just tip off the immigration department. But both of you guys are okay, though, so we wouldn't do that to you."

"Come on, Jennifer, what are you talking about?" Okezie asked. This was not going the way he'd hoped.

"Oke-zie, I know what I'm talking about," Jennifer responded casually, letting out her cigarette smoke in a circular pattern towards the ceiling. "I didn't ask you for a dime, but that was two years ago. Things have changed."

Looking at her friend Cynthia, Jennifer added. "You'll do it for him, baby, he's a good brother. He has a good job too, so a thousand bucks to get his African wife wouldn't be too much for him."

No one commented again on the issue. However, that last sentence, "a thousand bucks to get his African wife wouldn't be too much," kept resonating in Chinedu's ears. How accurately Jennifer had read his mind. He would even pay his one-year salary to get Nkechi to the US.

Jennifer had come with her car, so it was easy for her to leave whenever she wanted. Cynthia stayed the night with Chinedu. She was beginning to really love him, something that clearly troubled him. He also loved her, but would rather not encourage the relationship since he had just returned from Nigeria where he had formally taken Nkechi as his wife.

Cynthia finally agreed to marry Chinedu for the set price. The marriage and subsequent divorce took place without a hitch over the next six months. With Chinedu's green card in his hands, every effort was now directed to Nkechi's visa process. There were several problems along the road, which Okezie understood from his own experience. One of the potholes was the need to get a new marriage certificate for Chinedu and Nkechi in Nigeria. The date on that certificate had to be logically consistent with the so-called marriage and divorce with

Cynthia. That was, however, the easy part. One could easily get his own death certificate in Nigeria if it was necessary.

Chinedu and Okezie started to plot the subsequent moves with the help of Ijeoma. Ijeoma had been through the experience from the Nigerian angle, and Okezie had seen it all from the American end. The only concern now was to move speedily as the American embassy in Lagos was getting wise to these various moves by Nigerians in the United States.

"One important thing is that you must continue to be nice to Cynthia," Okezie explained. "You can't just disconnect. If she ever gets mad and opens her mouth, you will be in trouble, although she'd also be in trouble too."

"I understand that, and in all sincerity, that girl is good," Chinedu explained. "Now, I appreciate why, in spite of all the promises people make at home, they forget them and get married here. One runs into somebody whom he really loves and who loves him too. The question becomes, what else does one want?"

"I understand what you're saying, and that's what concerns every girl at home," Ijeoma explained. "No girl whose fiancé is abroad considers herself married until she joins him."

Okezie made a face at his wife. "So what are you saying? Do you mean that you still check out other guys?"

"I knew your mind was going to go there," Ijeoma responded. "If Nigerian men in the US could be half as faithful as the girls they left in Nigeria, you would have a lot of Nigerian saints in heaven."

"Is there a quota that Naija women at home aspire to?" Chinedu joked.

"Don't worry. I'm writing down everything you say. Nkechi will know about all of them when she comes," Ijeoma completed the apparent joke. "Any way, I respect these American women. I doubt that I could do for any man what Cynthia is doing for you."

"That's why I brought you from your village to see what American life is all about," Okezie joked. "Every morning, you should come and prostrate before me and thank me for bringing you to America. If it wasn't for me, you probably would still be in your village, waiting for a carpenter or a bricklayer to marry you."

"Chinedu, your friend should thank his stars that I agreed to marry him," Ijeoma countered. "Anyway, instead of this joke, let's concentrate on what's important. The problem in Nigeria is that once you go to the embassy and they deny you a visa the first time, then you're in trouble. You're better off bringing every paper with you the first time around."

"That's really not a problem," Okezie explained casually. "If they stamp 'denied' on your passport, you get another one. Once you properly grease the palms of the passport officers, you can have as many passports as you like. No big deal. Anyway, we want to make sure Nkechi gets through in one try."

It was easy for Chinedu to get all the papers needed by the embassy in Nigeria. There were a few difficult requirements, but Okezie had gone through this route and understood how to deal with them. For example, he helped Chinedu borrow money from a few friends to boost his bank account. The embassy liked to be sure a man had enough money to support his wife.

Nkechi was among the few lucky Nigerians who were issued a visa on the first visit. Although the embassy tightened things up by the day, a permanent resident husband who had a very good job with a reputable company appeared to satisfy the embassy. Therefore, Nkechi did not have many questions to answer. A few days later, she was on her way to Chicago.

PART III

17
THE NAIJA BRIDE IN AMERICA

The phone rang late at night. It was a Saturday night but Chinedu was quite alert. Would this be the call he was expecting?

"Hello. Who's calling?" Chinedu inquired.

"He-l-lo," a gentle, sweet, shy voice responded from the other end.

"Nkechi, where are you calling from, Heathrow or Gatwick?" Chinedu asked.

"Gatwick," she responded.

That phone call would forever change Chinedu's life. His wife was coming from Nigeria after such a long wait.

Okezie's number was on the speed dial, and in a moment, the two friends were rehearsing the plans for the big welcome party for Nkechi.

It was Sunday morning, and people were taking their time waking up. Many had spent long hours at parties the previous night, but the word spread quickly that Chinedu's wife was due in town shortly.

IK was a tall slim Nigerian who came to the US within the past year. Still in his early twenties, he was not married, but was a very good friend to Emmanuel. Emmanuel came to the US with Okezie and was one of the few Nigerians that came with their wives. It was through Okezie that Chinedu met Emmanuel who in turn introduced IK to them.

Because of his relative youth, IK had a care-free attitude to things. IK loved American music and liked to talk about American women. Emmanuel was more restrained but had a lot of sarcasm in whatever he said. In fact, friends always listened to him with suspicion because they felt there was a hidden meaning to whatever he said, no matter how innocent it seemed.

And so when IK heard that Chinedu's wife was due in town shortly, he decided to skip Sunday service and drove directly to Emmanuel's house so they could talk about the "latest news."

Emmanuel's wife, Onyinye, prepared a breakfast of scrambled eggs and bacon for her husband and IK.

"Emma," IK called. "Your wife is good with American food."

Emmanuel smiled but said nothing.

"Madam, thank you very much," IK greeted. "I'll skip McDonald's this morning."

Onyinye smiled and asked IK, "Do you want *fufu* this morning, I have good *ogbono* soup?"

"No, thanks. I'll rather visit again in the evening," IK responded.

Onyinye went into the room to prepare the children for Sunday service. IK and Emmanuel started to discuss Chinedu's wife.

"The girl tried," IK said. "You know she's been on lay-away for nearly three years. *Na wa o*," he added, indicating surprise at the fact that Chinedu's wife had stayed in Nigeria without her husband for so long.

"*Yaa,. . . yaa,. . . yaa*," Emmanuel admitted, throwing in one of his familiar wrench-like questions. "But who was she staying with all those years?"

"Emmanuel, that's why I don't tell you serious stuff," IK responded, allowing a little dirty smile. "Listen. Whoever she was staying with is now immaterial. When you put something on lay-away, there's no guarantee that other customers may not touch it, but they can only get a rain check provided you eventually pay up on time."

Chinedu and Okezie were at O'Hare airport hours before the British Airways flight from Gatwick arrived. The checkout was smooth. Nkechi's papers were in order, and in a short while, she was in Chinedu's embrace. Nkechi was still as beautiful as Chinedu remembered at their traditional marriage nearly two years ago. Chinedu held her out at arms' length, admired her, and both were locked again in a long embrace. Chinedu could have sworn he held a virgin in his arms, but he remembered that December afternoon when he returned for the marriage rites after two years in America.

Setting an eye on her during that marriage trip to Nigeria sparked a fiery fire in him. This was the girl he knew he really loved. When they got out of the bed that December afternoon, Nkechi was sobbing, but she was happy. Every second of that experience flashed through Chinedu's mind. But that was nearly two years ago. What had happened since his absence? Had she remained faithful?

As he was thinking these thoughts, Chinedu remembered what his father told him before his initial departure to the United States. Father and son had debated the pros and cons of leaving one's wife in Nigeria while he was in America. His father realized the anxiety in his son's mind. To calm him down, he told his son that the type of woman to be concerned with was the one who already "knew man," or as the Bible suggested, the one who had eaten of the "forbidden fruit." The woman who hadn't tasted of such fruit, it was generally believed, could be left in the midst of a million men, and she'd be just fine.

Chinedu felt that since prior to that December experience, Nkechi "didn't know man," then, she could be left in the midst of a million men for two years and she would be fine. But could Chinedu conclude that she had not been chaste these past two years, having once tasted the "forbidden fruit?"

"Jesus!" he heard himself mutter down his stomach. "Better a sweet lie than the life-threatening, bitter truth," he thought. There was a lot on his mind, but he needed something to give him strength.

"But remember, my son, that what you don't know, you don't know, and should never worry about, because you don't know it." Chinedu remembered his father's words. Those were the words to latch onto, he thought to himself. Whatever had happened in the last two years, he didn't know, and should never worry about. Stretching the argument further, since he didn't know, he could only conclude that nothing had happened.

All these thoughts raced through his mind as Okezie placed Nkechi's pieces of luggage in the trunk of the car for the ride home from the airport. Chinedu absent-mindedly opened the door for Nkechi, and with the renewed strength from that conversation with his father, he said aloud unconsciously, " *Ye-e-e-s.*"

"Chinedu," a sweet, gentle voice called. "Yes, what?"

"Nkechi," Okezie jumped in to the rescue, noticing his friend was blank. "Do you think you'll understand everything about America in one hour? Never mind, you're here to stay."

The drive from O'Hare airport to the north side of Chicago was smooth. Okezie was at the steering wheel while Chinedu and Nkechi sat comfortably in the back of Okezie's Ford Mustang. Okezie remembered Johnson, one of his very close friends in Nigeria. Johnson was a personal driver to their boss at work. He once gave Okezie the two cardinal rules a driver should obey to be successful driving "the big boss."

"You must be nice to Madam, the wife of the boss," Johnson had explained. "That's rule number one. If Madam is on your side, you'll be fine."

"And rule number two?" Okezie had asked.

"The second is like the first," Johnson had explained. "When you're out of town with the boss, and he's seated, not at the right hand of God, but in the back seat with his girlfriend, thou shalt not use the inside rearview mirror while driving."

"So, how do you drive?" Okezie had asked.

"You must turn the mirror away completely, so the boss knows you aren't interested in what may be going on in the back seat. Once he's assured you understand these two rules and can play along, you're fine."

Okezie recalled these rules very well and practiced the second rule during the drive from O'Hare to the north side of Chicago. Chinedu and Nkechi were thus left alone in the rear seat.

Although everything was ready at the apartment, Chinedu wanted to start impressing his wife immediately. He remembered how he felt when he was a Johnny Just Come, JJC, or one new at a place. However, he was now a pro in America.

"Okezie," Chinedu called, " *biko,* pull up by Uptown Bank, let me get some cash."

"Does the bank open on Sunday?" Nkechi inquired, recalling that in Nigeria, no banks were open that day.

"Oh, no. I have my twenty-four hour ATM card," Chinedu responded casually, yet consciously wanting to impress her. "With an ATM card, one can bank twenty-four hours a day, seven days a week, fifty-two weeks a year."

Okezie held back a little chuckle. He pulled up by the ATM machine, and Chinedu slipped in his ATM card, entered his personal identification number, and in a few seconds, several twenty dollars bills dropped into the bin. He folded them neatly into his wallet and they drove off.

"Is there always somebody inside to give you the money?" Nkechi half-asked and half-wondered.

"Nkechi, don't worry," Okezie answered. "Did your class not sing this song in elementary school?

Come and see, America wonder
you never know, America wonder . . . "

Nkechi didn't say anything again. She sat just as quietly as a mouse holding Chinedu's hand firmly as if it guaranteed her safety. She remembered that less than twenty-four hours ago, she was in a different world called Nigeria where if you had to go to the bank, that was your sole task for the day.

They were now in Chinedu's apartment and although Nkechi was tired, she was curiously going through the apartment identifying every appliance she had seen in the pictures Chinedu had sent to her. Many of Chinedu's friends came to welcome her. Some came out of curiosity, for although it was known that he was expecting his wife, no one was actually sure if Chinedu had a wife in Nigeria, since almost every Nigerian bachelor claimed to have a wife back home. It was common knowledge that Nigerian men preferred to travel back to Nigeria to choose a wife. Many of these marriages were arranged by the family. These men preferred to marry women they had never met, over single Nigerian women in the United States. These trips had become so commonplace that they became known as "missionary journeys" to Nigeria. A person making a second trip home, was like St. Paul on his second "missionary journey."

This did not fare well with many Nigerian women in the United States who were single. Why should Nigerian men treat them this way? They were not to be ignored.

IK and Emmanuel who had also come to welcome Nkechi joined the party already in progress. Nigerians were not used to "bringing something" to a party as was common in America. A Nigerian would provide for you if he invited you to a party, and would expect the same from you if you invited him. And so, Ijeoma, acting as the chief hostess had cooked a lot of food which she brought over to Chinedu's apartment. Chinedu and Okezie had bought drinks before going to the airport. As people ate and drank, pockets of discussion groups formed and people generally talked about how lucky Chinedu was.

"Iyke," for that was how Emmanuel preferred to address his friend IK, "Chinedu is in good hands with All State."

"*Dianyi*, that girl is worth the wait," Iyke responded. "If you look closely at Nkechi, you'd see that when you get down to it, it's like eating pounded yam."

"Shut up, Iyke."

"No, I won't. This isn't a matter of shutting up. That girl is fresh. That's why I've told other guys like me who're still looking around to go home and marry whenever they're ready. There're lots of sweet things still there."

"IK, it's now your turn," a female voice added from a dark corner of the living room. "I know that when you're ready, your parents will send one village girl to you via the US Post Office."

It was Leticia, the same Leticia who had helped Chinedu in the cafeteria during his first few weeks in America. Leticia had been vocal in criticizing men who went home to marry. Although single, she did not shy away from direct confrontations with men, unlike most other single Nigerian women. Leticia said what she felt.

"*Nne, biko,* who're you calling a village girl?"

Unfortunately, Leticia had not noticed Ijeoma, when making the "village girl" comment. Ijeoma had graduated from The University of Nigeria in Nsukka before coming to meet her husband. She had previously heard of this "village girl" stereotype made by Leticia and was looking for a chance to let Leticia know how offensive that classification was to her. Among Nigerians, a "village girl" was one who did not go to school or a girl who was unpolished. In contrast, a "modern girl," was well-educated and lived in a major city.

"Do I look like a village girl to you?" Ijeoma asked, hands on her waist as she looked down at Leticia. "I don't want anybody to let her frustration off on me. I didn't ask anybody to come to America without first finding a husband."

"Who's frustrated?" Leticia roared, and almost pounced on Ijeoma, but IK immediately restrained her. The verbal exchange was bitter and ugly, but luckily the presence of other people prevented a possible physical exchange.

Okezie had been inside the room unaware of what had happened.

"What are you doing here?" Emmanuel asked him. "Your wife was almost in a fight with Leticia." Okezie went over and talked to his wife, who immediately followed him into Chinedu's bedroom. Leticia went home and things calmed down.

"Somebody should marry that woman, so she'll stop annoying people," Emmanuel suggested. "Iyke, I don't think you need to go on another missionary journey to Naija this summer. We can all help and square you off with Leticia."

"That's really a good idea, IK," Chinedu said, supporting Emmanuel's suggestion.

"Look at Naija man," IK retorted. "He went home and brought his own 'chassis', and now Chinedu thinks it's time to give me advice. Your head isn't complete."

"No," Chinedu argued. "Mine is different."

Everybody in the room, including Chinedu's wife, liked that line and enjoyed the laughter that followed. Chinedu would probably never be able to explain how his own case was any different from IK's.

Emmanuel and IK left the room together and joined Alfred and Alexander, two other mutual friends who had also come to welcome Nkechi. They continued to discuss how lucky Chinedu was.

"*Dianyi*, when you see a sweet thing like Nkechi, you want to get married immediately," IK said to Emmanuel and his other friends.

"Go for it, Iyke," Emmanuel responded.

"Actually, I'm working on a target date of next December," IK said. "I've written to my father about it, and hopefully when I travel, I'll marry a girl as sweet as Nkechi from my village."

"So, after all these years in America, you still want a village girl?" Alexander joked. "I still don't understand why you guys want a wife you'll start paying school fees for, instead of ready-to-go women like Leticia."

"Alex, didn't you see Leticia before you went home and married, or is your own as different as Chinedu's too?" IK asked.

But he did not get a reply for the discussion stopped because Nkechi and Ijeoma came outside. Nigerian men always respected married women, and since Nkechi had just arrived, everybody was extra sensitive to her presence.

Emmanuel was one of those men who felt that one should never leave his wife in Nigeria. He believed it was almost impossible for such women to remain chaste. Emmanuel was also well-known for asking indirect questions. So when he engaged Nkechi is a dialogue, Ijeoma was suspicious and ready to intervene if need be.

"Madam, so you have joined us now in America?" he said to Nkechi.

Nkechi was too shy to say anything. She just smiled.

"Welcome to America and to Chicago, the windy city."

"Thank you."

"So, how were your parents when you left them?" Emmanuel further asked, shaking his head, a clear sign to close friends that mischief was on the way.

"They were fine."

"That's good. By the way, did you come straight from the village, or you were in Enugu with Chinedu's parents?" Emmanuel probed further.

At this point, Ijeoma felt that enough was enough and she immediately intervened. "Emmanuel, you have to leave this investigation until she settles down," Ijeoma said. "Allow her to rest. She has told you that her parents and Chinedu's parents were all fine. What else do you want to know?"

"See me trouble o!" Emmanuel exclaimed. "Ijeoma, you won't allow me to get the latest Naija news straight from the horse's mouth? OK. I won't ask again before I get into trouble with Ijeoma."

18
THE RULES OF PARENTING

Nkechi settled down quickly to life in America. She and her husband had learned from the stories about troubled marriages among Nigerian couples in Chicago and thus had considerable resources to draw from in their quest for a successful and happy marriage.

Nkechi spent the first few months at home watching daytime television, a luxury not then available in Nigeria. But she was now ready to get busy and Ijeoma was instrumental in preparing her for what to expect in the job market as an immigrant.

"The first thing is to get any job possible," Ijeoma explained. She was quite honest and always spoke directly. She was not the type to raise false hopes in others. "As a Nigerian who didn't study in America, it isn't easy to walk into a high school with your education diploma from Nigeria and expect to get a teaching position equivalent to what you had back home. No, it doesn't work that way in America."

Nkechi did not seem worried. Her mental state was as tough as leather. She was prepared to accept any job that kept her busy. "So, how do we proceed?" she asked.

"Here're the options," Ijeoma explained. "You could start the nurse's aid, or CNA training, or you could work as a cashier in a parking lot downtown. It'll be easy to secure that position. They seem to prefer women as cashiers."

"If you're sure it'll be easy, maybe we should go for that."

"It should be easy," Ijeoma assured her. "Systems Parking has an opening for a cashier at Illinois Center at Michigan Avenue. I can talk to the manager there. He was once my boss."

"Is it for the morning or the afternoon shift?"

"I think it's 3 pm to 11 pm. General Parking has a night shift opening at their Grand Avenue lot. However, night shift in a parking lot is better for men."

"I wasn't thinking about leaving my husband and spending the night in the parking lot," Nkechi half-said and half-joked.

"I don't blame you my dear," Ijeoma said, laughing as she did.

Nkechi sat quietly and listened, although her mind rapidly thought through the options.

"There're other options we can pursue, but I started out working for Systems Parking at Illinois Center," Ijeoma explained. "I worked as a cashier during the weekend and did the CNA training during the week."

Nkechi thanked her, but deferred her decision until she could discuss it with her husband. She eventually decided to follow in Ijeoma's footsteps, becoming a weekend cashier in a parking organization in downtown Chicago and doing the CNA program three days during the week, as well as taking college level classes.

In a short time, she was like any other Nigerian woman. She became pregnant, worked in a parking lot, and went to school. Nkechi's mood was often on a roller-coaster ride and as changeable as the weather. She would be happy one minute, sad moments later. Her ultimate comfort, however, was in the thought that, if other Nigerian women in Chicago went through it, she could too. Her due date shrank from a few months to a few weeks, then to only a few days.

Chinedu wanted to be with her during the childbirth. He promised himself not to miss any moment of his baby's birth. He attended the

Lamaze classes and was ready for the experience. Gossip in town circulated about another Nigerian who had passed out in the delivery room. But not Chinedu. He had witnessed deliveries by midwives in the villages in Nigeria. In those remote villages, there were neither hospitals nor doctors and babies were delivered by midwives.

Chinedu would not leave anything to chance and even took his wife to the hospital probably twenty hours too early during one false alarm.

"I think you should go home. Her contractions are still weak," the nurse in the maternity ward told them. "Once her water breaks, you can bring her to the emergency room."

"No, I think we have to stay. I won't risk a birth in the car," Chinedu responded, and reminded the nurse of the major road construction on Lake Shore drive.

"Well, you can stay if you choose to, but she won't be able to eat anything once she remains here. She'll be considered 'in labor' and, therefore, can't be fed solid food until her baby is delivered."

Chinedu and Nkechi chose to stay. It was a choice they would often laugh over in the future. Nkechi's baby came almost twenty-three hours later. With an empty stomach, she was as hungry as a starved wolf, and the contraction pains were as sharp as a needle. This was, after all, her first baby. She had had no prior experience, and depended solely on what her friend Ijeoma told her. Nkechi liked to eat and always resolved to start watching her weight after the next meal. However, the choice she had made with her husband meant that she had to survive the contractions on an empty stomach.

There was a story about a Nigerian woman who once bit her husband's ear during labor.

"He was bending over to comfort her," Okezie had told Chinedu. "This woman was screaming like hell. She was calling her mother, who, for all we know, was in their village in Nigeria. It wasn't clear why she thought her mother could hear her from there. She was yelling at her husband and blaming him because he was 'responsible for this.' When she went for his ear, the poor guy bent over, thinking she wanted to whisper something to him. He had to have over twenty stitches on the left ear. So, watch out when Nkechi starts to scream. You may still need your ear after your child is born."

Watching the birth of his son was an experience Chinedu always cherished.

Nkechi was now in the women's ward recovering after the delivery. Ijeoma believed she had prepared her very well on what to expect before, during, and after childbirth. She was becoming indispensable to her. She was her big sister, and now, she was almost like her mother. However, Ijeoma was human and could not remember every situation and every detail. So when Chinedu found Nkechi sobbing during lunch, a few hours after the childbirth, he was understandably worried. However, when he learned what the problem was, he did not know whether to sympathize with her, or laugh at her.

"What's this thing they brought for me?" she sobbed, pointing at the hospital food. They had served hamburger to an Igbo woman who had just had a baby. Apparently, Nkechi was expecting the Igbo delicacies prepared for women after childbirth, things like *uda, uziza, utazi, ji-mirioku.* These were the kinds of dishes a woman needed right after childbirth. They were medicinal and helped cleanse a woman's body after delivery. She was looking forward to these, but instead somebody was asking her whether she needed extra mayonnaise and pickles for her hamburger. It just did not make sense to the confused, new mother.

Nkechi's mother had sent all those food items from Nigeria a long time ago. Therefore, all she needed was to survive two more days in the hospital and she would be fine. In fact, that hamburger was the last food they served her. She told them not to worry and Ijeoma made sure to prepare the best dishes for her.

Nkechi shared a room with another newly-delivered mother. She was a white woman and was not used to the aroma of the food Chinedu and Ijeoma brought to Nkechi. It was lunch time and Nkechi ate her homemade dish while her roommate ate her American lunch.

"Isn't the food very hot?" asked the white woman as she watched Nkechi eat her *ji-mirioku.* "The aroma is pretty interesting too," she observed.

There was no doubt that the aroma of *ji-mirioku* cooked with *uda, utazi, uziza* and *okporoko* could often be more than "interesting" to people who were not used to it. In fact, this aroma was the cause for emergency calls to the police by non-Igbo tenants in apartment complexes where Igbo tenants lived.

Seeing how Nkechi concentrated on her food and realizing that she would rather not be disturbed, Ijeoma responded to the woman's comments.

"That's actually the way we eat it in Africa. We aren't used to a hamburger and a cold sandwich after we give birth."

She also explained to the white woman the medicinal values in the meal and the belief that it was good for a mother immediately after birth. In particular, it helped the womb to return to its pre-pregnancy position and size. "You may not need it here because there's medication for everything," Ijeoma added. "But in Africa, it serves both as food and medicine. African tree leaves have very high medicinal values."

"That's interesting," the white woman responded, alternately dipping her fries in ketchup and eating some very crunchy potato chips. She was no doubt enjoying her own meal too.

*　　*　　*　　*　　*

After the brief stay in the hospital, Nkechi and Chinedu found themselves raising a new born-child without help or guidance. Besides Ijeoma, who did not have much experience herself, Nkechi and Chinedu were like two blind people leading each other. Whenever the baby cried, they reviewed the notes they took in the hospital to try to determine what the cause of the baby's tears might be.

"Feed the baby well at the stipulated intervals. Make sure the baby is dry and stuff like that."

By now, they had memorized all the Lamaze notes, though the notes were not really a substitute for the type of help a new mother could expect. What made things more difficult was that every person was busy. Even friends who might have liked to help simply had no time. Consequently, Nkechi, with no prior experience, found herself taking care of her son Ikem all by herself. Although Chinedu was there, a Naija woman, could not readily agree that her husband was helpful in such situations.

"Sometimes it's better if he isn't at home," Nkechi complained to her friend, Christie, who had a day off from work and was visiting. "Once I give the baby to him, the baby starts to cry and the next thing is he hands the baby right back to me."

"My dear, they're all the same," Christie sympathized with Nkechi. "I went through the same thing with my husband. He doesn't know how to take care of the child, but I'll almost be fighting over my food with him. If you see him eating *ji-mirioku* cooked with *uda* and *utazi,* you'd think he just had a baby himself."

Nkechi and Christie laughed heartily at the thought of a man having a baby. Incidentally, they did not know that Chinedu had been listening to their conversation, and, as patiently as Job, was waiting for the right time to comment.

"Nkechi and Christie," he called. "Don't you know that what's good for a pregnant woman is also good for the person who impregnated her?"

"Did you hear that?" Nkechi asked Christie, laughing even more than she did before. "I asked him to return to his work and allow a delivered mother to eat her food."

"I thought he was sleeping," Christie chuckled gleefully, covering her mouth with both hands. "My dear, they're all the same."

Christie spent nearly the entire day with Nkechi and left in the evening. That was one of the best days Nkechi had had in a long time, for no sooner Christie left than Ijeoma came. Ijeoma's visit had become taken for granted. On coming back from work every day, she'd stop to see Nkechi and the baby no matter how briefly.

But things did not get any easier when Chinedu returned to work after a few weeks. Nkechi was now all on her own. Chinedu would periodically call from the office, but that did not help much. Ikem cried a lot and this was of serious concern to his parents. He did not sleep well and was constantly restless. Nkechi would go through the basics, feed the baby, make sure he was dry, and put him to bed. But Ikem was not cooperative.

The lesson notes given to Chinedu and Nkechi stated that, at Ikem's age, he should be fed four ounces of baby formula if his mother was breastfeeding, and six ounces otherwise. Nkechi was breastfeeding, and so Chinedu and Nkechi measured out four ounces of baby formula for Ikem. They looked at the markings on the feeding bottle so carefully that one would think they were in a physics laboratory, identifying concave and convex curvatures. They made sure the formula was precisely on the four ounce mark. In fact, Nkechi had suggested using a pipette to ensure that they were not off by more than a drop.

In spite of what the young parents considered their meticulous adherence to the instructions, Ikem drank his baby formula in the blink of an eye, played for a brief moment, and started crying.

"This child is a carbon copy of you when it comes to food," Chinedu told Nkechi allowing a broad smile. "When hungry, he's nothing but a wolf, like you when you're hungry. You don't remember anything or anybody."

"Everything good about a child comes from the father, and everything that may not be good comes from the mother," Nkechi sneered tauntingly at Chinedu. "A Naija man is still a Naija man even in America."

"There's no Naija thing in it," Chinedu argued. "You can see the speed at which Ikem swallows four ounces of formula. Just think about it. Is it like me or like you?" Chinedu laughed heartily knowing that he was annoying Nkechi.

"You can laugh until you break in two. I don't care," Nkechi shouted. "I'm not surprised. Isn't it true that in Nigeria all bad children have their mother's blood and the good children have their father's blood? Right now, Ikem has my blood, but when he grows up and becomes a good child, it becomes your blood. That's how it works for Naija men, isn't it?"

"I don't know where you get all this stuff," Chinedu smiled, wanting to end the conversation. "When is Ikem's next meal?"

Apparently, Nkechi had set the timer for the interval suggested by the hospital for the baby's meal times. If the hospital suggested a four hour interval for the baby formula, Nkechi's alarm went off every four hours. The fact that the baby cried did not matter. She tried to breastfeed in between the scheduled meal times, but that did not help very much. Ikem's constant crying was now a source of concern to his parents, and they planned to make it an issue during the next visit to the doctor's office.

One Sunday morning, the young parents were visited by Mazi Frank who was a respected member of the Igbo community in Chicago. He came to welcome their baby to the world, a tradition very common among the Igbo. Mazi Frank had lived in Chicago for many years, and his children were now in high school. He was carrying the baby when Nkechi's timer went off, indicating it was time to feed the baby.

"Is anybody working a night shift here?" Mazi Frank asked looking in the direction of the alarm clock.

"No, sir," Nkechi replied. "Why do you ask?"

"During my first years in America," Mazi Frank explained, "I worked as a security guard in a factory. I worked mostly from 11 pm to 7 am because I was also going to school. I went to bed about 7 pm and set my alarm to wake me up by 10:30 pm since I lived about fifteen minutes away from my workplace. I had this schedule for so many years that whenever I hear an alarm, that experience comes right back to me."

It was a sweet remembrance, and everybody laughed heartily commenting on how things had changed for Mazi Frank. He was now a very successful engineer working for Motorola in Schaumburg, Illinois.

"I always put the alarm to remind me that it's time to feed the baby," Nkechi explained, trying to take Ikem from Mazi Frank.

"Don't worry, give me the food, I'll feed him," he told Nkechi.

"The baby food will soil your clothes, sir. Let me feed him and then I'll give him back to you," Nkechi argued.

"Don't worry about my clothes. There're many dry cleaners in Chicago, and they have to pay their bills, too."

Nkechi smiled and handed Mazi Frank the bottle with four ounces of baby food.

Mazi Frank looked at the bottle and complained immediately, "This is too small, fill up the bottle."

"No, sir," Nkechi and Chinedu responded almost in synchrony. "They gave us a feeding chart in the hospital, and according to the chart, he should be fed only four ounces at this time."

"What kind of chart are you talking about? This is a boy. You have to continue feeding him until he sucks no more and starts to sleep with the feeding bottle in his mouth."

This was Chinedu's only son and he would not easily deviate from the hospital's directions. However, Mazi Frank was not ready to sit around and argue with Chinedu and Nkechi, whom he considered to be babies too. He walked over to the refrigerator and filled up the bottle with the baby food and started to feed Ikem. Ikem drank about seven and a half ounces and slept with the feeding bottle still in his mouth, exactly what Mazi Frank had predicted.

Chinedu and Nkechi were at a loss for words. They had never seen Ikem sleep so soundly after a meal. They stood there, looking foolish and feeling as silly as a sheep.

"Do you know that you guys nearly starved your son to death?" Mazi Frank joked.

"We were following the directions of the hospital," Chinedu tried to explain.

"Which hospital? Those directions are absolute nonsense. Ikem is an Igbo son and should be fed well. How much did he weigh at birth?"

"Nine pounds, five ounces," Nkechi recalled.

"That's what I thought. Therefore, don't feed him like a one-pound baby. Never measure his food again. Just fill up the bottle and continue feeding him until he pushes the bottle out of his mouth or sleeps with it in his mouth."

This was an experience Nkechi and Chinedu would never forget. From that day, they followed Mazi Frank's advice and Ikem never cried as he had before. Once well-fed and in dry diapers, Ikem played and slept like a normal child.

19

IKEM'S BAPTISM

A few months later, Chinedu and Nkechi decided it was time to have Ikem baptized. They discussed whether to defer the baptism until Ikem grew up. A grown-up Ikem would have the chance to choose his faith.

"I don't think that argument makes sense," Chinedu told Nkechi. "I was born into the Catholic faith and I intend to bring my children up in that faith."

"There goes the Catholic, always thinking that only Catholics will go to heaven."

"I didn't say that," Chinedu protested.

"Every Catholic believes that," Nkechi countered.

"No, every Catholic does not believe that. *Some* Catholics may believe that."

"What's the difference?" Nkechi asked.

"Between every Catholic and some Catholics?" Chinedu asked rhetorically.

Nkechi was immediately upset for this was not the first time Chinedu has played with words in a way she did not like. She reacted immediately.

"I didn't test for English as a native language," Nkechi said with a nasty smile and angry look from the corner of her eyes.

"I never suggested that Catholicism is better or superior to any other faith. They're all probably the same. So, why leave the one I belong to for another?"

Nkechi ignored the comment, apparently uninterested in continuing the discussion.

"I'm for the right of children and responsibility of parents," Chinedu continued, also ignoring Nkechi's apparent lack of interest in the conversation. "As a parent, it's my responsibility to provide moral guidance for my child. People tend to overly stretch children's rights. Should I stop feeding my child until he grows up and is able to make his own choice of food? Or should I stop taking him to the doctor until he is able to make that choice too?"

It was later decided to have Ikem baptized in the same church where Chinedu and Nkechi had celebrated their church wedding. A number of meetings were often held with parents and godparents to prepare them for the responsibilities of bringing up a child in the Catholic faith. This was the last meeting before the baptism. Chinedu, Nkechi and Ikem's godparents, Okezie and his wife, were seated in the parish office waiting for the Reverend Father. When finally he arrived, he apologized for this lateness and explained that he had been to a local hospital to administer the last sacrament to a dying parishioner. He went straight to the remaining issues that needed to be discussed before the baptism.

"What name do you plan to give the child?" he asked Chinedu.

"His name is *Ikem*, actually *Ikemefuna*, which in my language means 'may my strength not be lost'," Chinedu responded politely.

"That's a beautiful name," the pastor said, "but I'm talking about his baptismal name."

"It's Ikem," Chinedu added rather casually. "Is anything wrong with the name?"

"Not at all," the pastor replied. "I remember that you're originally from Nigeria and that must be a Nigerian name."

"Yes, Father, we're from Nigeria and Ikemefuna is a Nigerian name," Nkechi answered, trying to help Chinedu with some of the questions.

"The name is really beautiful," the pastor said. "However, the Church expects every baptized Catholic to have a patron saint who intercedes for him before God."

"A patron saint?" Nkechi asked.

"Yes," the Reverend Father explained. "If your son's baptismal name is Peter, for example, then St. Peter becomes his patron saint. Wouldn't you like St. Peter, St. Paul, St. Joseph, St. Christopher or one of the Holy Saints in heaven to be your son's patron saint?."

Chinedu was getting impatient.

"So Father, he can't be baptized unless we give him one of these names you mentioned?" Nkechi asked politely.

Her comment was quite timely, for it bought Chinedu a few more seconds to get himself under control.

"Not just the names I mentioned," the pastor replied. "I was only making a suggestion. I would be glad to give you a book that contains the names of all the holy saints in heaven."

Nkechi was getting irritated too, but she kept her cool. "So we have to pick a name from that book?" she asked.

"The important point here is the need to have a patron saint for your son *Aikim*, or can I just call him 'I' for now?"

"Sure you can," Chinedu responded.

"The patron saint will be his interceder before God and the Church considers this to be very important. His patron saint will pray for him, and he'll grow up to be a very good boy that you all will love."

"Father, who's really a saint?" Chinedu asked.

The priest allowed a relaxed smile. "That's a very good question *Chi*—ehm, I can't completely pronounce your name."

"That's fine, Father," Chinedu responded somewhat sarcastically. "Some friends just call me 'C'".

"Good," said the pastor, looking politely, yet suspiciously at Chinedu. "I think that when you understand the importance of the saints and their role in heaven, you'll see why it's so very important to choose a patron saint for your son. But to answer your question, when a person who has lived an exemplary life dies, there is a process that takes place.

We need not get into the details, but in time, if everything goes well, the person may then be canonized a saint."

"So Father, since there was a Peter who lived an exemplary life, died and later became a saint, doesn't it follow that if my son Ikem lives an exemplary life, and eventually dies, he could become Saint Ikem?" Chinedu's sarcasm was clear.

"Well, you're turning this into logic. That isn't what I'm here for. If you insist on giving him the name *Aikim* at baptism, that's fine with me. It was nice talking with you. See you on Saturday." The pastor walked away, with a little sad smile on his face.

"I was ready to get out of here and have Ikem baptized elsewhere if the priest had insisted on his St. Peter and Paul for my son," Chinedu told Nkechi as they walked out of the church with Okezie and Ijeoma, Ikem's godparents.

"My concern was that you were going to lose your cool. I was glad you didn't," Nkechi added.

"There's nothing to lose my cool over," Chinedu added. "For me, the issue is much broader than picking a name. It has to do with our African heritage. If we cannot pass on our names to our children, then it will only accelerate the erosion of African culture already in full gear."

It was a short drive to Chinedu's apartment. Their friend Emmanuel and his wife, Onyinye, who had come to visit Chinedu and his family but did not meet them were about to leave when Chinedu pulled the car to a stop.

"Where did you all go to?" Emmanuel asked.

Chinedu explained to Emmanuel that they had gone to the church because of Ikem's baptism.

"That's true," Emmanuel recalled. "When is his baptism?"

"Don't tell me you've forgotten," Nkechi said. "Didn't you get your invitation card?"

"I'm sure we did, but I've forgotten the date," Emmanuel said. "Don't worry, we'll be here. Even if I forget, Onyinye will not."

"My dear, don't mind him," Onyinye told Nkechi. "I remember it's a week from this Saturday, but I didn't know you had to go to the parish office today."

"I told you she'd remember," Emmanuel said and laughed as he did so. "How did the meeting go in the church?"

Okezie narrated the episode with the Reverend Father over the choice between Ikemefuna and an English name, for example, Peter. Chinedu also spoke about the impact of this on African heritage.

"That's actually what we were discussing just before we pulled up," Chinedu recalled. "I had expressed concern about the erosion of African culture."

By now, they had all settled down in Chinedu's apartment. Ijeoma carried the baby while Nkechi went straight to the kitchen to prepare food for her guests. Onyinye went to help her. The men carried on with the conversation.

"It's a very serious issue," Okezie said. "We must continue to resist any attempts to make us lose our heritage, and we must continue to inculcate the African way of life in our kids."

"True," Chinedu agreed. "Giving them African names is a very obvious and proud first step, but it's not always easy. I understand that Mazi Frank's eldest son, Chibuzo, refuses to be addressed by his Igbo name. He has taken 'Bill' as his name of choice."

"There's probably a good reason for taking American names," Emmanuel suggested. "I know many non-Americans in my place of work who took names like Peter and Cheryl. The argument is that it makes it easy for their American colleagues to address them by their names. Therefore, Chibuzo taking the name Bill may not be a bad idea. African names tend to stand out, and in some situations, they may be the determining factor as to whether one is hired or fired."

"Emma, I think you're over stretching it," Chinedu argued. "I'm sure that when your parents gave you the name, Emmanuel, it wasn't because they wanted to save anyone the agony of your Igbo name."

"I didn't suggest that, did I?" Emmanuel countered.

Chinedu ignored the question and continued. "Your parents thought they were doing the right thing for you by giving you the name, Emmanuel. We now know better."

"Are you sure?" Emmanuel interjected, but again, Chinedu ignored him.

"Our focus should be on bringing up our children so that they excel in whatever they do. Given that excellence, even the President of the United States will learn to pronounce their names, and correctly too. But if our children become social liabilities, whatever names they bear, become nothing than a set of character strings with which they'll be tagged in jails."

"Let's also look at this issue from another perspective," Okezie suggested. "Often people tend not to appreciate what they have and they spend tremendous energy chasing what they don't have."

"I agree," Emmanuel said. "I kept running after women who didn't care about me, neglecting those who flocked around me."

"You mean you're still playing away, even with your wife around?" Okezie joked.

"That's not what I said," Emmanuel protested.

"Am I hearing double? What then did you say?" Okezie asked.

Emmanuel's wife smiled but said nothing.

"You can run after whomever you like," Nkechi suggested cynically. "But don't forget you have your children to provide for."

"Nkechi, you're taking our jokes too seriously," Okezie said. "But returning to the issue of African names, has anyone considered the cultural assets inherent in us merely by being Africans? These are assets our African-American brothers continue to reach out for, and those of us who have them tend not to appreciate and nurture them. We can't allow our African culture to become a forgotten or forsaken thing. We must continue to advance our heritage in our names, in our way of life, and through all appropriate media."

"I don't get this argument about African culture when the rest of the world is talking about technology," Emmanuel said. "Okezie, can you make a case for not allowing African technology to become a forgotten or forsaken thing?"

"Must you turn everything into a joke?" Chinedu asked.

It was the Saturday of the baptism. Chinedu's family and Ikem's godparents were seated in the church when a middle aged-woman addressed the congregation from the altar. "My husband, Deacon Smith, will officiate at today's ceremony."

Nkechi and Chinedu looked at one another. Okezie and his wife were no less confused.

"*Dianyi*, this parish has two resident priests," Okezie reminded Chinedu. "What's going on? Do you think the priest was upset because you didn't choose St. Peter for Ikem?"

"No, I don't think so. We're only one of about seven families having their children baptized today," Chinedu explained. "I suspect this is the new thing going on in the Catholic Church these days. The Church likes to involve the deacons and the laity in many of its activities. It's a positive development, but in my view, I think the priests should continue to administer the sacraments, probably with assistance from the deacons."

The Reverend Father must have told Deacon Smith the episode with Chinedu, for the Deacon was quite prepared for Ikem's name. Unlike the priest who opted for "I", the Deacon pronounced Ikem so well that Nkechi was surprised. One by one, each child was baptized. When it was Ikem's turn, the Deacon carried him and pouring water over his head pronounced, "Ikemefuna, the Holy Scriptures tell us that John the Baptist baptized our Lord Jesus Christ. Following in their footsteps, I baptize you in the name of the Father, and of the Son, and of the Holy Ghost." Just like the children that preceded him, Ikem cried as soon as he felt the water on his head. His mother was, however, ready with his feeding bottle and the Deacon's wife had a warm towel with which she immediately wiped off the water. Ikem stopped crying as soon as his feeding bottle was put in his mouth.

At the end of the official ceremony, the parents and god-parents of all the baptized children went into the parish office to sign the church papers. The Deacon and his wife seemed anxious to ensure that Chinedu and his family were completely satisfied. In fact, the Deacon's wife even took time to praise Chinedu for the name he gave to his son.

"I think your son has a beautiful name," she told them.

"Thank you," Nkechi responded.

"My husband and I lived in Liberia for many years," she continued. "During that period, I learned a lot about Africa and African culture. Although your children born here are Americans, it's still true that their heritage is African." At this point, Chinedu and Okezie felt relaxed and were able to join the conversation. As Okezie later told Chinedu, "Mrs. Smith looked real."

"Yes, you'll know it when you see it or feel it," Chinedu responded.

"So, you mean you didn't believe her the first time?" Nkechi asked.

"She had said my son had a beautiful name," Chinedu said. "Was it any different from what the Reverend Father had said two weeks ago and yet almost insisted on St. Peter for him?"

Mrs. Smith was actually quite knowledgeable in Africa and African affairs. She discussed military coups and government instability in

Africa so intelligently that Chinedu was amazed. The rapport that existed between them was quite different from the one they had with the Reverend Father almost a fortnight ago.

A few hours after they came back from the church, friends started to arrive for the baptism party. As was typical with most Nigerian parties, it was an all-night event and the last group usually left very early the following morning.

20

OGBONO SOUP

It was one of those extremely windy days in the windy city. Alexander stopped by to see Chinedu and his family. There was nothing much going on in the Nigerian community, except for the steady stream of depressing news from home. The average Nigerian in diaspora was now maintaining two homes, one in diaspora, the other in Nigeria.

"Good afternoon," Nkechi greeted Alexander.

"Good afternoon, Nkechi." Alexander replied. "Where's Chinedu? Watching football?"

Alexander had guessed correctly. Chinedu was in the family room with IK and Okezie. They were watching a Chicago Bears, New York Giants game.

"I thought they were still playing baseball?" Alexander asked. "See how they keep you busy year-round with their sports—football, baseball, hockey, basketball, and what have you. Never a dull moment on the TV and the economy keeps moving."

"Of course, why not?" Chinedu said. "In your country, they're still discussing rotational presidency."

"Whose country?" Alexander retorted.

"That place is all messed up," Chinedu regretted. "It doesn't deserve to be called somebody's country. Every news item from there is more depressing than the one that preceded it."

"It's hard to understand what goes on there," IK said.

"Did you hear the story of a man who bought a custom-made car in Germany and had to rent a helicopter to drop it off in his village because there was no road to his village?" Chinedu asked.

"Wonders will never cease in that place," IK said.

"Although we joke about these things, the situation is becoming worse and worse by the day," Alexander said. "I just got off the phone with my people, and every time I talk to them, I get depressed. One fact people haven't caught up with is the rift the situation is causing in families. People at home think that those of us abroad aren't doing our best for the family. They see either a few lucky ones or a few drug dealers swimming in money, and they ask if our own America is any different from those people."

"Alex, I don't even want to think about that, because it's downright depressing," Chinedu said. "People have become so desperate at home that a person would kill his own brother just to survive. My wife once observed that these days, after you send one dollar to relatives in Nigeria, you spend ten dollars on phone calls to resolve the problem the one dollar had caused."

"It's a shame," Alexander agreed.

As the conversation continued, Emmanuel and Anselem walked it. "Remember our deal for today's game," Emmanuel reminded Chinedu. "On my part, I will cheer for the Bears instead of the Giants. On your part, there would be no discussion about Nigeria."

"Emmanuel, I support you," Nkechi said from the kitchen, where she was busy preparing a homemade dish for her guests. "This is what I suffer here everyday."

"Did you see that play action fake?" Emmanuel was determined to focus on the football game. "It's first and goal at the Giants' three yard line."

"What's the score?" Alexander asked.

"Chicago is up by a touchdown and the second one is knocking," Chinedu responded.

"I think there's somebody at the door," Nkechi indicated. "Emmanuel, did you lock the other people out?"

"No, I came with Anselem, that's all," Emmanuel said as he walked to the door and opened it for Chief Ogugua and a few others.

"T-o-u-c-h-d-o-w-n!" Chinedu exclaimed. "I saw it all the way. It was a well-designed and well-executed quarterback draw."

"Chinedu and football again today," Chief Ogugua said. He was often critical of Chinedu's love for American football in preference to soccer.

"Did you see the four wide receiver formation? They spread the defense and left a big hole in the middle," Chinedu said ignoring Chief Ogugua.

"It was a great call," Okezie added.

"And perfectly executed too," Chinedu said. "The quarterback just walked into the end zone untouched."

"Won't you greet your visitors?" Chief Ogugua asked Chinedu.

"The point after is good," Okezie said.

"Yep," Chinedu responded. "It split the upright. Fourteen zip."

"Chief, just take a seat and stop disturbing the game," Emmanuel told Chief Ogugua. "By the way, don't you call to inform people you are coming to their house?"

"Chief Ogugua, good afternoon, sir," Nkechi who just came out from the kitchen area greeted her guest. "It's football season and you know what it does to your friend, Chinedu."

"First-lady, peace be unto you and your household," Chief Ogugua responded. Chief Ogugua was very fond of Nkechi and always addressed her as "first lady," a nickname Nkechi cherished, given the special way she often treated Chief Ogugua.

"Chief, forget this, your first or second lady. My question is why didn't you call?" Emmanuel asked.

"First, this isn't your house, Emmanuel," Chief Ogugua responded. "Second, I'm not even sure you called before coming yourself. Third, if I come to Chinedu's house, and he asks me to go because I didn't call to inform him I was coming, then I know something is wrong. We have learned many things from America, but not to require our friends to ask for permission before visiting."

"You're welcome anytime in our house," Nkechi told Chief Ogugua. "Don't mind Emmanuel."

Chief Ogugua settled down with the other men, who were already enjoying the game. Okezie walked over to the refrigerator and served himself his favorite Heineken beer. A few moments later, Nkechi set before her guests a big bowl of steaming *ogbono* soup and farina which most Nigerian women used as a substitute for *fufu*.

"Perfect timing," Okezie said. "We can now welcome Chief Ogugua and his entourage during the half time."

"True," Chinedu concurred. "I don't want any distractions during the second half. This game has playoff implications."

"So you won't talk to me during the game?" Chief Ogugua asked. "Chinedu, this is sickness."

"Don't take it personally Chief," Chinedu told his guest. "This game is just too important. Home court advantage throughout the post-season is at stake."

"I have no idea what you're talking about," Chief Ogugua said.

"I can explain later, but I think Nkechi has an announcement."

Nkechi smiled. "The food is ready," she announced. "Chief, yours is in that room," she told Chief Ogugua pointing to a room at the far end of the house.

Incidentally, Chief Ogugua recently took the *ozo* title, and as such, tradition forbade him to eat in public. Nkechi was among the few Nigerian women who made sure Chief Ogugua was served in a manner that respected his title. Chief Ogugua stood, picked up his staff, placed it on Nkechi's waist, prayed for her and blessed her.

"Our wife, may you bear your husband as many sons and daughters as he wishes," Chief Ogugua prayed.

"*Isee!*" Anselem and a few others responded. Emmanuel didn't want to be part of the prayer. Instead, he picked up a copy of *Newsweek* magazine and started flipping through the pages. But that did not stop the Chief.

"When you train your children, they'll look after you in old age."

"*Isee!*"

"They'll never leave you in a nursing home."

"*Isee!*"

"It's your life."

"*Isee!*"

"It's your good health."

"*Isee!*"

"When you're in front, may our ancestors keep the evil spirits behind."

"*Isee!*"

"When you're behind, may our ancestors keep the evil spirits in front."

"*Isee!*"

Chief Ogugua murmured a few more prayers and walked into the private room to eat his meal.

"Nkechi, listen to me. Next time, I want my own food in the room also," Emmanuel chuckled. "I don't understand this *ozo* thing. I ate a Big Mac with this Ogugua guy at the Sheridan and Wilson McDonald's a few days ago."

"When you take the *ozo* title, I'll serve your food in a room," Nkechi told Emmanuel.

Emmanuel ignored Nkechi and continued to criticize Chief Ogugua. "If any of you knows that guy very well, let the person remind him that there're now prepaid nursing homes. From his prayer, which I think was said under the influence of *ogbono* soup and stockfish, it seems he is scared of nursing homes."

"Emma, leave Chief Ogugua alone," Nkechi protested.

"Although I don't know under what influence the Chief prayed," Okezie said, "I agree with Emmanuel that our people appear terrified of nursing homes. Let me tell you guys, the only way to avoid the nursing home is to go back to Nigeria now. America is a package. Take it or leave it. We must all be mentally prepared for prepaid nursing home and prepaid burial. There's no running away from them. No one should ever hold out any hopes that these American-born children will put up with us at old age. If you're lucky, they'll call you on Father's Day."

Everybody laughed heartily at the thought of a son remembering his father only on Father's Day.

"You must allow me to eat in peace," Alexander protested to Okezie. "Why do you have to bring up issues about nursing homes and prepaid burial at this time?"

"When do you want them to be brought up?" Emmanuel asked.

"Must you bring them up?" Alexander countered. "Whenever

these issues are raised, and I realize that my children will probably not take care of me the way I'm taking care of my old parents, I become depressed."

"It's not a big deal," Emmanuel told Alexander. "There're no nursing homes in Nigeria, so you have to live with your old parents. There are nursing homes in America, so all you have to do is start prepaying for your old age. You're not scared of getting old, are you?"

At this point Nkechi requested her guests to defer the conversation for some other time. It was one of those topics that made Nigerians sad, if not depressed.

Nkechi's guests settled down to *fufu* and *ogbono* soup. Although there was just one choice of food, it was nonetheless a buffet. Everyone served himself, taking as much as he wanted. They could not finish the food she prepared. If guests finished the food served by an Igbo woman, the interpretation would be that the quantity she'd made was small. Nigerian women often went out of their way to ensure that it did not happen; consequently, a lot of food was often wasted.

"Nkechi, you have cooked very well as usual. This soup is great," IK said, as he positioned a big lump of *fufu* with his right thumb. He formed a net with the remaining four fingers, using them to fish through the bowl of *ogbono* soup. With each lump of *fufu* that IK swallowed, he licked each of his right fingers carefully with his tongue, a sure sign that he was enjoying the *ogbono* soup. He also followed each lump of *fufu* with a bite of stockfish, coiled fish, or meat.

"I should thank you for eating. I'm happy somebody is enjoying it. Your friend Chinedu never praises my soup."

"Oh, Jesus! Are you back at this again, Nkechi?" Chinedu asked as he reclined on the sofa, and his left palm ran from his forehead through his hair to his neck. "Please, stop this, Nkechi. There's nothing to praise. I've said this to you many times and you pretend not to understand."

"Chinedu, why not?" IK asked. "The soup is great."

"If she spends a hundred dollars for a pot of soup, why won't it taste good?"

"That's not true, money doesn't make a pot of soup taste good," IK protested.

Nkechi winked at IK thanking him for the comment.

"My friend you can only discuss Big Mac," Chinedu told IK. "Wait until you're married before you understand and discuss these issues."

"There's nothing about marriage in this," IK protested. "The soup is good. Period."

"Listen, bachelor boy," Chinedu said to IK. "My grandmother, when she was alive, would start from almost nothing, go into the garden at the backyard, put a couple of things together, and there would be a delicious dish for the family. That's the soup to praise. You don't praise the soup where she has the internet and world wide web to assist her, if need be. There's absolutely nothing to praise."

"No, no, no, Chinedu, you got it all wrong," Alexander intervened.

"Thank you, Alex. *Biko* explain to him." Nkechi was happy at the defense. "Let me see if he'll tell you that you aren't married too."

"There's nothing to explain," Chinedu insisted, throwing out both hands almost in resignation. "You can put all these condiments in the pot, place the pot in a timer-controlled boiler, and in 30 minutes, the result would be the same as what Nkechi wants you to praise."

"Chinedu, the result can't be the same," Alexander insisted.

As the discussion continued, Chief Ogugua rejoined them, having finished his meal. At the same time, the second half of the game was about to start.

"Chinedu, can you switch to one of the Spanish channels that show South American soccer?" Chief Ogugua asked his host.

"You can go and use the TV in Ikem's room," Chinedu told Chief Ogugua. "No one is changing this channel."

"How did you become so Americanized?" Chief Ogugua asked. "What's interesting about fat men falling on themselves?"

"Chief, it's because you don't understand the game," Okezie told Chief Ogugua. "If you understand what's at stake when we say 'fourth and inches,' you'd see why the game is exciting."

"What's there to understand?" Chief Ogugua said. "There's no continuity or fluidity in your football. How can you compare it with soccer, where twenty two men are constantly entertaining you for ninety non-stop minutes? In football, you play for one minute and have a commercial timeout for ten minutes. It doesn't make sense."

"Oh my goodness!" Chinedu screamed. "This Chicago special team drives me nuts. Did you see that 80 yard kickoff return. The Giants are at the Bears 15 yard line. Shit!"

"So, Chinedu, you aren't listening to me?" Chief Ogugua asked.

"Don't waste your time, my dear," Nkechi told him. "Even if you pour hot water on him, he won't feel it until this game is over."

"Great defensive play," Chinedu said.

"How many yards were lost in that quarterback sack?" Okezie asked.

"About twelve," Chinedu responded. "The quarterback was in a shotgun formation on first down and didn't see the corner blitz from his blind side."

. "Second and twenty-two," Okezie said. "One more great defensive play, and they're out of field goal range."

"Chief, my dear, how's your family?" Nkechi asked. "Don't worry about Chinedu and Okezie. Give them one more hour and they'll return to normal."

At this point, the two groups in the house were well-defined, those watching the football game and those who were just not interested in the game. Eventually, the game ended and it became one crowd again. Those who watched the game were also happy because Chicago won.

"So, Chief, how's everything?" Chinedu asked the guest he had been neglecting.

"Everything is fine," Chief Ogugua replied. "My family will be traveling to Toronto in a few days. My wife and the kids want a small vacation."

"Hey, Chief, God bless you," Nkechi said. "You'll live forever, my dear. Everybody won't be Chinedu, who thinks he's the only person with family in Nigeria."

"I don't think the Chief wants to live forever," Okezie told Nkechi.

"I was waiting for it," Nkechi said. "You'll always defend your friend. Can you ask him if we have ever taken a vacation since we got married?"

21
FAMILY VACATION

After Nkechi's repeated protests about a vacation, Chinedu finally yielded, and the family started to prepare for a trip.

"I think there are a lot of places to go," Nkechi suggested. "We can go to Disney World, Busch Gardens, Six Flags Great America, or we can even take a cruise."

"All those places are theme parks," Chinedu countered. "When you see one, you've seen them all. Anyway, make your pick, and if that's going to bring peace to this house, I'll go reluctantly."

"Go reluctantly?" Nkechi asked.

"Of course," Chinedu was quick to respond. "I'd rather spend my time doing more interesting things."

Nkechi eventually decided on a cruise. She wanted something completely different from their everyday life.

"We've worked very hard this year, and we need to enjoy ourselves," she argued. "We can't always be thinking about sending money to Nigeria."

Chinedu pretended not to hear what she had said. It was clear to them that, although he'd given in to the idea of a cruise, his mind was not into it. Nkechi, however, was as excited as a two-year old as she made the preparations.

The day finally came. Okezie dropped them off at the airport for the first leg of their trip. The flight took them to Miami, where they boarded a cruise ship.

The ship was full of vacationers, both young and old. They were now in the open high sea and people walked about happily. Some were on deck, some watched life performances while others gambled away at the Casino machines. Chinedu preferred to work on his lap-top computer.

"I can't wait to get to the island," Nkechi told Chinedu. "I heard it's so beautiful there."

Chinedu was busy editing a document in his computer.

"Didn't you hear what I said?" Nkechi snapped angrily. "I'll throw that computer into the ocean if you'd rather work on it than talk to me."

"I heard what you said," Chinedu calmly responded. He was, however, in no hurry to exit the program.

"What did I say?"

"That the island is beautiful."

"And you said what?"

"There's nothing to say."

"Nothing to say?" Nkechi retorted. "Not even to agree or disagree?"

"Would it make a difference either way?"

"At least it shows you're here with me. Are you going to continue with your silent treatment even during our vacation?"

"Nkechi, don't make a case out of nothing," Chinedu pleaded. "You said the island is beautiful. I know your sense of appreciation is based on the price tag of an item. This stupid vacation is costing us an arm and a leg, so why should everything about it not be beautiful?"

"You're always complaining about money, money, and more money," Nkechi snapped. "Forget about money this week, and let's just enjoy our lives for once. We'll all die one day and leave this money behind."

A few moments later, Chinedu turned off the computer and walked over to the bar and asked the tender if he had Guinness stout. He did not, so Chinedu settled for an Amstel Lite. Halfway back to his seat, he changed his mind, went back to the bar and bought a glass of wine for Nkechi.

"Can you reason with me for a moment?" Chinedu asked Nkechi as he handed her the glass of wine.

" A glass of wine for me?" Nkechi asked excitedly. " Wow! Is this a vacation or is this a vacation?"

Chinedu ignored her and pretended to focus on the discussion.

" I was asking if you could reason constructively with me," Chinedu said.

"I've always reasoned with you," Nkechi responded. "But does reasoning with you mean I must agree with you?"

Chinedu took a sip from his glass and smiled. "Did you already decide not to agree with me even before I made my point?"

"Not true," Nkechi protested. " The problem is that you always want me to agree with you. If both of us agree on everything, then only one person is thinking. I can think too, can't I?"

" This discussion is getting us nowhere. Maybe we're better off simply enjoying our drinks."

" I'm already enjoying mine," Nkechi said. " I think the atmosphere is terrific and relaxed. Nigerian men should learn that this type of atmosphere helps to fend off the anxiety and tension that frustrate our lives in diaspora."

" So, looking out into the open sea is your therapy for our problems?" Chinedu stood up and walked over to the deck.

" Not just looking into the open sea," Nkechi said, leaving her seat to join her husband.

" What else are we doing here now, besides looking at the sea?" Chinedu asked.

" A lot," Nkechi responded. " I was amazed when you remembered to buy a glass of wine for me. Have you ever done such a thoughtful thing in the eleven years we've lived together?"

Chinedu put on a serious look as if to suggest that he did not see why Nkechi should be amazed over a glass of wine. For her part, Nkechi pretended not to notice the surprise on her husband's face. Instead, she moved closer to him. However, Chinedu moved farther away from her, in a way, marking off the same number of steps Nkechi had gained towards him.

"Are you running away from me?"

"I'm not running anywhere," Chinedu responded. "But we don't have to jump all over ourselves to carry on a conversation."

Nkechi smiled sadly, but opted not to inch any closer to him, at least for now. Instead, she continued with the discussion about the glass of wine Chinedu had bought her.

"All hope is, after all, not lost. If I can get a glass of wine today, I may get a dozen roses before long."

Chinedu eyed her suspiciously, but he said nothing. The next thing he realized was that Nkechi's arms were around his neck. He almost pushed her off, but realized that on that ship full of other vacationers, somebody must be looking at them. It would be rude to push his wife away. Speaking in a low tone Chinedu asked, "Can't you say whatever you want to say without standing toe to toe, waist to waist, and mouth to mouth with me?"

Nkechi ignored him and moved even closer.

"What's going on?" Chinedu asked, tilting his head sideways to avoid talking straight into her mouth.

"You can turn your face away if you like," Nkechi said, pulling him closer to her body. Before he could protest, Chinedu found she was kissing him. When finally, he was allowed a breather, he told Nkechi that this was her last vacation in the foreseeable future.

"The problem with Nigerian men is that they don't realize these things mean a lot to a woman," Nkechi explained. "Everything can't always be reduced to money, sending money to Nigeria, and saving money in the bank. Always money, money and more money."

"Nkechi, you're moving this trip off into a dangerous tangent. If what you brought me out here to do is to buy you a glass of wine and a dozen roses, then you'll be disappointed."

Nkechi smiled and kissed his cheek.

"This is the problem with Nigerian women," Chinedu told Nkechi. "So, the reason we're here is just for us to keep looking out at an empty sea, put our arms around our shoulders, and whisper to one another, 'I love you'."

"What's wrong with that? Don't you love me?"

"I do, but so what?"

"Why the difficulty in saying it then?" Nkechi asked.

Chinedu shook his head and rubbed his left palm over his forehead.

"Nigerian women are trying to be whiter than the whites," he told Nkechi. "Why are you carried away by all this kissing and hugging? They don't mean much. If they did, America would have the lowest divorce rate in the world. The last time I checked, that wasn't what I found."

Ikem, Kelechi, Nkiru and Obioha were sleeping in the cabin. Ikem was the first to join his parents when he woke up.

"The food service is buffet, so go over there and help yourself," Chinedu told his ten-year old son, Ikem. "Where are the others?"

"I think Kelechi is awake, but Nkiru and Obioha are still sleeping," Ikem said.

Nkiru was actually awake, only the three-year old Obioha was still sleeping. Kelechi was nine and Nkiru six. Obioha was allowed to continue with his sleep while the rest of the family went over to listen to a band playing Caribbean Calypso and Reggae music.

"Are you enjoying yourself?" Nkechi asked her husband.

"Why do you ask?" Chinedu responded.

"You seem to be looking at nothing in particular," she responded.

"My part is to bring you and the children here. I've done that. Once all of you are happy, I'm fine," Chinedu explained.

"Ikem," Nkechi called. "Tell your father to forget about Nigeria. The band is playing reggae, and your father won't even enjoy it."

"Who told you I'm not enjoying it?"

"I know you're not," Nkechi retorted. "I can read you like a book. I know there is nothing on your mind now but Nigeria."

"That isn't true," Chinedu responded. "However, if you want to talk about Nigeria, that's fine too. I can recall for you my years in Lagos and the weekend visits to Bar Beach at Victoria Island. Bar Beach was a lot better than this place, and as my father would say, I didn't have to cross seven seas and seven wildernesses to get there."

"Stay there and keep thinking about Nigeria until you have a heart attack," Nkechi told him. "Nkiru my daughter, let's go and enjoy ourselves. If Ikem and Kelechi want to stay with their father, that's their business."

"Why don't you guys also go with your mother," Chinedu told Ikem and Kelechi. "I'll stick around for Obioha to wake up. I know your mother has forgotten him. It's all part of enjoying herself."

"I haven't forgotten him," Nkechi retorted. "I know you'll find something wrong with me. Chinedu, if you don't want to enjoy yourself, fine, but I'll not waste all the money and still not enjoy myself."

The vacation days went by rather quickly for Nkechi and the children. For Chinedu, it seemed like an eternity.

"So, what have we done these past few days?" Chinedu asked as they sat in the lounge at the Fort Lauderdale airport, awaiting their flight back to Chicago.

"What do you mean by that?" Nkechi asked.

"Seriously, I'm trying to recap the highlights of these vacation days," Chinedu said. "We went to the beach and threw sand around like toddlers. We walked around the park, and you wanted me to hold your hand, because you saw other people doing that. We went on a cruise, and you enjoyed sitting down, while I served you a glass of wine. Then you put your hands around my neck although I forgot to tell you that you were slightly choking me. Anyway, did we do anything useful these past three days?"

"That glass of wine meant a lot to me. Moreover, I haven't been in the kitchen this past week. It was fun sitting in the restaurant and waiting to be served, instead of sitting by the oven preparing dinner. Chinedu, whether you agree or not, these have been among the best days since we became married. We must do this more often."

He eyed her as if something was wrong with her and simply responded, "You must be joking."

A few moment later, the attendants started to board passengers for their flight.

"Get the kids. They are boarding first class and passengers with children," Nkechi told Chinedu. "Since you won't buy a first class ticket for me, I'll still board with them."

"Nkechi, something is wrong with your head," Chinedu said. "So, the vacation isn't enough, it's now first class ticket?"

"Chinedu, you can afford a first class ticket for me for being your wife these eleven years," Nkechi responded. "The people who buy it for their wives don't have two heads."

"Jesus! Naija women," Chinedu muttered to himself.

"Naija man," Nkechi said, laughing as she did so. "You don't have to buy the ticket now."

"Let's go kids," Chinedu said, grabbing their carry-on luggage and urging the kids on. "Your mother has seen her last vacation in a long, long, time."

Shortly, their non-stop flight to Midway Airport in Chicago was airborne. The pilot apologized for the delayed departure, which he blamed on bad weather.

A frequent flyer, Chinedu realized from the position of the aircraft shadow that the aircraft was headed South.

"What's the problem?" Nkechi could easily tell something was wrong with her husband. Didn't she claim she could read him like a book?

"This plane is heading south," Chinedu responded worriedly.

"How do you know? Do you have a compass?"

Before he could respond, a voice came through the speakers. "Hello again. This is your captain. You may have realized that we're heading south. Be assured we aren't going to Havana, Cuba, but we're taking a south-west swing to avoid a big thunderstorm along what should have been our normal route through Gainesville, Florida."

The pilot turned on the seat belt sign and advised the hostesses to discontinue their beverage service until further notice. He planned to make a swing just before entering Cuban airspace. That swing would take the plane through Tampa, Tallahassee, and Atlanta, at which point they'd head north through the Ohio valley and straight into the Chicago area. Estimated arrival time into Midway was 6:30 pm.

"Jesus!" Chinedu quietly exclaimed.

"What's the problem?" Nkechi asked angrily. "Relax like every other person. The pilot said the weather is bad around Gainesville."

They continued heading south for a while. The deafening silence in the aircraft was only sprinkled with coughs and soft grunts. Not even the stewardesses could walk through the plane. Everybody was strapped to their seats.

"We should start saying our rosary," Chinedu murmured to Nkechi.

"Do you have your chaplet?"

"No, but I know the rosary by heart."

"You do?" Nkechi asked.

"Yes. It isn't hard. It starts with 'I believe in God, Our Father, Hail Mary and Glory be to the Father' repeated in some sequence. 'Hail Holy Queen' wraps it up."

"Okay, let's start."

Chinedu and Nkechi began quietly reciting the rosary. They were deeply absorbed in their prayers, allowing Chinedu to take his mind off the flight.

"The third sorrowful mystery," Chinedu intoned. "The crowning with thorns. We adore Thee, Oh Christ and worship Thee."

"Because by Thy Holy Cross, Thou hast redeemed the world," Nkechi responded.

But before Chinedu could start the next decade with the "Our Father," a voice came across the aircraft public address system.

"Hello, again. This is your captain."

Chinedu froze. He didn't know what he was thinking. Had the plane mistakenly entered Cuban airspace and was being trailed by Russian MIG fighters?

"If you've been following carefully," the captain told his passengers, "you will notice that we are now headed in a northeast direction. We've completed our southwest swing and are currently about 100 miles south of Tampa, Florida. I'm happy to announce that we've completely circumvented the bad weather that stretched from Miami to Gainesville. Thank you very much for your patience. At this time, I'll turn off the seat belt sign, and your hostesses will resume cabin service shortly."

It was only at this time that Chinedu realized that they were finally headed north. Life returned to the aircraft. A long line formed at the restroom. Chinedu remembered he had been pressed since they had started on their southward course.

"I need to go to the bathroom," he told Nkechi.

"I'm surprised you didn't wet your pants before now. Why were you so panicky? Did you think the plane was headed to Castro's Cuba?"

"Don't even touch that one," Chinedu responded. "Chicago is calling."

"By the way, why don't we finish up the rosary?" Nkechi asked.

"That's okay. We can finish it sometime later. There's no need to hurry."

"There you go," Nkechi joked. "People of small faith. Those who pray to God only when they're in trouble."

They were in fact out of trouble for the plane ride was smooth the rest of the way. Chinedu noted that the plane's touch down was one of the best he had ever experienced. His friend Okezie was impatiently watching the monitors at the airport for latest developments on the flight when Chinedu tapped him on the back.

"*Dianyi*, I know you must have been waiting for a long time," Chinedu said.

Chinedu's voice and the tap on the back startled Okezie who was deeply absorbed studying the contents of the monitor. On seeing his friend and family, Okezie heaved a sigh of relief. "I was becoming quite concerned about all the delay," he said to Chinedu. "You don't know if something had gone wrong but was being withheld."

"God forbid," Nkechi said. "The pilot said there was bad weather around Gainesville, Florida and had to make a big southwest swing to avoid Gainesville airspace completely."

"What kind of bad weather was that?" Okezie asked.

"*Dianyi*, I thought the plane was headed to Havana Cuba, but thank God all is well that ends well. How has everything been since we left?"

"Nothing has changed. Chicago is still windy and the holiday season is fast approaching. What else do you want to know?"

Everybody smiled as they put their luggage into the trunk of the car.

"Did you guys enjoy the vacation?" Okezie asked the kids.

"It was cool," Kelechi responded.

"It was okay," Ikem said.

"Dad, are we coming back tomorrow?" Obioha asked.

"Shut up," Nkiru said to him. "We are just coming back and you want to go back tomorrow."

It was a smooth drive home. Nkechi had one extra day off her kitchen since her friend Ijeoma hosted the family for dinner.

"I don't want this vacation to end," Nkechi said as they sat down for dinner at Okezie's house.

"Every good thing must end," Chinedu reminded his wife.

22

NIGERIAN-AMERICAN CHILDREN

C hinedu and his wife were experienced parents by now. For example, by the time their other children were born, no one told them the required quantity of baby formula. Moreover, the friendship between their family and Okezie's grew from strength to strength. They helped and supported each other in any possible way. For example, Ikem and Okezie's son, Nweke, played basketball together, and often one of the four parents dropped them off and picked them up. On this day, it was Okezie's turn, and he came to drop Ikem off at the end of the games. Nkechi had just returned from school, for in addition to raising four children, she was going to school full-time and working weekends. Surprisingly, she was pursuing a degree in nursing.

As they idled away waiting for Okezie to finish his beer before leaving, Chinedu explained to his friend why Nkechi was studying nursing. "I think we have to be more informed about the professions we get into," Chinedu told Okezie. "When we came to the United States, we just enrolled in engineering programs partly because that was what we were sent here to study and partly because every person we knew studied engineering. I think we're now better informed and should look at the job market before choosing a profession. I've asked Nkechi to enroll in a nursing program."

Okezie merely smiled and remarked casually, "How things have changed."

"What do you mean? What has changed?" Chinedu inquired. Of course, he understood to what Okezie was referring.

Okezie smiled again. "You don't know what has changed?" he asked rhetorically. "Did I ever hear you during our high school days say you'd never marry a nurse?"

Of course, this was not news to Chinedu.

"Nkechi is welcome to pursue any career she likes," Chinedu said. "I'm only here to advise, and I suspect I understand this society fairly well now."

"You understand the society, eh?" Nkechi questioned. "Did you tell Okezie what happened at the hospital last week?"

"*Dianyi*, I give Nkechi all the credit here," Chinedu said. "Ikem came back with a note from school the other day. His teacher reported that he was hyperactive, so we took him to the hospital for an evaluation."

"Why?" Okezie asked.

"That was the teacher's suggestion. To make a long story short, they wanted to put him on medication to slow him down. They gave us a few days to think it over, and then to sign the necessary papers. I must admit that I was confused. I didn't know what to do and I sought opinion from those who should know. The consensus appeared to be that we should give the medication a try. But Nkechi wouldn't even consider it."

"Why should I?" Nkechi interjected. "There's nothing wrong with Ikem. He's only being a child."

"*Nne*, you're the daughter of your parents," Okezie said, embracing Nkechi. "May God give you as many more sons as you can raise."

"Remember when we grew up in Nigeria," Nkechi further explained, "how we threw stones, fought, and covered our clothes with sand? Did that stop us from doing anything or living a normal life? Just because Ikem pushed another child while they were playing, that's why he should be placed on medication?"

"That's absolute nonsense," Okezie agreed firmly. "They'll give a child medication because he is playing. They'll give him a second medication to make sure he doesn't stop playing. They'll give him a third one to counter the effect of the first and second combined. They'll give a fourth, and so on and so on."

"Yep," Nkechi added. "That's why they have medicine cabinets. Too much medicine, my dear. Not for my son Ikem."

"You got that one right babe," Okezie added.

"Your friend Chinedu was beginning to waffle," Nkechi continued. "But I told him that only over my dead body would anyone medicate my son. It could potentially harm him in the long run."

"Okezie, I tell you the truth," Chinedu added, "I'm ever indebted to Nkechi for how she stood firm on that issue. That's what marriage is all about. If the husband is firm, the wife should follow, and if the wife is firm, the husband should seriously consider her viewpoint."

Nkechi chuckled. "So, if you're firm, I must follow, but if I'm firm, you only have to seriously consider, eh?"

"Nkechi, leave it at that," Okezie said. "Chinedu has put it as well as it should be. I think there's still one head in every family, isn't there?"

Nkechi recalled and pondered thoughtfully over her mother's admonition never to challenge her husband's leadership in the family.

"My daughter, don't ever challenge your husband. It'll destroy your marriage," her mother had told her on the eve of her departure to the US. "No Igbo man will stand a woman challenging his authority in his house. The only thing is that if you're smart about it, your husband will be the *head*, and you will be the *neck* of the family. Did you ever see a head without a neck?" she had joked. "So, my daughter, tell your husband that he's the head. Our men like to hear that. But you can secretly be the neck of your family."

*   *   *   *   *

Many years had passed and raising children in America turned out to be very challenging, especially for most non-American-born parents.

Chinedu and Nkechi found themselves saddled with the responsibility of raising American children in a Nigerian home.

One weekend, Nkechi and her husband were busy cleaning the house. The children were still in bed. No doubt, as soon as they woke up, they'd troop down to the basement to play Sega. Chinedu mopped the floor and Nkechi cleaned her kitchen. The oven was dirty and the dishes were not done.

"This is a tough place to raise children," Nkechi told her husband who walked into the kitchen to take a drink from the refrigerator.

"I agree," Chinedu responded. "Sometimes, it looks to me as if children are growing up without guidance. You and I grew up in a culture that had certain expectations of children and parents. In America, I don't quite understand what those expectations are. Actually, those expectations are in conflict with what you and I are used to."

"True," Nkechi agreed.

The American environment was clearly different from the Nigerian environment. What type of techniques would one use to deal with a child who needed to be refocused? In Nigeria, one option was for the parent to spank the child, an unacceptable option in America. In Nigeria, teachers spanked a child who needed to be refocused. In America, that was also unacceptable.

"Recall when we were growing up, all a parent needed to do was threaten to report a child to his teacher," Nkechi said.

"That's right. The word 'teacher' carried respect. No longer these days. Teaching was a special vocation but unfortunately, with the current trend in society, nothing distinguished teaching from any other job. Children, who needed slightly firmer control, found themselves herded between troubled homes and teachers whose hands were tied or who didn't care."

"That's unfortunate," Nkechi said. "Moreover, society frowns at parents who administer corporal punishment to kids."

"I can't help but feel that this society is too liberal in its child-rearing philosophy," Chinedu added.

Ikem and Kelechi woke up and as their parents had predicted, they went to the basement to play Sega. As they passed through the living room to the basement, their mother saw them and yelled, "Foolish boys, did you see us before? What do you say to your parents in the morning?"

"Good morning," Ikem and Kelechi said together.

"Good morning," their father responded.

"Next time I remind you to say good morning to us, I'll break your heads for you," Nkechi threatened.

The children went down to the basement.

"You should have responded to their greeting," Chinedu told his wife.

"You spoil these children," Nkechi complained. "Why do I have to remind old men what to say to their parents in the morning?"

A few hours later, after Okezie and Ijeoma had done their weekend shopping, they stopped by to spend some time with Chinedu's family. They came with their children, their oldest son, Nweke, who was thirteen, their daughter Nneka, twelve, and their youngest son, Enyinnaya, eight.

"How're you guys doing?" Nkechi said to Ijeoma's children.

"We're fine, and what about you?" Nweke asked.

"We're fine, my son," Nkechi responded.

"Why is it so quiet?" Ijeoma asked. "Where're your boys?"

"In the basement playing Sega," Nkechi responded, and raising her voice, she shouted, "*Ikem! Ikemefuna!*" There was no answer. She walked towards the door that led to the basement and raising her voice still higher, she shouted again, "*Ikemefuna!*"

"*What?*" answered a voice from the basement.

Ijeoma and Okezie started to laugh almost in synchrony.

"They're all the same," Ijeoma said.

Ikem ran up the stairs and stood looking at his mother.

"Didn't you hear me call you?" Nkechi asked angrily.

"I did."

"And what did you do?"

"I answered you, mom."

"You answered who?"

"Mom, I swear, I answered you."

"Shut up. How many times will I tell you to stop answering me '*what*' whenever I call you? What is '*what*'? Is that the only way to respond to me, 'what'?"

Nkechi fumed with anger. She was sick of getting the response "what" from her children. She was more used to a child responding "Sir", and "Ma" to parents. But this is America, and what a parent gets is "what."

"Don't you know what to say to your auntie?" she asked.

"Hi," Ikem said to Ijeoma, raising his right arm slightly as he said so.

"Hi," Ijeoma responded. "How're you guys doing?"

"Okay," Ikem responded.

"How are Kelechi and others?"

"They're fine."

"Where're they?"

"In the basement."

Ikem was about to dash to the basement as soon as the brief exchange ended but his mother cut in with a question.

"Didn't you see your friends, Nweke, Nneka and Enyi?"

"Hi," Ikem said to his friends.

"Hi," Nweke responded.

"Do you guys want to play games with us downstairs?"

"You're asking a rat if it'll eat fish?" Ijeoma said. But it wasn't clear that any of the kids heard her, for they all had dashed down the basement and were already arguing over who'd play the first game.

Once the kids were gone, Nkechi continued complaining about how Ikem had responded to her. "Who taught these children that 'what' is what they respond to their parents?"

"That's what they hear at school," Ijeoma explained.

"That's the kind of rubbish they learn," Nkechi added, "The other thing is playing video games. I've told their father to stop renting those games for them. These kids can play those stupid things for twenty-four hours without doing any other thing. They won't read their books. They won't even do their laundry. They expect me to do their laundry for them. No way. Let them smell in school."

"I thought it was only my children. Thank God it's a universal problem," Ijeoma added.

"Forget your universal problem, Ijeoma," Okezie said as he walked over to the refrigerator to serve himself a bottle of Heineken. "You women expect too much from these children. You expect them to do things you never taught them to do."

"All men are the same," Nkechi laughed, shaking her head in contempt. "That's exactly what Chinedu says here."

"So what?" Okezie asked. "Isn't he right?"

"He's not," Nkechi responded forcefully. "What am I going to teach them? Do they eat through their anus? Just walk up to Ikem's room. The clothes he wore to school two days ago are littered all over the floor. I have to teach an old man to wash his clothes? Even when he manages to wash them, it's like war to get him to fold them and put them away. He prefers to pick his clothes from the dryer, rather than fold them neatly."

"My dear, you're speaking as if you know what happens in my house," Ijeoma said.

"This is very serious," Nkechi continued. "When we grew up in Nigeria, we went to the stream or public pump to wash our clothes and fetch water. They don't have to do any of those things. They just need to put the clothes in the washing machine and dryer and fold them. I have to teach them that? No way."

Chinedu walked over to the refrigerator and served himself a bottle of Guinness stout and a can of Classic Coke. He looked at Okezie and both men exchanged understanding smiles. Unfortunately, Nkechi caught the exchange.

"Why are you smiling at each other?" she asked. "Can we know your secret?"

Her question was ignored. Everybody understood why.

"Just look at how both of you are drinking and neither remembered his wife," she added, pouting as she did so. She folded her hands across her breasts and shook her head in disbelief. "You wouldn't serve your wives, but you'd worship your American girlfriends."

One of Ijeoma's complaints when she came to America had been that her husband didn't open the car door for her. She noticed that in America, a man opened the car door, allowed the woman to get in, and then closed the door before walking around to the driver's side. That was something Okezie and Chinedu never did, although Ijeoma recalled that they did it for their American girlfriends.

"My sister, don't even touch their American girlfriends," Ijeoma said. "They remember their manhood when they return to us, but when they see American women, they worship them."

"My dear, I forgot to tell you that a picture showed up lately," Nkechi said.

"Who was it?"

"'Love, Cynthia.' That's what they wrote on the back," Nkechi said looking sarcastically at Chinedu.

"You talk about a picture showing up," Ijeoma said. "Somebody in this house has an album with pictures of Jennifer, sitting, standing, with the door of the car opened for her, you know the rest."

"You women are just being silly," Chinedu chided. "If it wasn't for those smart moves we made, you'd still be on lay-away in Naija."

"You call it smart move, eh?," Nkechi sneered at Chinedu.

"Don't mind them," Ijeoma said. "One day I'll show them how to really make a smart move."

"Ijeoma, you're veering off a cliff," Chinedu said. "Let's return to the drink you women requested. Here's the situation. Okezie wanted to drink, and he went to the refrigerator and took a bottle of Heineken. I wanted to drink and I took what I liked. If Nkechi or Ijeoma wants to drink, the refrigerator is right there, right Okezie?"

"Don't mind these Naija women," Okezie responded. "Maybe Ijeoma is already on her smart moves."

The women exchanged their own glances, but said nothing. Having given up on being served, Ijeoma preferred to continue with the discussion about the children.

"Let me return to the children we were talking about," Ijeoma said. "They're more important to me than American girlfriends. Sometimes, I try to compare the environment we grew up in with the environment these kids are growing up in."

"There's nothing to compare. The environments are completely different," Okezie told Ijeoma.

Ijeoma ignored him. Why discuss anything with a man who wouldn't even serve her a glass of Coke? She continued with what she was saying.

"You may recall all the chores we did before going to school in the morning. We fetched water from the tap, swept the yard, and sometimes washed the toilet and bathroom. We did those things and still got to school on time."

"They're the ones who spoil these kids," Nkechi said.

"Remember, there were no school buses," Ijeoma continued. "But here, all these kids do is just get out of bed, take a shower—if they know how to do that—eat their breakfast, and wait for the school bus to pick them up. They don't have to fetch water or clean the bathroom. Sometimes they expect us, their parents, to clean their rooms for them!"

"It's terrible," Nkechi added. "When we grew up, a family of seven couldn't afford anything better than a one room unit, and the family managed this and lived happily. There was no question of whether boys and girls slept in the same or different rooms. Today, my daughter Nkiru has a room all to herself. As a girl, she isn't expected to share a room with her brothers. Isn't this crazy? When I was her age, I slept on the floor with my brothers. I shared the same mat with them, and it didn't make any difference."

"My dear, this is America," Ijeoma said.

"No, this is madness," Nkechi insisted, her hands anchored at her waists. "Remember, we're talking about sharing a mat with my brothers, not with some people from outer space."

"Nkechi, listen," Chinedu added calmly. "I don't understand the point you and Ijeoma are making. You may have some good points, but you're mixing up the issues. What's your concern now? Is it that Nkiru and Ikem aren't sharing the same room, or that they don't fetch water in the morning?"

"Chinedu, you always ask your question in a way to make us look like we don't know what we're talking about," Ijeoma said angrily.

"Who said you don't know what you're talking about?" Chinedu hastily countered.

"That's almost what your statements mean," Ijeoma retorted strongly. "Whether the kids sleep in the same room or know how to clean their rooms are all related. We as parents must start to do something about this, otherwise, we're losing out on these children."

"Now listen, ladies," Chinedu said calmly. "I understand the concerns that both of you are raising. However, the solution isn't to scream at the kids or expect them to repeat, here in Chicago, everything we did in Enugu. I suggest talking to them calmly and giving them directions and guidance. They're good children and will obey us."

"I don't know about that," Nkechi countered. "They just don't like to do anything, except play video games, eat, and go back to the video games. It isn't a question of teaching them."

"It is," Chinedu insisted.

"It isn't," Nkechi countered.

"You forgot that we were also taught when we were at their age," Chinedu said as he walked over to the refrigerator and took another bottle of Guinness and two cans of Coke. He placed one can before

Nkechi and the other before Ijeoma. Nkechi angrily pushed away the can before her, looking away from Chinedu as she did so.

Ijeoma looked at Chinedu, then at Nkechi. She smiled at no one in particular.

"Chinedu," she called finally after a long minute had elapsed. "I don't understand the way you've served us. You brought this Coke as if you didn't want us to drink it. Isn't there any white wine in that refrigerator? Even Manischewitz?"

"Ijeoma," Okezie called. "First, you complained that you weren't served. Now after being served, you complain about the way you were served. Save everybody this pain and go to the refrigerator and take whatever you want."

Ijeoma ignored him. Chinedu also ignored Ijeoma's questions and Nkechi's anger. "As I was saying," Chinedu added, "we just didn't learn all these things in the womb. We were taught and so the discussion should be on whether we are doing enough for these children as our parents did for us."

Nkechi retained a suspicious look on her face. She was not convinced by Chinedu's explanation. "Chinedu, nobody taught me how to do very basic things when I was small. We didn't have a washing machine, and I knew how to fetch water from the pump and wash my clothes," Nkechi insisted.

"That's the one big mistake we all make," Chinedu explained. "Of course, somebody taught you how to do all those things."

"No, nobody did," Nkechi insisted.

"Believe me, somebody did," Chinedu countered. "It may not have been your parents, but the society then was different from the society now. It could have been another parent living in the same yard who taught you. Parents helped each other in those days. Except for Ijeoma and Okezie, who visit us, who else is our neighbor?"

Ijeoma listened attentively. Maybe she was buying the argument, Chinedu thought and continued with his explanation.

"Even if nobody taught you directly, it's possible that you could have learned things from other children who were taught by their parents. That was possible, because children played together and worked together. Children cross-learned through such interaction. But here in America, from which other children could Nkiru learn anything we don't directly teach her? If only you would listen, Nkechi, you'd understand that this is more complex than you think."

"Chinedu, I think you're really very patient with these women," Okezie added.

"There isn't much choice but to persevere," Chinedu added. "For example I know the effort it took me to show Nkiru that clothes can be washed by hand. I showed her that if she had only one underwear to wash, it could be done by hand and she could spread it on the shower curtain pole to dry. Prior to that she believed that only a washing machine could wash clothes and that even if she had only an underwear to wash she needed to startup the washer and dryer. But since I walked her through one session of washing clothes by hand, she does it as well as we did in Enugu."

"Good luck to you," Okezie wished his friend. "But I've given up trying to explain these things to Ijeoma because it is like talking to stone. I've tried without luck to point out the differences between the environment we grew up in, and the one these kids are growing up in. I've given up arguing that the kids don't know how to wash their plates after eating."

"Nkechi, did you hear that?" Ijeoma asked. "He has given up, so I have to wash their plates. I told you that these men are the problem. They spoil these kids."

"No, you don't have to wash their plates, Ijeoma," Okezie said. "And the kids don't have to wash them either."

"So who will wash them?" Nkechi interjected.

"My dear, ask him," Ijeoma said.

"We have a dishwasher," Okezie said. "Our parents didn't. But if you really wanted them to do dishes by hand, that'd still be okay, but you'd have to walk them through it."

"I think Chinedu did the walk-through on underwear," Ijeoma said with a sneer. "Maybe it's your turn to do the walk-through on plates."

"Don't mind them, my sister," Nkechi added.

Okezie ignored the comments and continued. "These children don't know how to do these things. For example, the children think that all one needs to do is to pour liquid soap on a dirty plate and turn on the tap, and the plate is washed. They have to be taught. That's all Chinedu and I are saying. Yelling, screaming, and cursing won't help. But, if you women think we're only supporting ourselves because we're men, that's fine too."

"Nkechi, my dear, we'll have to open a school to teach them everything," Ijeoma joked.

"I'm not teaching anybody anything. They're human beings. They know exactly what they want. Do I teach them to eat pizza or hamburgers?" Nkechi asked.

"Don't even start," Ijeoma added, throwing up her hands in the air. "That's the one thing that drives me crazy. After spending all my time to prepare good *egusi* or *okro* soup, these kids will tell me they won't eat *fufu* and expect me to call Domino's pizza for them."

"Once I prepare *fufu*, everybody gets his or her own in a separate plate. You eat yours or you go hungry. I just don't have time for nonsense," Nkechi insisted.

Chinedu conceded that getting the children to eat *fufu* or even rice was always a problem. He found it interesting that his American-born children didn't like these two main Nigerian dishes. Eating rice used to be a big thing in Nigeria, but here in America the children would rather eat spaghetti.

"It's only what they're exposed to," Okezie noted. "Spaghetti and pasta aren't necessarily American. They're Italian. However, spaghetti, pasta and pizza feature in their school menu just as often as hamburgers and sandwiches, and the kids get used to them and eventually love them. When they get home, it becomes difficult to convince them to eat other types of dishes."

"It's tough," Nkechi added. "I agree that they're exposed to these dishes at school, but sometimes it goes beyond that. I also think it has to do with the type of African image they're exposed to at school. They learn that Africa is all jungles. I think that if you tell them pizza is really from Africa, there's a good chance they may dislike it."

"We're out of the decision-making loop," Chinedu noted. "To combat these negative images, we must get into the loop. We must be in the room when menu decisions, curriculum decisions, and in fact, all decisions, are made in their schools. Otherwise, we'll be complaining forever."

"I don't know how we'll get into the loop," Nkechi said. "For now, my immediate concern is how to deal with the problem. Ijeoma, what do you normally do? Do you go to Burger King or McDonald's everyday?"

"Oh, no," Ijeoma responded. "Even if I wanted to, we can't afford it."

"So what do you do?" Nkechi asked.

"I use a variety of techniques," Ijeoma explained. "I may be forceful, I may cajole them, or I may strike a deal. A deal could be something like, if you eat *fufu* for lunch, you'll get ice cream or yogurt with your dinner. I'll try anything that works. It's tough, though."

Okezie had discussed this issue with his wife before and wanted to make his point again.

"But do we really need to force them to eat *fufu*?" he asked.

"What else would they eat?" Ijeoma snapped. "These men don't understand that it's difficult deciding what to cook everyday. And when you ask them to suggest a dish, the answer is that it's a woman's decision to make."

"We can offer at home whatever they feed them in school," Okezie explained.

"So when they go to Nigeria, what will they eat?" Nkechi asked. "Or have you joined Chinedu, who thinks these kids may never return to Nigeria? He always says these kids are Nigerian-Americans just like there're Polish-Americans around Pulaski Avenue. That's a very scary thought, because I want my children to be Nigerians, no more, no less."

Chinedu and Okezie exchanged another understanding smile.

"I agree with you, my sister," Ijeoma concurred. "My parents keep calling to find out when we'll bring them home. I was hoping that one way to address the problem would be to send them to Nigeria to go to high school. If they can spend five years going to high school in Nigeria, then they'll have gotten the Nigerian culture inculcated in them. They can then return to America to finish a university degree. But at the rate Nigeria is decaying, that option is ruled out completely."

"The sooner you women start orienting your minds as to who your children really are, the better for everyone concerned," Chinedu added.

23

NIGERIAN HEART, AMERICAN BODY

It was another weekend and this time Chinedu's family visited Okezie's family. This had become a common practice. Either Okezie and his family visited Chinedu and his family, or vice versa. Quite often, these visits always took the same form. The kids went to the basement to play video games. The games were interrupted only at meal times. The parents engaged in discussions that ended up as the husbands versus the wives. This day was no different from the other days. As this particular visit was coming to an end, Okezie wanted to know if he could keep a date with Chinedu the following night. "Sometimes, we need to take a break from these women and discuss issues from a male perspective," he suggested to his friend.

"Before you commit to any plans," Nkechi told Chinedu, "remember we're going for Ikem's first grading conference tomorrow evening."

"True. I almost forgot that," Chinedu admitted.

"Do you have time for those things?" Okezie inquired. "I hardly have time for them. Actually I consider some of them a waste of my time. I guess Ijeoma alone can handle them."

Ijeoma, who was in the restroom, somehow overheard the conversation and hurried out as if not to allow this to pass her by.

"I think it's a mistake not to go," Chinedu argued. "In the past, I looked at it exactly the way you do, until I discovered how important they were."

"What's important?" Okezie asked.

"Oh, yes, those things are really important," Chinedu explained. "Most parents attend the conference and if you don't, it might become a social problem for your child."

Ijeoma repositioned herself on her seat. She sat very attentively with her left elbow anchored on her thigh and her left palm cupped in her chin. Her attention and calmness could have made a mouse seem restless. Chinedu observed how attentive she was, but he didn't know why and didn't want to ask.

"Your child needs the kind of support other kids get from their parents," Chinedu continued. "Moreover, the conference affords the chance to reassure the teachers that the home environment is supportive of what's being done at school. There's also another reason to become involved in what goes on at your child's school."

Ijeoma could not believe what she heard. Could Chinedu and Okezie see an issue differently? Something was not right. She sat quietly but attentively in disbelief. Chinedu was still making his point.

"This may seem funny," he said, "but it's true. Do you know that sometimes you can influence the grade your child receives at school?"

Something about this discussion made Ijeoma really excited. However, she remained uncharacteristically silent. She hadn't said a word. Could it be that Chinedu was making her point? No. That would be too unusual. It was always the men who held identical views, and the women whose views were sure to differ from the men's.

"What do you mean?" Okezie asked. "How can you possibly influence your child's grade?"

"It's a very simple concept. You get involved in what goes on at school and you get rewarded with a good grade for your child."

"I don't understand," Okezie added.

"Let me illustrate with one example I'm familiar with," Chinedu suggested. "A number of schools encourage this concept. They call it 'a classroom parent'."

"What does that mean?" Okezie interrupted.

"A classroom parent is a parent who volunteers time to help a class in whatever way the teacher requests. One of the benefits of this is a close union between the parent and the teacher. Although no one openly admits it, such a union potentially influences the attitude of the teacher towards the child of the classroom parent. This may reflect on the child's grade. In fact, I'm aware that this is being overdone in some instances to the extent that it would appear that the sole intent is to influence the grade a child gets in a class."

"Why do you want to do that?" Okezie asked. "You should allow a child to get the grade he or she deserves."

"That would be true in Nigeria," Chinedu added. "But this is America. Remember that when it's time to give out the scholarships, you and I wouldn't be there to explain that our child got a 'B' and the other child an 'A' because his or her parent volunteered as a classroom parent. The important factor will be that one child earned an 'A' and the other a 'B'. Please tell me who gets the scholarship, other factors, of course, being equal?"

At this point, Ijeoma could not hold back any longer.

"I'm glad you observed these things," she said to Chinedu. "I've quarreled with your friend over this issue many times. I feel so bad, because when we don't attend, or worse still, I attend alone, the teacher believes the child is from a troubled home."

"Why is it worse when you attend alone?" Okezie angrily asked. "So, no parent showing up is better than one parent attending?"

"Yes, it is," Ijeoma snapped. "Both of us should be there."

"I'm not surprised," Okezie sneered. "You've always reasoned like a baby."

"Say whatever you like," Ijeoma taunted. "But the truth is that whenever both parents don't show up, the impression is that no one really cares about the child at home, and consequently, no one expects the school to care."

"This is a silly argument," Okezie said with a cynical tone.

Ijeoma was not deterred. She continued with her argument. "The other untold message sent whenever I attend alone is that they believe I'm a single parent. I know that single parenting is becoming a way of life here, but it isn't common in our own culture. I've tried to explain these things, but you know your friend, if he doesn't want to listen, he won't."

Okezie saw this as a chance to put the single parenting issue to rest. This was not the first time Ijeoma had brought it up and Okezie just did not like it.

"I'm glad you realize that single parenting is becoming a way of life here. What, then, are you complaining about?" he asked. "This is America, not Nigeria. I've repeatedly asked you to stop discussing issues you don't understand. America has many great sons and daughters raised in single parent homes. Here's the problem, Ijeoma. Stop transplanting America onto Nigeria or vice versa. It isn't going to work. I don't understand why you women reside mentally in Nigeria, yet physically in America. Our current society is American, not Nigerian. You must understand that. This mental habitation in Enugu or Owerri, when you're about ten thousand miles away, won't do anyone any good."

"I also don't understand Ijeoma's point," Chinedu said, but was immediately interrupted by Nkechi.

"Naija men will always defend themselves. Whatever one does, the other will support him," she complained. "Do you know that Chinedu expects me to go to a restaurant alone with our four kids?"

"What's wrong with that?" Okezie asked. "Does he have to leave work to take the kids to the restaurant? Or is that defending him?"

"Yes, you're defending him," Nkechi would not yield. "We'll wait for him to come back from work, and we can all go together. Aren't we a family?"

"So, he'll be busy dealing with issues at work and factoring in that he has to go to a movie and a restaurant with you?" Okezie asked cynically.

"Don't I work too?" Nkechi countered. "Is his work more important than that of every other American parent who makes time for his family?"

"My dear, don't mind them. They're the only workers in America," Ijeoma said mockingly.

"I'm not going to a restaurant with four kids again if he isn't with us," Nkechi fumed. "First, they drive me nuts in the restaurant. Second, everybody looks at us and thinks here comes another one of those welfare mothers who does nothing but breed children."

Chinedu's patience exceeded the limit and he snapped. "Nkechi, stop! Time out! What's the difference between what you're saying now and basketball thrash talk? How do you know what people are thinking? Are you a mind reader?"

"Chinedu, you just don't understand," Nkechi responded. "About three weeks ago, I took the kids to Red Lobster. It was a Friday evening and the restaurant was packed. It seemed like all eyes were on us. I had no idea what the food tasted like because I was so embarrassed. I'm not doing it again."

"You always make silly arguments," Chinedu said. "You don't have to go to a restaurant. It just saves me money. By the way, I thought you were all Nigerians. Nigerians cook and eat at home. Americans eat out. Which one are you? Or you become one or the other when it suits you? But listen, what I want to discuss with Okezie is this school conference, not restaurants and movies."

"All these issues are important. School conferences, movie, the cinema, restaurants, hotels, the market, whatever you call them, they're all important. You don't stay in your office playing computer games and having fun on the internet, and then claim you're busy. Don't leave these children to me alone. It took two to create them," Nkechi argued.

Chinedu rubbed his left palm on his forehead. This always helped him to refocus on the conversation. "Okezie, as I was saying before Nkechi started recalling how she enjoyed Lobster at Red Lobster last Friday, these school conferences are important."

"Your husband knows how to reduce somebody's concerns to nothing," Ijeoma complained to Nkechi. "You see how he reduced everything to your dinner at Red Lobster."

"I'm used to it by now," Nkechi responded. "I knew it was coming. I can read him like a book. Anyway, I've made my point. I'm not going to a restaurant alone with these kids. Whether the restaurant is Red Lobster or Burger King isn't important."

Chinedu ignored his wife's comments and continued with the school conference topic. "I think that when the teachers see both parents, it's very reassuring to them and that can be helpful. I know that when we went to school in Nigeria, our parents didn't have to leave their work for any conference. But, if I may use your argument, we're in America, hence we must continue to fight our mental habitation in Nigeria."

"No, don't fight it. Leave it for Nkechi and Ijeoma." Nkechi taunted her husband with a sneer.

As usual, Chinedu ignored her. "That's one major problem Nigerians in the United States must address, and quickly too. Many of them are mentally living in Nigeria. Whatever problem or issue a Nigerian parent is faced with in America, the first thing he or she does is compare the situation against a hypothetical situation or memory of Nigeria. That's dangerously wrong."

"But it isn't just the conferences, it's also the games," Okezie complained. "The schools expect parents to be there when their daughter is playing softball or their son is playing football or soccer. These things drive me nuts."

"Okezie, every man in America does that," Ijeoma said with a shrill. "You aren't any different from them."

"That may be true," Chinedu added. "However, allow him to finish making his point."

"I thought we were on the same side on this one," Ijeoma said to Chinedu. "So, you can't refrain from defending your friend?"

"Let me continue, Chinedu," Okezie said. "In Nigeria, we would go out and play soccer after school. You mix with other children, make your share of mistakes, learn from them, and grow up. But not here. As a parent, you may have to buy insurance for your child because another parent may sue over an injury sustained on the playground."

This time, it was Nkechi who was thirsty. She walked over to the refrigerator and brought out a bottle of her favorite wine, Manischewitz. She filled two glasses, one for herself and the other for Ijeoma. Nothing for the men. Chinedu looked at Okezie and scratched his head, but said nothing.

"If anybody has lice on his head, let him buy camphor and treat them," Nkechi said sarcastically.

"Don't mind them, my sister. We're in America and everybody's eyes will clear," Ijeoma said, offering her support for Nkechi's rebellion.

Neither Chinedu nor Okezie responded to the comments. "They keep telling parents to make out time to play with their kids," said

Chinedu. "Nonsense. How can a forty-year-old man play with a four or five-year-old child? Leave the child to play with other children his age and let parents use their time more gainfully."

Nkechi and Ijeoma exchanged glances. Maybe they were surprised that neither of the men had complained about not being served. Maybe they would have preferred a complaint, but they didn't get one.

"That's exactly my point," Okezie added. "I have to play softball with my daughter, play soccer with my son, and still do other things expected of me as a father. Don't forget that Ijeoma wants her own time too."

"I was waiting to see if you won't eventually put the blame on me," Ijeoma cynically added.

"You want your own time, Ijeoma, don't you?" Chinedu asked, laughing.

"Yes, she does, and I want mine too," Nkechi added.

"Or, if they're now too old to take care of business, well . . . ," Ijeoma added, allowing herself to laugh.

This time, Chinedu rubbed his forehead with both palms. One palm would not do. Okezie struggled with a choking cough that suddenly seized him. Ijeoma was still laughing at her suggestion, and Nkechi suspiciously watched Chinedu and Okezie. In the end, Chinedu broke the silence.

"Being men, our duty is to keep this discussion focused," he told Okezie.

"Chinedu, there's nothing to focus," Nkechi laughed.

"I agree with you, my sister. All these things are now auto-focus," Ijeoma joked, offering a very strong Igbo-like pronunciation to the word "auto."

Okezie looked at Chinedu again. It was getting worse and worse. He shook his head. "I give up," was all he could say.

"Then try Viagra," Nkechi suggested.

"Jesus! What a day," Chinedu added in a desperate tone. "You know, we're here discussing how to save our children, not realizing that we've lost our wives too," Chinedu said.

"In fact, we should refocus this discussion on how to save our wives first," Okezie suggested. "Naija men are ending up like Aaron in the Bible. We're going home empty-handed."

"Anyway, let's stay focused on the children for today," Chinedu suggested. "However, that bottle is the last bottle of Manischewitz Nkechi or Ijeoma will bring into this house or my own house. We're all living witnesses of what a glass of Manischewitz can do to two otherwise homely women."

"I agree with you," Nkechi countered. "We've also seen what dark Guinness stout and Heineken can do to two otherwise homely men."

Okezie and Chinedu exchanged glances. It had been a long day.

"Whenever Nkechi agrees with me, something must be wrong," Chinedu suggested.

"The more I think about these issues, the sorrier I feel for our children," Okezie said, steering the conversation back on track. "Our children have been denied their childhood. We're living in an environment where a child isn't allowed to be a child. It's a tragedy."

"I agree with you," Ijeoma said. Apparently, everybody had enjoyed the digression and was now ready for serious talk. "These children are being robbed of their childhood. One other problem is that you men believe that we, their mothers, are at fault."

"I don't know how you arrived at that conclusion," Chinedu countered. "Anyway, it's the nature of the society. That's where the blame lies, not necessarily on the parents, although we cannot be completely absolved of all the blame."

"It's a tough situation for parents," Okezie added. "Especially men."

"That's correct. We take care of the kids. We take care of the wives, too," Chinedu joked.

"Don't start again," Ijeoma warned, laughing.

This time, her warning was heeded.

*   *   *   *   *

Almost immediately there was a knock on the door. Mazi Frank was let in. Mazi Frank was a leading member of the Igbo community in Chicago. He had lived there for many years. Chinedu and Nkechi had remained indebted to him following the episode over the quantity of formula to feed Ikem.

Mazi Frank was the current President of the Igbo Association in Chicago. In a week's time, the Igbo Association would celebrate their

New Yam Festival. Among the Igbo, yam was the king of crops and many years ago, a man's wealth was measured primarily by the number of barns of yams that he had. In those days farming was the principal occupation of men. Before the planting season, the Igbo offered sacrifices to the god of the soil to bless the soil. When the new yams were harvested, the Igbo held a big festival to thank the god for the "new yam" and good harvest. But with the influence of western culture, wealth in Igboland was no longer necessarily measured by barns of yams. However, the Igbo still believed that yam was their most important crop and hence the New Yam Festival had survived even the influence of western culture. Every Igbo, regardless of profession or place of abode celebrated the New Yam Festival.

For the Igbo living in diaspora, it fell on their various cultural organizations to ensure that the New Yam Festival was celebrated. In his capacity as the current President of the Igbo Association in Chicago, it was Mazi Frank's responsibility to ensure that the festival was successful. In fact, over the past several weeks, Mazi Frank had been visiting every Igbo family in the Chicago area to ensure that everybody participated in this year's festival. It was this "meet the people tour" that brought him to Okezie's house.

"Good afternoon, sir," Ijeoma greeted their guest.

"Good afternoon, IJ. How are you?" Mazi Frank often referred to Ijeoma as "IJ." He exchanged greetings with everybody. "Chinedu, I'm glad to meet you and your family here, so I'll kill two birds with a stone. I was planning to stop by your house once I leave here."

"That's fine," Chinedu said. "But this is Okezie's house. We'll still like to have you over."

"I'll definitely visit once this New Yam Festival is over. I want to make sure that First Lady fills Ikem's feeding bottle."

Everybody laughed heartily for they all remembered very well the episode over feeding Ikem four ounces of formula. That was many years ago.

"I told you guys not to worry," Mazi Frank said. "The young shall grow. First Lady is now one of the experienced mothers in Chicago. What a difference a few years make."

Nkechi smiled and said to Mazi Frank, "Papa Chibuzo, we see you once in a blue moon. You're a very busy person."

"First Lady, not really. I've been around quite a lot, especially since the last few months that we've been working on our new yam festivities. You know it's a week from tonight."

"That's true," Chinedu said. "How are the plans coming along?"

"Pretty well so far. It isn't easy, but don't they say that only fools do easy things? That's actually why I'm visiting everybody, looking for advice and making sure everybody is ready to play his own part."

"That's true, sir," Nkechi said. "I've no doubt that, with your presence, everything will be fine."

"Thanks for that compliment, First Lady," Mazi Frank responded. "I hope it'll be a success."

"Papa Chibuzo," Ijeoma called. "There's something that I'd like to ask an experienced person like you."

"Experienced person?" Mazi Frank asked smiling.

"Yes. When we consider Igbo men in Chicago, most of us look up to you," Ijeoma said. "I know there are two other men in this room, but you know what I mean," she added, coughing and laughing.

Okezie cleared his throat, went over to the refrigerator and brought a bottle of Guinness Stout for Mazi Frank. Ijeoma was probably disappointed that neither Okezie nor Chinedu had responded to her provocation.

"I didn't know I was that experienced," Mazi Frank joked. "Anyway, what do you want to ask? If I don't know the answer, maybe one of the two other unnamed men you mentioned may have the answer."

Nkechi smiled and pouted. "All men are the same. I'm looking forward to the day when women will defend and protect themselves the same way that men do."

Chinedu and Okezie exchanged glances but said nothing.

"Nkechi, my sister, don't mind them," Ijeoma said lending support to Nkechi. "Papa Chibuzo, my son Nweke is now in high school. I'm very worried about the friends he keeps. Not that he keeps bad company or anything like that, but he has no Nigerian friends. There's a beautiful girl who often calls him. God bless her soul, but I'd rather Nweke was dating a Nigerian-American."

Mazi Frank lapsed into uncontrollable laughter.

"Why are you laughing?" Ijeoma asked.

"IJ, this is America," Mazi Frank responded. "There's nothing wrong with his dating a non-Nigerian, is there?"

"If Ikem brings any of those girls into my house, I will break their heads," Nkechi threatened. "He knows better than to try it."

"You know this is exactly the same issue I was discussing with Chief Ogugua earlier this morning," Mazi Frank told them. "To be quite honest with you, it's a serious problem that we have to address."

"What do we do then?" Ijeoma asked.

"Many parents feel frustrated over the issue, but it needs a systematic solution," Mazi Frank said.

"Nkechi probably thinks that threatening to break Ikem's head is as systematic as it can get," Chinedu said, eyeing his wife out of the corner of his eye and knowing that he was annoying her.

"Chinedu, I won't argue with you," Nkechi further threatened. "Let him try it and we shall see whether he's in charge or I'm in charge."

"I guess I'm out of it, eh?" Chinedu joked.

"This is very serious, Chinedu," Nkechi said. "It's nothing to joke about. You think Ikem is still a small boy? He's not. He can impregnate a woman now. I married from Nigeria and I want him to follow in my footsteps."

"First Lady, I know how you feel about it," Mazi Frank said. "And you're right. But it isn't as simple as it seems. You may remember that when we went to high school in Nigeria, we used to socialize a lot during vacation and in the dorms. Many friendships and marriages started there. But that isn't the case with our children. They're missing that fun we had during our high school days, and in the process, missing out on many friendships."

"You're absolutely right," Okezie said. "Ijeoma, when did we meet the first time?"

"I can't remember precisely when, but I know it was at a Sunday jump during vacation," Ijeoma recalled.

"That's true," Okezie said. "That was what we used to call Sunday dances, they were Sunday jumps. I remember them very well. I remember the Wings, Hygrades, the Strangers and a host of other bands of that era."

"Those were great days," Chinedu added.

"I know. I was there," Mazi Frank concurred. "Anyway, let's make sure we all understand what the problem is."

"It's our children," Nkechi interjected.

"We know, but listen first, and talk later. Not the other way," Chinedu urged.

"It's our children, as First Lady correctly pointed out," Mazi Frank continued. "As parents, we're concerned that our high school kids in particular aren't having the type of social interaction we would like for their development."

"Yes," Ijeoma concurred.

"Quite often, on returning from school, they're locked up in the house until the following day. They interact mostly by phone and electronic mails with their classmates."

"True," Nkechi agreed.

Mazi Frank continued. "Incidentally, most of the friends they have are non-Nigerian-Americans. One of the reasons for this is that there is no concentration of Nigerian-Americans in any part of Chicago. We're dispersed as an unidentifiable minority in this country."

"Tell me about it," Chinedu said. "Everybody wants to live on his own."

"Our primary concern now," Mazi Frank continued, "is what the fate of these children will be when it's time for them to get married. They'll very likely end up with the friends they know, and these friends aren't of our people."

"You pretty much summarized it, Frank," Okezie said.

"That's our problem," Mazi Frank continued. "We must find a solution."

"We must, my dear," Nkechi said. "Ikem must marry a Nigerian."

Chinedu sneered at his wife but said nothing.

"Our culture in Nigeria supported arranged marriages," Mazi Frank noted, "but the American culture to which these children are exposed doesn't support that. Unless we start to help them know themselves, we're in for a shock. They'll marry into foreign cultures. It isn't enough to instruct them to marry a Nigerian-American. They won't obey that instruction. We should start helping these kids to develop a network of Nigerian-American friends."

A deafening silence overtook them turning the atmosphere in Okezie's house into that of a graveyard. There was something about the reality and seriousness of the current discussion that weighed heavily on these parents. After a long silence, Nkechi stood up, clapped her hands in hopeless resignation, and asked, "So, I have to find a woman for my son? This is serious. Our parents did the opposite, warning us against premature dating."

"The times are changing," Mazi Frank added calmly. "But, actually, what we're proposing to do isn't really different from what our parents did. I don't know about Chinedu and Okezie, but in my own case, my parents kept focusing me towards the girls and families they wanted me to eventually choose from. In a sense, that's what we are proposing here, to direct their focus towards the group we want them to choose their spouses from. That way, we aren't really pushing women on them."

"Nkechi, do you have any idea what Frank is talking about?" Chinedu asked his wife casually.

"About what?" Nkechi retorted, pretending not to understand where Chinedu was headed.

"About a parent, actually, a mother directing a daughter to a potential husband," Chinedu responded, clearing his throat and scratching his head.

"Chinedu, my mother didn't direct me to you, if that's what you're implying," Nkechi said with a sneer on her face. "You and your people were chasing *me*."

Chinedu cleared his throat again, scratched his head some more, and went over to the refrigerator to get a drink. He said nothing to his wife's challenge.

"Frank, not to worry," Okezie said to Mazi Frank. "This episode may be new to you, but the four of us call it *Chichi* special or *Chi*nedu/Nke*chi* special."

Mazi Frank merely smiled, but passed on the topic. "One of the projects the Igbo Association is planing for next year will start to address this problem," he declared. "We're looking for volunteers. One thing I plan to do for my son's next birthday is to organize a party for all Nigerian-American teenagers. My wife and I will ask parents to drop off their kids about 4 pm and pick them up about 9 pm. We've promised our son Chibuzo that we won't bother them. We'll provide them a safe environment and allow them to feel free and get to know each other. It doesn't matter whether they play only rap or other American music. That's okay. The key thing is that we start to encourage this Nigerian-American environment for them."

"Papa Chibuzo, you have my support," Nkechi said. "When is

Chibuzo's birthday? Ikem, Kelechi and Nkiru will be the first to get there. If it means calling out of work, I will do it. This is very important to me."

24

THE GOOD OLD DAYS

It was a hot summer afternoon. Okezie and Chinedu were in the parking lot of Truman College on the north side of town waiting to pick up their children who participated in an intensive Igbo language program designed for Nigerian-Americans and run by the Igbo Association in Chicago. Moreover, it was also the day of the Igbo New Yam Festival in Chicago and the two friends were to go to downtown Chicago to buy a few things their wives had requested, presumably for use during the festivities later in the day. Given that their wives had worked as cashiers in a parking lot in downtown, Okezie and Chinedu had first hand knowledge of how expensive parking a car in downtown was. Their wives no longer held those jobs, so they couldn't park their cars for free, a benefit usually extended to the parking lot employees and their spouses. Incidentally, their mutual friend Emmanuel had also come to Truman College to pick his own children.

"Let's ask Emmanuel to drop off these kids," Okezie suggested.

"We're better off using the El to go downtown. Parking in downtown is a nightmare."

"Excellent idea," Chinedu said. "Wilson is an AB stop and it wouldn't be long before the next train arrived." Emmanuel gladly accepted the responsibility of picking up all the kids while Okezie and Chinedu went to downtown.

As they waited on the El platform for the downtown-bound train, they continued their conversation where they had left off.

"I'm becoming tired of this place," Okezie said. "Ijeoma and Nkechi have infected me with their despair."

Before Chinedu had time to respond, the train pulled up at the station. The speakers on the platform came to life with the conductor's voice.

"This is a Howard Englewood A train. Last change for the B train to Addison Wrigley field. All aboard. This is Wilson and Broadway."

The doors opened. Chinedu and Okezie stepped into the train and were just settling down when a voice bellowed angrily at Chinedu.

"Hey man, don't match on me. Fuck, shit!"

Chinedu turned around to face a tall black male carrying a bottle wrapped in a paper bag in one hand and a quenched, half-smoked cigarette in the other. The anger in his face could have made Job restless. Accidentally, Chinedu had stepped on his foot.

"Hey man, don't look at me like that. I'm not your carpet, man. Don't match on me no more. Shit!"

The man was furious. Chinedu was both terrified and frightened. Without saying a word, he moved away from his antagonist. Okezie followed behind him closely.

"*Dianyi*, I told you I don't like these trains," he told Okezie.

"You don't want to pay for parking in downtown," Okezie replied.

"I'd rather do that," Chinedu responded.

They quietly moved to the next car. The Dodgers were in town for an afternoon game with the Cubs. The smell of hot dogs and the gaiety of the crowd at Wrigley singing to "Take me out to the ball game" were felt in the train as it sped past Addison.

Okezie realized that his friend was slightly shaken by the encounter that had driven them from the previous car. The current car was less crowded and they were seated, so Okezie could refocus his friend's mind and thoughts.

"You know, today is the big day for all the chiefs and titled men," Okezie reminded Chinedu.

"True," Chinedu responded. "You're talking about the New Yam Festival tonight."

"Yes."

"Fine. We can discuss their chieftaincy titles later, but I have more important things on my mind that I'd like to bounce off you."

Okezie sighed sadly. "Everybody has a lot on his or her mind," he told his friend. "Let's hear yours."

The train was now leaving Belmont. "This is a Howard Englewood A train. Smoking radio playing is not permitted on the train. Fullerton is next. Last change for the Evanston train. Fullerton is our next stop. Fullerton." The operator's voice clicked off the speakers.

Chinedu looked casually out of the window and noticed that the temperature display on top of the Chase Manhattan building, visible from the Belmont El stop, read 90 degrees.

"Today is one of those 100 degree days."

"Yep," Okezie responded.

Chinedu returned to their discussion. "I'm thinking about our conversation with Nkechi and Ijeoma," Chinedu said. "Although Nkechi in particular would shout away her points, making it difficult for you to differentiate noise and information, there's no doubt that they do have some points worthy of serious consideration. I'm very concerned about us and our children, what our futures and their futures hold."

"True," Okezie agreed.

"When I look at what's happening to our generation in the diaspora, I get depressed," Chinedu continued. "Quite often I feel totally confused about what to do about our children. Are we here now forever? Will our children never return to Nigeria?"

"Chinedu, those are tough questions," Okezie responded.

"How do we bring these children up? The American way or the way our parents brought us up in Enugu? Either way, I feel I have an obligation to bring them up in a way in which they'll at least understand their Nigerian heritage. I sincerely don't think they'd ever go back to Nigeria, but they can't be allowed to completely lose their identity. That's what distinguishes them from the rest."

They were engrossed in their conversation, but Okezie noticed that the train was no longer on the elevated tracks, but rather, underground.

" Where're we now?"

" I don't know, but I guess Washington and State is still ahead," Chinedu responded.

Just as they were talking through that, the conductor announced the stop.

" Clark Street and Diversey. Watch your steps and have a nice day. Clark and Diversey. Chicago and State will be our next stop. All aboard."

" When did we pass North and Clyborn?"

" I don't know," Chinedu responded. "But it seems you aren't thinking about what I've been saying."

" Why do you say that?" Okezie asked.

" You're thinking about the train stops. Do you plan to become a train conductor?"

Okezie smiled. "No. It's been more than a year since I rode the El."

" Actually, this conductor is okay," Chinedu said. "Some of them are so taciturn, they don't even announce the stops."

" True," Okezie agreed. "It can be annoying to a newcomer to town."

They returned to their conversation.

" The fate of our children is a tough one," Okezie said. "Honestly, I don't have an answer to it. Even if we concede that they'll live their lives in America as Americans, do we also concede that they'll never visit Nigeria again?"

" You remind me of something interesting," Chinedu hastily added. "Last year, I took my children to Nigeria. We stayed with my sister in her flat in Ikenegbu layout, Owerri. I'm sure you know Ikenegbu layout, probably better than myself. My family was among those that moved to Owerri after the creation of Imo state."

" The same was the case with my immediate family," Okezie responded. "However, my uncle lived there before the civil war. I know the city quite well, but the place is also decaying, like the larger society."

" Tell me about it. That's actually part of my story. My sister's flat had the usual shower, sink and the so-called water system in the bathroom. Only heaven knows the last time water ran through it's pipes."

"The first morning after our arrival," Chinedu said, continuing with his story, "Ikem wanted to brush his teeth. My sister handed him a glass of water. Ikem held the toothbrush in one hand and the glass of water in the other. He couldn't understand why he was given a glass of water when there was a tap in the sink."

"Oh, boy," Okezie laughed. "So what happened?"

"He turned on the tap, but it was dry. He dipped the brush into the glass of water and started to cry because he didn't know how to use the brush and glass of water to brush his teeth. I won't even bother to tell you what happened when he was given a bucket of water for his shower."

Okezie lapsed into uncontrollable laughter. He had heard of similar experiences from a number of Nigerians who visited home with their children. "Chinedu, we're all in trouble," was all he managed to say.

"Yes, we are," Chinedu agreed. "However, as my father would say, let me tell the second part since they were two that created me."

"Is there another side to the story?" Okezie asked.

"Yes, there is," Chinedu said. "Despite their obvious disappointment with the state of utilities in the house, my children loved their grandparents very much. You may remember we extended our visit by a week because Nkiru didn't want to return."

"True, I remember you had some problems with rebooking your return flight," Okezie said.

"Mama Nkechi was crazy about her grandchildren. She wouldn't let Nkiru walk. Can you imagine lapping a girl as big as Nkiru?"

"What about your mother?"

"She was no less excited. But since Mama Nkechi wouldn't let anybody touch Nkiru, my mother settled for the rest, especially Obioha. Our parents really spoiled the kids. I wouldn't leave the children with their grandparents."

"That's strange in a sense," Okezie noted. "I would have thought their grandparents would have been concerned because the kids couldn't do the type of chores we did when we were young."

"Not at all," Chinedu said. "Mama Nkechi in particular supported everything they did and even spoiled them further. Moreover, the village kids were too excited to do things for them."

"True, I forgot to ask," Okezie said. "How did they get on with the village children?"

"It was great. There was the initial language problem, however, in a week or so, they could understand most things spoken to them in Igbo, though they responded in English."

"What about your father and Nkechi's father?"

"They were no less excited. At the end of the trip, my father was so overcome with joy at seeing his grandchildren that, like Simon in Luke 2:25-31 he declared: "Lord, now you are letting your servant depart in peace, according to your word, for my eyes have seen your salvation which you have prepared before the face of all peoples.""

"That's funny," Okezie said. "Everybody that traveled home had a similar experience."

"Yep. My father couldn't believe he was alive to see his grandchildren."

"He'll see his great grandchildren."

"Amen," Chinedu prayed.

"By the way, I know you'll now accuse of me of train conducting, but I think we're at Washington and State," Okezie said. The conductor bore him out.

"This is Washington and State. Change for the Lake Dan Ryan. Change for the State Street Subway. Change for the West side Douglas O'Hare train. Washington. Washington and State. Next stop is Madison and State. Your attention please. This is an Englewood bound Howard Englewood A train. Smoking, radio playing is not permitted on this train. Madison is next."

Just before the conductor lowered the window, a young couple in their mid-twenties stepped into the train. He was a black male, carrying a radio with disproportionately-sized speakers. A half-smoked, unlit cigarette was held in place between his lips. His oversized baggy pants were held in place by his buttocks. Standing next to him was his light-skinned partner. She stood close to him, her large breasts bolting out of her undersized brassiere.

"Look at those kids," Chinedu told Okezie.

"What about them?" Okezie retorted.

Chinedu did not follow up. However, the couple had attracted many eyes in that car. She didn't look restless, but was behaving that way. She couldn't stand still, but was always moving either sideways, towards or away from her partner. A man reading *The Wall Street Journal*, standing behind her, took a few measured steps away. Her buttocks had clearly won the battle with what passed for the short pants she wore. She kept shaking her head, causing her loose long hair to fling backward. Her left fore and middle fingers held an unlit cigarette in place. She was about three inches shorter than her partner who could have been an effective center in the NBA. Her lips kept moving up to his, begging to be kissed. He obliged a few times. For his part, his free hand continuously worked its way from her thighs up her back, up to her hair and made its way down her front side.

"Are those kids crazy?" Chinedu asked Okezie.

"Just mind your business. It's legal to be in love in the US of A."

"Isn't this the type of thing Nkechi sees and starts complaining to me about in public?"

"It isn't her alone," Okezie said. "Try and talk to Ijeoma."

The train was at another stop.

"Aren't we getting off here?"

"No, let's get off at Jackson," Okezie responded. "The stores we want are between Jackson and Washington on State street. So we'll work our way from South to North and re-enter the subway at Washington or Madison for the ride home. You were talking about your visit to Nigeria and your parents' reactions to their grandchildren; actually you had started with how Ikem used the toothbrush."

"True. I almost forgot what we were talking about," Chinedu responded.

"You accused me not too long ago of not considering what you said seriously. Now, you almost forgot yourself."

"OK. You're right," Chinedu joked. "But let me continue with what I was saying."

"Go right ahead," Okezie told him.

"In a sense, these issues are a manifestation of the conflict and tragedy of our generation. Time is passing and we're all getting old."

"That's scary," Okezie added.

"I think our generation is on the wrong side of history."

"I don't know about that," Okezie argued.

"Yes, we are," Chinedu countered. "If we were in Nigeria today, we would be ruling and leading the country. Here we are, some with multiple advanced degrees, wasting away in America."

Okezie felt that the phrase "wasting away," was rather too strong. "Come on, Chinedu, we aren't wasting away. We're making a useful contribution to the economy."

"Which economy?"

"The economy we live in. Don't you know we have Nigerians in top places in almost every sphere of American life?"

"True," Chinedu acknowledged. "But we are easily dispensable in those places. It's Nigeria that really needs us. Instead, we live in economic exile in America, which could replace us anytime if she wants."

"So, do we start packing and heading back home?"

"It isn't outside the realm of possibility," Chinedu answered tartly.

Okezie chuckled. They were on the escalator at Jackson, riding up to the street level.

"Please be careful when we come out," Chinedu said. "I get disoriented sometimes here in downtown. That was why I wanted to get off at Washington. I have some landmarks there to properly orient me."

"That's okay," Okezie reassured him. "We'll be fine. You were talking about returning to Nigeria."

"Yes."

"Well, whenever anyone talks about returning to Nigeria," Okezie recalled, "I remember this stupid woman who lived in the same apartment complex I lived in when I came to the United States. Her primary concern was whether or not she'd find 100% Florida orange juice for her children in her village if she returned to Nigeria. She was proud to announce that her children no longer drank water, just orange juice."

Chinedu gave Okezie a funny look. "Okezie, I'm discussing something important, and you're talking about a woman and orange juice. Listen, our generation is wasting away. We can't fold our arms and hope God will solve our problems for us."

They were now at Marshall Field on State street having been to Sears without finding the perfumes they were looking for.

"Nigeria's problems are complex," Okezie agreed, "but you must give credit to Nigerians for surviving all the hardships they face everyday."

"Stop," Chinedu snapped. "This is where I get impatient with your logic. There's no credit due to any Nigerian, including me."

"What do you mean?" Okezie appeared perplexed.

"About what?" Chinedu asked.

"About what you just said," Okezie responded.

Chinedu concentrated on the Avon perfume they were buying.

"You can test it," the sales clerk told Chinedu handing him another bottle of the perfume which was used as a tester.

"No, thanks," Chinedu said.

"Isn't that women's perfume?" Okezie asked the sales clerk.

"Yes, it is," she responded.

"And you want a man to spray it on his body?"

"Not necessarily on his body," the sales clerk responded. "He can spray it on his palm to appreciate the smell."

"A woman's perfume?" Okezie asked again.

"Of course," the sales clerk said. "His wife is going to wear it for him. Who's going to appreciate it but him?"

Okezie scratched his head and took a few measured steps away from Chinedu and the sales clerk as if to minimize the risk of a woman's perfume being sprayed on him. Chinedu was in no hurry to try the perfume either. He merely cross checked the name against the one Nkechi had given to him. Satisfied that it was the right perfume, he gave the sales clerk his credit card. She swiped it through the machine and in a few seconds she got the authorization for the sale. Okezie also bought another bottle of the same perfume for Ijeoma. They exchanged parting greetings with the sales clerk, left the store and walked down the subway stairs onto the platform to wait for their train for the ride home. As they waited for the train, Okezie continued the discussion.

"Chinedu, I'm still listening because sincerely, I think you're the only person who doesn't understand that Nigerians deserve credit for surviving all the hardships that they face."

"Okezie, let's skip this topic. We'll get no where with it."

"Seriously, I don't understand what you're talking about," Okezie said.

"I'm surprised that you don't understand. Consider a Nigerian and an American. Can't you see some startling differences in their attitudes towards life?"

"No, I don't," Okezie responded strongly.

"Don't you see that an American and a Nigerian have different beliefs?"

"Chinedu, I refuse to be interrogated," Okezie said emphatically. "I'm ready to listen to your viewpoint, but I don't want a cross examination."

Chinedu smiled at Okezie's apparent seriousness. They stepped into the first train that pulled up, not caring whether it was an A or B train. Wilson was an AB stop.

"Since you don't understand, let me explain," Chinedu told his friend as he sat in the first available seat. Okezie sat by him.

"If you're ready to explain, I'll listen," Okezie responded.

"My main point is that we're here in diaspora because of the situation at home," Chinedu stated.

"There isn't much argument about that," Okezie agreed.

"Consider what goes on in Nigeria," Chinedu continued. "Do you think it could happen in America?"

"Why not?" Okezie asked.

"It won't, and the reason is simple," Chinedu explained. "In this society, when a person is faced with a serious situation, he confronts the problem head-on. He can either solve it, and everybody is happy and learns from it, or he dies trying to solve it. The result is still the same; the problem is solved. People give their lives in search of solutions to problems and for what they believe in."

Chinedu paused, and since Okezie had nothing to say, he continued. "Now consider what happens in an analogous situation in Nigeria. What does a person do when confronted with a problem, such as a scarcity of electricity, gas or pipe-borne water?"

"What do you want him to do?" Okezie asked laughing.

"There's a lot he can do," Chinedu added. "But what does he actually do? Does he confront the problem head-on in attempt to find a solution? Of course not. He avoids it and opts for a way to work around the problem. In the absence of electricity, he steps down to cooking with kerosene stove. In a short time, there's no kerosene, and what does he do? He becomes philosophical and reminds himself that our forefathers cooked with firewood. Ultimately, with no firewood, there's talk about the ability to adjust to cooking with sawdust a.k.a. the *Abacha* stove. Thus, instead of focusing on the inability to tackle existing problems, there's a deceitful emphasis and praise on the ability to survive very harsh conditions."

Chinedu paused again allowing his friend time to absorb the information. He stood up and moved towards the door.

"Where're you going to?" Okezie asked.

"We just passed Montrose. Wilson is next," Chinedu responded.

As they walked to the Truman College parking lot to pick Okezie's car, their discussion continued. "I hope you get the picture that I'm painting," Chinedu said. "We started with a middle-class family. By most measures, this is a fairly comfortable family, living the Nigerian dream. They live in a flat. They have a car and a stable marriage with healthy children. In addition, they have a house in the village and a good job providing income to cater for parents and in-laws at an old age."

"They have it made," Okezie joked.

"That would have been true," Chinedu regretted. "But notice what's happening to them. They no longer have electricity or pipe-borne water. They now carry their cooking pots down the stairs from their flat on the third floor to the ground floor where the Abacha stove burns. Nobody complains. Everybody keeps adjusting and surviving. The problem is never resolved, and the quality of life of a once free, proud, and prosperous people becomes worse than that of slaves during the slave era."

"Sounds true to me," Okezie sighed. "The net impact is that we're all here drinking orange juice in America."

"Don't turn this into a joke," Chinedu said rather strongly. "This is serious stuff."

"Who says it's a joke?" Okezie countered. "The solution is simple though. My plan is to get all my family over to the United States. You should be thinking along the same lines."

The drive to Okezie's house was short. On entering the house, Chinedu went straight to the refrigerator and served himself a bottle of Guinness Stout and Coke. Okezie, as usual, went for Heineken. They continued with their discussion, ignoring Ijeoma and the kids.

Ijeoma had prepared homemade *ugba* for them. She noticed the intensity of the on-going discussion. She was by now used to it, for whenever Chinedu and Okezie were together, Nigeria's problems and politics were most likely the topic of conversation. She quietly placed the *ugba* on the table and snuck away as if not to stir up any trouble. Chinedu absent-mindedly thanked her and continued talking. "Are we going to empty Nigeria into America?" he asked.

"If that's the way you want to look at it, so be it," Okezie responded.

Chinedu shook his head. "It's a tragedy."

"True," Okezie admitted. "The situation is serious, and that's why I have to bring my parents out of that place. Things are worse in Nigeria today than during the civil war."

"Of course," Chinedu agreed. "During the civil war, wives left husbands and daughters left their families. To some extent, one could rationalize that because of the war. I'm not aware there's a war going on in Nigeria today, but what do we have? The situation looks more desperate than during the war. Sons no longer respect their parents and our daughters are loose on the streets of Rome, London, Accra, Johannesburg, and Los Angeles. Nigerians, dispersed all over the world, are willing to settle for anything and anywhere, except a free ticket back to Nigeria."

Okezie looked at the clock on the wall and saw that it was almost 5 pm.

"We'll not solve all of Nigeria's problems today," he told Chinedu. "I'm switching gears now. Remember that the New Yam Festival ceremonies start at about 6 pm. Let me drop you off because Nkechi must be getting impatient by now. I also need to do a few things before going to the festival."

25

THE NEW YAM FESTIVAL

The Igbo Association in the Chicago area had put considerable time and energy preparing for this year's New Yam Festival. For the first time, the *Izaga* masquerade would perform, in addition to the *Ojionu* and *Okwonma* masquerades. The Igbo Association women's wing would also present their dance.

Parents brought their children to the festival. It was not only a way to expose them to the Nigerian culture, it was also a way to bring the children together so they could meet each other. Even the children looked forward to the festival.

"I'm really looking forward to the festival tonight," Ikem told his parents as they prepared to leave for the occasion.

"This is the first time I've heard you say something reasonable," Nkechi responded. "Kelechi, what about you? Are you looking forward to it?"

"Yep," Kelechi responded. "I guess I know why Ikem is all

excited, though."

"Why?" Ikem challenged him.

"Since you got an 'A' in that project about dad's childhood, you always want projects that have to do with Nigeria. You told me your teacher loved those stories about Africa. Are you going to write about the festival in your next project?"

"You bet, I will," Ikem responded. "You know I received the best paper award for that essay on dad's childhood. I think it was neat. My teacher loved how I compared all the stuff Dad and Nweke's dad told us, with all the stuff that we do today. One that my teacher really enjoyed was where I discussed how Mom shared a mat with her brothers when she was young. I contrasted it with Nkiru having a room alone. My teacher is really interested in African stuff. Actually, I told her about this festival and she can't wait to read my experiences. I also told her we may all be visiting Nigeria next year. Dad, are we still going?"

"You better believe it," Nkechi responded, even though the question wasn't meant for her. "That's why I'm working all the overtime."

When Chinedu and his family arrived at the festival venue, they found a seating area that allowed a good view of the podium where the ceremony would be held. Ikem was particularly interested in the event and didn't want to miss anything that happened. Although the occasion was yet to officially start, pockets of groups were forming. As always, Nigerians discussed their problems. In one of the groups were Chinedu's friends, Emmanuel, Alexander, Anselem, IK and Okezie. Once his family had settled down, Chinedu left them and joined his friends. He exchanged greetings with his friends and joined the discussion already in progress.

"The problem is that Nigerians in diaspora have no sense of direction," Alexander told Emmanuel.

"*Oga Elegi*," Emmanuel responded. "What direction are you talking about?" Alexander's friends often preferred to address him as *Elegi*.

"Emma, leave *Oga Elegi* alone," IK added. "He's always opposed to everything organized by the Igbo Association. Maybe we'll make him President next year to see if he'll change."

"You guys are talking nonsense," Alexander forcefully said. "Do you see me as one interested in running for office?"

"How can we know?" IK responded, scratching his head. "*Oga Elegi*, you know that since all lizards lie on their stomach, it's difficult to identify those with a stomach problem."

"IK, I have no idea what you're talking about. Let me talk to Emma, I think you're still a child."

"*Oga Elegi*, talk to me, sir," Emmanuel joked. "Leave Iyke alone."

Everybody took a cheap shot at IK because he was the only unmarried person in that group.

"Emma," Alexander called. "Can you tell us the amount of time your wife spent preparing for this so-called dance. For the past two or three months, the only thing the Igbo women in Chicago have done is to discuss the special clothes for this dance."

"What's wrong with that?" Anselem jokingly asked.

"It shows the kinds of things that occupy our minds. We have too much time on our hands."

"I think this is even a more serious problem for men," Okezie noted. "Imagine the time our men spend preparing for the *Ojionu* dance. The common explanation is that it is our culture. I don't quite get that."

"What don't you get?" Anselem asked. "I did the *Ojionu* and *Atunma* dances when I was a kid. I don't see what's wrong with doing them here in America."

"I'd have agreed with you completely if we used the *Ojionu* dance as a prelude to a larger goal," Okezie said. "But if we assemble here every week only to watch the dance, then it's a waste of time."

"Okezie, it isn't a waste of time," Anselem insisted. "You and Chinedu always criticize everything that people do. But you won't start anything to make an example. It's so easy to criticize. Lead us by example and we'll follow you."

"Anselem, don't bring me into it," Chinedu protested. "You don't love the *Ojionu* dance as much as I do. But that isn't the point Okezie is making. If you don't understand an issue, then don't argue it."

"Chinedu, there's nothing to understand," said Anselem. "*Ojionu* is *Ojionu*. No more, no less."

"That isn't the issue," Chinedu insisted.

"What is it then?" Anselem asked.

"If you listen to him carefully, you'll understand the issues," Chinedu said.

"But you won't say what they are?" Anselem retorted.

"OK. Here's one of them," Chinedu said. "Let's use these *Ojionu* and *Atunma* masquerades as an avenue to organize ourselves into something productive for our people. If you think carefully, you'll observe that, between May and October, there's no weekend in which at least one Nigerian party isn't held. Your namesake who came from New Jersey, has a similar story for the tri-state area of New York, New Jersey and Connecticut."

"What's wrong with that?" Anselem interjected.

"We can't just keep partying every weekend. After a party, we disperse, only to reassemble the following week. If you participate in any conversation like the one we are having now, you'll hear the same problems discussed over and over. No one ever asks what decisions were made the previous time a particular problem was discussed, and what follow-up actions were agreed upon and implemented."

"Chinedu, do you think you'll win an argument against Anselem?" Alexander asked. "I think it's a doomed effort on your part. I gave up debating him years ago. Once he latches onto a view, he becomes as obstinate as a mule defending that view."

Anselem looked at Alexander, smiled, and said, *"Oga Elegi,* I don't want your trouble."

As with most Nigerian parties, it was irrelevant what time it was scheduled to start. People arrived when they wanted, often not before 9 pm. It was quite common for a Nigerian invited to a 4 pm party to call the host at 9 pm to inquire if the other guests had started to arrive. He probably didn't want to be the first to arrive.

It was about 9 pm and most of the chiefs and titled men were still arriving. Given the number of chiefs coming to the occasion, it looked as if there were more titled men in Chicago than in all of Igboland. At about 10 pm, a good number of people had come, and Mazi Frank, the President of the Igbo Association was about to formally start the proceedings. Once Mazi Frank went up to the podium, Chinedu left his friends and rejoined his family so he could explain to his children anything they didn't understand.

"Che, che, che, Igbo kwenu!" Mazi Frank greeted the crowd.

"Yaa!" the people responded.

"Kwenu!"

"Yaa!"

"*Nigeria kwenu!*"

"*Yaa!*"

"*America kwezuenu!*"

"*Yaa!*"

Mazi Frank was aware that time wasn't on their side and so he briefly explained what the occasion was about. In conclusion, he added, "I will now call on our very own Dr. Chief Ogbuefi Ezennia, the Ezeudo I of Nanka to lead us in the breaking of the *kola* nut."

Dr. Chief Ezennia wore his full traditional regalia. The shiny gold beads on his chieftaincy staff matched the gold rings that decorated his wife's (*lolo*) fingers. Feathers of very special and rare birds were pinned on his cap. It was once rumored that some animal rights groups demanded to know from where such exotic feathers had been obtained.

Waving his staff and cutting through the air, Ezeudo greeted the crowd.

"*Igbo kwenu!*"

"*Yaa!*" the people responded.

"*Kwezuenu!*"

"*Yaa!*"

"I know that this is a mixed audience," Chief Ezennia said. "I appreciate our American friends in our midst. Some of them are our spouses and in-laws. There're also other non-Igbo Nigerians among us. To all of you I say, welcome."

"Thank you," some of those being addressed responded.

Chief Ezennia continued. "We're now about to bless and break the *kola* nut. This is one of the most significant customary rites we perform before any important occasion in Igboland. We pray to our ancestors to guide us in whatever we're about to do. So, we're about to call on them now for their guidance."

He cleared his throat, looked around, and continued. "Incidentally, neither our ancestors, nor the *kola* nut, understands the English language."

The crowd cheered and clapped.

"*Ga niru,*" someone shouted from the crowd. This was a popular phrase used to urge a person to continue with whatever he or she was doing. It was an indication of appreciation and support.

"You're the son of your father," another excited person added. This was a high praise in Igboland. To be assured that one was the son of his father was very important because while the identity of one's mother was never in doubt, one's father may be a different case.

This time, with his staff in his left hand and his chieftaincy fan in his right hand, Chief Ezennia waved to the people and greeted them again.

"*Igbo kwenu!*"

"*Yaa!*"

It always worked like magic. He got the attention and silence he wanted. "I'll, therefore, ask your indulgence as we call on our ancestors in the language they understand. Our President, Mazi Frank, will take a few moments later and explain to you what went on."

Chief Ezennia whispered and exchanged words in Igbo with a few people, then continued in English. "I'm inviting all the titled men in this hall to join me on stage for the breaking of the *kola* nut."

As already indicated, there was no shortage of chiefs in the hall. Typically, the titled men greeted themselves by touching the back of their hands three times and concluding the greeting the fourth time by grasping and shaking hands. They showered greetings and praises on each other and called each person by his title.

"*Ochi agha, eze dike,*" Chief Ezennia greeted his compatriot, Chief Uzondu. "*Odozi obodo Nbawsi. Udo diri gi.*"

"*Aka ji aku,*" Chief Uzondu greeted. "*Eze ukwu, eze udo. Ya gazie.*"

After the exchange of greetings, the breaking of the *kola* nut began.

"Anyaogu, will you please lead us in breaking of the *kola* nut?" Chief Ezennia asked Dr. Chief Tobias Uchendu, the *Anyaogu* I of Mbieri.

At the distant end of the podium, a few of the titled men still murmured and exchanged words in low tones. It was later learned that someone in the crowd had objected to Ezeudo inviting titled men instead of chiefs to join in the blessing of the *kola* nut. The problem was that women could also take chieftaincy title in Igboland. Before now, a woman could only be *lolo,* that is, the wife of a chief. However, there was a female chief in the hall. But, Chief Ezennia recognized that women couldn't bless *kola* in Igboland, hence, he was clever enough in wording his invitation. Chief Tobias Uchendu, the Anyaogu I of Mbieri rose to his feet, about to start the blessing of the *kola* nut.

There was a common consensus that Chief Uchendu understood

Igbo tradition better than anyone in Chicago. His eloquence was second to none. He prayed to the ancestors for guidance. He prayed for the children, so that they would grow up to be good children. He prayed that the children would stay together, marry among their own people and not become lost in the big ocean of America. He prayed that the Igbo would all find the good things they sought in America and return to Nigeria in good health. He prayed to God to help Nigeria in her current difficulties.

It was at this point that IK allowed a cough that he had been suppressing.

"*Nna*, tell that Chief of a guy to wrap up his prayer quick," he murmured to himself, but loud enough that it could have been meant for Emmanuel, who stood next to him. "Naija people always forget that God helps those who help themselves."

"Don't mind them," Emmanuel whispered back. "They're deceiving themselves."

Finally, Chief Uchendu concluded his prayers, pouring libation and asking the ancestors to drink before the people drank. The *kola* nuts were cut and distributed.

After the *kola* nuts were eaten, the actual new yam ceremony was performed. In Nigeria, the New Yam Festival ceremony varied slightly from one village to another. However, its core remained the same across towns and villages. At this time in Chicago, the Igbo belonged to one umbrella organization, the Igbo Association, and hence celebrated one New Yam Festival. As a result, effort was made to ensure that the festival captured the core ceremonies common to the Igbo.

The New Yam Festival marked the beginning of the eating of new yam, or yam harvested in the current farm year. Prior to the ceremony, nobody ate a new yam, only old yam, or yam harvested during the previous year was eaten. New yam was eaten with a cock during the festival, a tradition similar to eating turkey during thanksgiving celebration in America. Titled men ate the new yam first before the people did.

Ikem sat next to his father who explained to his children the significance of every action that took place. Ikem was very attentive and took notes in a small pad he held. Moments later, a group of about twenty women walked in, each carrying a small basin on her head. They sat at one corner on the stage. Chinedu explained to his son, that those women represented *umu ada,* or the first daughter in every family. Their mother, Nkechi, being the first daughter of her parents, was in the group.

"Look at Mom there," Ikem said. "Where's Nweke's mother? She isn't there."

"Your mother is the first daughter of her parents, so she's an *ada*, and hence belongs to the group," Chinedu explained to his children. "Ijeoma, Nweke's mother, has an older sister, so, she isn't an *ada*, and hence doesn't belong to the group."

"Cool!" Kelechi said. "I guess they have some stuff in those basins?"

"Yep," Chinedu responded.

"So what part will the *umu ada* play in the ceremony?" Ikem asked.

"That's a good question," Chinedu said, but before he could explain, Chief Ezennia started the actual ceremony.

"In Nigeria, the oldest titled person present performed the ceremony Chief Ezennia is about to perform," Chinedu whispered to his children. "But some of these rules are relaxed because we aren't at home. He's going to kill one of the cocks and offer it to the god of harvest and thank the god for the new yams."

"He's going to kill the cock?" Kelechi asked. "That'd be cruelty to an animal."

In fact, that part of the ceremony had been slightly modified, and hence no cock was actually killed on stage. But in Nigeria, a cock would have been killed in everybody's presence and its blood sacrificed to the gods.

"The god of harvest, you know that we have killed a cock for you," Chief Ezennia said.

"*Ise-e-e!*" the people agreed.

"*Onye kwe, chi nya ekwe!*" one person shouted, indicating that everything was by faith, and that if a person believed in something, the person's god or *chi* also believed too.

"The god of harvest, you gave us fertile soil and new yam," Chief Ezennia continued. "We've come to thank you and ask you to bless the yams before we eat them."

"*Ise-e-e!*" the people cheered.

"We must thank you because we need your continued protection in the future."

"*Ise-e-e!*"

Chief Ezennia completed his prayers offering libation to the god of harvest and praying for good health and long life. After this official ceremony, the *umu ada* carried the new yams and the cocks away to cook them. The yams had been brought from Nigeria for this occasion.

"What'll happen next is this," Chinedu explained to his children. "The titled men would eat the new yam first and after they'd eaten, everybody would then be free to eat the new yam."

"That's a neat tradition," Kelechi told his father.

"Yes, it is," Chinedu responded.

"It's cool that the people thank the god of harvest so that in subsequent years, he'll give them richer harvests," Ikem observed.

"That's the idea," Chinedu said.

"I like the ceremony, but I know that they changed many things because this is America," Ikem said. "Maybe next year we can go to Nigeria and observe the unabridged ceremony."

"That'll be cool," Kelechi said.

While those ceremonies proceeded inside the hall, some people outside waited for the music to start. Others were engaged in discussing politics, for in Matthew 18:20 of the Nigerian version of the Holy Bible, it was recorded that "For where two or three Nigerians are gathered in diaspora, Nigeria's problems and politics are in the midst of them."

Chinedu joined his friends as they continued their discussions.

"Why did someone not ask the city to close off Broadway Avenue for us today?" Alexander wondered.

"Why do you want it closed off?" Anselem asked.

"Why not?" Alexander countered.

"I didn't suggest that they close the street. You did, so tell us why," Anselem argued.

"Have you ever been to Chinatown during the Chinese New Year?" Alexander asked.

"*Oga Elegi*, this isn't the Chinese New Year. It's the Igbo New Yam Festival. Both of them are *new*, but they're different," Anselem joked.

Alexander ignored the joke. "Look at the Uptown Bank parking lot. It's full. Go down a few blocks to Truman College, their parking lot is also full. Do you know there are enough of us in Chicago to influence what goes on in City Hall? It isn't difficult to request that the city detour traffic for us off Broadway and redirect it through Sheridan Road, between Argyle and Montrose. What we're doing here today is important, and we have the numbers to demand more respect. We only need to realize that we can ask, and be strong enough to insist that we're heard."

"How can you influence City Hall if you don't vote?" IK asked. "Are we going to annul American elections, too? By the way, you have to be a citizen to vote. Are you?"

"Yes, I am," Alexander responded. "What about you?"

"*Oga Elegi*, I am, but suppose we vote, what difference would it make?"

"A lot," Alexander responded. "In this country, everything is politics. Power belongs to the people, to the big corporations and political donors. As an interest group, if we can show a mayoral candidate the number of votes we can deliver for him or her on election day, he or she will listen to us. That's what counts, not chieftaincy titles. We must find a way to pull our resources together and thereby compel people to respect us and listen to us," Alexander added.

"What do you mean?" asked IK.

"Did you ever hear of Chinatown or Polish village? Don't you admire how those people live together? If we can buy a majority of the homes in a community, then it may become Naija town or Igbo town, and we can have it as the Chinese have Chinatown," Alexander explained.

"You mean Ndigbo or Nigerians living together?" IK asked. "Count me out of that. I won't live there, though I'll still visit you if you prefer to live there."

Chinedu followed the discussion with interest. He had strong views on the topic and couldn't restrain himself any further.

"Alex, I'm really excited about the views you are advancing," Chinedu said. "I think I understand what IK is saying. While I respect it, I suspect it's self-defeating. Let me take your model a little further. Does IK realize that, unless we start to take control of our lives, our generation will waste away in the diaspora?"

"You guys have started Chinedu, now you must hear him to the end," Okezie said, scratching his head.

"It isn't a question of starting me, Okezie," Chinedu responded. "It's more of taking care of our destiny. We must develop a more strategic and long-term view of our lives and the lives of our children in diaspora. While I applaud all those people who put these traditional festivities together, they'll be fruitless if all that they achieve is to make us feel good and dance away our pains."

"So what's the answer?" Emmanuel asked.

"We aren't in Nigeria," Chinedu continued. "We're in America, yet we aren't really in America. We must find our footing somewhere, otherwise we'll all die away in this self-imposed economic exile."

"We have to start educating our people. Many just don't understand," Alexander added. "Our people appear to think only one thing: party, party, party. Nothing more. We don't seem to have anything serious to excite or challenge our minds and brains."

"True," Chinedu added. "Consider what the Cubans have done in Miami. I don't know if you guys know Miami well. I visited a friend there last summer. There's this place they call Little Havana. Although it's no substitute for Castro's Havana in Cuba, Little Havana provides the Cubans in diaspora the closest thing to the real city. If you go to Little Havana, the language is Spanish, the food is Cuban, the dressing is Cuban."

"Brother Chinedu, you're always theorizing and philosophizing," IK said. "So what's next? Shall we all move to Little Havana?"

"No, that isn't what I mean," Chinedu protested. "We should concentrate and coordinate our own efforts. Our people say that when we urinate together, it foams."

"Chinedu, I understand that unity is strength, but maybe I will allow you to finish your point first," IK said.

"I will live to see the day when Nigerians will stop interrupting a speaker," Emmanuel said, excusing himself to go to the restroom. That was a clear reference to his friend IK, but IK preferred not to contest it.

"So, the question becomes whether or not we should emulate the Cuba-Miami model," Chinedu continued. "For example, should we start a gradual movement to, say, Houston, Texas? A small community, *Little Enugu*, that we develop there will afford our children the closest to Igbo life in diaspora. Not too long ago, some of us had a related discussion with Mazi Frank. We were all concerned about the real likelihood of our children picking non-Nigerian-American spouses. But why wouldn't they? They don't know other Nigerian-Americans. They don't go to school with them because they don't live in the same neighborhood. Isn't that enough reason for us to live together?"

"Many of our people can't understand this very important point you're making," Alexander added. "For now, everyone is preoccupied with becoming the only black person in his rich, white neighborhood. That's fine, but we can't have our cake and eat it too. We can't live in those neighborhoods and want a Nigerian spouse for our son or daughter. No, it doesn't work that way. They'll pick their spouses from the friends they keep."

"Thanks Alex," Chinedu said. "I can't say it any better so I won't belabor that point. Instead let me move on to another reason why we may want to live together. This has to do with political power."

"Political power?" IK asked. "Are you now into American politics, Chinedu?"

"Just hear me out, Iyke," Chinedu admonished. "Shouldn't we start to congregate in small suburbs so that our numbers would be strong enough to elect, for example, a mayor of such a small city, or influence the senatorial seat in the district? We must realize that we're here in America to stay. Many people feel offended by this thought. While I respect such people, I think they're wrong."

"Chinedu, how can they be wrong?" Emmanuel asked. "You're either an American or a Nigerian. Since they're Nigerians, it's fair to assume they'll return to Nigeria."

"You're wrong, Emmanuel," Chinedu insisted. "That's really one of the advantages of these discussions."

"I don't see the point," said Emmanuel.

"Just bear with me. Allow me to land," said Chinedu.

"Moments ago, he was criticizing me for interrupting you as if he wasn't a Naija man. He probably landed from outer space," IK said, happy that he had his chance to get even with Emmanuel.

"Most of the people influencing American policies towards various regions of the world are immigrants from those places. Why can't we look at ourselves as immigrants from Nigeria and work towards influencing American policies towards Nigeria and Africa? That's the way to go."

26
PARTY TIME

C hinedu and his friends joined the big party going on inside the hall. The Igbo women's association had just completed a great traditional performance and the DJ, Dr. Brutus was mixing the latest from Nigeria's "oldies." Rex Lawon's "Jolly Papa" was preceded by "Susana Pango" by the same artist, and the hall was rocking. Okezie's daughter, Nneka, admired her parents who, no doubt, had grown up in Rex Lawson's era.

"Mom, look at you!" she screamed at her mother, Ijeoma. But Ijeoma was too busy to be disturbed. Although a devoted mother, those who understood Ijeoma knew she would rather not be disturbed whenever she was enjoying a Rex Lawson tune.

"Nneka, come and dance with us," Okezie told his daughter.

"No, dad. I don't like that Nigerian music."

"You don't know a good thing," Okezie said, giving up and concentrating on the memories that flashed like lightning through his mind. He remembered the great Nigerian musicians, Rex Lawson at the top of the list, IK Dairo, Osita Osadebey, Celestine Ukwu and a host of others. "Why can't these kids appreciate the music of these great artists?" he thought to himself.

Dr. Brutus was one of the best in the business. He had given the "old" group about an hour of non-stop music and most of the women were literally drenched in perspiration. Okezie, like the other men was also having a good time. He was still wondering why his daughter couldn't appreciate Rex Lawson when he felt his feet frozen on the stage. He had lost the rhythm and was trying to pull himself out of the trance when he saw Nneka, her two hands in the air, really swinging. Okezie heard the children in the hall screaming *"uh-huh."* Dr. Brutus had switched to the children's favorite and was rapping and hypnotizing them from "Life After Death" by the Notorious B.I.G. The children swung and sang along:

> *Biggie Biggie Biggie can't you see*
> *Sometimes your words just hypnotize me*
> *And I just love your flashy ways*
> *Guess that's why they broke, and you're so paid (uh)*

Now the stage really rocked and vibrated. Okezie quietly snuck out with other members of the "old" group.

"Dad, *com'on*," Nneka screamed at her dad. "This is the Notorious B.I.G."

Okezie pretended not to hear. Somebody preferred this "uh-huh" to Rex Lawson?, he thought to himself. Something was wrong. He walked up to Chinedu, shook his head in disbelief and said, "We're in trouble. Are these Americans or Nigerians?"

"It's serious," Chinedu comforted him. "I don't know where we're headed to."

"Hey man," IK who was standing by, chuckled. "You guys are too old to enjoy the Notorious B.I.G?"

Okezie and Chinedu ignored him and decided to go outside hoping to wait out the youth's rap session. The session lasted about an hour and then it was parents' time again. The crowd mover "Ihe Oma" by the Orientals had just played and as was his habit, Dr. Brutus used "People's Club" to recognize every important person in the party. There were quite a few of them and this was where Dr. Brutus excelled. Once he called a person, the crowd joined him in recognizing the presence of the individual with the response—"In the house"—an indication that the person was present at the party.

Nigerians loved titles, and the DJ, Dr. Brutus, himself not lacking in title, lavished titles generously on all. This was part of his popular appeal among the Nigerian community. Many Nigerians had become "Chief," "Dr.," and "Professor" though no one took those titles any seriously at party time. In fact, IK recently joked that every Nigerian was an MD—the "Managing Director" of his family!

In any event, with Dr. Brutus on the microphone, it wasn't the time to justify titles. It was time to feel good and have a good time. With "People's Club" at the background, Dr. Brutus proceeded to pump up the crowd.

"Chief, Dr., Professor Ezennia, the *Ezeudo I* of *Nanka*," Dr. Brutus called.

"In the house!" the crowd cheered.

"Sir, Honorable, Chief, Dr., Professor Uzondu, the *Odozi obodo I* of *Mbawsi*."

"In the house!"

"Mazi Emmanuel Okongwu, M.B.A., Pharmacist, Managing Director, Progress Pharmaceutical Group of Companies, Harvey, Illinois."

"In the house!"

"*Ezi Ada*, Chief, Madam Ifeoma Okoli, B.S.N., Registered Nurse, Certified Independent Beauty Consultant, Mary Kay Beauty Products, Opa Loka, Florida."

"In the house!"

"Dr., Professor Chinedu Emezie, *Eze-nwata*, The *Eze Aro I* of cyberspace."

"In the house!"

"*Obi-die, Ezi nwayi,* Madam Nkechi Emezie, First Lady."

"In the house!"

"Dr. Okezie Obioha, *Ocho nma obodo ya,* traditional Prime Minister, Chicago, Illinois."

"In the house!"

"*Ada-ugo, Enyi-die,* Madam Ijeoma Obioha."

"In the house!"

"Chief, Dr. Henry and Dr. Mrs. Stella Umerah, Ph.D., MD., Cardiologist, Surgeon, the *Ezeafulunaya* and *Lolo I* of *Etiti*."

"In the house!"

"Our very own, Sir, Chief, Dr. Ikenna Uchendu, Certified Public Accountant, the *Anyogu I* of *Mbieri*."

"In the house!"

"Dr. Alexander Okonkwo, *Ome oka chie*, our indigenous entrepreneur, Executive Director and sole Proprietor, ONE STOP African Foods and Textiles, Gary, Indiana."

"In the house!"

"Chief, Dr. Cletus Okoye, *Eze di ndi onachi nma*, Attorney at Law, Immigration and Green Card Specialist, General and International Law, Bronx, New York."

"In the house!"

"Mazi Frank Nwankwo, Distinguished Engineer, Able Chairman, Igbo Association of Chicago and Environs."

"In the house!"

With Dr. Brutus behind the microphone, everyone was guaranteed a good time. Nigerians in diaspora lived under unusual stress. Almost everyone worked more than one job to maintain both the nuclear and extended families. As if that was not enough, there was the added pressure of raising children in a culture that was quite alien to them. These parties were among the few occasions that they felt at home. People danced their hearts out and had opportunity to tell their problems to understanding ears.

The parties were also beginning to resemble the launching ceremonies in immediate post-war Igboland. The parties had become the forum where people sought donations and raised funds for various projects at home.

Mazi Frank was on the stage making a few closing comments while people were still sober. After a few more drinks, it might become difficult, if not impossible, to get his message across.

"I will want to use this opportunity to thank everybody here for helping our people at home," Mazi Frank told his audience. "Gone were the days when our parents sent money to us from Nigeria. Things have turned 180 degrees, and we must now support them from here. It's our culture. It's our way of life for we take care of our own."

"These guys just make me sick to my stomach," IK told Emmanuel. "Everything is our culture."

"Don't mind them," Emmanuel responded. "Let them keep deceiving themselves."

"Can you imagine what Frank is saying?" IK continued. "Our country is screwed up. Our people can no longer feed themselves and he's telling us that it's our culture, it's our way of life. I think he has no idea what he's talking about."

But Mazi Frank was still on his feet. "My appeal today is that we go beyond thinking just about our parents," he continued. "It's time to start thinking globally about the society our parents and brothers live in. I'm thinking about our schools, our hospitals and our markets."

Mazi Frank paused, then continued. "To those of us who are college professors, this is my challenge: there must be old books in your school libraries that are no longer needed and are just taking up space. These books will be great treasure for our universities at home. To those of us in big companies, please encourage them to make donations to our schools and universities."

"*Igbo kwenu!*" Mazi Frank greeted.

"*Yaa!*" the people responded.

He continued.

"This challenge isn't just for men. It's for all of us, men, women, and children. In particular, a good number of our women work in hospitals and nursing homes. Think about those old wheel chairs lying around in your facilities. You and I know that they're gold to many of our handicapped at Orthopedic Hospital in Enugu. So, the challenge becomes how to make them available to our hospitals at home. Let everyone here today commit himself or herself to find a way to help our people. The Americans are rich and generous and will help if only we ask."

"*Che, che, che, Igbo kwenu!*"

"*Yaa!*"

"*America kwezuenu!*"

"*Yaa!*"

GLOSSARY

A GLOSSARY OF SELECTED IGBO WORDS AND PHRASES

( ) indicates suggested pronunciation

agbada (ah.bwah.dah)	a large deep frying pan
agbogho (ah.bwoh.hoh)	a young girl with mature, standing breasts
agu (ah.goo)	a lion
aguba (ah.goo.bah)	a very sharp, razor-like knife used to shave hair
aju (ah.joo)	a pad that provides a cushioning effect to the

	head when a load is carried
aka ji aku (ah.kah.gee.ah.koo)	a name of praise: the rich one.
aka mere (ah.kah.meh.reh)	a locally brewed gin. *Aka* means "hand," *mere* means "made," hence *aka mere* means "gin made by hand" to differentiate it from machine-brewed gin
akawu (ah.kah.nwoo)	salt petre
ano (ah.nor)	four
anu (ah.noo)	meat; *anu okpo* is dried meat
biko {bikonu} (bee.koh {bee.koh.noo})	please
chi (chee)	a personal god, or sometimes God. *Chi-mo* is an exclamation, "Oh my God."
chukwu (chu.kwoo)	God. *Chi* and *chukwu* are often used interchangeably, especially in Igbo names.
Chukwu ekwena (chu.kwoo eh.kweh.nah)	God forbid
dianyi (dee.ah.nyee)	a generic salutation among male colleagues and friends
dibia (dee.byah)	a medicine man
eke (eh.keh)	one of the four market days. The others are

orie, nkwo, afor;
eke Ohafia is the market in Ohafia which is held
on *eke* days.

enu (eh.noo)	"up" or "high" depending on usage
ewo-o (eh.who)	a scream as a result of some discomfort or pain
eze (eh.zeh)	a king or chief
eze dike (eh.zeh dee.keh)	a phrase of praise: great king
eze udo (eh.zeh oo.doh)	a phrase of praise: king of peace
eze ukwu (eh.zeh oo.kwoo)	a phrase of praise: great king
iba (ee.bah)	malaria
igba afa (ee.bwah ah.fah)	communicating with the spirits
igwe (ee.gweh)	In the context used in the book, it is a generic name for a machine; thus *igwe okpa* is a machine for grinding *okpa*.
ikeji (ee.kay.gy)	The new yam festival in Arochuku.
iro (ee.row)	a fairy tale
isee (ee.say)	a response indicating concurrence in what was said
isii (ee.see)	six

ito otu aka n'abo
(ee.tow.to
ah.kah.na.bhor)

Ito otu is a palm wine container; *aka* is hand; *n'abo* is a reference to two, indicating that the palm wine container has two hands, hence *ito otu aka n'abo* means two gallons of palm wine.

iyanga (ee.yah.gah)   pride, showing off

izu ato {asaa}
(ee.zoo.ah.toh   {ah
sah})

three {seven} native weeks; *ato* is three; *asaa* is seven; *izu* is week. In some dialects, *ato* is *ito*, and *asaa* is *issa*.

ji (gee)   yam; *ji mirioku* is yam porridge

ji-oyibo
(gee.oh.yee.boh)

white man's yam, or potato

jigida (gee.gih.dah)   waist beads

juju (joo.joo)   a native medicine

ka ka ka
(hak.kah.kah)

the sound of gun fire

ka obanye
(kah.awe.bah.nyeh)

let him/her enter

karam, karam, karam
(kah.rahm   kah.rahm
kah.rahm)

the noise when a crunchy item is chewed

ka-gbim, ka-gbim
(kah.bwim kah.bwim)

a heavy sound, for example, of a bomb

kwenu (kweh.noo)	a greeting or salutation
lijua nsi onu (lee.jwoh.nsee. ah.noo)	a curse; translates roughly to "shut your mouth"
mama (mah.mah)	a mother; example, Mama Chinedu means Chinedu's mother.
mama iwota (mah.mah ee.who.tah)	a sea mermaid, often used as a symbol of extreme beauty
mazi (mah.zee)	a salutation reserved for men; connotes status or respect; *ndi mazi* is the plural form of *mazi*
mba (m.bah)	no
mechi onu (meh.chyeh. awe.noo)	a curse, "shut your mouth"
na wa o (nah.wah.oh)	a colloquial expression of surprise
ndi iche aro (n.dee.ee.ch.eh. ah.roo)	elders and ancestors of the Aro people
nna (n.nah)	father; for example, *nna* Chinedu means Chinedu's father
nne (n.neh)	mother; for example, *nne* Chinedu means Chinedu's mother.

nri (n.ree)	food
nsisa (n.see.sah)	a type of food made from cassava
nwa (n.wah)	son of, daughter of, or more generically, child of
nwayi (n.way.yee)	a woman
nwoke (n.who.keh)	a man
nzu (n.zoo)	a whitish stone, very much like chalk used by medicine men
obi-die (oh.bee.dy.eh)	the husband's heart
ochi agha (awe.chee.ah.yah)	a phrase of praise: war leader, commander
ocho nma obodo ya (awe.ch.awe m.mah oh.boh.doh yah)	a phrase of praise: one who looks out for the good of his people
odighi (awe.dee.yih)	Arochukwu dialect for *mba* or no
odozi obodi (oh.doh.zee oh.boh.doh)	a phrase of praise: one who looks after his people
o-gini (awe.gih.nee)	What is it?
ofu (oh.foo)	one

oga (oh.gah)	a colloquial reference to someone as a boss or a senior
ogene (oh.geh.nee)	a musical instrument; a gong
ogbuagu (oh.boo.ah.goo)	lion killer—a title earned by men who have distinguished themselves in unique ways
ogwu (oh.gwoo)	medicine
oji	The meaning depends on how it is used and pronounced; when pronounced *awe.gee*, *oji* means kola or kola nut which every Igbo presents to welcome a guest; however, when pronounced *oh.gee*, *oji* means a very powerful *juju* in a rattling staff carried by a masquerade.
ojugo (awe.joo.goh)	a disease that afflicts hens
okuko (awe.koo.koh)	a hen; *Okuko ojugo* is a sick hen that should be disposed of immediately
ome oka chie (oh.meh. awe.kah.chyeh)	a phrase of praise: one who acts big
ome ka nna ya (oh.meh.kah. n.nah.yah)	a phrase of praise: one who behaves like his father
omu aro (oh.moo ah.roh)	a type of wrapper worn by the Aro people
onye kwe, chi nya	if a person believes in something, the person's

ekwe
(oh.yeh.kweh,
chee.yah eh.kweh)

god believes too

ose (oh.she)

pepper; *ose oji* is a special type of pepper for eating *oji* {kola}

ozugo (oh.zoo.goh)

it is enough

ozuzu   {ije   ozuzu}
(awe.zoo.zoo)
({ee.jey
awe.zoo.zoo})

training {to go to training}

papa (pah.pah)

father; for example, Papa Chinedu means Chinedu's father.

phew, phew, phew
(few, few, few)

sound of a fast-moving object; for example, a jet fighter

shi-i (shhh)

a call for silence

tufiakwa
(too.fyah.kwah)

a curse

ube (oo.beh)

a popular fruit in the pear family that is eaten with roasted corn

uda (oo.dah)

a medicinal seed used in cooking for a newly delivered mother

udala (oo.dah.lah)

a delicious fruit with a pebble-like seed

udu (oo.doo)

a musical instrument made of clay pot

udo diri gi (oo.doh dee.ree gi)	peace be upon you
ugba (oo.bwah)	a local delicacy served as an appetizer
uka (oo.kah)	Sunday, or church, depending on context
uno (oo.noh)	house; *uno enu* literary translates to "a house that is high," a reference to a multi-story building
uziza (oo.zee.zah)	another type of seed used as *uda*
ya gazie (n.yah gah.zyeh)	may everything go well for you

A GLOSSARY OF SELECTED IGBO NAMES

{*} denotes the same name in a different dialect.
The second of two names separated by a slash denotes the
complete or formal version of the first name.
( ) indicates suggested pronunciation.

Ada / Adaku (ah.dah / ah.dah.koo)	daughter/daughter of wealth
Ada / Adaugo (ah.dah/ ah.dah.oo.goh)	daughter/the daughter of the beautiful bird, the egret
Amechi (ah.mey.chee)	no one knows tomorrow
Chibuzo (chee.boo.zoh)	God is in front or God leads

Chika / Chukwuka {}* (chee.kah/choo.kwoo.k ah)	God is greatest
Chinedu (chee.neh.doo)	God guides
Chinelo (chee.neh.loh)	God is thinking
Chinwe (chee.nweh)	God's own
Dibugwu (dee.boo.goo)	husband is prestige
Ego / Nwakego (eh.goh /n.wah.keh.goh)	a child is greater than money
Enyi / Enyinnaya (eh.yih/ eh.yee.n.nah.yaa)	his father's friend
Ezennia (eh.zeh.nyah)	his father's kingdom
Ezeudo (eh.zeh.oo.doh)	the king of peace
Ijeomà (ee.joh.mah)	a good journey. The actual meaning depends on the context. It could be used to indicate that the journey a woman took to her husband's home is a good one.
Ike / Ikechukwu (ee.keh/ ee.keh.choo.kwoo)	God's power, the power of God
Ikem (ee.keh.m) *(Ikemefuna / Ikemefula) {*}* (ee.keh.meh.foo.nah/ ee.keh.meh.foo.lah)	my strength or my power; for example, a man sees his son as the product of his "strength." It is a prayer to God that "my strength" should not be lost or go in vain.

Ike / Ikenna (ee.keh/ee.keh.nah)	the father's power
Kelechi / Kelechukwu *{*}* (keh.leh.chee/ keh.leh.choo.kwoo)	thank God; be thankful to God
Mgbokwo/Mgbeke/Mgb orie/Mgbafor (mboh.kwoh/ mbek.keh/mboh.rye/ mbah.foh)	a common name given to a female child born on the corresponding market day; the daughter of *Nkwo/Eke/Orie/Afor*
Ndidi (n.dee.dee)	patience
Ngozi (n.goh.zee)	blessing
Nkechi/Nkechinyere (n.keh.chee)/ (n.keh.chee.nyeh.reh)	the one given by God. Its real meaning depends on context. For example, a couple looking for a male child could give the name to their daughter suggesting that this is the one God has given. It could also mean, this belongs to God.
Nkiru/Nkiruka (n.kee.roo)/ (n.kee.roo.kah)	what is ahead or what is yet to come is greater
Nneka (n.neh.kah)	mother is supreme
Nwankwo/Nweke/ Nwoye/Nwafor (n.wah.kwoh/ n.weh.keh/ n.who.yeh/ n.wah.foh)	a common name given to a male child born on the corresponding market day; the son of *Nkwo/Eke/Oye/Afor. Orie* and *Oye* are different dialects of the same word.

Obioha / Obiora {}*
(oh.bee.awe.ha/
oh.bee.aw.ha)

the heart of the people

Ochonma
(awe.choh.mah)

the beauty seeker; one who takes time to make himself look handsome

Ogugua (awe.goo.gua)

console me

Okezie/Chikezie {}*
(okay.zyeh)/
(chee.kay.zyeh)

a good creation by God

Okugo (oh.kwoh.goh)

the big beautiful/handsome bird, the egret

Olunwa (awe.loo.wah)

Caring for a child is never tiring.

Onwuasoanya
(awe.woo.ah.soh.
ah.yah)

Death respects no one.

Osita (Ositadinma)
(oh.see.tah)
(oh.see.tah.dee.ma)

if it starts being good from today, it's fine

Uche / Uchechukwu
(oo.chee/
oo.chee.choo.kwoo)

God's will

Uche / Uchendu
(oo.chee/ oo.chee.doo)

the thought of life

Ugo / Ugochi
(oo.goh/ oo.goh.chee)

God's grace

Umeh / Umerah
(oo.meh/ oo.meh.rah)

may child death stop

Uzo / Uzondu (oo.zoh/ oo.zoh.n.doo)	the way of life
Uzunma (oo.zoo.n.mah)	the sound of beauty

ABOUT THE AUTHOR

Cyril U. Orji

Cyril U. Orji is currently a Member of Technical Staff at Lucent Technologies, Holmdel, New Jersey.

Cyril was born in Enugu, Nigeria. He attended St. Patrick's Primary School, Iva Valley, and St. Patrick's Primary School, Ogbete (Coal Camp), both in Enugu. Cyril's experience with the American way of life started when he entered Government Comprehensive Secondary School, Gborokiri, Port Harcourt, Nigeria. This was a joint high school project between the then Government of Eastern Nigeria and the University of California, Los Angeles (UCLA). But the express train to UCLA was derailed by the Nigerian civil war, 1967-1970. At the end of the war, Cyril completed his high school education at St. Teresa's College, Nsukka. He worked for the Nigerian Posts and Telecommunications (P & T) before coming to the United States for further studies.

Cyril earned a Bachelor of Science (College Honors), Electrical Engineering, a Master of Business Administration (MBA), a Master of Science and a Doctor of Philosophy, Computer Science, all from the University of Illinois, Chicago, Illinois. He is married to Adanma Orji (nee Adanma Ohiaeri), a registered nurse. Both are blessed with four children, Uzoma, Obinna, Uzoamaka and Uchenna.